HOW TO
KILL
YOUR BEST
FRIEND

HOW TO KILL YOUR BEST FRIEND

LEXIE ELLIOTT

BERKLEY

NEW YORK

BERKLEY
An imprint of Penguin Random House LLC
penguinrandomhouse.com

Library of Congress Cataloging-in-Publication Data

Names: Elliott, Lexie, author.
Title: How to kill your best friend / Lexie Elliott.
Description: New York : Berkley, [2021]
Identifiers: LCCN 2020052591 (print) | LCCN 2020052592 (ebook) |
ISBN 9780593098691 (hardcover) | ISBN 9780593098714 (ebook)
Subjects: GSAFD: Suspense fiction. | Mystery fiction.
Classification: LCC PR6105.L588 H69 2021 (print) | LCC PR6105.L588 (ebook) |
DDC 823/.92—dc23
LC record available at https://lccn.loc.gov/2020052591
LC ebook record available at https://lccn.loc.gov/2020052592

Printed in the United States of America
1st Printing

Cover art: Window drips © Savvapanf Photo / Shutterstock

For Leigh
(with assurances that I have never considered killing her).

And for the swimtrek gang.

And, again and forever,
for Matt, Cameron and Zachary.

HOW TO
KILL
YOUR BEST
FRIEND

HOW TO KILL YOUR BEST FRIEND

Method 1: Accident

Yes, but what kind of accident? It's so easy in the movies: a pleasant walk along a cliff top, then—bam!—a sudden shove . . . In real life, there's no handily accessible cliff, and if there was, nobody in their right mind would walk so close to the edge of it. And supposing, just supposing, those two obstacles were somehow resolved, there's always the chance that somebody would see you. A dog walker, probably. There's always a bloody dog walker around.

It's just like they say: it's not the murder that's the problem; it's getting away with it.

No, wait. The murder is a problem, too.

ONE

GEORGIE

The hotel is beautiful—of course it is; it topped the Condé Nast list of the best small hotels worldwide—but that barely registers with me because I'm late. Hideously, terribly late. It's not my fault: the plane was delayed, and it took forever for the luggage to be unloaded; but that hardly matters. All through the teeth-clenchingly slow two-hour journey from the airport, I've been fervently hoping that something might have delayed the start, but now that I'm here, spilling out of the cool taxi into the hot, humid reception area—open on all sides to allow any breath of wind to waft through—I'm abruptly aware of how slim a hope that is. There's a smiling woman, local in appearance, waiting for me by the enormous bamboo sofa; there's a tray laid on the table in front of it with a moist towel and some kind of tropical drink complete with a cocktail umbrella. I cut off her welcome. "Has it started?"

"Oh." She's visibly startled. "You're here for the, um, you mean—Lissa?" I nod tersely. "But yes, it started already."

"Where? Where do I go?"

"Down to the beach," she says, pointing, her own gaze following her finger. Then she looks back at me, and her brow furrows in consternation. "But ma'am—"

I'm already rushing past her. "I'll check in after. Hold on to my bags, please," I call over my shoulder.

"But ma'am—" she calls after me. I don't stop, though, because I'm late. I'm late, I'm late, I'm terribly late.

The reception area is set up on a hill. I hurry down the (charming, but steep) stone steps, pushing my sunglasses back up my nose repeatedly and bemoaning my precarious wedge sandals, with barely a glance at the azure blue of the sea, shimmering in the late-afternoon sun. The path twists and turns as it picks its way through the tropical foliage. I can't see the beach that it's surely about to spit me out onto—but then I turn a corner, and the horseshoe-shaped cove is laid out before me. The cliffs near the mouth drop straight into the sea, but in the main belly of the cove, there's a beach, some thirty meters wide at this tide, and perhaps one hundred meters long. Set out in the middle of it are rows of chairs, with an aisle down the middle. Next to what I can only imagine is the priest, I see the unmistakable figure of Jem facing the sixty or so attendees, his sunglasses hooked on by one arm at the open neck of the white linen shirt he's wearing.

And then a breath of wind takes the skirt of the lightweight halter neck summer dress I'm wearing—black, but scattered with scarlet flowers—and streams it out sideways, as if a flag. Jem's head turns toward me, and after the merest of beats, he lifts his hand. It's a small gesture, but nevertheless, the priest tails off and most of the crowd turns reflexively, and I realize with dawning horror that every one of them is wearing white. White. All of them.

Jesus. It looks like a fucking wedding, not a funeral, I think. *Jem could be a groom waiting for his bride.* A wave of nausea swells inside me. I stamp it down ruthlessly; this is not the time to fall apart. I force my shoulders back against the weight of all these pairs of eyes and walk deliberately down the last few steps, ignoring the mutters I can already hear, my scandalous black and scarlet cutting a path straight down the aisle, which is thankfully paved by wooden slats. White linen shirts, white sundresses, white wide-legged beach trousers . . . How did I miss that detail? There are one or two pairs of pale beige tailored shorts, but other than that, everything is resolutely snowy. Behind my sunglasses I'm searching for Bronwyn, or Duncan, who will surely be near the front. I spot Duncan's height first, in the second row, with Bron's wayward chestnut curls next to him, barely reaching his shoulder. As I get closer, I see that Jem means to step forward to greet me before I can duck into the row, and I can't think of a single thing to say that is worth saying.

"You made it," he says, reaching out with both hands to clasp mine. I haven't seen him for months—actually, over a year; not since the last time all the gang got together for one of our regular swimming holidays. Except no, that wasn't the last time for everyone else: the last time was when Lissa drowned, but I wasn't there. For once he looks every second of his forty-plus years. His mouth is smiling, but there's no energy in it, and his pale green eyes look worn. It's as if he's pulled on the suit of his skin and found that he doesn't quite fill it anymore.

"The plane was delayed. I'm so sorry," I murmur inadequately.

"No matter, you're here. She would have wanted you here."

Hardly. Nobody wants their funeral at thirty-five; she wouldn't have wanted this at all. She would have wanted me to be there that night, to stop her from going for a swim alone in the dark. But I wasn't. I squeeze his hands mutely, then let Duncan pull me into the row, my wedges sinking awkwardly in the sand. "Quite an entrance, as usual," he mutters as I squeeze past him to a chair next to Bron. Her eyes are puffy, but then, all of her seems puffy; I can feel the give in her waist as I slip an arm round her and pull her against me. There's been gradually more and more of Bron over the half of my lifetime I've known her, and less and less of Lissa. And now there's nothing left of Lissa at all.

Bron catches my eye as the priest starts up again. "Making a statement?" she murmurs quietly, gesturing at my dress.

What on earth would that statement be? "I didn't get the memo."

Her eyebrows lift briefly; I'm not sure she believes me. To her, I'll always be the girl she first met, or a mere step away from that. Careless, reckless—with myself and others; a bullet ricocheting. Maybe she's right; maybe I'm the one fooling myself. Perhaps one step is all it would take to fall back into that. Today, that step is perilously tempting.

Focus, I tell myself. *This is not the time to fall apart. I have to hold up Bron.* She is crying now, as silently as she can, one of my hands gripped tightly in hers. There's barely a breath of wind on this beach, and we are entirely exposed to the tropical sunshine. There's something extraordinarily *wrong* about this weather for a service like this. It should be cold, bone-piercingly so, but instead I can feel a dampness where Bron's forearm touches mine, and it's possible those behind me can see a sheen of sweat on my exposed back. I'm also starting to need the bathroom. How strange that Lissa can be dead but our bodies don't seem to know; they just continue on with their own petty concerns.

It was cold for Maddy's funeral. And for Graeme's.

Focus.

I force myself to concentrate on the priest, but suddenly I can't hear what he's saying because I've caught sight of a large photograph of Lissa, displayed on an easel as if a painting. It's not one I've seen before, and it must be a professional shot: it's black-and-white and artfully lit so that her eyes stand out, but the rest of her features are almost bleached away. She looks unfinished.

Lissa is dead. She's dead, she's dead, she's dead. How can she be dead? It's been a constant tattoo in my brain over these past three months, since Bron called to tell me, though she couldn't get the words out. Duncan had to take the phone off her.

There's been an accident, he said. His voice was raw but steady. *She went for a swim the other night by herself, at Kanu Cove, and—*

Wait—She? Who? Who went?

Lissa.

Lissa? But . . .

She's missing, Georgie. Lissa is missing; she didn't come back. They're still searching, but by now there's really no hope, he said. *And the water at Kanu—you haven't seen it, but . . . Christ, I don't know what she could have been thinking. The police will record it as missing, presumed—*

No. I wouldn't let him say it. *I don't believe it.* I didn't believe it then, and I don't know how to believe it now.

Duncan is nudging me; I belatedly realize everyone else has risen. I lurch to my feet, and my wedge sandals sink unevenly into the sand, tipping me awkwardly against Bron, who is still fixed to my side. I think of all the photos I have of the three of us: sixteen years of posing for the camera. Pictures from university—swimming galas, black-tie events and celebrations, pre-mobile-phone era—yielding to shots taken at weddings or christenings or on our numerous swimming holidays. In almost every one, I'm in the middle. There isn't a middle anymore.

I sense we're nearing the end, but I still can't make sense of the priest's words, not with the photo right there. It could be a painting that the artist has stepped away from for a moment, perhaps to give the model a cigarette break; he hasn't had time to paint in what she was thinking. I think of Duncan's words—*I don't know what she could have been thinking*—and the puzzlement in his voice. I don't know what she was thinking, either. None of this makes sense. Lissa is dead, and it doesn't make sense.

It seems to be over; Duncan is turning to me. I don't know what he sees in my face, half hidden as it is by my sunglasses, but he says, almost helplessly, "Oh, Georgie."

I shake my head abruptly, take a deep breath and pull Bron against my side. "No Ruby?" I say, to head him off.

He looks at me searchingly, as if he has something to say, but then he sighs and shakes his head. "She wanted to, but with the twins . . ." Duncan's twins can't be much more than seven months old. He looks like he's carrying all of those months in the lines on his face and in the slight paunch I can see beneath his loose shirt. "Maybe if it had been somewhere easier to get to . . ." It's true that many more family and friends would have been able to attend had the service been held in London. I glance back at the departing crowd. At a guess, the last few rows, perhaps even half of the congregation, were occupied by locals, many of whom are wearing staff uniforms. "It's not like you can build a holiday around a funeral."

"Memorial," I say. Duncan looks at me. "No body. Memorial." No body, but also no doubt. A teenager in some kind of light fishing craft hauled up a blond-haired corpse in a red swimsuit with his net a little over a month later. He was so shocked, he didn't actually get it on board, and it slipped back into the depths. It was the swimsuit that erased all doubt; he saw the logo. TYR. A swimmer's swimsuit, not the type of thing the average woman would be wearing on vacation.

TYR. Lissa's favorite brand. That *Baywatch*-red suit was familiar to us all. I wonder where she is now; I wonder what that red swimsuit looks like after months in the salt water. I don't want to think what Lissa might look like.

"Well, trust Lissa to demand a *memorial* on an exotic island in Southeast Asia," says Bron, in a valiant attempt to sound like her normal self.

"Demand?" I ask.

"It was in her will," Bron explains. "Jem said so. They got them done when they bought this place, and she put it in then."

"Jesus," I say. "That seems . . ." Prescient? Macabre, to be that specific at her age?

But Bron, ever practical, is thinking along different lines. "No, it was very sensible. You really ought to have a will, especially if you own property." She looks at me keenly. "Do you have one?"

"I rent." My words are heavily soaked in vinegar.

Duncan looks at me sharply. "Come on," he says quickly, either to forestall Bron from pressing me or to stop her quizzing him on the status of his own will and testament. "There's a thing now. Up at the main reception."

I glance back at the photo. One of the staff is preparing to lift it from the easel. It's not Lissa, or not my Lissa. I turn back to Duncan and Bron. There is nothing to be done but forge on with this awful day. "Yep. Let's go."

We are among the last to traipse back up the hill to the main reception, retracing the steps of my earlier mad dash. The sun is sinking hastily, without the fanfare of any dramatic colors; it will be dark in mere minutes. Lights hidden within the foliage that flanks the path are flickering into life. As we approach, I can see that the thing seems to involve a meal. There's a buffet laid out beneath the shade of the traditional wall-less pavilion, with staff behind multiple stations for different types of food that is being cooked on demand on the spot. I'm not in the least bit hungry.

"Georgie," says a voice behind me, in a soft Northern accent. *Adam,* I think; then, even as I'm turning, *Surely not.* But here he is.

"You came," I say, unable to hide the surprise.

"You thought I wouldn't?"

Yes. But I don't say it. He must have been here for a few days, as he has the start of what I know will become a mahogany tan, accentuated by his crisp white shirt. He looks like he always does, lean and efficient—there's never any excess to Adam—and moves to greet me with kisses on both cheeks. I feel absurdly self-conscious during the ritual.

He gestures at the buffet line. "Can I get you anything?"

"No thanks." I glance at my watch. 6:30 p.m., but it doesn't feel like it to me. "It's nowhere near dinnertime for me. How long have you been here?"

"Two days. I flew with Duncan and Bron."

It's stupid to feel a stab of jealousy at that—after all, I live in New York, and they all live in London, or thereabouts; of course I couldn't fly out with them—but nonetheless, I feel it prick at me. We are hovering at the edge of the covered pavilion, watching people lining up for food and settling at the white-clothed tables scattered through the space. Duncan is helping Bron at the salad buffet. Jem is deep in conversation with someone in a uniform. "Whose idea was it to set this thing up like a fucking wedding?" I mutter. Adam glances at me, and I feel myself blush defensively.

"Jem wanted it to be a celebration of—her. Though I don't expect the staff have much experience of planning memorials, hence . . ." He gestures with the fingers of one hand, the smallest of movements that somehow seems to sweep in the tableau in front of us and the staff behind it all. I don't see Lissa in any of it. "It's quite different to Graeme's funeral, isn't it?"

Graeme. Kind, funny Graeme. Lissa's first love and first husband; Adam's best friend. But the last thing I want to do is talk about Graeme. "Who is that?" I nod toward Jem and the uniformed man. Behind them, I can see Lissa's parents, sitting at a table with several other people, their plates loaded with food. Lissa's father is tucking in, but her mother hasn't even picked up her cutlery. I wonder if she's even aware of the plate in front of her. I look away quickly.

"The chief of police. I can't for the life of me remember his name, but he's decent; he did all the right things after she went missing." I look at him, nonplussed, and he explains. "You know, search parties with all the local fishermen—the ones that weren't too scared to go out, that is—and interviews with all of us, that sort of thing. There was a vested interest from the locals to find her; they're all terrified that Jem will close the hotel now."

"Will he?"

He shrugs. We lapse into silence for a moment, and then his words tweak at me. "Too scared to go out. What did you mean by that?"

"There's a local legend about Kanu Cove. Some kind of sea serpent is supposed to frequent there: a snake or a dragon or something like that. Some of the traditionalists think she was taken as tribute. Or punishment—"

"Punishment?" I swing round to him. "For what?"

"It's a centuries-old myth, Georgie; it's not exactly big on detail. This snake-thingy likes them young and female, I'm told, but beyond that, the story varies. Anyway, one or two of the fishermen didn't want anyone to go searching for her at all. Apparently they thought it might be unwise to look like you're asking for your tribute back." I realize my mouth is open and close it sharply. Adam's lips twist wryly at my expression. "Yeah, I know, but don't worry, the search was really thorough. Two more fishing boats wouldn't have made any difference."

A waitress pauses by us with a tray of mixed cocktails; Adam waves her on. "Hey," I exclaim, even though I wasn't planning to take a drink at all. "What if I wanted one?"

"You're not stupid enough to drink today of all days."

I grimace. "I hope you can still say that at the end of the night."

He shrugs. "I'll be here." To stop me, or regardless of what happens? I can't tell what he means. He rubs at his jawline, and I suddenly remember how it felt when his stubble scraped over my bare shoulder. Was that the last occasion when I had a drink? No, that would have been when I last saw Lissa, of course. I stare resolutely out over the milling crowd. After a moment, I gesture at Lissa's father, Philip. He's by a drinks station now, grinning at a very pretty young waitress, who is looking up at him rather coyly. Philip is an actor of some repute. Right now I would guess he's playing charmingly debonair Englishman with just a hint of lovable rogue. It's not a new role for him. "Christ, is he at it today of all days?"

Adam glances over. "Mmm. Can't teach an old dog new tricks."

"Yes, but you can neuter them," I say viciously.

"I don't think his wife is the neutering kind." I glance across at Diane again. She's as beautifully put together as ever, in white of course, sitting perfectly upright at the table; I'm not sure she's moved since I last glanced at her, though her table companions have melted away. I thought perhaps she was in shock, but no—there's something about her posture, about the set of her mouth. She seems too tightly reined in for shock.

Adam observes quietly, "You know, you didn't call me back."

I glance at him sharply, then just as quickly I look away. "No." Oh dear God. Where's a rug to brush things under when you need one? I hadn't expected him to bring that up—I hadn't expected to see him here at all. He was never the biggest fan of Lissa. He wasn't at university with us; he was really just part of the swimming gang as Duncan's friend—and also Graeme's, originally. I'd anticipated a period of British awkwardness when we next met, while we resolutely ignored what happened between us the last time we were together; I'd expected a certain discomfort that would have to be endured until we found our way past it. But he's waiting for more, and I find myself actually offering it, acutely aware of the color rushing to my face. "There wasn't anything to say."

"No?"

I hadn't expected him to push the point, either. "You live in England. I don't."

"We could have talked." I'm looking out across the sea of people, but I sense he's almost amused by me.

I think about that for a moment. "I'm not good at that."

"No kidding." This time I do look at him, and I find myself laughing—as much at his wry expression as his words. Then the waitress passes again. She has glasses of champagne mixed in with the cocktails. Cold beads of water have formed on the outside of the glasses. "Come on," Adam says, pulling my attention away. "Let's go speak to all the people we need to and then we can slip away for the swim."

I draw back in horror. "We're swimming? Surely not where—"

"No, not there. Of course not there; we'll be swimming where the ceremony was." He reads my face. "You didn't know? Duncan and Bron thought it would be a fitting send-off, and Jem was all for it." *Duncan and Bron and Jem and Adam. All here, all making plans together. And I didn't even know about the white dress code.* "Look, it's not compulsory. If you're not up to it—"

"No, it's fine." I swallow. He tips his head quizzically. "Really. It's a good idea. You're right, though. I'd better go speak to her folks before I get my swim stuff." I recognize I've been putting it off. Spending time with Lissa's parents has always felt awkward, and I can't imagine the present circumstances will improve that.

"Philip actually said he might swim, too," Adam says. "I should tell him it's almost time."

We can't immediately see Philip, so Adam heads off to find him, but Lissa's mother, Diane, is exactly where she was before, still alone at the table as I approach hesitantly and slide into the chair next to her. She turns her head slowly to look at me. It always surprises me how little she looks like Lissa: dark haired and athletic in a posh, horsey sort of way, whereas Lissa is blond and china boned. *Was.* "Georgie," she says. Her voice is entirely flat.

"I don't know what to say."

"Yes." We look out at the crowd. After a few moments she says, "No white for you, I see."

"I—"

13

"Quite right, too. It's not a bloody party. But Philip said I shouldn't make a fuss." Her mouth twists bitterly. I should say something, but I can't think of anything that would fit. "Do you believe in fate?"

"What?"

She waves an impatient hand. "Fate. Destiny. Was this preordained?" I look at her blankly; I can't seem to find solid ground in this conversation. She's still staring out at the milling crowd. "All that time invested, all that—love. Sleepless nights and schools and ballet lessons, swimming lessons . . . Was this the end point all along? Or was it something I did? Or didn't do? Or Philip?" She looks straight at me, suddenly fierce, and I finally see Lissa in her, in the hazel eyes they share. In the accusations they hold. "Or you?"

I can't find a breath. "I don't—"

But she's already looking away, her sudden energy entirely dissipated. "I think I'll go back to the villa."

"Should I . . . should I find Philip for you?"

She barks an entirely mirthless laugh and pushes her seat back abruptly. "No, thank you."

I watch her walk away from the pavilion, her back militarily straight, and I wonder if Diane is the only person alive who might be capable of understanding what I'm feeling.

Twenty minutes later, after collecting my swim gear, I'm back in the horseshoe bay, which I have since learned is rather boringly named just that: Horseshoe Bay. Jem, Adam, Duncan and a handful of people I don't know are looking rather businesslike in Speedos at the shoreline. Someone has put thought into this endeavor: there are Chinese lanterns strung up on the piers that jut out on either side at the widest point of the bay, and lights on a series of buoys that span the water between them. There's enough light, from the unobtrusive lamps that light the path skirting the beach and from the moon, for us to see what we're doing, but the sea itself is a dark mass, darker even than the sky above it, only occasionally lightened at the shoreline by flashes of white from a breaking wave.

"What's the plan?" I ask Bronwyn. She's already shrugging out of her white dress to reveal a dark-colored Speedo swimsuit underneath.

"No fixed plan, I shouldn't think. It's about five hundred meters across, pier to pier. We usually swim straight out to the buoys then do laps along the buoys between the piers."

We. We usually. We, but not me; I am not part of that collective, though surely they can't possibly have done this swim more than half a dozen times. I peel off my own dress, throwing it carelessly onto a sun lounger, and adjust the shoulder straps of the swimsuit I'd put on underneath. "No sea serpent myths for this particular bay?"

"None that I'm aware of."

"Where is Kanu Cove anyway?"

Bron's hand falters as she tucks her hair into her swim cap. "Farther round, past the headland. Maybe seven minutes' walk."

"Then why didn't she swim here?"

Bron exhales. "I don't know, Georgie. Maybe she wanted somewhere peaceful. Some time alone."

"Lissa? At night? Really? On our Malta trip we could barely get her to put a toe in the water after dark."

"People change." There's an edge to her tone that surprises me. "She was living here; I guess she got more comfortable with it."

"That's just it: she was living here. So she must have known Kanu Cove was danger—"

"Stop it, Georgie." She whirls away from me, then just as suddenly turns back. The moonlight isn't strong enough for me to see her face, but I can hear the tears in her voice. "She went swimming and she drowned. It was stupid, it was senseless—and she died. And you're not the only one trying to come to terms with it."

LEXIE ELLIOTT

She turns away again. I put a tentative hand on her shoulder.
"Bron. Bron, I'm sorry."

She turns into me and hugs me fiercely. "I know," she says into my
shoulder. I can feel her tears on my skin. "It's just . . . you weren't here.
It was awful. We were all asking those same questions at the time,
and the police were asking things; it was nonstop. And none of it mat-
tered because in the end she was still gone. It was . . . Well. You weren't
here."

"I . . . I couldn't be," I say, but that's not entirely true. I didn't dare
come. I was too scared of what I might see in Lissa, in Jem. Even now,
my mind skitters away from it. I was buying myself time by not coming, and Lissa died. "I'm sorry."

We stand together, Bron's head at my shoulder, my hand stroking
her hair. It always surprises me how much taller I am than her. Is it
that which shapes the balance between us; is it merely height that
casts me into the role of protector? Even though, in many ways, Bron
is far more robust than I? Then Duncan calls, "Are you two coming,
or what?" and Bron releases me.

"Coming." She runs ahead of me to the water's edge where Duncan, Jem and Adam are waiting for us. I scoop up my swim cap and
hold my goggle straps in my teeth, tucking my hair into the cap as I
follow her. A group has already set off and is starting to string out; in
the dark, I can't see the swimmers properly, but I glimpse intermittent flashes of pale arms or the white froth from a kick. We will catch
them quickly enough; they don't possess the swimming pedigree of
our little group. I know the water ought to feel beautifully warm, but
without the heat of the sun, it still chills me, and I suck in my breath
when it reaches my stomach. Bron throws herself into a dolphin dive,
and I force myself to do the same, feeling adrenaline flood through
my body as my head submerges; then I break into an easy front crawl,
popping my head up occasionally to check for Bron and the others
without breaking stroke. Within ten strokes or so, my heart rate has

16

settled as my body starts to adjust to the water temperature. Now I'm following the pale bubbles of somebody's kick trail—probably Duncan's—so I don't need to lift my head to sight. Within a minute or two we've passed a swimmer with an awkward stroke, then two more, then the whole pack of the first group. Bron has settled in on my right, only a meter or so from me; I can see the windmill of her pale arms every time I breathe to that side. Jem and Adam will be on our feet, following our kick trail. This is how we normally swim together, like a pod of dolphins: Duncan up ahead, Jem and Adam at the rear, Bron on my right and Lissa on my left. Only every time I breathe to the left, Lissa isn't there.

Duncan, who is the quickest out of all of us, is setting a leisurely pace by his standards, whether out of thoughtfulness to Jem, who is the weakest, or because he's not in his usual shape, I can't tell. Whatever the reason, I'm grateful for it: I'm feeling the effects of both the jet lag and the emotional exhaustion of the day; I don't feel as if I have another gear to slip into if Duncan were to pick up his pace. My eyes are adjusting to the dim light: I watch the trail of silvery bubbles from Duncan's feet; I watch my arms cut rhythmically through the darkness beneath me. I feel the cool water slipping past my limbs, the swell of it beneath me when a bigger set rolls in. Three strokes and look for Bron. Three more strokes, don't look for Lissa. Bron, no Lissa. Bron, no Lissa. Slowly I am being cracked open. You can't hide from yourself in the water; it doesn't allow it. It seeps into even the finest of hairline fissures and soaks off the shell.

Duncan's feet drop down, and I realize he's called a halt by one of the lit buoys, presumably to let Jem, who is lagging now, catch up. Adam, by contrast, hasn't lost any ground. He was never really a competitive swimmer—he played water polo instead—so he must have been putting in some training of late. We tread water by the buoy, which gently rocks as the water beneath it swells and ebbs, its circle of light wandering to and fro, painting faces then receding, as the faint rhythmic slap of Jem's arms against the water grows nearer. There's a solemnity to the silence that grows with every additional second that it remains unbroken. Jem has reached us now, breathing a little hard. I tip my head up toward the stars above. I will remember this forever, and I don't want to have to. It's so extraordinarily hateful to be here without her.

"Lissa." I don't realize I've said it out loud until Jem's voice joins mine. "Lissa," he says hoarsely. "To Lissa."

And then we are all saying it, our murmured words rolling out across the black velvet sea. "To Lissa." "Lissa." "To Lissa."

After we all swim back, Adam comes to settle on a sun lounger beside me, still in his trunks with a towel in his hand.

"You didn't find Philip?" I ask him, awkwardly pulling my dress over my towel. It takes a feat of coordination to remove the towel without exposing myself, but I'm practiced at it.

"I did." There's something in his voice that pulls my attention to him. "He was . . . ah . . . otherwise engaged." I shake my head, not understanding. "Quite deeply engaged, in fact."

Realization dawns. "Oh my God. With the waitress?"

"The very same."

"Jesus." It's beyond revolting, but somehow I can't help giggling. "That's appalling." Then a thought sobers me. "Poor Diane."

"She's not blind to it. At some point she must have made a decision to stay regardless." Lissa wasn't blind to it, either. But children don't get the same choice. He stands, wrapping his own towel round his waist, and then shucks off his trunks underneath it. I look out across the bay. Someone has extinguished the lights on the piers. "Though, on today of all days . . ."

"Maybe it's a reaction to it. An affirmation of life. Or something."

"Maybe." He sits back down beside me and starts to pull on dry shorts. "I heard you with Bron. Asking about Kanu Cove."

"Bar?" Jem calls across to us.

"In a minute," I call back. I turn back to Adam, my hands busy bundling my wet hair into a bun. "I didn't mean to upset her; it just doesn't make sense." I sound defensive. I have no reason to sound defensive. "But then, I wasn't here when it happened." *As Bron made clear.*

"I know, but you're right. It doesn't make sense." He pauses. "Tell the truth: when you got the call, did you expect it to be Jem that was missing?"

Yes. I stop, my hands still full of my twisted hair at the nape of my neck, my mouth full of words I can't say, that I don't dare voice. *Yes, I thought it would be Jem. Not then, exactly; not quite so soon, but at some point. At some point I would get the call, and it would be about Jem.* My eyes are fixed on the darkness of his face. I deliberately slide them away, looking at my lap as I finish securing the bun. The silence that sits between us has a weight to it.

He nods once, twice, as if to himself, then reaches out a hand to lay it carefully on my shoulder, his thumb rubbing gently along my collarbone. "You know," he says thoughtfully, as if we haven't just been discussing—well, whatever we've been not discussing. "I could kind of get behind the life-affirmation thing."

"Adam." It's barely a whisper, and I don't know what it means. His thumb travels along my collarbone and back once again. *Is this a good idea?* I want to ask, but just as suddenly, I really don't, because I know I'm going to take this careless, reckless step anyway. He's waiting for me to move. I lean into him and it's done.

TWO

BRONWYN

Breakfast. Breakfast on my own, on a terrace overlooking a bay with colors so brightly saturated that it's as if someone has applied an Instagram filter to the whole vista. Breakfast that has been cooked—cooked, not poured from a cereal box!—by somebody else and delivered by a young man with a smile and skin so perfect it's ludicrous that he isn't starring in a face cream commercial. I would give anything for this normally, so why can't I enjoy it?

"Morning." It's Georgie, looking exactly right for the setting in a pale sleeveless shirtdress and flip-flops, with enormous sunglasses hiding half her face and damp hair pulled into a messy bun. Time marches on everywhere, except around Georgie.

I pull out a chair for her. "Where did you get to last night?" I ask, though I already know. It wasn't hard to put two and two together when neither Adam nor Georgie appeared in the bar after the swim; though it made for a tamer evening than I'd anticipated. Or perhaps Lissa's absence would have done that anyway. She was always the match to Georgie's touch paper. But Georgie makes a noncommittal gesture with her hand. "Adam?" I press, then immediately feel gauche.

"Yes," says Georgie, but then she's turning to order muesli and a black coffee from our wondrous-skinned waiter. I wonder where Adam is. What does it say about their tumble if they aren't even eating breakfast together afterward? I've never known how to handle Georgie and Lissa's casual approach to men—as if they are toys to pick up and put down, as if those men have no feelings of their own; I could never quite work out if I was appalled or impressed by it. Though Lissa at least evolved enough to marry. Twice, in fact.

"Adam was asking the other day about how we met," I say. Georgie doesn't answer, but I'm fairly sure she's paying close attention. "Sometimes I forget he wasn't at uni with the rest of us." *Us*, meaning Georgie, Duncan, myself and Lissa—and Graeme, once upon a time. Five, then four; now three. "Anyway, what was it: sixteen, seventeen years ago that we met?"

"Something like that. I've known you as long as I haven't." A short laugh bursts out of me unexpectedly, and she arches her neck slightly and smiles, enjoying my reaction. How typically Georgie. The sly twist she puts on things, that halts you in your tracks. She never quite says what everyone else would, but she *almost* does. If you weren't paying attention, you'd miss the difference.

"Ah," I say wryly, "but I'm wysiwyg, remember?" Wysiwyg: what you see is what you get. That's what Lissa used to describe me as. It was affectionately meant, and I took it as such, even if I sometimes wished to be just a little mysterious. Though only a little; mystery must be so exhausting. "You don't need long to get to know me."

"I don't know. You still manage to surprise me from time to time." She's still smiling, still pulling me into the bright circle of Georgie. She could be the exact same girl, not a cell different, from the one I met seventeen or so years ago.

"Working?" I gesture at the laptop she's placed on the chair beside her.

"Yep. We're having IT issues, though, so I'm not sure how successful I'll be at logging in remotely." Her hand moves as if to chop off that conversation—*too dull*—and then she tips her sunglasses up on her forehead and focuses on me with her green eyes. "Anyway. It's so good to see you, despite . . ."

"I know. You too. We still miss you in London, you know." I try to cajole her back every time I see her, but it never works.

Her smile is rueful. "I miss you guys, too. New York is great, but you can never make friends as close as the ones from uni. Nobody has the time after that." The rueful smile makes a brief reappearance.

"Tell me about it. All these new friends I supposedly have—all the mums at the school gate—they're lovely, and they're almost all of them really friendly; they'll happily grab your child for you if you're running late, but it just feels superficial when the only thing you have in common is kids the same age." We smile at each other, a smile that somehow echoes through all the years: all the training sessions, the competitions, the nights out and the parties; those years when we saw each other absolutely every day. Then after uni, when Georgie was still in London, all the catch-up lunches and coffees and dinners and phone calls, when the frequency was still at least twice weekly. All that time invested in a relationship such that it can now survive a distance of three and a half thousand miles on a diet of only emails and calls and a visit or two a year.

"Tell me everything," Georgie says. "What's going on with you?"

"All good, really. Well, apart from—well, this, of course. The move to the dreaded burbs has actually worked out really well. I knew it was the right thing for the future, for the kids' schools, but I thought I would miss London, and actually I don't at all. It helps that the house is lovely, I suppose." Her head is inclined to me, and she nods as she listens, but I still wonder if I sound boring—harping on about schools and the suburbs, while Georgie dons designer clothes for work, drinks cocktails in Manhattan bars and goes home with whoever she feels like. Or maybe she's envious of family life: grass is always greener and all that. Rob would tell me I'm being silly, but even he turns up his smile a notch when Georgie and Lissa are around. Sometimes I think that's what the attraction was with Graeme: that he had Lissa but he wanted *me,* even if only in that moment.

But there's no point in thinking about Graeme. I slide my knife decisively into my croissant. "You must come stay next time you are over. See your goddaughter; Kitty would love that." Kitty adores Georgie, and Georgie is brilliant with her. The expression of unmitigated outrage on Kitty's little face when she realized I would be seeing Georgie without her was priceless. I feel a pang. Kitty and Jack will have climbed into our bed this morning for a cuddle, like they always do. I can almost feel the warmth of their little bodies against me, still heavy with the remnants of sleep, before the energy that fizzes through them for the rest of the day has had a chance to take hold.

"That would be lovely. It's been too long since I've had a trip back." She doesn't say *home.* We all know Georgie never goes *home,* and we all know she won't talk about it. Even I, with my famous lack of tact, know better than to tackle that subject. "So you and Rob are better now?" she asks.

"Yes." She tips her head sideways, a mild telegraphing of her disbelief. "No, really; we are. I think that—episode—was a good thing, actually. It made me appreciate him more, appreciate what we had." It's terrifying now to think of everything I jeopardized. My marriage and my family, even my friendships. If Lissa had ever found out . . . And all for what? I didn't get whatever I thought I would from it, if I was thinking at all. "I mean, he's still rubbish at—well, all the things he's rubbish at, but it doesn't drive me quite so mad now."

She thanks the waiter, who has brought her order, then turns back to me. "Your wysiwyg-ness didn't extend to telling him, did it?"

"God, no. What on earth would that have achieved?" I stare at her, confused. Did she expect that I would have? Surely the only people who confess are those who are looking to walk out the door but need a push?

One shoulder shrugs in the smallest of movements. "And you don't think Graeme told Lissa?"

"Are you kidding? Do you think Lissa would have ever spoken to me again if he had? Do you think I would even have been allowed to live?"

She winces, and I wish I could drag back the words, but it's too late now. "God. Sorry." An odd thought strikes me: is she asking because she herself told someone? "You didn't tell her, did you? Or anyone else?"

"Of course not. I promised you I wouldn't." It's so simply put: she promised she wouldn't, and therefore she didn't. End of discussion. And it really is: if I have to trust someone with my secrets, there's no one better than Georgie. Though not *all* my secrets. Not that.

"I know. Yes. Anyway." I find I'm rubbing my temple where a headache is forming. It's the brightness of the sun, maybe, or the wine from last night. Or maybe it's just this conversation. I want to drag it somewhere less fraught with obstacles, for either one of us, but I can't suddenly start talking about the weather, or Brexit, or Trump. Lissa died. It's why we're here; there's no escaping it. "When did you last see Lissa in person, then?"

"When she came to New York. I was planning to come out a month after you guys came; we had it all arranged for when my work eased up. But . . . anyway, I last saw her in New York. That must have been, oh, five months ago." She looks sideways, a little furrow forming between her eyebrows as she squints against the sun; when she turns back to me, there's a trace of it there still: the first evidence that Georgie is not immune to time. A teeny burst of something akin to triumph blooms inside me and is followed immediately by hot shame: I am mean and petty and not worthy of being her friend, this girl who has never been anything other than utterly supportive to me. "She seemed . . . happy. For Lissa, I mean." She shrugs and her lips twist ruefully. "It's all relative. But given how—broken—she was after Graeme died, she really seemed to be doing well. She was pretty absorbed in the hotel project. I know it had been Jem's dream for—well, forever, but it really seemed to be hers, too."

"Yes, she and Jem stayed with us for a bit when they were sorting out some of the financing in London, and it was literally all she could talk about." It had been an odd visit. She stayed for a fortnight, and yet we hardly seemed to find a moment to properly catch up. Was she happy? I would have said so. With hindsight, though . . . But perhaps hindsight casts shadows that were never really there. I pull myself back to the present. "Well, they've done an amazing job with it—not that you'd expect anything else." Both Lissa and Jem made careers out of high-end hotel management. They actually met at a professional conference. "It's quite something, isn't it?"

"Yes." She looks around, as if taking in the view for the first time, then back, dismissing it entirely. "I can see how it suited them. As a couple, I mean."

I know what she means. The glamour of this place is undeniable. "Yeah, I couldn't see Graeme here." Graeme again. *What's wrong with me?*

"I know." She has barely touched her muesli, which is unlike her. Despite being almost as lollipop thin as Lissa, Georgie likes her food. "He was better for her, I think."

"Hardly. Graeme and Lissa were fighting like cats and dogs before he died." I sound truculent; I try to soften my tone. "And remember, her dad never much liked him."

Georgie huffs out a breath. "Did you ever see him approve of anything Lissa chose to do without consulting him? As if his opinion was ever worth counting."

I shrug. I know Georgie's opinion of Lissa's father, and whilst I don't exactly think she's wrong, it still seems somewhat . . . disrespectful. "Well, anyway, Jem adored her."

She looks at me in that way she has, as if she's peeling back the surface to see what's underneath. *Nothing*, I think defiantly. *I'm wysiwyg, remember?* "I suppose. Though Duncan said Jem and Lissa were arguing that night, the night she—"

"You were talking with Duncan?"

"Yes. This morning. Adam and I ran into him at Kanu Cove." I see the cove in my own mind's eye, a narrow tongue of a bay, shaped more like a fjord, all dramatic cliffs and almost no beach; it's exactly the sort of place that would have a serpent myth attached to it. She doesn't miss the shudder that goes through me. "Exactly. The water there—there's not a chance you'd get me in there. So it doesn't make sense that Lissa would opt to swim there—"

"Jeez, Georgie." My words are too strident. An elderly man in a frighteningly bright orange shirt looks up from the next table, but I can't help myself. "Do we have to? Go over everything?"

She looks at me quizzically without saying anything for just long enough for me to feel myself start to flush. "Bron, are you okay?" she asks quietly.

"No!" I take a breath, then two, before I risk a glance at her. I'm pushing her away, I know it, but I just can't bear the questions . . . "I mean yes. Sorry. Yes." I dash a hand at the tears that have spilled out. "I'm just on edge today; I don't know why." She hands me a napkin and strokes my upper arm while I wipe away the tears, trying not to mess up my eye makeup. Though I don't know why I'm bothering to take care, given that in this heat my mascara will have smudged into panda eyes by lunchtime anyway. I take another deep breath and let it out slowly. Georgie is waiting patiently for me to say something. "Maybe it's being away from home. I know it sounds lame, but I really miss the kids."

She shakes her head. "It doesn't sound lame at all."

"When I'm with them, I'd kill for a little alone time, but the minute I get it, I'm wishing they were here." I force a laugh. "They ruin you twice over." But Georgie has her head tipped to one side again. "What?"

She shrugs. "Nothing, just . . ."

"What?"

"I thought maybe it was my questions—"

"Georgie—"

"—I know I'm upsetting you with them, and Duncan, too; I'm not meaning to, I'm just trying to understand—"

"Why? What difference does it make if you understand? She's still dead, and there's nothing you could have done." My volume has risen again: the elderly man is looking at me once more, and now the occupants of a few other tables are, too. "What difference does it make?"

"It makes a difference to me. It should make a difference to all of us." I stare at her, and suddenly I feel slightly afraid. When she's set her mind on something, Georgie doesn't bend. Lissa had that about her, too. Maybe I did once, but that was a long time ago, before marriage, and kids. "Don't you think we owe it to her to try to understand? To make sure the same thing never happens again?"

"How could it ever happen again?" I'm genuinely bewildered, but Georgie has dropped her sunglasses back into place, hiding those intense green eyes of hers. All I can see is the azure of the sea and the white of the terrace wall reflected in her dark lenses. I look away, across the bay, to where the horizon blends into the sky. The blues are so bright that they make my eyes ache. I reach for my bag and push my chair back. "I'm going to call home. I'll see you later."

She purses her lips, then shrugs, reaching for her laptop. "Duncan, Adam and I are planning on swimming this afternoon, sometime after lunch." Her tone is excessively polite. "Dunc was going to see if he could get a boat to take us out to the nature reserve island, so we can do a swim round there."

"Oh," I say, equally stiffly. "Well. I might join you."

She's opened up the laptop now and is firing it up. I feel dismissed, despite the fact that I was the one to get up from the table. I turn back when I get to the edge of the terrace, but she's entirely focused on something on her screen. She's not looking at me at all.

Only I can't call home, because it's not even four in the morning, as Georgie no doubt worked out because nothing much gets past Georgie—when she's sober. Which, come to think of it, is the only way I've seen her this trip, in stark contrast to our university years, though she hasn't said anything particular about it. Georgie is the direct opposite of wysiwyg—except no, Georgie isn't as binary as that. She's the strangest mix of wide-open rooms and locked doors. I had just started at uni when I met them both—Lissa and Georgie together, as they always were—and full of desperation to be more interesting than in my staid years at a girls' private school, being diligently studious and enthusiastically sporty and utterly ordinary; the only thing that held me apart was my swimming. It was swimming that brought me to Lissa and Georgie, but Georgie's was the arm that pulled me into their circle. It took me a long time to figure out that that same arm holds people away. Everyone except Lissa, that is. But I was an academic year younger; it felt natural that they would be closer.

Ordinary. It's not the insult now that I felt it was at eighteen. I'm not even sure it's damning with faint praise. So many well-lived lives are ordinary; so many enduring loves, too. It took me an even longer time—and Rob pointing it out—to realize that my very ordinariness is why Lissa and Georgie and I fit together so well. *You're their voice of reason,* he said. *They need a point of reference, a true north.* A wave of longing to hear his voice sweeps through me—but he won't much thank me for waking him at this time; I'll have to wait a few hours.

I could go and lie by the pool, I suppose, and maybe I will later, though I'd better stick to the shade. Georgie hasn't even been here a day, but already her skin has acquired a golden glow. The only things I've acquired are more freckles and an uncomfortable sunburn on the backs of my knees; I'll need factor 50 there if I'm to swim later. But for now, for want of anything better to do, I head toward my room, winding my way up the hill on the paved stone path, occasionally having to move to one side to allow one of the fleet of what looks like adapted golf buggies to pass, laden with dirty bed linens or gardening equipment or some such. It can't be more than two hundred meters, but it feels much farther in the heat. Jem has put us all up in amazing villas—I have one all to myself, with a private plunge pool, no less—at no cost to us, though it did make me wonder if maybe the hotel isn't doing so well as I thought. Surely he ought to be putting paying guests in these accommodations?

There's a local man coming down the steps from the entry to my villa as I approach; presumably one of the staff. There are more staff than guests here, it seems; I must remember to get some local currency to leave a housekeeping tip when I depart. I smile politely, and he bobs his head back, before setting off quickly down the path. The cool shade inside the air-conditioned suite is a welcome relief to my sticky skin, but I know that nothing short of the ibuprofen that's in my toiletries bag will help my headache.

The slide door to the bathroom has been closed, presumably by housekeeping. It sticks a little; it takes both my hands to yank it into motion. Then those hands fly to my mouth. Scrawled across the mirror, which spans the width of the bathroom, in six-inch-high letters are the words:

IT'S YOUR FAULT
BITCH

I whirl around, my heart thumping in my ears, as if I might find the culprit right beside me, but the bathroom is completely empty. I reach for the bathroom phone and am midway through pressing the button to dial reception when my brain catches up to me. If I report this, I will have to answer questions, more and more questions. Questions like, who could have done this, and why? Like, what exactly is it that's my fault, and why might I be a bitch? I slowly replace the receiver in its wall-mounted cradle and stare at the words, fighting the urge to run screaming back down to the main reception while I try to formulate a plan. *Safety first:* I need to check the rest of the villa. I listen for a minute, then two, straining to hear above the rasp of my own breathing. Even my heartbeat is too loud, and too rapid. But the villa sounds empty. There's a slight nasal hum from the bathroom light, and a low-frequency whirring from the air-conditioning unit, and now that I'm concentrating on it, I can hear something from the minibar, too, but nothing that indicates the presence of a person hiding somewhere. It feels empty, too.

I slip off my noisy flip-flops and move slowly into the bedroom, trying to move soundlessly as I run my eyes over the perfectly made super king bed, the chair in the corner with the nightdress I'd dumped on it now neatly folded. In here the air-conditioning unit seems extraordinarily loud; I keep glancing over my shoulder. Would I hear anyone behind me? I force myself to check under the bed—nothing. Nothing in the walk-in wardrobe, either. The safe there is still shut; when I type my code in, which I have to do twice as my fingers are trembling and clumsy, my jewelry and passport are safely intact.

The living area is similarly empty, and the French doors that open out onto the plunge pool area are locked. Whoever came in did it through the front door, and they could have done it at any point after I went to breakfast. Though surely after housekeeping came in, given the neatly made bed; I doubt the housekeeping staff would have missed six-inch-high letters across the mirror. I think of the man I saw leaving. Was it him? Was he dressed correctly for a staff member? He had a dark blue smock on, in some kind of light material, and matching trousers. Is that what the housekeeping staff wear? I can't think. But why on earth would a staff member write this? This is personal. This comes from someone who knows something. Or thinks they do. I find I'm shaking. *It's your fault.* Lissa's death, surely—but who would lay that at my feet?

I go back into the bathroom and approach the writing cautiously. The missing apostrophe glares at me, though I can't imagine it says anything significant about the writer's origins: native English speakers are just as likely to have made that mistake. It looks like it's been written in browny-pink lipstick—my own lipstick, I realize, as I spot my MAC Verve tube wrapped in a tissue on the bathroom counter, the protruding lipstick mashed and misshapen. On further inspection I spot the missing cap on the floor. It seems particularly spiteful to have used my lipstick. Or opportunistic. I should probably bag up the lipstick tube. It's unlikely to have fingerprints on it, assuming the culprit used the tissue when holding it, but there's a chance—and then I stop. What's the point in bagging it up if I'm not reporting this? But what if this is the start of something more sinister? Surely I ought to bag it anyway? In the end I repurpose the plastic bag that holds the complimentary shower cap and gingerly transfer the tissue and the lipstick tube to it, taking care never to touch them directly. Then I store the bag in the minibar; I'm not completely sure, but I think I read once in a crime novel that cold preserves fingerprints.

Lastly I take my mobile phone and carefully photograph the words in the mirror. *It's your fault. Bitch.* I stare at the photo on my phone. My own reflection, holding the phone in front of me at shoulder height, is in the image. *Bitch* is written across my face.

I pick up one of the pristine white facecloths and set about cleaning off the lettering.

THREE

GEORGIE

Sender: Kateb, Melissa.

I read it twice, because I can't believe it, adrenaline coursing across my skin, and my heartbeat rushing in my ears. *Lissa.* It can't be. But I haven't made a mistake; I'm definitely looking at the inbox folder of my email, and the sent date is yesterday . . . Oddly I find myself looking around at the sun-drenched terrace, but none of the other guests enjoying their breakfast are paying me the slightest attention, and Bron has already left. I turn back to my laptop and move the cursor with glacial speed to click on Lissa's email—*Lissa.* I'm not breathing.

The email pops open immediately—a part of my brain recognizes that the Wi-Fi is excellent here in the restaurant—and immediately I realize what has happened. The email got caught in a quarantine; there's explanatory information on that above the body of the message. The installation of our new IT system has not been without issues, one of which is a firewall system so enthusiastic that for a short while absolutely all of the email traffic of one of my colleagues was caught in it because the messages apparently contained profanity

33

(his surname is Cockburn). In fact, Lissa sent her message months ago; it has only just been released to me now. I check the actual sent date again. Four days before she died. My breath comes out in a long, slow huff, and I feel my shoulders drop several inches. *Relief.* I don't want to analyze why I feel it, but I know that's what I'm feeling.

I look around again, and a waiter spots the movement and starts toward me, then he relaxes when I quickly shake my head. I could delete the email, but I can't delete my knowledge of it. I'm going to have to read it, these words from beyond the grave—no, not the grave, from beyond the watery deep. I think again of the waters of Kanu Cove, as Adam and I saw them this morning. There was a boat there, no more than a skiff, really, with the helmsman fighting to hold position while simultaneously pulling in a lobster pot. It was high tide, and the water streaming past the bow on its way out to sea was breathtakingly fast. *Apparently it's something to do with the combination of the narrow neck of the cove and the topography of the seabed just beyond,* Adam said, small crow's-feet appearing at the outer corners of his eyes as he squinted against the sun. *Christ, what was Lissa thinking?*

I take a deep breath and look again at the email. *Kateb, Melissa.* Once *Williams, Melissa* and before that *Dashwood, Melissa,* but *Kateb, Melissa* last of all and forever more. I know I have to read it; there's no point in delaying. I find that I'm glancing around again; I force myself to focus on the laptop, scrolling down past the quarantine information to the start of her words.

Hiya honey,

How are you? Hope things are settling down for you at work. Are you sure you can't make it out? I know you're coming next month instead, but everyone else arrived this afternoon, and I can't tell you how lovely it is to see them, but it's not the same without you . . . Hop on a plane! You know you want to! And in case you were wondering, Adam is here too. Just saying. ;-)

Actually they've all gone to bed now. I'm the last one standing, just like you and I always are. Jem used to stay up with me, but he's exhausted now, what with the hotel going gangbusters. That, or he's bored of me. I'M JOKING. Though he still makes such a fuss of the female guests, even after I took your advice and spoke to him about it. They practically cream their underwear in front of him, even the married ones. Especially the married ones, actually— Bron too; she lights up like a bloody light bulb around him— and doesn't he know it. He says it's good for business (which is shorthand for shut-the-fuck-up-about-it). Is it me, do you think? I can't help thinking it must be; something I'm attracted to initially, or something about me that attracts that type. I wouldn't have stood for it when we were younger. I don't know that I should be standing for it now, but I just don't have the energy to fight again right now. Or "discuss," as he calls it. He wants us to try IVF—as if it's that easy when you live in the middle of an ocean! But even if there was a clinic down the road, you know what that was like for me. It's as if history is trying to repeat itself, and I won't let it. I can't face it all again.

I'm being appallingly maudlin. It's the wine, and missing you. We're fine, really. Come, please. Pretty please. If you can.

Love Lissa x

Lissa. I read it again. I'm about to read it a third time, when a voice beside me makes me physically jump. It's the waiter. "I'm sorry," he says, smiling even while speaking. I wonder if Jem tells the staff to smile incessantly or if it's just in his nature. "Can I get you anything else?"

"No. No, thank you. Just the bill, please." I return to the email. What did she mean by history repeating itself—which part of history? Was she just talking about the IVF, or something . . . else? Her tone is odd; she sounds like Lissa, but not quite. More . . . no, not more; less. Less attitude, less fight. Less bravado, even. Less Lissa. I try to see this particular version of her walking along the stony path to Kanu Cove in the dead of night, pausing on the stone jetty to put on her cap and goggles, but even she won't do it. It's madness.

I shut the lid of the laptop smartly and sit back in my seat. A moment later I flip it open again to fire off an email to the head of IT; if there are any other messages languishing in quarantine, I'd rather like to know about them.

"Georgie." It comes from behind me. I whip out a hand to slam the laptop shut again, even as I'm turning to the voice. It's Jem, in what I think of as his managerial uniform: a loose linen shirt and artfully tailored shorts that sit right across the line between smart-slash-casual. Did he see Lissa's email? But he's smiling, or trying to, as he bends to kiss both my cheeks.

"Join me?" I ask brightly.

He pulls out the chair that Bron was sitting on only minutes ago. "A coffee wouldn't go amiss." He takes off his sunglasses and hangs them on the front of his shirt, then runs both hands over his face, before turning his remarkable pale green eyes on me for barely a second. His gaze is already off and roaming around the terrace as he asks, "How are you doing?"

"Do you know," I say thoughtfully, "I think you may be the first person to ask me that."

"Christ, lucky you. People are asking me that nonstop." He turns to the waiter and rattles off an order in the local language. I wonder how many languages he speaks. He turns back to me. "It's not because they don't care."

"I know. It's because they're afraid I might answer."

Jem's lips quirk upward. "Maybe. Nobody knows how to pigeon-hole you in the grief stakes. Husband is easy, but the two of you . . . there was always something so intense between you." He's still easily the handsomest man on the terrace—in the whole resort, probably—but he's not quite his usual self. His eyes won't rest; his edges are frayed. Even his French accent is stronger. He glances at me briefly as if waiting for an answer, but I didn't hear a question. "I didn't quite understand it myself. The—the *dependency*."

I shrug with deliberate nonchalance. "Maybe at uni. But we haven't even been living in the same country for nigh on five years."

"Really?" He looks like he's about to challenge that, but at that moment the waiter brings him an espresso. He raises a hand briefly in thanks, then takes a sip, those strange eyes wandering once again across the terrace. *Sea glass*, I think, finally realizing what they put me in mind of. Broken bottles rubbed into smooth pebbles by the bottom of the ocean; pale enough that you almost think you can see through them, that they might allow you to see the same world with a different filter—but you never quite can. I wonder if it's his eyes that are the clincher with the married women. "You know," he says, as if there hasn't been an interruption, "it didn't feel like the distance made a difference. You still spoke all the time."

No, I think, though I simply shrug. *No, we didn't; not anymore, not in a way that counts.* There are things you can only talk about in person, late at night, softened by a blanket of darkness and alcohol. We hadn't spoken like that since Graeme died.

"Tell me something about her," he says. "Something I don't already know." He finally fixes me in his gaze, and it's a shock when I see what he's no longer trying to conceal: the naked, ugly resentment toward me. "Something nobody else knows."

"Jem—"

"Tell me," he insists.

"Jem, I could tell you a hundred things, but it wouldn't—"

"One thing, Georgie. That's all I'm asking." His words are a challenge, and as my shock recedes, it's hard not to rise to it. He has no right to lash out at me this way. And maybe I'm angry with him because of Lissa's email, too. Is he still flirting with all the female guests now that he's a widower? Does that add to or detract from attractiveness? "Just tell me one. Just—"

"All right!" I sit back in my chair in frustration. He raises his eyebrows: *Well?* I take a moment, as if to collect my thoughts, but I already know what to say. If he wants a story, I'll deliver one he won't forget. I let him stew for a beat or two more, then sit forward again, my elbows on the table. "All right. Well, in our third year, there was a party. Actually there were lots of parties, but this was *our* party, at the house that we were renting—"

He's nodding, all of his attention fixed on me. "With Duncan, right? And a couple of others."

"Yes, Martin and Julia." I can't think when I last spoke to either of them. I got the impression they were rather relieved when the year was up: it's one thing to be around the party crowd when you choose to join it, but it's quite another to live with it the morning after.

"I never did understand how you guys could party like that and also be on the varsity team." Varsity: it betrays his American college education. Nobody called it the varsity team.

"It wasn't like the US setup. Nobody had a scholarship; we didn't even have a paid coach. Don't get me wrong: we had some great swimmers, and we all put in a fair amount of training, but it was just another strand of university life. And, actually, it was usually the sports teams that threw the best parties." He's frowning slightly; it still doesn't compute for him. "Anyway, at this particular party, everyone was hammered on shots of vodka jelly, and Lissa was high, too. I don't remember what she'd taken." He looks away, but just as quickly he looks back, unable to call a halt to the car crash that he's asked for. "It got late. Almost everyone had left; the ones that were still there were either copping off or passed out. Bron was throwing up in the bathroom upstairs—she never could hold her drink. Her boyfriend at the time had gone AWOL, so I wound up looking after her; I put her to bed in my room. And after that I went looking for Lissa." I can see the hotel terrace, but now it's overlaid with the five-bedroom student house. I feel myself walking unsteadily down the narrow stairs, one hand on the wall for much-needed balance after all those virulent jelly shots. Nobody has yet bothered to turn off the speakers in the lounge, and *Pure Morning* by Placebo is still pumping out: *A friend in need's a friend indeed...*

Jem clears his throat. "Where was she?"

"In the kitchen. With Bron's boyfriend, Scott." I see them now: Lissa is on the counter, her long hippie-dippie skirt bunched up at the top of her thighs and her slender legs wrapped round Scott's waist, the ankles locked. Her bare skin is painted an unhealthy yellow from the streetlight just outside the kitchen window; it's the only light in the room. My hand flies to my mouth, and I'm turning to leave, but Lissa's head tips back as Scott buries his own in the curve of her neck. I see her face, and it's the disconnect between the two of them—Scott urgent and hungry, Lissa entirely flat—that stops me in my tracks. "It looks like they're fucking—or about to, but something seems . . . off." One of her hands is busy at his fly, and the other is reaching behind her, stretching for something . . . I'm too slow to make sense of it until it's too late. "And then I realize she's picked up a bread knife. One of those long, serrated ones." I'm peripherally aware that Jem is leaning toward me. I'm not sure he's breathing. "And she puts it to his dick." Jem recoils involuntarily, murmuring something like *Jesus*. "She says—I can't remember exactly, I wasn't entirely sober at the time, but something like: *Bron is one of my best friends. Did you really think I would let you do something like this?*" All those years ago, it takes a second or two for the situation to dawn on Scott. The instant it does, he tries to buck away, but she has him held too tightly, the knife pressed against the base of his penis, on the underside, and all he succeeds in doing is forcing the blade more firmly against himself.

"Christ," breathes Jem. "Did she—did she hurt him?"

Are you fucking psycho? Scott yelps in the dimly lit kitchen. *You're cutting me.* And she is: I can see drops on the blade. They look black in the dim light. The music is still playing: *A friend with weed is better.* "She cut him a little. I stepped in at that point and tried to get her to put down the knife." Fifteen years ago, I'm slowly lowering my hand from my mouth. *Lissa. Put it down. I think he's got the message.* They both turn to me. Lissa's face isn't expressionless anymore. It's strangely dreamy, as if she's floating. Scott's is a mix of outrage and fear—and shame, too, when he sees that it's me. He starts to plead even though he can't meet my eye. *Georgie. She's gone nuts. Please. Get her off me.*

"Did she? Did she put it down?"

"It took a bit of persuasion. Quite a bit, in fact." There was blood on the linoleum floor as well as the knife by the time she relinquished it. Afterward I washed the blade in the kitchen sink, watching the sticky dark rivulets thin, then disappear, under the running tap water. There was a wiry black pubic hair caught on one of the serrated teeth. The water took that, too, eventually.

I wonder if it worked. I wonder if Scott ever tried to cheat on a girlfriend again.

"Did he go to the police?" Jem asks.

"Of course not. He threatened to, but I made him see it how the police might see it." Jem shakes his head, not comprehending. I adopt an arch tone. "Lissa was one of his girlfriend's best friends, and she was high as a kite. He took advantage, forced himself on her. She was defending herself. And of course, I saw it all." Jem opens his mouth, then closes it again. I shrug. "Anyway. I doubt he's told a living soul. He broke up with Bron by phone the next day; I'm not sure I ever actually saw him again." I see him now, though, surly and defeated, his shoulders rounded as he gingerly stuffs himself back into his jeans. His mouth is working to hold himself together. *She's fucking psycho,* he spits out as he passes me on his way out of the kitchen. I can hear the presence of the tears that he's fighting. *And you're a twisted fucking bitch as well.*

Jem sits back. I'm back on the terrace, too, now; the darkened kitchen has faded away. "Jesus Christ, Georgie." He runs both hands over his face again, ruffling his Hugh Grant–ish flop of hair as he does so. His resentment toward me has gone, at least, although I'm not sure what he's replaced it with. His jaw is tight as he looks across at me with those strange eyes. "She was just scaring him, right? She wouldn't actually have cut it off?"

I almost laugh. That he could have married her—married her!— and be so oblivious. Are all marriages like this? Is it in fact a neces- sary attribute in order for a marriage to survive: some kind of willing suspension of critical thought, so that the person you see before you is the person you *want* to see? But I'm not angry at him anymore. "Of course," I say, with a casual shrug. He looks at me uncertainly, and for a moment I think he's grasped the equivocation: of course she would, or of course she wouldn't? But whatever he reads in my face must be reassuring; his slight frown clears.

We've planned to meet up for lunch—Duncan, Adam, Bron and I— though not at the main restaurant, where I ate breakfast; there's ap- parently another, much more informal one down by Horseshoe Bay that I didn't notice yesterday. I take an utterly illogical route there that goes past Kanu Cove and don't bother trying to justify it to myself. The cove is empty this time: no Adam with me and no boat struggling in the water. Lissa's email is on an endless cycle in my mind: *It's as if history is trying to repeat itself, and I won't let it. I can't face it all again.* I should have come on the trip. I should have been here, to hear her tell me what she meant by that, to talk her out of whatever hole she was digging herself into. To save her from herself.

I walk along one side to the stone jetty and then, on impulse, take my sandals off and sit on the edge, dangling my feet in the water. The shape of the cove, like a deep, narrow fjord, means that it's a sun-trap with nary a breath of wind, and right now the sun is at its highest and strongest; I quickly find myself wishing I'd brought a hat. The stones beneath my bottom are uneven and gritty and uncomfortably warm; the water cooling my feet and ankles is just water, just the same seawater as at Horseshoe Bay. Why would Lissa have chosen to come here particularly? Is it perhaps a different place in the dark? I sit until I'm intolerably hot and sticky, but nothing reveals itself to me. Finally I give up and scramble back to my feet, bending double to fasten my sandals.

When I straighten up, there's a man only inches from my face.

A shocked gasp escapes me as I step back involuntarily; how did I not hear him? He looks local in appearance, and small and wizened, with possibly the most rotten front teeth I've ever seen on display, in what I hope is meant to be a smile. He's wearing a ripped sleeveless T-shirt of indeterminate color and incongruous basketball shorts. "Sorry," I say weakly; though why am I the one apologizing? "You gave me a fright."

He nods. "Kanu," he says. "Not safe."

"It's okay. I wasn't going to swim."

He shakes his head impatiently. I wonder if he's as old as I think he is, or if the hardness of life has added extra years. "Kanu." His

English is broken, but that word is clear enough. I don't understand his hand gesture, though: he's wiggling one hand, almost in a wave-type gesture, but somehow not quite. "Swim, no swim, Kanu not safe." His hand, brown and leathery and small as a child's, moves again, in that same odd gesture. Side to side, not up and down. "Leave."

I look around involuntarily. "Not safe? Why?"

"Kanu takes. You leave now. Kanu takes." He's shooing me now, insistently, such that I have to step back away from him, and away from the edge of the jetty.

"Takes? Takes what?"

"Kanu takes. Takes who wants taken."

"I . . ." I stare at him, appalled, but he's actually touching my arm now, with those warm, dry, leathery hands, and pushing me with surprising strength. I give up and turn, half running, for the path.

HOW TO KILL YOUR BEST FRIEND
Method 2: Poison

Poison. Specifically, recreational drugs, given that I can't think how I could possibly get hold of cyanide, strychnine or—I don't know—nightshade or belladonna or something equally ridiculous and straight out of a nineteenth-century gothic novel. But pretty much all of the obvious twenty-first-century recreational substances are deadly in large enough quantities.

So: recreational drugs.

Pros:
- Believable
- Executable: I can definitely get hold of them.

Cons:
- Traceable: I have to buy the gear off someone, and that someone would know that I had.
- Depends on her being in the right kind of mindset to actually take some; unless you can administer it in a drink or food?
- I'm not one hundred percent certain it would be effective: she could survive an overdose. Of all people, she could.
- I might have to travel with it, which gives a higher than average chance of getting banged up for possession. It's one thing to take a chance for the actual murder, but I'm not keen on it happening before the opportunity to commit the crime presents itself.

This is madness. But what else is there?

FOUR

GEORGIE

The others are just arriving when I turn up at the restaurant in Horse-shoe Bay, having only just calmed myself after my Kanu Cove en-counter. Surely he was just an old man who's probably not actually allowed to be on resort land—most guests would rather not confront the yawning chasm between their luxury holiday lifestyle and the desperate poverty of the islanders, and he wasn't wearing a staff uni-form. Just an old man with a questionable grasp of English. He couldn't possibly have meant it how I interpreted it.

And anyway, she didn't want to be taken. She couldn't have wanted that.

This restaurant is very different to the main one; it's styled in beach shack chic with tables set directly on the sand under a light-weight trellis for shade, and chairs made from old surfboards. We're the only guests there for the moment, so we have our pick of the ta-bles. Duncan chooses the most shaded one, and I sit down next to him, then immediately regret it: Bron, directly opposite, won't meet my eye, and I'm absurdly aware of Adam sitting diagonally across the table from me. He hasn't shaved. It suits him.

I would have known if she wanted that. Surely I would have known. But the words from her email needle remorselessly in my mind: *I can't face it all again.*

Duncan picks up the wine list. "Anyone for rosé? Yes? Bron, Georgie, you'll have a glass, right?" He doesn't wait for an answer before beckoning over the waiter. We usually save any drinking until after swimming; Adam glances at him briefly, then at me. I look at Bron. Bron doesn't look back.

I'm overthinking it. It was just poor English. He just meant to scare me away from a cove with a dangerous riptide. I have to shake it off; I have to concentrate on my lunch companions.

"Is Jem joining us?" Bron asks nobody in particular, without lifting her eyes from her study of the menu.

"He's working," Adam says laconically. I wonder if that's a welcome escape for Jem or a constant reminder of Lissa.

"Oh, I managed to book the boat," Duncan says, with a burst of enthusiasm. "Two thirty, at the jetty over there. You're coming, right, Bron?"

"Erm, sure. I suppose Jem will still be working, though?" She puts down her menu and crosses her arms in front of her, as if cold, though it must be over eighty-five degrees Fahrenheit today. The action particularly highlights her ample cleavage, more ample than ever before given her extra pounds, framed by a red bikini under her scoop neck sundress and dusted with almost as many freckles as her shoulders. It's a different dress from the one she was wearing at breakfast; she must have changed specially. I think of Lissa's email again: *She lights up like a bloody light bulb around him.*

"I think so," Duncan replies. The waiter has already returned with a bottle of rosé, sheathed in beads of water. He pours a glass for Duncan to taste. I look out over the bay, to the hazy shadow I can see across the open strait. From memory of the map, that's the island nature reserve where we're going to be swimming. It lies like a long, thin bullet shape parallel to the coastline, perhaps four and a half miles offshore, though it looks farther away from here.

The waiter has moved round the table, bringing the bottle toward my glass. I put my hand over the top of the glass. "No, thank you." Duncan turns to me, raising his straw-colored eyebrows and his pink-filled glass. "I'm not really drinking anymore." If I were a grown-up, I wouldn't feel defensive about it. If I were.

The straw eyebrows shoot up even farther, almost reaching the thatch of his hair. "Yeah, sure. You're not drinking anymore—but you're not drinking any less, right?" He's grinning, but the jollity doesn't ring true, and suddenly I remember that he knew Lissa for longer than even Bron or myself; he knew her from his high school days. I force a laugh and lift my hand, letting the waiter pour. I don't look at Adam. After a moment's hesitation, Bron accepts a glass, too, and then Adam.

"Isn't this place stunning?" says Duncan, his eyes sweeping panoramically around the bay. "There's something to be said for an island pace of life."

"Planning early retirement?" Adam teases.

"Maybe." He shrugs a little defensively. "I mean, I don't want to work like I am right now for the rest of my life. There could be worse retirement plans than getting involved with managing a place like this."

"Where is everyone?" I ask, looking around at the empty tables.

"I think most people are flying out on the Lufthansa flight this afternoon," Duncan replies. There are only three direct long-haul flights a week from the island: one British Airways flight to London, and two Lufthansa flights to Frankfurt. For anywhere else, you have to take a tortuous route, like I did, via at least two international hubs and a local carrier. All four of us are booked on the next BA flight back to London, in two days' time.

"What about . . . proper guests?" Non-memorial guests. There isn't a neat way to say it.

Duncan grimaces. "Not all publicity is good publicity. With Lissa's death, there were quite a lot of cancellations. Most of the clients come through luxury travel agents, and I'm guessing they're waiting to see what impact this has on the management." The management: Jem. "If you take out everyone who's here for the memorial, there are only three villas booked out of the thirty-two." The hotel is really a collection of discretely arranged villas, carefully planned so that each one feels secluded and has a sea view. Some are single bedroom; the largest—the presidential villa—sleeps ten. I look around again, noting all the staff that lie within a casual glance: four waiters, a gardener and two people manning the towel station, and those are just the ones I can see. God knows how many are working behind the scenes. If the hotel closes for a period of time, it will be a disaster for the micro economy.

"Can he ride it out?" Adam asks Duncan.

"I don't know." Duncan grimaces. "I'm going to take a look at the figures with him tonight." For a moment he appears lost in thought, but then he visibly shakes himself and takes a large swallow of the wine before turning to Adam to start up a conversation about bikes, a topic on which Adam can hold forth all day, seeing as he runs his own bike shop. I drink from my water glass rather than my wineglass and look across at Bron, meaning to catch her eye and share a laugh at their boring preoccupation—*middle-aged men in Lycra!*—but her eyes are fixed on her glass.

"Miss Ay—Ay-ers?" asks a voice hesitantly, and I glance up. It's one of the reception staff. I'm starting to distinguish the differences in the uniform depending on the role; the reception staff have loose scarlet dresses, or shirts and trousers, whereas the waiters are in a deep blue. His eyes are flicking uncertainly between Bron and me.

"Ayers," I say. "That's me. Like air, but with an *s*."

"Ayers," he repeats, smiling. "This came for you." He hands me an A4-sized envelope. It has some heft to it; there must be a document of tens of pages inside.

"Oh. Thank you." I wasn't expecting anything, but I've recently been made partner of the patent company I've been with for years, and the step-up in workload has been noticeable. The others are looking at me curiously. "It can only be from the firm." I grimace, pushing back my chair awkwardly against the sand the legs are buried in and taking my table knife to slice along under the flap of the envelope. Then I step away for privacy, curious to see which enterprising soul has managed to get something across to me here. The first sheet is blank except for a bold title in large font in the center:

FOLLOW THE MONEY

Frowning, I flick to the next page, but it says exactly the same. And the next, and the next. I look around for the man from reception, but he's already gone. I leaf through the entire stack again. There's nothing else, and absolutely every sheet says exactly the same thing. *Follow the money.* Which money? Follow it where? And who wants me to do the following?

"Okay?" asks Adam, his voice pitched a little louder to reach me.

"Ah—yes. Ish." I give him a bright smile. Too bright, judging from the mild raise of his eyebrows. "It'll be fine; I can deal with it later." I rejoin the table and stuff the envelope in my beach bag, where it lies incongruously alongside sunscreen and my Kindle. *Follow the money.* To what end? Adam looks at me thoughtfully, then asks Duncan whether he still has his Chelsea season ticket. I look across at Bron. She's staring out to sea, whether out of preoccupation or a determined effort to avoid my eye, I can't tell. Is she sulking? But it's not like Bron to sulk—and then I realize that her fingers are methodically shredding her own cuticles. A thin line of blood is apparent by her left thumbnail, but her left forefinger keeps working at it.

"Did you get hold of Rob and the kids?" I ask lightly. *Follow the money.* Whose money?

She looks across, blinking, as if I've dragged her out of a deep sleep, and her fingers still. "Oh. Yes. Well, not after breakfast; I was confused on the time difference. But I spoke to them just before I came here." She finds a smile; it lacks wattage, but it's definitely a smile. *Preoccupation, then.* Or perhaps it's the strangeness of what we are now; I feel it, too. We're a three-legged stool that's lost a leg. We have to find a new way to balance. "Kitty sends *all* her love," she says.

"Bless. Send mine back." I really should take a trip back to the UK soon. She is my goddaughter after all. Bron's attention has wandered back out to sea, and her forefinger starts its merciless attack again. I can't bear to see it: my hand shoots out to cover hers, stilling it. "Bron," I say gently. *What money?* And then I think: *Lissa's money?*

She looks down at her hand, with mine on top of it, and blinks several times before she lifts her head, her hazel eyes suspiciously bright. "Yes. Right," she says briskly, giving my hand a small squeeze before she releases it to reach for her glass of wine.

The boat Duncan has booked is apparently more usually employed towing water-skiers, but it's perfect for what we need, with cushioned seating running around the back and sides, and a wide platform out the back that will make it easier to climb back in afterward. The driver is a burly thirtysomething Australian called Steve, who has thick stripes of white zinc paste across his cheekbones—which seems too little and too late given the leathery look of his skin—and an easygoing can-do attitude; he's already known to Bron, Duncan and Adam from previous swimming outings, which goes some way to settling the unease I've felt all through the lunch. Duncan drank perhaps two thirds of the wine himself, but he's six foot two with plenty of frame to spread it across, and he also ate a hearty lunch. That means Bron had the rest, since Adam and I were more or less pretending to drink, and she's only five foot three and barely picked at a salad. She immediately wedges herself in one corner of the boat and drops into an instant nap.

I choose to sit at the front next to Steve and watch as he expertly maneuvers us away from the wooden jetty. We're moving so slowly that there's hardly a wake behind us; there must be a speed limit in the cove. As we draw nearer to the mouth of the bay, the land rises on either side of us to form cliffs of striated pale yellow, with smatterings of gray, above the clear blue-green of the sea. The sky above us is entirely cloudless. It's almost laughably picture-perfect.

As we exit the shelter of the bay, the boat begins to pitch and roll and the wind picks up, teasing strands of hair out from my chignon and whipping them around my face. Steve turns the wheel so that we are tracking the shoreline, and opens up the throttle; the boat noticeably lifts. The wind, warm and welcome, becomes a constant buffeting pressure, as if I'm being deliberately massaged by it. I start to feel the freedom that always comes on the water at times like this, when there is nothing else I should be doing, nothing else I *could* be doing, as if the whole essence of my self expands. Even the manila envelope with its curious contents begins to drop away. I look back at the others. Bron is still napping, despite the bumps and thrusts of the boat, her feet in Duncan's lap. Adam has taken off his T-shirt and is sitting in Bermuda shorts, with one arm stretched casually across the back of the seat cushions. There's a scar on the underside of his arm that I hadn't noticed before: perhaps he got it whilst he was in the army? He sees me looking at him, and his face breaks into a slow half smile beneath his sunglasses. *In this moment, I am happy,* I think, and it's too shocking to contemplate. I have to look away. How dare I be happy when we are here because Lissa is dead?

I look instead at the shoreline, and suddenly it dawns on me where we are. "Is that the mouth of Kanu Cove?" I ask Steve, trying to pitch my volume for his ears alone, but I misjudge it and the wind steals my words. Steve bends toward me from his upright position at the wheel, and I try again, half standing to reduce the distance. I see his face clear as he comprehends the question and starts to nod enthusiastically, and then I see the moment when he remembers we are all Lissa's friends.

"You'll be swimming on the other side of the nature reserve. The current is just too wicked round here," he yells, his eyes watchful, and I nod, but my gaze is drawn back to the cliffs bookending the opening. They look almost the same as those of Horseshoe Bay, but there's a curious glassiness to the center of the strip of water between them. A rip current, most likely, the deceptively smooth surface hiding a fierce tow out to sea. *Kanu takes. Takes who wants taken.* Steve is leaning toward me again, and I mirror him to catch his words. "If you got swept out, the current would most likely take you right past the tip of the nature reserve—I guess that's what must have happened. After that it's about two hundred miles before there's another shore."

I sit down abruptly, my mind full of Lissa, in that red swimsuit, floating facedown a couple of feet below the surface with her blond hair clouding around her. I can't see the current pulling her inexorably on, but I know it must be there. She's turning slowly, lazily, spinning around in the dark waters with that hair fanning out—in a mere handful of seconds I will see her face, her eyes; dear God, I can't bear to see her eyes . . .

Steve is touching my arm. It's the merest of brushes, but it drags me back to the boat. "You okay?" he's yelling, his eyebrows drawn together in concern. "Seasick?"

I shake my head. "I'm fine," I force out, and he nods, though not as if entirely convinced. Then, because I can't stop myself asking, "Is that where the fisherman found her? Near that shore two hundred miles away?"

Steve waggles his head equivocally. "Not quite. It was a fair bit farther west. Lots of different factors can affect the currents, especially round here; it's so hard to predict. The search area that the police came up with was impossibly huge."

I settle back down in my seat and look at Adam again, but it's too late. The freedom has gone.

FIVE

BRONWYN

I couldn't be less in the mood for a swim. The wine from lunchtime—more than I should have had, but less than I wanted—followed by my nap has induced a low thumping headache. I know a swim will be just the thing to clear it, but still, I can't quite gear myself up for it; I feel like a reluctant teenager as I sluggishly find my goggles and swim cap and look for Vaseline to slather over the areas that chafe. Georgie, on the other hand, is already prepared, and Steve is explaining the swim route to her. "Just remember you can't land on the island at all; it's protected. There's a special kind of cormorant that breeds here, and some kind of ducks. Technically you're supposed to keep at least twenty meters from the shoreline even when you're swimming, but you'll be okay so long as you don't actually go ashore."

"But I can see people on the island—look, there," Georgie objects, pointing. I glance up to follow her finger and see a group of five or six people walking on the island, up on the high ground, intermittently hidden from our view by trees.

Steve nods. "Yeah, there's a tourist ferry that lands at a specific site three times a day; that limits the numbers. They have to stick to the paths."

Georgie looks back at the map, studying it. She's swimming in a bikini today. Sometimes she takes off the top, depending on the country we're swimming in and how relaxed she's feeling. Lissa used to do the same, but neither of them has much more than an A cup to worry about. Or had. My own swimsuit feels tight and restrictive; it's already cutting into me under my arms and across my back. I grit my teeth. It's no use wishing that I had been swimming more of late and was three-quarters of a stone lighter; it's not going to melt off overnight.

"Jem loves it here," throws in Duncan. He is slopping globules of Vaseline along his jawline in what I know is a vain attempt to prevent his stubble from rubbing his shoulder. For a blond man, he grows unexpectedly dark facial hair, and remarkably quickly too: his five o'clock shadow makes an appearance around noon. He adds mischievously, "Did you know he's a closet twitcher?"

"What, Jem?" Georgie sounds skeptical. "Really?"

But Duncan is nodding vehemently, his blue eyes twinkling at the incongruity of it. "He and the chief of police like to go off on bird-watching trips together." I've heard him point it out before, as if it somehow belittles Jem, as if it makes him less "cool," when really it only belittles Duncan.

Steve is tapping the map, trying to pull Georgie's attention back to it, given she's the only person who hasn't done this swim before. "At this end—here—there are some lovely caves you can dip into, but just make sure you stick together when I can't see you. Motorboats aren't allowed within one hundred meters, to protect the reeds and whatnot, but most of the time I'll be able to see you. And don't go beyond the headland—here—because the currents start to pick up, and you might get swept round and caught up in the currents on the other side." Georgie looks uncharacteristically anxious, and

Steve moves quickly to soothe her. "Don't worry, I'll make sure to signal you all to stop well before that point."

Georgie is nodding, then she turns to me. "All okay? You sure you want to swim?"

"Not in the least," I say, yawning, "but I'll be glad I did afterward."

"That's the sort of enthusiasm I like to hear," calls Steve wryly, but Georgie is still looking at me searchingly. I know I ought to tell her about the message in my bathroom, but somehow I can't. She'll ask me all sorts of questions in her dog-with-a-bone way, and I can't take any more of that. I already have questions running in a constant loop in my head that the wine did nothing to disrupt. *Who wrote it? Why did they write it? What do they think is my fault—Lissa's death? And if so, why do they think I'm to blame?* The trouble is that even trying to answer the last one feels like accepting the premise; accepting that someone might reasonably think I *could* be to blame, when I'm *not*. It's ludicrous. Nobody could reasonably think that I am.

I step onto the platform out the back, pulling my goggles into place. "Come on, guys, let's get this thing over with," I call, and then I throw myself in.

For the first few instants, my pulse races frantically, but then my body works out that it's not actually cold at all. I hold myself a couple of meters underwater without surfacing from my entry and watch the blurry shape of Georgie on the boat dissolve and re-form as the waves shift the water above me. Then her feet burst through the greenish ceiling of my world, bubbles blossoming around her and rushing up the length of her body, seemingly multiplying as they race for the surface. I come up for a breath then submerge again, sculling with my hands to keep from floating up. The water here is clear and deep, and there's no bottom to be seen, just a gradual darkening that must surely become black at the point where the light can no longer penetrate at all. There could be all manner of creatures living down there, devoid of the sun, and I wouldn't be able to see them. Do they look up and watch us, as I watched for Georgie only moments ago? An image crosses my mind of a giant serpent, slithering sinuously through the depths, its ancient gnarled head reaching upward, its ink black eyes searching—and I kick sharply for the sunshine of the surface just as Adam and Duncan explode into the water beside me.

"Okay?" Georgie asks me. The sun is so bright that it would be easier to close my eyes. I shouldn't have had the wine. That's what's making me susceptible to ludicrous flights of fancy. That, and the writing on the mirror. Though to be fair, it was the writing on the mirror that made me susceptible to the wine. Who wrote it? What do they want? And possibly the most important question: *What happens next?* Or is whoever wrote that message content to leave things at that?

If something else happens, I will tell Georgie. If something else happens.

"Okay?" Georgie asks again, somewhat impatiently, and this time I nod. She gets cold if we don't get going quickly; she doesn't have any body fat to speak of for warmth. The men have surfaced now. "Ready?" she asks them.

"Give me a sec. Still peeing," says Duncan. Georgie makes a face as, on the boat, Steve laughs. "Right, done." And we're off, in our little pod that lacks the symmetry that it used to have. Georgie positions herself on the trail of bubbles from Duncan's feet, and I sit off her right shoulder. Adam won't fill the gap of Lissa, because he breathes to the left, and he won't be quick enough in the long run to sit on Duncan's right-hand side, so he's following on Georgie's feet. We are an arrowhead with one blade missing.

I'm battling a little to stay level with Georgie, hoping that either I find my stride soon or that she slacks off the pace. It used to be that no matter how rough I felt at the beginning of a swim, I would be confident that my strength would tell in the end; front crawl was never my stroke—I was a butterfly swimmer—but whilst I could never beat Georgie in a front crawl race in the pool, in open water conditions, where sheer strength as well as technique are important, I used to be able to just about match her. Now, I'm not so sure. I feel fitter than I was before I flew here—swimming here every day has done that—but I'm nowhere near the shape I ought to be in. Maybe I never will be again; another clause in the contract I hadn't realized I'd signed by having kids.

I twist my wrist awkwardly mid-stroke under the water to see the time on my watch; we've only been swimming for ten minutes. I should have settled by now, if I'm going to settle at all. Duncan is keeping us some one hundred meters or so from the shoreline, presumably on instruction from Steve, which is far enough away that we may as well be in open ocean. I try to give myself over to the rhythm, but everything is off-kilter. The waves are coming in from my left and ought to be blocked by Georgie, but occasionally one washes over my face, forcing me to break rhythm by throwing in a quick recovery breath to the other side; and whenever I turn to breathe, the sun is too bright. And the greenish-black depths beneath me are too dark, too secretive.

After some time (Two minutes? Five? Twenty? I won't let myself look at my watch again.) I realize we are now angling toward the shoreline. The darkness below me is losing its saturation, and then, only a few strokes later, I can discern a sheer cliff face sloping beneath us, an extension of the rock face that's above the water. Duncan has slowed his pace, which surprises me because it's not the most interesting viewing, but then I realize that there are schools of small silver fishes darting with impossible swiftness along the sloping shelf; Duncan has a good appreciation of the treasures of the seas, whereas if I'm honest, marine life doesn't hold much interest for me, except to know which species might bite or sting. I've swum here before, and it's starting to come back to me: the shoreline here breaks up into nooks and crannies, and then just a little farther on, we should hit the caves—and then we do.

Duncan pauses, treading water before a yawning opening in the cliff face, so that we can all group up, though Adam was right on our heels the whole time. Georgie is already moving slowly into the cave, holding herself upright in the water by using an eggbeater kick for stability, with each leg alternating in a breaststroke corkscrew motion as she cranes her neck, her goggles up on her forehead, looking up at the vaulting cave ceiling that soars above; it must be at least the height of a two-story building. I remember there's a small pebbled beach at the back of it, and I start toward that, but as I move into the shadows I feel the abrupt change of temperature and pause on the border between the light and the dark. It's deep here—surprisingly so, so deep I can't clearly see the bottom—or perhaps that's because I have my goggles up and in this spot, half in and half out of the sun, my eyes can't adjust. The movement of the water is playing disturbing tricks on my eyes as I look into the depths. I could almost believe something is moving down there; all this focus on Kanu Cove and that ridiculous myth is making me embarrassingly open to suggestion. The ebb and flow of the sea is moving me rhythmically to and fro, though more to than fro: I have to work a little to keep myself from being swept in. Then something cold slithers past my leg, and I let out a strangled yelp.

"What's up? Did I kick you?" It's Adam, unexpectedly close behind me.

"You just about gave me heart failure." But he's on the wrong side; how could he have kicked me? I stare into the depths again. They shift and move with every back-and-forth of the seas. I find I've drawn my knees up impractically high for treading water; I'm being swept inexorably from the sunshine into the gloom of the cave. "Is there . . . Adam, can you see something moving down there?"

61

"What? Did you see a jelly?"

Jellyfish. The scourge of the open water swimmer. It could have been a glancing touch from one, I suppose, though it lacked the electric feel of the Mediterranean variety. Those can leave vicious welts; I've no idea what they can do in this area, as I haven't encountered any yet. "I don't know. I'm heading out." I'm already fixing my goggles in place and turning for the sunshine, kicking hard to leave the cave behind.

The penetrating warmth of the sunshine on my shoulders is an instant tonic. I stop some thirty meters from the cave mouth, still reluctant to extend my legs into the depths. I'm simultaneously scared to look and afraid not to, which results in snatched glances that can't possibly be effective; I know I'm being entirely ridiculous, but I don't seem to be able to put a stop to it. Instead I look around for the boat. Ordinarily Steve would always stay within sight of us, often only ten meters or so away, but right now I can't see the craft at all. I can't hear it, either, and I can't see any of the others; they must be deep within the recess. I scan around slowly—Steve can't be far away—surely the higgledy-piggledy shape of the coastline here is hiding him from me? I lie back flat in the water to stick my ears under without sinking my legs, in an attempt to pick up the noise of the engine through the water—but nothing. And when I right myself again I realize I've been swept along a little, parallel to the shoreline, toward a distinctive arch, which has a series of diminishing stacks trailing into the ocean from it—I remember swimming through that arch before. Probably Steve is waiting on the other side; I think that's what happened last time. Did he tell us that he would be waiting there today? I wasn't paying quite as much attention as I should have been when he briefed us.

I should wait here for the others. It's stupid to swim alone. I'll wait.

And then a long shadow moves below me.

Or it doesn't, I can't be sure, but I'm not about to wait and find out; I've already broken into a fast front crawl, heading for the arch and trying to scan the depths beneath me as I swim, a high, choppy six-beat kick keeping my legs almost out of the water. I stick my head up quickly to locate the archway and catch sight of a flash of sunlight off metal: the boat! It must be on the other side. Forty meters to the arch. Thirty meters. I'm breathing hard now, gasping air every second stroke. Twenty meters. The water is getting shallower as I near the arch, and I can see that there's nothing below me, but I still can't bring myself to ease up on this panicked dash—not until I've safely hauled myself onto the boat. And now I'm swimming through the arch, without the slightest easing of pace to pay heed to the impressive geological feature that the sea has carved. The boat must be just ahead, it must be just—

A roar fills my ears—an engine—so loud and close that it seems like it must be right on top of me. I stick my head up, desperate to spot the source, even as my brain tells me that it's a trick of the water; speedboats always sound closer underwater than they actually are. But as I lift my head I realize with horror that there really is a boat bearing down on me—a small motorboat— heading straight for me, its dirty blue bow lifted out of the water by the speed at which it's traveling. There's no time to shout or wave or even take a breath; I throw myself sideways and down, pulling frantically with my arms and kicking with fast, hard dolphin kicks in a frenzied attempt to get below the propeller. Seen from beneath the water, the shape of the hull is growing darker and broader as it races closer, filling almost my entire field of vision, a turbulent flow of water streaming out behind it. I'm not deep enough, it's going to hit me, I'm sure it's going to hit me—and then it's right over me, the propeller mere inches from my trailing legs, so close that I feel the tug of its suction. And then the boat has passed. I hang underwater for a second or two, then shoot to the surface, pulling my goggles off to peer after the vessel. It's turning in a short, tight arc to go through the arch, in the opposite direction to how I swam through, the engine at what sounds like full throttle. I have only the briefest of moments to catch a glimpse of it. A shabby-looking long-nosed craft, of what I would guess is traditional design, where it seems as if the engine has been added as an afterthought. Two on board, the driver and one other. The driver had a baseball cap on and was looking back at me; I could swear he was laughing. And suddenly I'm afraid they're going to circle round and mow me down again.

I need to get out of the water. Swim to shore? Climb the walls of the arch? Though I'm not sure I could get enough purchase on the rock. Even as I try to make a plan, my mind racing at breakneck speed, I become aware of an engine coming closer; it'll have to be the arch, as there's no time to get to shore. I start to swim back toward one of the sides, water polo–style with my head up, looking round for the craft. It sounds like it's behind me; could it have circled round that quickly? But before I can reach the rocky wall, I hear the engine cut back and a familiar voice call: "Bron. Over here! Quick!"

Duncan. It's Steve's gleaming white boat, not the shabby blue craft—and he already has the others on board. I swim toward them, dimly aware that I'm sobbing as I chop through the water. Duncan and Adam are hanging over the side, grim faced, with arms extended: as soon as I'm close enough to touch, they haul me unceremoniously into the boat, without a care for the skin I'm scraping. Georgie has a towel and wraps me in it without letting go so that I'm wrapped up in her arms, too.

"We thought it had got you," Georgie says into my hair, her arms tightening around me.

"It nearly did." The horror of it—the looming shadow with the deadly propeller behind it, getting closer and closer—makes me shudder. "It nearly ran me over. I thought I was going to lose an ankle."

"What?" asks Adam. His tone is oddly puzzled. "Ran you over? What did?"

"The boat. The blue-hulled boat." I become aware that all four of them are looking at me, with varying expression of confusion. "I had to duck under; I thought I was going to get sucked into the prop. I swear they saw me, too, I swear . . ." I trail off. "Why, what were you talking about?"

"The creature," says Georgie simply. "There was something in the water."

Despite the fact that we've swum for barely a third of the intended time, there is no question that we're done for the day. Steve takes the boat round the island to a secluded cove with exceptionally shallow, clear water, where nothing could lurk without us seeing it, and cracks open the post-swim snacks of melon and cookies, washed down with hot chocolate from a large flask. We eat mechanically and listen as Steve informs the coast guard of what the others saw; not that they seem at all sure of what they saw. Adam calls it a creature, and Georgie is using that word, too, but sometimes she calls it a serpent instead. Steve has been wondering if it was some kind of harmless basking shark, but I see the doubt in his own eyes as he says it, and the others all agree it was far too long—Adam estimates almost twenty meters —and much too thin for that; they got enough of an eyeful of it streaming under them to at least agree on that. I think of the cold brush of my leg in the cave; I think of the shadow that passed beneath me. For all my much-lauded practicality, it may be some time before I can get either out of my head.

Steve is radioing in to the hotel now. "It must have been in the cave," I say to the others. "That must have been what I felt."

"Maybe," says Adam. "Or maybe that was just me bumping you."

"No, I think it was in the cave. Perhaps it followed me out and then circled back. You saw it on your way out of the cave, right?"

"Yes, but we were a ways out from the cave."

Steve is signing off on the radio. "They're going to warn the nature reserve about the boat that nearly ran you down," he says to me. "It was well within the exclusion zone." As was he, when they scooped me up, but under the circumstances I don't think anyone will make a complaint. "Sometimes you get idiot tourists tearing round here looking for an Instagram shot under the arch; I bet it was one of those. Too busy dicking around to even see you."

But I'm certain they saw me: I picture the driver once again, his head turned back, laughing. "Wouldn't they have a nicer boat?" I argue.

Steve shrugs and pours some more hot chocolate into my cup. "Anyway. Feeling better yet?"

No, I think, but he's a kind man, so I smile back at him and say, "A bit." And in truth my pounding headache has receded, at least, and the endless loop of questions has been supplanted by the events of the afternoon. "Though for once I can say I'm actually *not* glad I swam." He smiles ruefully at my attempt at humor, and then the boat lapses into silence, with everyone settling for a snooze. *Like toddlers,* I think, with a pang for Jack, who at three shows no sign of wanting to drop his afternoon nap and is at his most delicious when he pulls himself out of his bed, his hair askew and his mouth still slack with drowsiness. Duncan stretches himself out across the seats on one side of the boat. Adam is sitting sideways along the back seats, parallel to Georgie, who is lying on her back on the platform at the rear, sunglasses in place. One leg is hitched up and the other trails into the water. I want to tell her to pull her leg in; I want to tell her to sit in the boat proper, not on that ludicrously open platform, but I don't want to betray my unease—or sound like a scolding schoolteacher. Instead I reach for the sunscreen, conscious I've already had more sun than intended today. Suddenly music bursts out loudly: Steve has connected his iPhone to the boat speaker system.

"Sorry," he says, dialing down the volume and scrolling for a different song. The unmistakable first chords of *Suspicious Minds* blare out. Before Elvis gets through the first phrase, Duncan has pulled himself upright, chopping sharply with his hand. "Not that." Steve looks across, surprised. "It has connotations for us all," he explains awkwardly. "Graeme—Lissa's first husband—used to sing it. He had a great voice . . ." He trails off as Steve turns off the music altogether.

"I don't think I ever heard how he died," says Steve.

"Nut allergy," Duncan says succinctly. He runs a hand over his face and then elaborates. "He had a severe nut allergy, and he ate a cookie that had hazelnuts in it; they never figured out where it came from. Probably a local café or something, but they couldn't trace it from the paper bag it came in. The chains have got much better at labeling their food now, but even those weren't so great a few years ago. Anyway, he always carried an EpiPen, but on this one occasion it wasn't in his jacket. Maybe it had fallen out somewhere . . ." He trails off, then shrugs self-consciously. "I don't know. But he was alone in their house—Lissa's and his—and he couldn't get help in time." He looks away, into the clear, blue water. Graeme was one of his closest friends; they'd known each other since high school. Something in my chest is swelling so abundantly that surely I will burst, and all my secrets will erupt into the light. I look at the sunscreen bottle in my hand, gripping it tightly.

"He dialed 999, but the emergency services couldn't get there in time," I hear Adam say.

"Christ. How awful." This is Steve. I stare at the sunscreen bottle, resolutely not thinking of Graeme, not imagining what it must have been like for Lissa, getting the call at her work . . . "Poor Lissa," Steve murmurs.

I force myself to take the cap off the sunscreen. The small movement reminds my body that I *can* move. I glance across at Georgie, still prone on the platform. She could be a statue. She might be asleep, I suppose, but her stillness seems more deliberate than that.

"Maybe no music today," I suggest to Steve, trying to soften it with a rueful smile. "Just to be on the safe side."

"Fair enough."

The boat lapses back into silence. Duncan resumes his stretched-out position. The snippet of *Suspicious Minds* has dredged up a memory of Lissa on her wedding day—her first wedding day. We overheard that very song emanating from a convertible passing the church as the three of us climbed out of our limousine. That's also when I heard Lissa's agitated whisper to Georgie—*He hasn't seen the dress yet*—and I hadn't understood at all, because of course Graeme hadn't see the dress; grooms don't, in advance. But then I saw the look on her face—half proud, half defensive—as we joined her father in the vestibule of the church, and I realized that I'd ascribed the wrong person to *he,* though I still didn't understand.

Duncan's leg twitches abruptly, as if he's nodding off. Georgie still hasn't moved. Then: "Do you think it was the Kanu serpent? That we saw?" she asks suddenly, without moving anything but her lips. Adam, half sitting, half lying across the back seats, flips up his sunglasses and shoots her a glance that she probably doesn't see; I don't think her eyes are open underneath her sunglasses.

"That's a load of nonsense," says Duncan sleepily. "Just a tale that parents tell to stop their children from swimming in a dangerous place."

"Is it? We all saw—something."

"We were nowhere near the cove, though."

She pushes herself up on one elbow. "And you think that thing couldn't make the journey? You saw how fast it moved." She watches her own hand moving sinuously from side to side, in a snakelike motion, as if oddly fascinated by it. Duncan and Adam keep silent. How is it that she could be completely immobile during the Graeme conversation and yet so animated by this sea creature? "It changes the playing field, doesn't it? Nobody has been saying it—"

"Georgie—" Adam says quietly, but it's not enough to throw a wall in front of her words.

"—but surely we've all been operating under the assumption that there are only two reasons why someone would be in the water at Kanu Cove." She pushes her sunglasses up on her forehead and appeals directly to Steve, who's already shaking his head in his pilot's chair. "Right, Steve?"

"Uh-uh. Leave me out of it."

"Jeez, Georgie," says Duncan, though there's not much frustration in his words. I realize he's turned his head and is looking at me. They're all looking at me.

I shrug, concentrating on rubbing the sunscreen in. There's no point trying to hold back the tide. "Say it, then." It doesn't change anything. That's my whole argument: it doesn't change anything, so what's the point of going over everything? But I've realized I can't derail Georgie. She's on a mission.

Still, my head is already running ahead of Georgie: *Accident or suicide,* that's what she's about to say. And she of all people must know that Lissa was about as likely to kill herself as Georgie would be, or me. And anyway, we went over all of this with the police before. But Georgie is arranging herself cross-legged with a businesslike air, her elbows on her knees, with apparently no care for the shallow blue behind and beneath her. I find I'm searching it for shadows and force myself instead to focus purely on her.

"Okay then," Georgie says. Now that I'm directing my attention straight at her, it's hard not to look at her crotch, given her cross-legged position. Her black bikini briefs are perfectly in place, without a hair, or even a follicle, to be seen. I wonder if she waxes everywhere? Or if she's had electrolysis? I've heard that's the norm for singletons in the US—the Tinder generation. A doctor friend told me that even in the UK, everybody he sees under the age of thirty is entirely devoid of pubic hair these days. "Okay then," she repeats. "Two reasons: murder or suicide."

My gaze jumps straight up to Georgie's face. *Murder?* What is she talking about? But before I can speak, Duncan is objecting. "Wrong," he says mildly. "You've missed out fatal hubris: a miscalculation leading to a tragic accident. Which is what happened."

"I'd buy that—maybe—in daytime. Not at night," Georgie says decisively, as if her word is the last word. As if *any* word could make a difference. Which, again, is my point. But: *Murder?* Where did that come from? "But we should start at the beginning. How do we know for sure it was actually Kanu Cove where she got in the water?"

Duncan sighs and sits up, adjusting his sunglasses on his nose. "Your shoulders are going red," I say, but he ignores me.

"There were flip-flops left on the jetty. Jem thought they were hers, but she had like a hundred pairs, so . . ." He shrugs. I can see Georgie about to speak, presumably to argue that that's hardly conclusive, but Duncan holds up a hand to forestall her. "And she was seen in the water there."

"She was seen?" Georgie sucks in a breath. Apparently she didn't know that. "By who?"

"By Arif." This is Steve. He sighs, evidently reluctant to go on, but Georgie makes a gesture and he continues. "One of the gardeners; he's a good lad. He'd only been on the job a few days at that point. Most of the staff quarters are out that way, and he was on his way there. He's not from round here; he didn't know that swimming there was so dangerous."

"He could tell it was her? He could see that in the dark?"

"He could tell it was a woman, swimming crawl. He'd heard the boss's wife was a big swimmer, so he didn't think anything of it until the next day."

"The boss's wife?" Georgie says mildly, but there's an archness to her tone, and Steve flaps a hand in a semi-apology. "I know they owned it together," he says, his ears reddening, "but most of the staff thought of Jem as the boss. Lissa wasn't so involved in the day-to-day personnel management; she concentrated more on reservations and accounts."

"Mmm," says Georgie, flipping her sunglasses back down and somehow conveying in that one sound that she'll forgive him—but just this once. Poor Steve. I don't suppose the "woke" work environment of Manhattan has quite caught up to him yet.

Steve hurries on. "Arif said she looked fast and strong, she was kicking hard." I've heard this before, though not the fast and strong part. But Lissa *was* fast, and she *was* strong; we all are, compared to the average person. Compared to the average swimmer, even. Even if she was setting a leisurely pace by her standards, Arif would have been impressed.

"Which direction?" asks Georgie. Steve shakes his head, not understanding. "Which direction was she swimming in?"

"Oh. Toward the mouth of the cove."

"I doubt that was her intention; she was likely aiming for the other side, but at night, and with the current, she probably got disoriented," observes Duncan.

"Maybe," says Georgie. "Or maybe she didn't care what direction she was swimming in. Maybe she was trying to get away from the creature. Maybe—" She stops. Her bottom jaw moves from side to side as she tries to work something through. "Where was her dress?"

"Her dress?" Duncan sounds confused, but I can see where Georgie is going with this.

"Her dress," Georgie repeats impatiently. "It's hardly likely she walked through the resort at night in just her swimsuit."

"I don't . . ." Duncan looks at Steve, who shakes his head. "I don't think they found a dress."

Georgie is absorbed in what might have been. "So she could have taken off her flip-flops to sit on the pier and dangle her feet in the water, and then . . . well, then either she falls in, is pushed in . . . or is dragged in."

"But then she'd be wearing a dress," Duncan objects. "She wasn't when the fisherman found her."

"She wasn't wearing a swim cap or goggles, either, was she?"

Duncan shakes his head. "No. I don't believe so. Though they could have been torn off."

"So could the dress," argues Georgie. Torn off? By what? The fishing net, or waves, or rocks? Or is she thinking of that sinister shape in the water again?

I've been silent thus far; both Duncan and Adam are doing very well without me, but they're both missing the point. "But Georgie, why are you so reluctant to believe that she climbed in of her own accord? That it was an accident?"

"Because it doesn't make sense. Because none of us would have done it." Georgie unwinds her legs and climbs to her feet in what seems to be an entirely liquid motion. The sun is behind her; when I look at her, she is simply a dark shape hovering over me. "Because I like to think that if the tables were turned, she'd be standing here looking for answers."

"Looking for someone to blame, you mean." I glance at Duncan in surprise at his words. There's an unfamiliar hardness to the set of his mouth. Then I look at Georgie, but she's still simply a dark silhouette. She doesn't speak, but her hand moves up to her face and drops back down clasping her sunglasses, which she tosses into the boat. Then she throws herself backward into the water.

"Shit, Georgie!" I scramble to standing, leaning out over the edge of the boat, looking into the water around us for the merest hint of a moving shadow. Adam has moved even quicker than I and is on the back platform, calling her name, but she's still underwater. Then she surfaces.

"Get back in the boat, Georgie," says Adam. I've never heard him so clipped. Steve, Duncan and I are calling out variations on the same theme, but Adam's are the words that carry.

Georgie is wiping the seawater from her eyes as her legs work in eggbeater circles. "There's nothing here—"

"Get back in the fucking boat."

She looks up and locks hold of his gaze, and for a second or two I think she's going to protest, but then she takes two swift strokes and grabs the arm he's extending. He yanks her out with one strong pull, her legs scrambling to get purchase. I turn to find her a towel and hear him bite out, "What the hell was that?" Turning back with the towel, I see her close her eyes briefly. The misery on her face is a kick to my gut. Then she opens her eyes and takes the fluffy blue-and-white hotel towel I'm offering, wiping it across her face, and when she emerges from behind it again, she's entirely expressionless.

"Nothing," she says to the boat at large. "I just wanted to cool off."

SIX

GEORGIE

Steve makes no allowances for the comfort of his passengers on the journey to the resort. When we finally reach the pier, I'm stiff from bracing myself against the bone-shuddering thumps of the boat over the waves, which seem to have become more substantial over the course of the afternoon, along with the wind. I climb awkwardly onto solid ground, still feeling the sway from the boat in my body and a scratchy tightness on my skin where I've had too much sun. Nobody had anything to say on the boat—in any case it would have been snatched away by the wind—but now that we're on dry land, wearily tramping up the path from the bay, it seems that nobody has anything to say anyway; and none more so than Adam. He's rigid with all the things he isn't saying.

"Bar at seven?" says Duncan, when we reach the split in the path that leads to his villa, and to Bron's.

"Sure," Adam says, and Bron and I nod.

Adam and I continue along the path. It takes me a moment to realize we've passed his own turnoff. He cuts me off as I start to point it out. "Yeah, I know. We need to talk."

Even if I was actually willing to discuss my impromptu dip, the bite in his tone would have made me bristle. "Do we, though? What if I don't want to talk?"

He barks out a short, utterly mirthless laugh. "Georgie, you *never* want to talk. That's a given." We've reached my villa door now. I scrabble in my beach bag for the key and then freeze. The manila envelope isn't there. I rummage through again. How can I be over-looking something so substantial? But how can it be gone?

"Looking for this?" I look up at Adam's words. He's leaning against the wall beside the doorframe, one hand holding up the sheaf of papers. The manila envelope is half shredded around them.

"You—you went into my bag?" I'm too astonished to be indignant.

"No—well, technically yes, but not how you think."

"How, then?"

"Your bag was getting soaked from the spray. I moved it to a better position, and this envelope fell out. The paper was so wet it pretty much disintegrated—I honestly wasn't prying, but I couldn't avoid seeing . . ." He opens and closes the fingers of the hand that isn't hold-ing the envelope, as if he might grasp the right words. "Whatever this is." He's holding my gaze. "What is this, Georgie?" I break contact and hunt for the key again, successfully this time, and unlock the door. Adam follows me in uninvited and repeats his question. "What is this?"

"I don't know." I walk quickly through the living area of the suite to the minibar. Adam is right behind me.

"Who gave it to you?"

"I don't know." I take a Coca-Cola can from the minibar and pull the ring. It's cold and sweet and not at all what I'm craving to drink.

"What does it mean?"

"I. Don't. Know." Suddenly my frustration spills over. "Jesus, Adam, you were there when I received it. It came from reception. I have no idea who sent it."

Adam swears quietly under his breath, then reaches past me to open the minibar himself and take a sparkling water. "Please, help yourself," I say with faux sweetness. He raises an eyebrow, his expression loaded with exasperation, and I feel myself redden at my childishness. I take another drink of the cold Coke and turn to face the room, leaning my bottom against the beautiful wooden sideboard. "I was thinking I'd go and ask at reception about it," I offer. It's the closest thing to an apology that I can muster.

He nods. "There was nothing else inside?"

"Nothing."

"Someone is trying to tell you something."

"No kidding. It would be helpful if they were a little less obtuse about it."

"Mmm." He turns to copy my own position, resting against the waist-height sideboard less than a meter away. He lifts the bottle to his lips again. A triangular hollow forms at the base of his throat as he drinks. I look away. It's too strange, having him in here, in my own suite. Just the two of us, in daylight hours, with no blanket of darkness to shelter under—it's too intimate. "You know," he says thoughtfully, "that's a fair point. Why are they being so obtuse? It seems like it's important to them that you discover whatever it is for yourself."

"Or it's a game."

He turns his head to look at me oddly. "A game? You think someone is having fun?"

I shrug. "Maybe. Though not everyone plays games for fun. Some just play to win."

"You don't have to play. You could just . . . not engage." He looks at my face. "Yeah, okay, I get it. So. First action point: ask at reception. What's next?"

I twist to point at the papers that he's dumped behind us on the sideboard. "Take the bait. Figure out how to follow the money."

"Whose money? Lissa's?"

"I suppose. Though it all went into this place. And everything is Jem's now anyway."

"So we're looking at Jem?"

"I guess. I can't think what else would fit."

"Did she have life insurance?" he asks.

Jesus. We really are looking at Jem if we're considering that angle. "I don't know."

He's silent for a minute, thinking. "I suppose there's no way this could really be connected with your work instead?"

"None that I can think of. And before you say it, there's no point in going to the police, because I literally have nothing I can tell them except I received some utterly inoffensive sheets of paper."

He's nodding. "Yeah, I came to the same conclusion." He takes another drink from his water. I look out through the French doors to the plunge pool, and beyond it, the sea, peppered with white tops; the wind must be growing even stronger. Inside the room, the silence grows, too. There's a weight to it; it has substance. It's heavy with all the things that neither of us dares to say.

I have to speak. He will reach for me if I don't speak, and I know I won't stop him. "I thought you were mad at me for going in the water again."

"Believe me, I'll get to that." There may be a trace of humor lurking among the dry delivery. I risk a glance at him. His head is cocked toward me, and his eyes are warm. He reaches out his arm to put his bottle of water down very deliberately on the sideboard inches from me, then pivots around that point to bring himself right in front of me, his arms bracketing me. His forehead is almost touching mine.

"Careful," I say, not entirely sure if I'm joking. "This is getting to be a habit."

His face instantly shutters, and he pulls back a few inches. "Relax, Georgie. I still live in England." The edge in his voice floors me; I don't understand what I'm navigating here. I look up at him, at the hard line of his jaw and the tight line of his mouth, and I can't think of a single thing to say. We are stuck in that moment for a second, for two, and then he breathes out slowly and his edges soften. "Sorry," he says. "I just—sorry."

I still don't know what to say. I look down to the side and watch my left hand as it lifts to cover his where it rests on the sideboard. It could be someone else's hand. Perhaps it should be someone else's hand.

Later we walk to the reception. I wonder if Adam might hold my hand, or perhaps that's too much—and then self-mockery kicks in. *We've just had sex in daylight hours, but public displays of affection? One step too far!* But he doesn't try to take my hand, and I don't take his.

"Why did you never like Lissa?" There's no thought behind the question; it simply propels itself into being. *Why do I care? Why does it matter?* But it does matter. I know that it does.

"I didn't dislike her." He laughs softly at my snort of disbelief. "No, really. She was fun to be around; she made every event feel like a party. When she spoke to you, she really spoke to *you*—and listened, too." Yes, Lissa had that knack. "And I truly believe she adored Graeme. I was just . . . very wary of her, too."

"Why?" The sun, even this late in the day, is so very warm on my skin; it's like a protective barrier against this conversation that I didn't mean to have. God, I would love to live somewhere like this, drenched in sun with the ocean mere meters away. Not actually here, though; not with Lissa spinning slowly under the water somewhere off the coast.

"You know that I knew Lissa a little at school."

"Only vaguely, I thought." They were at different high schools; Duncan was the one who was at school with Lissa. And Adam was still living up in the north of England until he was sixteen or so.

"Yeah, only vaguely. She dated someone in my year for a while—a guy I knew through cycling. Anyway. They split up, and he got a new girlfriend; it was never clear if there was overlap. He would say not, but . . ." He waggles a hand equivocally. I can feel myself tensing. The rays of the sun may not be sufficient to insulate me against what's coming. "His brand-new time trial bike, his absolute pride and joy, ended up in the river. Beautiful bike, that." He shakes his head, as if in mourning. "He thought it was stolen, but when the river level dropped in spring, he saw it there, on the riverbed." *Not theft, then. Malice, or vengeance.* "And then, sometime later—maybe a year, I don't exactly remember—his new girlfriend was the victim of an acid attack." I take a sharp despairing breath inward: *Oh, Lissa.* "She flung an arm up to protect her face, so she doesn't have many scars there, but her whole forearm had to be grafted. Nobody saw who did it; the police never charged anybody. But my friend always thought Lissa was behind it." He shrugs. "Hence my being . . . wary."

Wary. Such a careful choice of word, from a careful man. He's not telling me this by accident, either. He'd have found a way to weave the tale into conversation no matter what words spilled out of my mouth unbidden. Was it Lissa, though? *Probably.* Though as soon as I think that, I realize that it hardly matters. The point is that both he and I think it could have been.

"Did you ever tell Graeme that story?"

He shakes his head. "No. But he knew about other stuff." My cheeks are hot; I can't imagine that I came off very well in any of those tales. In truth, I could barely hold myself together at the time, let alone do more to manage Lissa—but still, I see it differently now. There's a clarity now that was entirely missing at the time, and that clarity is riddled through with guilt. "He wasn't under any illusions about her. He just loved her anyway. Like you did." My throat is impossibly tight, constricted by everything I failed to do. Most of all, I should have come on the last holiday. Such cowardice in delaying;

how can I ever live with it? I'm saved from having to say anything by our arrival at the reception, which, like the rest of the resort, is deathly quiet. It's manned by a young receptionist, who greets us with a gentle smile.

"I had a delivery of some documents from reception today," I say. "I wonder if you could tell me how they got here."

"Is there a problem?" Her brows have gathered together in instant concern.

"No, no problem. I just wanted to understand who delivered the documents."

"They didn't reach you?" Her brows are still maximally gathered.

"No, no; they did. I have them. There's no problem; I just wanted to understand how they got here. To reception, I mean. Did someone deliver them? Or did they come through the post?"

"Ah." Her expression clears, and she turns to rattle off a question in the local tongue to her colleague, who is manning the desk marked *Concierge*. Their animated exchange seems overlong for what I'm asking. Eventually she turns back, her expression oddly apprehensive. "He thinks that Cristina would know, but she is not here."

"When will she be back?"

"She is . . . ah, she is not coming back. She is gone."

Adam suddenly speaks up. "Cristina is gone? Gone where?"

"She is left. She is . . ." The poor woman is flustered, searching for the right word, and the right grammar. "She is quit."

"Who's Cristina?" I ask. Whoever she is, Adam seems stunned by that news. So does the receptionist, actually.

"Hey, guys," calls a voice, and I turn to see Duncan ambling toward us, his sandals shuffling a little with every step. His linen shirt looks like it could use an iron, too. It occurs to me that he's turning into the sort of mildly bumbling Englishman that his father was. "Evening," he says, smiling amiably at the receptionist. "Is Cristina about?"

"She's quit, apparently," Adam says baldly.

"What?" Dunc's head whips round to Adam. "No! Really?"

I try again. "Who is Cristina?"

"Jem's assistant manager," says Adam in a quick aside, then he turns back to the receptionist. "When did this happen?"

She hesitates, and for a moment I think she won't answer, but then she offers quietly, "Just one hour ago."

"I was supposed to be meeting her now," Dunc says, still sounding shocked by the news. Then he visibly regroups. "Where's Jem? Is he in his office?"

She shakes her head. "He went back to the villa." She bites her lip as if she wants to say more.

"Perhaps we should go and check up on him. A bit of moral support and all that," I say casually, watching her reaction. Relief floods her face, and she nods quickly. I surmise Jem must have taken the news rather badly.

"Wait, we should tell Bron where we're going," I say, as Adam and Duncan turn from the reception. "Can you put me through to Mrs. Miller's room, please?" The receptionist obligingly taps on a computer, and then on the phone before handing me the handset, but there's no reply. I let it ring through to the answering service and leave a message. Then Duncan leads the way out of the reception, in a direction I haven't been before. Out of the shelter of the building, the strength of the wind is more apparent, and the sun has set whilst we were occupied in the reception. For the first time since I arrived, I'm in danger of feeling cool.

"Why were you meeting Cristina anyway?" Adam asks Duncan, a smidgen too casually.

"Oh. Well, I promised Jem I'd take a look at the figures, and he said it was probably best to start with her, as she was doing a lot of the budget creation work. This way, Georgie," he says, steering me onto a path marked *Private*. Ahead of me, a steep staircase ascends into near-total darkness; Jem and Lissa's villa must surely be at the highest point of the resort.

"It's going to be a blow for Jem," Adam comments.

"I'll say," says Duncan, with feeling. "I don't know how he'll manage, with both Lissa and her gone."

It sounds utterly heartless, putting the resignation of an employee on the same footing as the death of a wife, but I suppose they both amount to the same thing for a business: a gaping hole. "Why do you think she left?" I ask. "Was there tension before?"

"Nothing I was aware of," Duncan tosses over his shoulder, panting a little as he climbs. "I didn't really see her as the confrontational type, to be honest."

The dimly lit villa is well nestled in the foliage. Even as we approach the entrance, I can't get any sense of the scale of it. It's built in exactly the same style as the rest of the resort accommodation, but somehow there's an air of permanence to it. Perhaps it's the somewhat shabby bikes propped against the wall to the left of the front door, just under the shelter of the roof. One of them is smaller. I wonder who will ride it now.

The door of the villa is ajar. Dunc raps his knuckles on it in a brief tattoo, then walks in, calling, "Knock knock."

"In the lounge," calls Jem's voice. His accent is the strongest I've ever heard it. Duncan obviously knows this villa well enough; he walks through the hallway with purpose, but I jerk to a halt mid-step, as if caught by a fishing hook, staring at the photos on the console table. Adam follows him, then pauses at a doorway to look back for me.

"Are you—ah," he says, catching sight of the same photos. The one in the foreground is Lissa and Jem on their wedding day: a staged shot I remember being taken. Jem, grinning, has hoisted Lissa in the air by way of his hands on her waist, and she's looking down on him and laughing. The *Dirty Dancing* shot, the photographer said. A good photo, certainly, but it's the one behind that has a genuine sense of intimacy. It's also from Lissa's wedding, but not to Jem. To Graeme.

Adam has come to stand beside me, his eyes drawn to the same photo. It's a group shot, unstaged and unplanned, of us all in the bar very, very late in the evening after the wedding. Lissa, in her wedding dress, is seated on Graeme's knee, one arm wrapped round his neck and the other holding a champagne flute which she's using as if a microphone. Bron, her husband Rob, Adam (in his army days, so with noticeably shorter hair) and myself are standing behind, arms slung across one another's shoulders as we join the happy couple in belting out the song. I remember it distinctly: *We can't go on together with suspicious minds* . . . Duncan, a little thinner and with a little more hair, is in an armchair just to one side, Ruby perched on the arm with her shoeless feet in his lap. They're both looking across and laughing. In fact, everyone has laughter in their eyes. "God, we were young," Adam says quietly.

"You don't look so very different, apart from the hair." It wasn't so many years ago. My brain can't seem to do the simple mathematics, though.

"None of us do, really." *Except Lissa and Graeme.* I can't help imagining her again, floating lazily in that red swimsuit, clouds of blond hair billowing in the slightest of currents. Before she can spin round to face me, I see there's a silent shadow approaching, long and fluid, impossibly fast in its sinuous path. A wash of creeping dread is building up inside me, starting from the very center of my core and sweeping outward—but Adam is talking again. "Though I feel it. I feel the years." He looks at me, considering. "Don't you?" The serpent has stolen my voice; I manage the smallest of nods. "Come on," Adam says gently, taking one hand and tugging on it. "We should go in." So we do, into a large rectangular space, with glass doors running the length of the side facing across the ocean, which is a dim dark gray now, not quite as dark as the sky above it. It would be impossible to spot the serpent in this light; it could come right up to the shore, and nobody would ever know—

"Georgie?" Adam touches my arm gently, and I drag my eyes away from the windows and focus on the rest of the space, but that offers no relief. This room, too, is reminiscent of the rest of the resort accommodations, but the soft furnishings are different—no longer an innocuous bamboo and beige, instead there's a three-piece sofa set in pale turquoise with vibrant patterned scattered cushions and a driftwood coffee table: statement items. I can't tell if it's Lissa's statement, or Jem's, and I can't do the detective work to answer the question, either; I can't bear to let my eyes rest where there might be another photo or object or trinket that reeks of Lissa, or I might scream and never stop. How can Jem still live here? But he can, he must be able to, for he's here on the sofa, his elbows resting on his knees and his hands dangling between them. A glass of something golden brown is in one hand, and the bottle from whence it came is open on the coffee table in front of him. He's in what looks like a serious conversation with Duncan, who's standing on the other side of the coffee table. Then he turns as we enter, and I see that he's not alone on the sofa: someone, previously hidden by his body, is beside him.

"Bron," I say, startled enough to snap back into a semblance of my normal self. "Did you get our message?" But no, of course she didn't. She was here already.

Bron starts to mumble an answer without meeting my eye, but Jem cuts across her. "Drink?" he asks. I glance away from Bron and find him dragging himself to his feet, gesturing toward the bottle with his crystal glass; the viscous liquid inside comes perilously close to sloshing out. "I was saving it for a special occasion. And there's nothing quite so special as witnessing your entire livelihood— Christ, the only thing I've ever really wanted in life—going down the fucking tubes."

"It's just one employee," says Duncan, in his most reasonable tone.

"No. No, it's not," Jem says savagely; Duncan blinks at his ferocity. "It's not just one employee. There's been a steady stream out the door since Lissa—and with Cristina gone, all faith will evaporate. And it's not just one cancellation. There is only one booking remaining—one—after you guys leave." He pauses for dramatic effect. He's been drinking, but he's not drunk. He's too measured for that, too aware of the impact of his performance. "And, as it turns out, there hasn't been only one fraud. There have been many."

"What? Fraud?" Duncan looks shocked.

Jem's smile is an exercise in ironic bleakness. "Frauds." He stresses the *s*. "As in, multiple. Cristina found them. She thought it was me." He picks up another crystal glass and hands it to Duncan, who takes it heedlessly, shock still writ large across his face. "Looks like you chose the wrong hotel to invest in." Invest? Duncan invested in the hotel? *Follow the money.* I look at Adam for the briefest of moments; from the stillness in his face, I would guess this is news to him also. But Jem is pouring from the bottle into Duncan's glass and then into his own. The liquid flows out as if runny honey: cognac, I presume. Not a tipple I would ever choose for myself. "Have a drink." It's a command, not an invitation. Duncan looks down as if seeing the glass for the first time, then takes a short, sharp swallow. "Anyone else?" Jem asks, waving the bottle around, but nobody speaks up. I look at Bron again, still seated on the sofa. She's in another halter neck sundress that I recognize from previous holidays, which once again emphasizes her cleavage.

Duncan takes another sip. "Wow." He looks at the bottle label. "Hennessy? Jesus. That *is* special." His mind appears to have kicked back into gear, because he adds, "Wait, why would Cristina think it was you?"

"Because only she and I have access to our payment systems."

"How did you find Cristina in the first place?" I ask. "Was she local?"

"No, she's Brazilian. I worked with her at one of the Four Seasons properties, in the Maldives."

"You really never met her?" Duncan asks me. "Dark hair? Small?"

"That narrows it down." Nobody even cracks a smile at my drollery.

"Hot," says Duncan decisively, as if that might be the very detail to jog my memory. "In a pocket rocket kind of way."

"She's not *that* hot," Bron objects. Duncan mutters something that might be, *Yeah, she is.* "Extraordinarily white teeth," Bron continues, deliberately ignoring Duncan. "She must bleach them." I glance at Jem involuntarily; I'm sure Jem does exactly that.

"Regardless, could she be behind this?" I ask Jem. Right now his very white teeth are occupied, gaining a fresh cognac coating. We wait while he finishes his sip. "Until today, I would have said absolutely not. Now . . ." He raises his glassless hand and spreads the fingers wide, palm up.

"Like I said before, show me," says Bronwyn earnestly to Jem. She's standing, too, now, her hand laid lightly on his arm. He doesn't shake it off or move away. How long was she here before us? And why? "I'm an accountant, remember? I might see something."

"Can't hurt," Adam says blandly; it's the first thing he's contributed since we entered. I look at him quickly, and he looks back, deliberately keeping his face neutral. Jem shrugs and moves to the corner of the room where a MacBook is sitting open on a desk, Bron trailing behind him. After a second or two I follow nonchalantly, wondering if I can find a way to work in a question about Lissa's life insurance, though I can't think how to do that without it sounding like a blatant non sequitur. Jem sits at a swivel chair and clicks through to some kind of application that causes Bron to murmur in recognition: a form of accounting software, presumably.

"We only installed it this month," Jem is saying. "It lets you slice and dice your data much more efficiently, apparently. Cristina's been loading all the historical data onto it, and that's how she found it."

"Found what?" This is Adam.

"Fake supplier payments. Referencing suppliers that we do use, for F&B and the like, and for fairly typical amounts, but they don't tie out to any actual invoices."

"Going back how far?" Bron asks, shooing him out of the chair to take control of the computer herself.

Jem shrugs. "Several months, I think. I can't be sure. Here, look—that's one of them." He points to a line on the screen that looks no different from any other line.

"When is your accounting year-end?" Bron asks.

"December."

"It must have started after last December, then. It would have been picked up in your year-end financial audit otherwise," she says, clicking through screens and applying filters as she speaks. "Can you put me onto your bank accounts? Let's see if I can figure out where it's all been going." Jem leans over her to take control of the mouse, resting his left hand on her bare shoulder, ostensibly to brace himself. Would I do that if I was in his position? If it was Duncan sitting there, or Jem, or Adam? I can't tell. At the very least I know Jem wouldn't do it if it was me in Bron's seat.

"How much?" asks Duncan.

"One second," Jem says. He pulls open a drawer and rummages around, then pulls out some kind of electronic security card and starts to read off some numbers to Bron, but her attention is fixed on the still-open drawer, her face oddly still. "What?" says Jem, following her gaze. I lean in to look. Lying among the jumble of pens and assorted stationary items is a yellow cylindrical object, too thick to be a pen, with a snub-nosed conical orange tip. "Oh, that. It's for my niece; she left it by accident. She's allergic to bees." He looks at Bron, puzzled. "You've seen an EpiPen before, surely?"

"I . . . Yes. Of course." She takes a deep breath and pushes the drawer closed, shaking herself with a quick smile. "Go ahead." *Graeme*, I think, with a wave of sympathy for her. *It reminded her of Graeme.*

Jem is now reading off the numbers again, for Bron to input for access to a mobile banking system. "I'm in," she says briskly, then starts to mutter to herself as she skims through the accounts.

"How much?" repeats Duncan.

"I don't know yet." There's a reluctance to Jem now; he's no longer performing. He leaves Bron's side and moves back across the room to slump on the turquoise sofa. I take his spot, looking over Bron's shoulder—pink from the sun with a pale negative of a swimsuit strap in sharp contrast—but I keep my hands to myself.

"Roughly." The edge in Duncan's voice has real teeth now. He drops onto the sofa, too, but sitting on the edge, as if poised to leap up at any moment. I glance at Adam and see that he's watching Duncan. How much did Duncan invest, I wonder? Strange that he didn't mention it the other day at lunch, when he touched upon his retirement dreams.

Jem mutters a number that only Duncan can hear, then scrubs both hands down over his face. "At least," he adds more audibly, then reaches for his drink. I can't tell from Duncan's reaction whether that's more or less than he was afraid of. "We could absorb it easily enough—well, not easily, but we could absorb it—were it not for the cancellations. Though I suppose your sighting of the creature from the Black Lagoon, or whatever it was, wouldn't have helped, either, if it got around."

I watch Duncan process that. It's like watching a calculator: nothing, then an answer; there's no indication of the operations between input and output. "You need to bring in your accountants," he tells Jem. This is the Duncan who works in private equity and more or less runs the firm he's with; I'd almost forgotten this version. "You probably also need to inform any lenders, since I'm sure you will have an information undertaking in your loan doc, and you certainly need to inform any other equity investors."

"That last bit is done. You're it." The bleak smile has returned, though he can't seem to look Duncan in the eye. Shame? Wounded ego? Or am I wrong, is this now the performance? Could Jem have been stealing from his own business?

Duncan sinks on the sofa next to him. "Listen," he says authoritatively, pushing his straw-blond hair back from his forehead. "This is not the end for you. We will get to the bottom of this." He claps a hand on Jem's shoulder and leans in, still talking. I can't quite hear all of what he is saying, but nevertheless I'm filled with a rush of warmth for Duncan. He's so very nearly a caricature of a person—no, of a certain type of Englishman: so very predictable in his outdated, laddish comments, so very traditional, so very *straight*—and yet, all of those are his best qualities, too. So very loyal. So very dependable in a crisis. Of course he would have helped Jem and Lissa with a financial stake when they asked, if he could; though not blindly—he's far too smart for that. He would have fully researched the opportunity. Of course he's trying to help Jem now. Though not blindly for that, either.

I look back at the screen, over Bron's chestnut curls, over her mildly sunburned shoulder; across the swell of her ample bosom, barely restricted by the dress. Jem must have had precisely the same view. I wonder if his grief will have stopped him noticing. I think of all the times I've encouraged Bron to be more adventurous in what she wears: *If you've got it, flaunt it.* It's just that in this case I'm not sure who she's flaunting it for.

She's switching back and forth between the accounting and the bank account systems. "Yikes," she mutters. "There's like a thousand payments for around the same amount." She sighs, then murmurs: "Follow the money."

My head snaps round instantly. "What did you say?"

"Follow the money. The accountant's job." She turns to glance up at me. "Are you okay?"

"I—yes. Fine." Coincidence. Pure coincidence. I take a deep breath and let it out slowly and silently, feeling the adrenaline subside. *Follow the money.* The accountant's job—Bron's job—so why choose *me* as the message recipient? And who would send an anonymous message? I can only think that it came from someone too scared to raise their issues directly. If Cristina found the fraud, could it be that another employee also found it and wanted to anonymously raise an alert? Or is the message in fact nothing to do with the company? In which case, why do it anonymously? An employee of the hotel, someone who can't afford to upset Jem, is the only category I can think that would fit.

I'm just going round in circles. "So, um, how come you were here already?" I ask Bron.

"Oh." She's looking straight ahead again. The blue-tinged wash from the screen somehow seems to highlight her freckles. If she was blushing, would I see it in this light? "Well, I ran into Jem on my way back from the spa. I was going to book a treatment." Suddenly she leans in to the screen.

"Found something?"

"Maybe." She's flicking between the two systems too quickly for me to see what she's looking at. "Twenty-fourth, twenty-fourth, yes . . . there it is. Now where did you go?" She's on the banking system again, scrolling down. I risk a glance at the windows. It must be entirely dark outside now; all I can see is the reflection of ourselves. Jem and Duncan on the sofa, in a golden pool of light provided by the floor lamp behind them. Bron and myself lit in cold blue by the computer. And Adam, barely visible in the shadows.

"Here you are. Let's see . . ." Bron mutters. I wonder if she misses this. I'd been taken aback when she quit her—very successful—

accountancy job; it didn't seem in character at all, but I hadn't felt able to ask. There wasn't a way to do it without sounding judgmental, as if I, the unmarried, childless friend, was accusing her of betraying the sisterhood. I'd even wondered if it was a knee-jerk reaction to her interlude with Graeme, a statement of sorts: a very public commitment to family above all else. Not that she and Graeme were public.

Duncan calls across suddenly. "Time for dinner, surely? Jem? Soak up a little of this Hennessy?" I glance across and see Duncan signaling, none too subtly over Jem's head, that he needs us all on board.

"Absolutely. I'm starving," I say obediently. "Right, Bron?" I glance down at her, but she's frozen, staring at the screen with none of her previous efficient motions. "What's up? Did you find something?"

She starts. "No." Then she glances up with a quick smile. "No, nothing. A red herring. I'll try again tomorrow; this is probably going to take a while. Let me log off."

As Adam and Duncan coax Jem off the sofa, I move to scoop up my shoulder bag. "Ready, Bron?" I ask, turning back to see her stuff a piece of paper in her pocket, a pen on the desk next to the MacBook behind her. She smiles brightly as she joins me at the doorway, but there isn't a smile in the universe that's bright enough to blind me to the fact that she's hiding something.

HOW TO KILL YOUR BEST FRIEND

Method 3: Hire a hit man

Hire a hit man. As if. Where would you even find someone like that? And anyone willing to kill for money would also be willing to sell me out, too, so in all likelihood I'd end up thousands of pounds poorer and in jail to boot.

I can't involve anyone else. That's how people get caught: the stupidity of others. That, and random chance. It's funny how many affairs are discovered because the wife who never goes anywhere happens to pop into a pub that's miles from her normal patch, or the husband who has never paid attention to the bills happens to read a credit card statement. The universe takes a perverse joy in making sure our secrets don't stay secret for long.

SEVEN

BRONWYN

This dinner is going to be a car crash. Adam is trying valiantly to talk to me, but I can't think straight, let alone hold up one end of a conversation. My mind is entirely focused on the two sets of eight-digit numbers, on the slip of paper in my pocket, and the third number of only six digits scribbled beneath them. Account numbers—UK ones, specifically; I saw the IBANs when I clicked through to see the full payment details. Two accounts, exactly the same except the last two digits; two account numbers with the same bank, hence the same six-digit sort code for both. Like a pair of accounts opened at more or less the same time.

They can't be. It makes no sense. I've misremembered.

And after all, it's been quite the day—and, at the risk of sounding melodramatic, all of it somehow stacked against *me*. That vile message on the mirror, followed by too much alcohol and too much sun (admittedly both my own fault), and then that terrifying boat bearing down on me—and, even before that, the awful shadow slipping beneath me in the sea . . . When we first reached the restaurant, I overheard the boat pilot, Steve, giving one of the waiters short shrift for having asked him about his sighting of "Kanu," which seems to have run like wildfire through all of the staff already, but for all of Steve's robust bluster, I could detect the same self-doubt we've surely all been feeling: what was it we saw, or felt? What can we actually be sure of and what did we imagine? It's ridiculous to feel like the creature—or serpent or thing; whatever we're calling it—is part of a deliberate campaign against me, but under the circumstances perhaps I can be forgiven a little paranoia.

But anyway, the point is that on a day like today, anyone would be putting two and two together and getting five. Nevertheless, as soon as I reasonably can, I slip off to the toilet, the pressure of Georgie's eyes lying heavily on my back; I'm sure she's clocked that something is up, though she's been acting somewhat oddly herself. If I can just get into my email folders; surely I have a record of the account numbers there. If I can just see them in black and white, prove to myself that there's not a match . . . But no, an email search on my mobile finds emails from the bank, no account numbers on them. I'm pretty sure I can remember the password to log on online, but the ordinarily impressive Wi-Fi doesn't appear to be working; I sit on the loo seat cover and watch the spinning circle of doom on my phone, debating whether to turn on data roaming and risk the wrath of Rob with an egregious phone bill (what on earth would I tell him?), and then I realize I don't even have any signal at present. I stare and stare at the spinning circle until the fear that someone will come looking for me forces me out of the cubicle. Then I wash my hands, watching myself in the mirror, bathed in the oddly sickly light of the bathroom—not enough to allow touching up of any makeup and yet too much for mood lighting—as if watching a stranger: someone who looks like me, almost, but the finer details are wrong; they don't quite knit together.

They can't be. I've misremembered. And anyway, literally nobody would remember account numbers for accounts they barely touch.

And then: *I would. It's what I'm good at. I'm good with numbers.* The stranger in the mirror straightens abruptly and turns away.

Back at the table, Adam has shifted to sit next to Georgie, filling my spot. Their heads are together, and even though one is blond and one dark, there's something remarkably similar in their lean, sparse bone structure, in the tilt of their necks. They look up to see me at exactly the same time, reflected lamplight gleaming in their liquid eyes, as if they are two heads of the same beast. Suddenly I think again of that shadow racing under me in the ocean.

"Sorry, Bron, I didn't mean to usurp you," Adam is saying, but I'm too unsettled to do more than flap a vague hand as I circle the table to slide back into the seat he's now vacating.

"You can't usurp Bron," Georgie says, smiling as she puts an arm round my shoulders, squeezing me against her briefly, and this at least penetrates. I laugh, but not for the reasons she thinks: of course I can be usurped. Of course that's what Adam wants to do; it's completely normal. Boyfriends, who later become husbands, who, later still, spawn one's children—they all usurp friends; that's just how it works. How can Georgie be so clueless?

Because it wasn't like that for Lissa and Georgie. Nobody could replace what they were to each other. Even I didn't understand it.

I look around the table. Steve has joined us; as there's hardly anyone else in the restaurant, it would have been odd for him to remain at a table alone. His earlier unease has vanished, and he looks relaxed and expansive, a beer in one hand as he regales the group with a story from his previous life, something about trying to teach surfing to an oligarch's daughter who refused to paddle a single stroke. Jem has probably heard it before, but he laughs in the right places regardless, though he's looking a little ragged at the edges; he's a tall, broad man who can hold his drink, but nonetheless, it's starting to catch up with him.

"Is everything okay, honey?" asks Georgie, in a low murmur beneath the table conversation.

"Fine," I say brightly. "Why?"

"You just seem a little distracted today. Even before that thing in the water."

"Oh." Of course she would notice. "I'm just . . . I'm just finding it a bit difficult. Being here, all of us, but no Lissa."

Georgie is nodding, but before she can say anything, the waiter appears between us. "Wine, ma'am?" he asks, proffering a bottle. I shake my head quickly. I'm still feeling too fragile after my lunchtime efforts to contemplate anything other than water. Georgie and Adam allow the waiter to pour them a glass, but neither actually moves to taste it. Jem, on the other hand, is half a glass down before the waiter has got around the whole table.

"Is the Wi-Fi working on your phone?" I ask Georgie, before she can return to her line of questioning.

"What? Oh." She scrabbles in her bag and fishes out her mobile, frowning. "No, doesn't look like it. Actually, I don't have any reception at all." She cocks her head, looking up at me again. "Why, did you need something?"

"Oh, it's nothing, really. I just wanted to check on something for Kitty's school."

They can't be. It makes no sense. I've misremembered.

She looks at me for a moment, and I think she's almost about to say something, but the food arrives just then. I eat what is put in front of me mechanically, resisting the urge to check my phone yet again for Wi-Fi connection. Steve moves on to another story, which pulls Georgie's attention away from me. I hope he has a lot of them, enough to let me sit here and laugh when everyone else does and pretend to be absolutely fine. I'm not practiced at it, that type of pretense; the subterfuge nearly killed me when I was with Graeme. Well, not *with* Graeme. Whatever it was we were doing, we weren't exactly *together*, except in those certain moments when we were very much exactly that . . . Like in the utility room at the old house, where he first kissed me, with all our friends outside in the garden for Kitty's first birthday party. He and Lissa had had another blazing row; he was decompressing from it by downloading to me whilst I hunted in the freezer for the ice cream. And then he kissed me: not like Rob kisses, as if nothing more than a brief overture to be efficiently dispensed with before the main event, but as if trying to quench an endless thirst. Like the Elbow song: *Kiss me like the final meal. Kiss me like we die tonight.* That was a moment when we were together, Graeme and me.

God, what's wrong with me? I can't be thinking about Graeme. I haven't thought about him in years. Perhaps it's Steve's fault, with all those questions on the boat—

"Wow, you were hungry," says Adam. I glance at my plate and realize I've plowed through everything, though I couldn't say what I've just eaten, whereas Adam looks like he's barely taken two bites. His brow knits together in concern. "Is everything okay? You seem a little—"

"I'm fine," I interrupt brightly. Too brightly, I realize. "Except— well, it's been quite the day. All that excitement in the water." I shudder a little, not entirely forced, and he makes a sympathetic noise. "Is Jem doing anything about it?"

"He reported it to the relevant government body, but they're not going to advise that people stay out of the water given what we saw was so inconclusive. I think Steve said they're going to double up on lifeguards in Horseshoe Bay for the time being. And nobody is supposed to swim at Kanu Cove anyway." I shudder again. "Are you cold? Did you get too much sun?"

"I think maybe I did," I say ruefully, pulling a wrap around my shoulders, which do in fact feel a little like fiery sandpaper.

He nods seriously. "You're smart to stick to the water, then." I glance at his own ruby-red filled glass, and then at Georgie's. Both still look untouched. It suddenly occurs to me that I've barely seen Georgie take a sip of alcohol since she got here, a far cry from the Georgie of old; I remember, at university, Duncan once complaining that she was never sober after 9 p.m. I glance at her inadvertently. Surely she can't be pregnant? But no, she's stick thin—her stomach could have been used as an abdominal muscle anatomy lesson in her bikini today—and I have to believe she would tell me something like that. Surely she would tell me.

"We were at this very table that night," Adam says suddenly. "Do you remember?" I nod. I know which night he means: the night that Lissa drowned. "Swap Steve for Cristina and Georgie for Lissa and we're all in exactly the same seats, actually."

He's hooked George's attention with this; her head swings round from Steve's latest anecdote. "How did Lissa seem that night?"

"A bit tense, maybe," Adam offers. "She and Jem had been fighting."

"She told you that?" I ask, surprised.

"Yes—no, wait. I think Cristina told me that."

"Cristina again," murmurs Georgie. There's a scrape of chair legs on the floor, and we all look up to see Jem pulling himself to his feet. "Bathroom," he says laconically, then turns in that direction, bumping the table so forcefully that a bottle teeters then tips over, red wine blossoming from it across the white tablecloth. I leap to my feet and grab a napkin to dab at the mess while Jem leaves without a backward glance. I'm not even sure he's aware he knocked the bottle.

"Leave it," says Duncan. "They'll sort it." And it's true: two staff members are fussing at me with various hand signals to leave it be.

"Habit," I say, with an attempt at a smile as I relinquish the red-soaked, sodden napkin. "That's what mothers do; they clean up the mess." I glance at Jem, weaving ever so slightly as he threads his way through the tables. "It's not great for guests to see him drunk."

Duncan looks across at my words. "S'okay." Duncan has had more than a few himself by now. "Look at the place." I glance around again. He's right: there's only one other occupied table.

"What were they fighting about?" Georgie asks, as if there's been no interruption. Duncan looks nonplussed. "We're talking about that final night; Cristina said they were fighting."

"Oh." Duncan pauses, remembering. Steve is listening, too, now. "I don't actually know."

"The business, maybe?" presses Georgie. "Everything was going okay, right? Financially?"

"Absolutely. It was all looking good before—" Duncan waves a wrist in circles as if the motion might conjure him the right words. "Well, before."

"She was definitely jumpy that night," contributes Adam. There's a small frown on his face as he tries to remember. "And kind of down; she kept saying that she wished you had made it out." He glances at Georgie's face, then hurries on. "I actually wondered if she had taken—" Now it's Steve that he shoots a look at as he stops himself abruptly.

But Georgie has no such qualms. "Drugs? Can you even get them out here?"

"For sure," Steve pipes up, nodding grimly. "You get the wealthiest sections of society coming through this part of the world on their holidays. You better believe there's a thriving market in supplying them. That's despite the fact that the drug laws are properly harsh here; even possession for personal use can lead to the death penalty." He frowns. "I never heard any rumors about Lissa using anything, though." He looks round the group. "Did she . . . ah . . . Was that her thing?"

After a beat of silence, Georgie says, "Not especially," in a casual tone, and Steve nods as if understanding, but how could he, really, when Georgie has told him nothing at all? Suddenly Steve's face changes, and I realize that Jem is almost back to the table. "Boss," he says easily. "Thank God you're back. I've long since used up all my decent chat. Now I'm just boring these good people; we need your famous raconteur skills."

"Ah, but these good people all have stories of their own, don't you?" Jem settles himself back in his chair. "Just this morning Georgie was telling me quite a tale." I suddenly realize Jem's eyes are fixed on Georgie's.

"C'mon, share," says Duncan, apparently oblivious to the tension.

"I don't think now is the time and place for that one," Georgie says with too-careful disinterest.

"What? But we're all friends here." Jem throws an arm wide to indicate the table, making me anxious for all the wineglasses near him. Stupid, stupid man. A cornered Georgie is a lioness. Utterly dangerous and genetically incapable of backing down.

"Are we?" muses Georgie, toying with her untouched wineglass for an uncomfortably long moment. Then she fixes Jem with a look that could skewer fish even as she says sweetly, "Then perhaps, as the famous raconteur, you'd like to tell it?"

Jem holds her gaze for a beat or two, then leans back in his chair and throws his napkin on his plate. "I'm done," he says with absolutely no finesse. "I'm going to the bar."

"What on earth was that about?" I ask, watching as Steve follows Jem to the bar.

"Nothing," Georgie says quickly.

"Wait, is this the Loretta Bobbitt story?" says Duncan, understanding dawning on his face. "He was spouting off about that earlier—"

"Later, Dunc," Georgie says, her words so heavily loaded with meaning that it's a miracle that he misses it, but he does.

"What?" I ask, but Duncan is talking over me: "Why on earth would you tell him something like that?" he asks Georgie.

"He asked."

"What?" I ask again; finally Duncan looks at me and says, "Jem is spouting off about some Loretta—"

"Lorena," breaks in Georgie.

"—whatever, *Lorena* Bobbitt story that Georgie told him about Lissa."

Adam is frowning. "Wait, Lorena Bobbitt: wasn't that the woman who—"

"Cut off her husband's dick," says Duncan. "Yes."

"I don't understand. Lissa never . . ." I catch sight of Georgie's face and stop talking.

"It's okay, she didn't," Georgie says quickly to me.

Duncan snorts. "Not for want of trying, the way Jem told it."

Georgie rounds on him. "And was Jem actually there?"

"And you were?" I ask, completely baffled by now. She nods slowly. "Whose dick?"

"Your ex. Scott. Before he was ex." She delivers it in one clean punch. I open my mouth. Then close it again.

Adam looks even more confused than I. "So Lissa tried to cut off Bron's boyfriend's dick?"

"Not exactly. She threatened to. She held a knife to it." Adam's eyes widen, and he visibly swallows. "With a certain amount of force." Now Duncan shudders slightly.

"But . . . why?" I ask helplessly.

Georgie looks at me, and I can see from her direct gaze that I'm not going to like what she's about to say. But Georgie is a pull-the-Band-Aid-off-in-one-go kind of girl. "Because he was trying to cheat on you."

"Cheat on me." I'm finally putting it together. "With Lissa." She nods, sharp and fast. Scott Mayhew. He was even more of a creep than I'd imagined him to be, for disappearing without a trace. Except that now I understand why he disappeared without a trace. All those years ago, I was furious at him for entirely the wrong reason.

"How were you there anyway?" Duncan asks her. "Was it a three-some thing?"

"No!" Georgie half laughs, then sobers again, shrugging. "I just walked in on it. On them. Just as she grabbed the knife."

Dunc shudders again. "Even for Lissa, that's completely over the top," he says.

"Really? Tell me, Dunc, what is the proportionate response to infidelity?" Georgie asks with faux sweetness.

"Oh, come on—" Dunc starts.

"A slap in the face? Or is that just for kissing? What about a blow job, is that two slaps?"

"You're being ridic—"

"Is it more or less if the girl that you try it on with is your girlfriend's best friend?"

"Come off it." Duncan's finger is pointing at Georgie, across the table, to the middle of her chest. He's a big guy, and he's using that to intimidate, consciously or unconsciously. It's like a red rag to a bull with Georgie; she seems to swell toward that very finger.

"And what if she's actually high at the time? How does that change the scale?"

"This isn't a women's lib, Me Too thing; women cheat, too, you know—"

"Not as many as men," she shoots back.

"People make mistakes." He's almost yelling. "They shouldn't lose a body part over them—"

"Jesus Christ, you two; behave," orders Adam sharply. Duncan pulls back abruptly, lounging back in his chair, though the tension still visible in him is entirely at odds with his deliberately casual position. Georgie picks up her glass of water and takes a sip, holding the glass with both hands and sitting up tall and prim, with both elbows on the table and color still high in her cheeks. Nobody speaks. Duncan picks up an unused knife and swings it lazily, holding one end between thumb and forefinger, before he seems to recognize what it is and drops it abruptly. "You're right, Adam," he says, after a beat or two. He looks across at Georgie and offers a half smile. "Drink at the bar?"

She smiles back—not her usual smile, but it is at least a smile. "Come on then."

Adam and I watch as they leave the table, Duncan slinging an arm round Georgie to pull her against him. After a moment Adam eyes my face. "Well. That was intense," he offers.

"Yes."

"Are you okay?"

I shrug. "It was a long time ago."

"Even so, that sort of thing can still sting."

He doesn't miss much, Adam. He and Georgie are well suited in that regard. "It's okay." I shrug. "Scott was a shit even before I knew he was a cheating shit."

He laughs, and it totally changes his face. If he laughed more, I might feel more at ease with him; or if I could just read what he was thinking. Maybe it's an ex-military thing: he always seems to be assessing. Constantly preparing to maneuver.

"Don't you wonder, though," I start, then stop. Adam cocks his head. "Don't you wonder how Scott's dick got into Lissa's hand?" Adam looks down. "Wouldn't there have to be some kind of action first? It seems pretty late in the day to start an impassioned defense of the sisterhood when your hand is actually down his pants."

"That did cross my mind," he admits, meeting my eye. "I'm guessing his version might describe it as entrapment."

"Yes, I would think it might." Duncan and Georgie have reached the bar now; Dunc still has Georgie pulled against him. He's a good man, to have offered the olive branch first. "If he hadn't been such a shit—and a cheating shit—I might even feel sorry for him."

Adam's lips twist briefly. "I wouldn't. Good guys don't lunge at their girlfriend's friends, even if it's offered on a plate."

"Now they don't. I'm not sure even the good guys thought that way at twenty." *Especially if that friend was Lissa, who everyone wanted to screw.* And then: *Graeme lunged at me, and I wasn't offering anything on a plate.* But that was different. We were both struggling in our own relationships. Perhaps it was a way of weathering the storm.

"Your faith in men is heartening," Adam says dryly, but I notice he's not arguing. "Shall we move to the sofas?"

I follow him across to the area he chooses to commandeer, checking my phone en route. Still no bloody Wi-Fi. I flop into an armchair, and Adam takes the sofa opposite. I don't know where Georgie has disappeared to, but Jem, Duncan and Steve are up at the broad counter, in conversation with the bartender. Jem is still drinking steadily; Duncan appears to be trying to keep up. And Adam is watching everything because that's what Adam does. Which is really starting to irritate. "What on earth is up with Jem?" I ask him.

"You mean besides his business falling apart?"

I grimace. "Yeah, I get that, but why is he taking it out on Georgie?"

"Well." Adam shrugs. "Jealousy, I think."

"Jealousy?" I stare at him. He's looking back at me calmly. Once again, I can't tell what he's thinking. Can Georgie? Or is that part of the attraction? "I don't understand."

"He didn't understand the dynamic between Georgie and Lissa."

"Nobody did." I sound peevish. I feel peevish.

Adam looks at me closely. "Even you?"

"Even me."

He pauses as if thinking that over, then moves forward on the edge of the sofa, his elbows resting on his knees, his long forearms pointing toward me. "Well, anyway. He didn't understand it, the intensity of it. Then there's the story you've just heard, and then Duncan said something a few days ago, I don't even know what exactly, but some throwaway comment that's had him wondering if they were maybe—" He stops and replaces his words with a slight twitch of his fingers, and just as I'm starting to shake my head, to say *I don't get it,* then suddenly I do. "I think all he can see is Georgie and Lissa, all tangled up in their schemes together."

I let that sink in for a moment. Georgie and Lissa. They used to talk late into the night and end up falling asleep in the same bed all the time, but I never saw anything specific— certainly nothing that couldn't be explained away by just being the very closest of friends, with *that* sort of interest in them stemming from unbridled male fantasy, and yet . . . "Why doesn't he just ask her?"

"He can't. And"—he spreads his hands wide, and his lips twist wryly—"it's Georgie. Even if she deigned to answer, I'm not sure he would believe her."

"If she answered, she'd be telling the truth." He nods in agreement. "Why don't *you* ask her?"

"It doesn't feel like any of my business." I blink. Really? I can't imagine thinking that the sexuality of who I'm sleeping with isn't my business. He cocks his head. "But just to warn you, Jem might ask *you,* though."

"Well, I'll just say no. Regardless." He goes oddly still at *regardless,* and I suddenly realize how he's interpreting that. "Wait, I didn't mean . . ." I stop and try to regroup, though there's a slight perverse satisfaction in seeing that he's not as buttoned-up as he'd like to be. "In all honesty, I don't have an answer. I really don't. But he needs to hear a solid no, so that's what I'll tell him." Adam nods. "Though maybe that's kind of worse for him, don't you think?"

"What do you mean?" His gleaming eyes are trained on my face.

"Isn't it simpler if you can explain away their connection as sexual? If it was something else, something deeper and more, I don't know, more unfathomable—well, how could anyone ever compete with that?"

Adam sits back on the sofa and throws an arm casually along the back of it. "But there is no competition. Lissa is dead."

I shake my head; his logic is flawed. "You're looking at it the wrong—"

But Duncan and Steve are joining us. "So I've been trying to work it out," says Steve in a teasing tone. "Swimming is the connection between you all. So which of you lot is the best swimmer?"

"Duncan," Adam and I chorus together.

"Well, no, it depends," says Duncan, though I can see he's flattered by our immediate response—and by the fact that Steve looks like it's what he was expecting to hear. He settles next to Adam on the sofa, and Adam shifts up to give him space. "Pool swimming is different to open water. Lissa was the best at breaststroke; Bron was the best at two hundred meters butterfly."

"I'm really good up to, oh, all of ten meters, at head-up front crawl," Adam tosses in, self-deprecatingly.

Steve looks confused. "He's really a water polo player. Played for England under eighteens," explains Duncan. "Graeme, too." Steve looks suitably impressed. I look at my phone. Still no reception; still no Wi-Fi.

"And for the open water stuff?" Steve asks, transparently searching for a lighter topic than Graeme.

"Duncan again," I say. "And then Georgie. She's always the fittest out of all of us."

"Training has always been like a religion for her," Duncan says. "She didn't have the easiest home life, our Georgie. She once said that without swimming she'd have never resurfaced after her sister died."

"She said that?" I ask, unable to hide my surprise. Duncan nods. "Wow. She literally never talks about Maddy." I look around: where *is* Georgie anyway?

"Well, she was drunk at the time." He grimaces briefly as if to add, *Plus ça change.*

"Maddy was her sister?" Steve is looking around expectantly, awaiting more.

Duncan explains. "Maddy died when Georgie was about fifteen; she was much younger, only about five. Georgie adored her, apparently. Anyway, Georgie was out with friends, and Maddy had a seizure. Her parents didn't even notice; they were pretty heavy on the . . ." He tilts his hand toward his mouth, miming drinking from a bottle. "Georgie found her when she got home." Adam is looking across at Duncan, too, his face indecipherable, though I'm sure this can't be news to him. Or can it? I'm never sure what men really tell one another.

Steve puffs his cheeks and then blows out slowly. "Christ."

"Sorry," Duncan says to Steve. "Didn't mean to get so serious. Jem!" he says, catching sight of him approaching. "Come join us." He hooks the armchair next to mine with his ankle, pulling it out for Jem.

My phone is suddenly chiming. I scramble to grab it. "Wi-Fi! At last!"

Adam's eyebrows quirk up minutely. "I didn't have you down as an avid Instagrammer," he teases.

"Hardly. I just need to check on something for Kitty's school. Rob's not on the email list." I briefly debate disappearing off to a quiet corner, but that would look odd; why would I want to hide a school missive? Instead I stay where I am, in the large armchair opposite Adam, Duncan and Steve, with Jem on my left now, while I Google the bank's mobile site, wondering when I last logged on and whether I can remember the password. I probably haven't done this since the accounts were first created; they're not with the bank that holds Rob's and my current accounts. These are the kids' Child Trust Fund accounts, designed especially for tax-free savings—literally the only activity is that money is dripped into them each month, by way of the standing order I've set up; the money can't even be withdrawn until the child turns eighteen. I've never bothered looking at the balances online; I just glance at the annual summaries when they arrive by post.

It's a damning testament to my poor password security—almost every online account has the same one—that I gain access on my first attempt. I find I'm holding my breath as the page loads. And suddenly there, on the account summary page, are the eight-digit numbers for Kitty and Jack's accounts, in bold black.

They match.

It's impossible, but they match. With scant concern for who is watching, I pull the scrap of paper out of my pocket to double-check. Two clicks take me to the account details page.

They match.

Every single digit; the sort code, too. They match. Just like I somehow always knew they would. From not breathing at all, I find I'm almost panting; I have to deliberately calm myself before anyone thinks I'm having a seizure. I glance around quickly, but the men are engaged in a conversation about US politics, and Georgie still hasn't reappeared. I'm almost too afraid to click through to the account balances, but I force myself. The total on Kitty's account is just a jumble of digits that is meaningless to me, until suddenly the position of the separator resolves into sense and I have to stifle a gasp. There's tens of thousands more than there should be in there—and the same in Jack's. Far more than the tax-free allowance—I find myself wondering if that jeopardizes the tax-free status of the allowable savings, and then realize with rising hysteria that that is the very least of my worries. There's no question that it's real now. There's no question of it being an accident, either. Somebody did this. Somebody did this deliberately; somebody did this for a reason, targeting me with sly, malicious, targeted intent. Because this isn't just a case of money laundering, of using these accounts as a temporary step in a layering process, part of an attempt to hide the origin of the cash. Nobody would steal money to put it in an account that they absolutely, positively couldn't get it out of. Nobody would do that. And yet, there it is.

I need to think. I need to take a moment and think this through.

"Everything okay?" Adam asks, turning away from the group, and suddenly I hate him and his dark, watchful eyes with a passion beyond reason. I hate him, and I hate Duncan, and I hate Jem, and Georgie and everyone and anyone who could possibly be behind this. Because, whatever the reason, whatever the intent, surely it has to be someone who knows me. "Bron? What's wrong?"

"Lice," I say brightly, scratching theatrically at my scalp. "There's nits at the school again. Even just reading about it makes my head itch." I cock my head. "Where's Georgie? Shall I check on her?" And without waiting for an answer, I get up from the armchair and leave the bar.

I get as far as two twists along the path before I have to throw myself into the dark foliage and bend double, my entire meal spewing from my mouth in one spasm of extraordinary force. Some of the vomit spatters back at me off the thick, unfamiliar leaves, gray-black in the darkness; I feel it pebble-dashing my bare legs and feet. I stand up shakily, tears leaking from the corners of my eyes, though I don't even have the energy to screw my face into an accompanying grimace of misery. The wind has dropped since the sun went down, and the night is silent except for the odd chirping of some kind of cricket-like insect and a low undertone of music from the bar. My eyes are clearing now: I can see in sharp relief the vivid greens of the bushes where the low lighting of the path touches them every five meters or so down the pathway. My head is clearing, too. The acrid smell of vomit is crusted in my nose, around my mouth, and like a perverse kind of smelling salts, it provides unexpected clarity. I have nowhere to go, literally nowhere is safe. And if nowhere is safe, then any place is as good, or as bad, as any another. Which means that I may as well go to my room, since I have to clean myself up.

And then, once I've done that, I'll have to clean up whatever kind of mess I'm in.

EIGHT

GEORGIE

I don't think about where I'm going; I just go. It's a trick I discovered as a teenager, when I had to find a way to get myself to all those early-morning swim sessions. A 5:30 a.m. wake-up is brutal; a 5:30 a.m. wake-up as a teenager without supportive parents to chivy you along is almost impossible. The trick I discovered, though, is beautiful in its simplicity: you just don't think. No questioning, no internal debate, not a single moment allowed for contemplation: you simply get out of bed, dress, grab your bag and leave. Unthinking, unquestioning, uncaring. An automaton.

The trick is easier at the crack of dawn, though, when one's mind is not exactly primed for analysis. Here and now, at the other end of the day, my brain is suspicious; it doesn't take long before it fears it's being hoodwinked. But I manage to make it three-quarters of the way there before the internal debate hardens into solid thought. Not that there's so very much to debate.

This is stupid and pointless.

Yes, but I'm going anyway.

And then there's no point at all in debating, because I'm there.

Here. Kanu Cove, again. It *is* different at night; I knew it would be. There's the same low, unobtrusive lighting that's present along all the pathways in the rest of the resort, though somehow it seems even dimmer here. And it sounds different here, too: there are still faint noises from the rest of the resort, but they seem dampened, whereas the water itself sounds louder, more urgent; the waves run and race and crash on the small beach at the head of the cove. There are lights at either end of the narrow stone pier that runs for some meters along one side of the tongue of water, where I had my encounter with the local man previously. I find my way there again, though thankfully alone this time, sandals in one hand, bare toes flexing against the still-warm stone beneath them as I squint at the inky blackness of the water. I'm not sure if I'm seeing, or imagining, occasional white tips out in the center of the expanse of water. The only solid marker is a light on a buoy, perhaps the same buoy that marked the lobster pots. Is the serpent in this cove, slipping soundlessly in and out of the narrow mouth between the cliffs to wind itself around the metal chain that leads ever deeper, link by link, to secure the buoy to the seabed? Or does it sleep at night, coiled in a deep, dark cave somewhere—or stretched out on the ocean floor, moving gently like a standard in the deep currents? Or perhaps it hunts at night. Perhaps even now it's preparing its next attack—not in the way that we humans do, out of malice or fear or driving anger, but with emotionless calculation, relentlessly driven by implacable animal instinct that cannot be appealed to or appeased.

Kanu takes. Takes who wants taken. The ambiguity of those statements has been a stray thread for my mind to constantly worry at. It was surely just poor English, but still . . . Did he mean Kanu the cove, or Kanu the serpent? Did he actually mean to say that Kanu takes what it wants to take, or that it takes those who want to be taken?

If I wanted to be taken, this would be the place. Not Horseshoe Bay, with its air of sanitized domesticity—no self-respecting serpent would haunt Horseshoe Bay. This cove, though, has a wildness to it, not just in the water, but also in the land, in its abrupt drop from cliff top to water's edge, more fjord than bay. I was so sure at first, that Lissa didn't want that, that she couldn't have wanted that, but my subconscious has been tugging away at that loose thread nonetheless: sifting through every line of every email, every word of every conversation, over and over, constantly looking for the meaning that I missed the first time round, trying to see afresh from every angle. But after all of that endless mulling, all I can say is that I'm sure I don't know. How can it be that I don't know?

I've been thinking, too, of the beginning: the beginning of Lissa and me. Perhaps that's natural at the end of something, or perhaps it's because of Jem's questions about—how did he describe it?—our *intensity.* But Lissa was literally the first person who truly understood me; who would always be on my side. I don't think either of us had forged strong friendships at school; in my case, most likely because I was so full of grief and anger, after Maddy's death, that I was numbed to feeling anything else. There were plenty of people at school that I called friends, but none that I would have opened up to. Maddy's death: that's another thing that Lissa understood. I told her about it very early on, perhaps only a couple of weeks into the first term; that's how instant our connection was, forged initially through us both quite clearly being not just the keenest on a party, but also having the stamina—nay, sheer determination—to keep the party going when others fell away. But it was the conversations we had when everyone else fell away that bound us together.

Everyone kept saying it was just a terrible tragedy, I told her bitterly. *And all I could think was, if I had just been there—I mean, I know it wasn't my fault—*

God, no, she said, somehow clear-eyed despite it being long past midnight. *Of course it wasn't your fault.* But everyone would have said that. It was what she said next that was important, the thing that nobody else would have said even if it did cross their mind: *It was your parents' fault. They're the ones to blame.*

I bend to take off my sandals, thinking that I could sit on the edge of the pier again. I could dangle my bare feet into the black, secretive water, as surely she must have done. I could do that, maybe I *need* to do that, to put myself in her place—after all, it was what I intended to do in coming here—but now that I *am* here, I'm too scared. Because what if it works? What if I feel what she was feeling? What if, even if only for the briefest of moments, I find myself wanting to be taken, too? What do I have to stop me?

Something flickers in the corner of my vision, and I look right, toward the inland beach. It takes me a second or two to realize what has happened: the pathway lighting has gone out. Surely it's not on a timer? Or if it is, surely it can't be so very late already? I twist my wrist to look at my watch, and as I do, the lights around me on the pier flicker once and then die completely. It's instantly very, very dark.

It's a power cut, I reason. I stay still for a few seconds, waiting for the lights to come back on, or a reserve generator to kick in. But the darkness remains complete; there are no stars or moon to paint their silver on me tonight. Only the weak glow of the LED on the buoy provides any kind of landmark. Above the sound of the water, I can still hear snatches of music from the somewhere else in the resort. Not a resort-wide power cut, then. If it's a power cut at all.

Suddenly a shower of small stones comes from the cliff face behind me; I gasp as I feel a couple hit my toes even as I hear them, then take a few involuntary steps before common sense halts me. A small animal dislodged them, surely? Though what type of animal? I strain to listen for it, but I can't hear any movements above the rushing that's started in my ears. I don't want to be in Kanu Cove in the dark; I don't want to be here at all anymore. My eyes have adjusted a little, but there's simply not enough light to find my way back safely; I might trip and fall—worse, I might fall into the water. I fish in my shoulder bag for my phone, my fingers scrabbling at every single useless item before they bump up against the familiar rubber edge of the protective case. There isn't enough light for the phone to recognize my face: I have to tap in my PIN code, in a flurry of mildly panicked fingers; I get it wrong twice before I get it right, and the two-fingered swipe action that's necessary to find the torch function takes several attempts also. But finally I have a bright, cold beam of light streaming from my device, which reveals that I've got myself turned around somehow. I sweep the torchlight around me to get my bearings, the circle of warmthless clinical white picking up the jetty with its impotent lamps, then the crumbling stone of the cliff face, and finally finding the pathway that leads back inland.

Something hits my shoulder. I'm being showered again by soil and small stones, and it's enough to make me drop all pretense at calm and start to run, the phone held in front in my right hand, like a talisman, and my left hand reaching across myself to grab at the crossbody shoulder strap to stop my bag banging, which means that the sandals looped over my thumb by the ankle straps bash away at me instead. The path here is gritty and uneven, being only very roughly paved, and with my movements the torchlight bounces and flares, flooding the near ground in too much light and rendering everything two-dimensional, yet throwing ludicrously large shadows for the smallest of pebbles in the periphery, making it near impossible to choose where to place my feet at the pace I'm moving. Gravel jabs at my bare soles and digs painfully into my heels, but I'm not going to stop to put on my sandals—I'm not going to stop until I'm away from here, back where there's lights and music and people. My breathing is harsh and ragged in my ears. I'm nearly at the head of the cove now, where the path splits, and even though I'm looking for it, I almost overshoot the fork and have to turn sharply, my ankle protesting vehemently. Now I'm on a wider track, one that the little golf buggies drive along so it's much better paved, though with cobbles that aren't any more comfortable to run on—but every stumbling step is taking me farther from the source of my panic and closer to the holy grail of civilization: in the distance I can see the lights of the restaurant. I've overreacted, I know—the first pricks of shame are making themselves felt—but that's not nearly enough to stop me running.

Some sixth sense turns my head, just in time to see a dark shape bearing down on me, and I leap sideways, simultaneously twisting to face the danger. And it is danger: as I turn, the talisman of the phone rotates with me, washing light over . . .

A man.

Or a man's chest, at least: arms stretching forward, reaching out for me. He's so close that the circle of light is too small to show his face. The next second he has knocked my arm aside and the mobile is sailing through the dark, its light sweeping round like a beacon as it tumbles. I flail out with the hand that's holding the sandals, swinging hard at where I think his head might be even as I start to run, but my blow doesn't seem to land, and then I'm jerked back so abruptly by the strap of my bag that I almost come off my feet. He's saying something, but I can't hear it properly through the ragged shrieks that are bursting from me as I twist to extract myself from the bag, and then a scything leg sweeps one of my own out from under me, and I drop to one knee, still caught up in the bag. We've veered off the path in our struggles; there are leaves and branches thwacking my face as his arms go round me, and even though he's not a big man—I sense he can't be very much taller than myself, and his torso against me feels skinny—even despite that, it's like being wrapped in a steel vise. For the first time it crosses my mind that I may not be able to get out of this—this what? mugging? assault?—and the ensuing panic provides enough fuel for me to throw myself backward, pulling him awkwardly down with me. He has to free one arm to brace himself, and that is enough: I twist from under him and swing again with the sandals, and this time I have a better idea of where his head is. The wedge heels connect with a thump followed by a harsh grunt. I scramble to my feet, backing away and desperately seeking out the path, and out of sheer luck I can see a circle of light: the mobile torchlight; it's landed such that it's illuminating paved stones. I grab it on the run, heading for the reception area, that nirvana of lights and music, screaming as loudly as I can manage in between the breaths needed for running. I daren't look behind me; he must surely be catching up—and then it occurs to me he will be able to track me by the pool of light from the phone, and I toss it hard into the vegetation off to one side and keep on running without the screaming. I can run for a very long time, but not at this pace, and not in the dark—but suddenly I'm not in the dark. The low-level path lighting has sputtered back on, and the restaurant lights are getting closer, too, now: I can make out the long counter of the bar, the sofas; I can see Adam and the barman in conversation, and I yell something wordless that comes from somewhere I didn't know was inside me, and Adam looks up.

Instantly his face changes and he's on his feet, rushing toward me. "What happened?" He's scanning me all over. "Your knee—you're bleeding."

"Someone—someone attacked me." I'm gulping in breaths, and I'm not crying—I know I'm not crying—but my voice isn't my own. Adam shepherds me toward the sofas; I feel the ground beneath my feet change from the stone and sand of the path to the wooden floor of the restaurant area, and it feels like entering a magic circle of safety. The barman is hovering awkwardly beside us both. "I don't know who—someone tried to grab me."

"What?" says Steve sharply. I didn't see him before, but he's here now, looking behind me as if he might see the culprit there. "Who? Where?"

I gesture where I've come from, hands on hips, bent over, trying to catch my breath. The adrenaline that has been coursing through me is abating: I know this because I suddenly feel extraordinarily like throwing up. Adam pushes me gently onto the sofa, then turns to grab a napkin and some water. "I don't know who. Back there—ouch!" Adam mutters something that might be an apology; he's on his knees in front of me trying to clean the sand out of the wound on my knee with a now-soaked napkin.

"Were they after you or your bag?" Adam asks, tipping his head toward my side.

I look down at the shoulder bag and realize that the contents must be scattered along my flight path, because one side of the bag has been ripped at the seams and is hanging open. "Me. Definitely me. The bag was collateral damage." I remember being yanked back by the shoulder strap, then the horror of those arms closing around me, the realization that, strong as I am, as I always have been, I might not be able to escape the viselike grip of what were, after all, just thin and unremarkable male arms. What unforgivable hubris I have been operating under, to think that my strength, my fitness, would make me capable of swatting away something like this.

"Could you recognize him again?"

I purse my lips, then shake my head. "The lights were out; it was dark. I was using the torch on my phone. I could describe what he was wearing, but I didn't see his face." Adam calls to Steve, who has stepped away a few paces to issue rapid instructions that I can't quite hear to the barman and another staff member. He comes over, and I recount what little I can of my attacker. Only a little taller than me, possibly a local from the skin color of those reaching arms, wearing a T-shirt with very thin gray and black horizontal stripes—the circle of torchlight told me that, but no more. It's a pitifully scant description.

"Where were you when he attacked?" asks Steve, calmly business-like, while Adam continues to clean my knee.

"On the way back from Kanu Cove." Adam's hand stills, and he looks up at my face. I can't read what I see there; I'm not equipped to interpret such things right now. But almost immediately he turns his attention back to my knee. Steve nods and returns to the staff, who, serious-faced, turn to immediately carry out his instructions, some at a run.

"Hold this against it," Adam instructs, pushing my hand against a new napkin on my knee. I wonder if they will get the blood out of all these previously pristine linen squares. Perhaps hotels have secret methods to manage tough stains? I'm starting to assess the damage to myself, too. Besides the knee, I have cuts on my feet, and my ankle and shoulder are aching in a way that suggests nothing good, and one shoulder strap of this dress might give way at any second. How long did the whole encounter take: two minutes? Less? Only two minutes to entirely crumble the image I had held of myself.

"So," Adam says. I suddenly realize it's just us. Steve and the rest of the staff have melted away. Duncan is nowhere to be seen. Were he and Jem ever there? I can't remember seeing them when I ran up. "Tell me. From the beginning."

I start to, but suddenly my brain catches up to me, and I interrupt myself abruptly. "Where's Bron?"

"She went to check on you. But"—Adam frowns as he checks his watch—"that was ages ago. She must have gone back to her room."

I stand, ignoring the lancing pain through my knee. "We have to check on her. We have to go now." I turn, uncaring of whether he's with me or not. I can't explain the dread that has resurfaced inside me, as if it never really left after the attack, as if it never will leave— not truly; and I can't explain the sudden fear for Bron in particular.

Adam looks as if he wants to say something else entirely, but he stands up, too. "I'll call her. From the phone at the bar. Stay here." But I follow him, briefly marveling at the set of his shoulders ahead of me. Was he always like that, or was it the army that put that inside him? There's nobody manning the bar; presumably whoever should be there is off doing Steve's bidding. Adam leans over and grabs the phone, pulling it up to the counter and punching in the number for Bron's room. I can hear it ringing out in low electronic hums. He lets it ring for a very long time, his eyes holding mine through all the unanswered rings while the dread inside me roils and turns, a turgid, cooling mass.

Finally, reluctantly, he puts the receiver back in the cradle. "She's probably asleep," he offers, but the thin line of his mouth shows that he doesn't believe it, either.

"We have to go there."

He nods, just the briefest of movements; a minimum of effort. "You can tell me what happened on the way," he adds as we cross the bar area to take a path from the other side, moving as quickly as I'm able without actually running, which is a lot less quickly than I'd like. There's an umbrella stand at the end of the pavilion, with one hotel-branded umbrella in it. The wooden handle looks sturdy. I pull it out and hold it by the other end. Adam looks at the upside-down umbrella in my hand, then at my face, and then he picks up the umbrella stand itself, which is made of bare metal struts without any panels. He wraps his fist around the midpoint of one of the long struts and flexes his arm, getting the measure of the heft of it, then nods at me. Then we take the path to Bron's villa, which is thankfully not suffering from any power outage, and Adam asks me questions, which I answer briefly because that's the best I can do under the present circumstances. The resort is different to me now. I'm no longer charmed by the paths which twist and turn in meandering fashion through the foliage, presumably to give the guests a permanent sense of seclusion. Instead I see every bush, every dark patch of foliage, as a place where an intruder could be hiding. The path lighting is not sufficient; nothing short of full midday sunshine could be sufficient. The dread inside me hasn't receded with activity—if anything it's growing and hardening with every step, even though I know there's no logical reason for it. I can't even ascribe it to a protective instinct; the now granitelike weight in my stomach is far too excessive for that. Adam falls silent beside me. I can't tell if he's run out of questions or if he has just given up.

Then we reach the steps to Bron's villa. I can't see any lights, other than the standard dim resort lighting around the exterior, but it would be difficult to see interior lights from this side anyway. Adam presses the electric bell; we hear it chime within, my eyes finding his as we listen, just as we listened before to the telephone ringing. There's a stillness to the villa that makes my stomach clench around the granite inside. Adam tries the handle—a futile gesture, since all the doors lock automatically when closed—and then presses the bell again, but without waiting for a response to the chime. I bang sharply on the door with the umbrella handle and call out, "Bron? Bron, are you there?"

There's the faintest of noises from inside, and then the door swings open, to reveal Bron—thank God!—in a bathrobe, with her hair wrapped up in a turban of towel. Bron, blessedly alive and well, her cheeks damp and flushed, presumably straight out of a bath or shower. I spill into the room, reaching out to hug her. "Bron. Thank God. You're okay—" And then I stop, because oddly, she's backed a couple of paces away from me, and I've seen a flash of something silver in her hand as she hastily shoves it behind her back. And then I know the granite in my stomach is there for a reason: I've been right to be afraid. Bron is not *okay*. None of us are *okay*. "Bron." It's barely a whisper, but it doesn't need to be more than that; my urgency shouts for me. "Why are you holding a knife?"

NINE

BRONWYN

Why am I holding a knife? Why, indeed—and then, as Georgie steps farther into the light, my jaw drops and I've got the perfect excuse to delay answering that question. She's a mess. Her mascara is smeared across one temple, there's sand in her hairline, she's barefoot and her dress is hanging lopsided off one shoulder, as if the fabric has become misshapen beyond repair. There may even be smatters of blood marring the misty green fabric at the hem, and she's rather incongruously carrying an umbrella, held upside down. "Oh my God, Georgie, what happened?"

"Somebody attacked me," she says, unexpectedly dismissively. She drops the umbrella, and the wooden handle clatters heavily on the tiled floor. "Bron—"

"Where? When?" And what does it mean? How does that connect to the message on my mirror and the money in the accounts? For a moment I consider saying I was attacked myself, and that's why I have the knife, but just as quickly I discard that. They'll never buy it; I would have raised the alarm at the time.

"Never mind that. The knife, Bron?"

I look down at it in my hand. It's hardly the kind of weapon I might have hoped for. The new bread knife from home jumps to mind for that: long and serrated and kept wickedly sharp by Rob, who is very particular about that sort of thing—but this is just a bog-standard dinner knife, one that was left with the complimentary fruit. If I hadn't instinctively tried to hide it, I suppose I could have claimed I was about to cut into an orange when they banged on the door. "Come on in," I temporize, stepping back and turning to put the knife carelessly on the nearby console table. Adam closes the door behind them. I could tell them everything, right from the very start—well, perhaps not the *very* start, but nearly. I'm almost about to—and then a look passes between the pair of them, one that I'm not invited to share, and the words turn to ash on my tongue.

"Bron?" Georgie says again.

"You'll think I'm completely paranoid." I grimace as if mortified. I've only got the side lamps on, and Georgie's eyes are liquid black in the dim light, and fixed entirely on my face. I reach for the main light switch to snap it on defiantly, and she blinks, her eyelids lifting on green eyes. It's oddly disconcerting, as if her eyes have changed rather than the ambient light. "It's just, I . . . It's stupid, but I thought I saw someone in here when I got back after dinner. Well, not inside, but out back, in the pool area. I didn't know who was banging on my door all in a hurry, so . . ." I shrug. That last sentence at least is true. I didn't know who was banging on the door, and until I've figured out what's going on, I can't trust anyone. I'd have put the knife in my pocket and it would be there even now, if Georgie hadn't spotted it.

Adam speaks first. "Could you describe them?"

"Who?" I say blankly.

"The person you saw." His words are dripping with deliberate patience. "Out by the pool area."

"Oh. Not really. I doubt I could pick him out of a lineup." Georgie's fingers make a frustrated gesture. I sigh. If I'm going to have to make something up, I may as well describe the man I saw leaving the villa before. "Okay, well: local. Youngish. Taller than you, Adam, but not by much. Thin."

"Clothing?" Georgie asks.

"I couldn't really say; there isn't enough light out there. He was probably one of the staff and I'm being ridiculous. I mean, it's been quite a day . . ." That much is certainly true. My arms have wrapped themselves across my middle, each hand hugging an elbow.

"He probably wasn't," Adam says, as if musing aloud. "Something alarmed you. Surely your subconscious wouldn't have been on the alert if he was wearing the right staff uniform." He looks at Georgie. "Could it be the same guy?"

She shrugs. "Possibly. But, clothing apart, Bron's description probably fits two-thirds of the men in this area."

"Was it a mugging?" I ask her. "Was he after your bag?"

She shakes her head. "I don't think so. I don't know what he wanted." She reaches out a hand to the wall as if to steady herself, and I suddenly realize that, like her dress, she's only just about held together. Now that I've made the room brighter, it's clear that the stains on her dress are indeed blood, and there's more blood streaked down one leg.

"Come and sit down," I urge her. "Can I get you some water or something?" She lets me lead her to the sofa and sinks down into one corner of it, grimacing as she bends her knee. "Ouch. That looks really nasty." There's thick, partially congealed blood oozing from the livid cut, and angry purple bruising around it. "We'll need to clean that up."

"Cleaning up the mess again?" she says, but it's a very weak attempt at humor.

"Well, that is what mothers do. Let me see if I have some Band-Aids." I hurry off for the bedroom, for the brief respite it will offer from their birdlike gazes, picking away at the surface of me. I need to take my own counsel right now. The account numbers are not accidental. I need to be smart; I can't just spill my thoughts because of the insistence of Georgie's gaze. I reach the en suite bathroom and catch sight of myself in the white dressing gown, my hair still in the stupid turban—as if I've been spending the afternoon at a spa. I pull off the towel and twist my damp hair into a knot secured by a scrunchie; it will frizz beyond all belief without immediate application of serum and straighteners, but I'm beyond caring. The question I've been thinking about since my stomach contents spewed from my mouth, the question that's been wearing a groove in my mind is: who would have access to those account numbers? The list is not long, but it's not pinpoint specific, either. It includes my parents, because they pay a small amount into those accounts each year, and Rob, and—actually, and Georgie. Georgie, who is the godmother of my child, and who, like my parents, drip-feeds Kitty's account on a regular basis. Would I have sent her Jack's account number, too? It's possible. But to be perfectly clinical about it, the list should include anyone who has visited the house and who might have felt inclined to slip off to the study to rummage through my files—it would have taken them less than three minutes, if they knew what they were after. I am nothing if not organized. Everything is well labeled; an identity thief's delight.

Am I really considering Georgie? Rob, or my parents—well, that's frankly ridiculous. None of them would have the required access to Jem's business accounts in any case . . . As I stare at myself in the stupid white dressing gown, I realize that's the crucial factor. I've been looking at this wrong: it's a Venn diagram problem. Who had access to Jem's business accounts *and also* access to those account numbers? That's a much smaller list of people.

A smaller list indeed, and most likely all of them are on this island right now. I need to think this through. I need to be smart.

I hear a mobile phone ring and then Adam's voice, too faint for me to make out the words, and it spurs me into opening and shutting some cupboards, as if looking for something, though I know exactly where the Band-Aids are. Then I take a deep breath, exhale and turn for the living area. The knife on the console table glints at me as I pass. *Once more unto the breach, dear friends . . .*

"Here," I call, waving the Band-Aid box. "I think the largest one should just about be big enough." Georgie is still sitting on the sofa, almost crumpled in on herself; I'm slightly shocked by how much the attack seems to have shaken her. It would shake anyone, of course, but Georgie isn't just anyone. At uni, everything bounced right off her; she was invincible. But she doesn't even straighten as I cross the room. Unless . . . unless she wasn't attacked at all? Is this some elaborate hoax and she's overacting? I falter and almost stumble as the thought crosses my mind: it's so completely ridiculous, and yet, I can't unthink it . . . Adam is still on the phone, speaking in short, clipped phrases and staring out through the glass doors to the pool, lit sky blue against the almost pitch-black surrounds. I wanted to close the drapes as soon as I got back here, but I didn't. It's always better to see what's coming.

I kneel before Georgie and size up the bandage against her cut. "Yep, this should work." I'm half listening to Adam's side of the phone call, too, but it's not very enlightening: *Yes. Okay.*

"A regular Girl Scout," Georgie says, forcing a smile. *We should check again in the morning.* Check what?

"I also have a spare pair of toddler underpants in my handbag, should you ever have a need for them." I smooth the bandage carefully over the cut. Fake or not, it's going to hurt to no end, every time she flexes her knee. *Yep. Will do.*

"Good to know." She smiles again, her head almost level with mine given she's slumped down on the sofa. We're trying hard, both of us; I can feel it. Too hard.

Adam has finished his call; he turns to join us, standing at the end of the sofa and bending to briefly lay a hand on Georgie's shoulder. She surprises me by snaking her own up to try to clasp it even as he's withdrawing. For a second their fingers are tangled in midair. Then I blink and they're separate, but the image still lingers for me. They're a pair—but Georgie doesn't *do* that. Not ever. But what I say is, "Who was that?"

"Steve. He's had the staff searching the whole property, but nothing." He stops as if reluctant to go on, but Georgie glances up at him and he continues. "It would have been pretty easy for an intruder to get in, as it happens. Only one of the three security guards was at his post."

"What? Why?" I climb back to my feet.

"Apparently there's a rumor going round the staff that Cristina left because nobody is going to get paid. Some of the kitchen hands disappeared mid-shift this evening, too."

I groan. "Oh God, that's the last thing Jem needs. Where is he now?"

"His villa. Duncan took him back earlier, before all of this. He was pretty plastered—actually they both were. Steve's already checked on them; he said they're both passed out on the sofa snoring fit to wake the dead." He shoots a glance down at Georgie as if regretting his choice of words, but she doesn't react. "Anyway, Steve has the remaining staff running security patrols around the property, and he's doing his level best to try to combat the rumor."

"If it is a rumor," I say, without really thinking.

Adam cocks his head at me. I have the sense, without looking, that Georgie is doing the same from her spot seated a few feet below. "Do you know something? Did you see something when you were looking at the accounts?"

I shake my head. "No, nothing; I didn't have time, and I wasn't looking at the payroll system anyway." But Adam is still waiting for more. "It's just—well, does this place feel like a going concern right now? Maybe the best thing he can do is shut down for a while then relaunch. Or sell. Duncan can probably advise him." I'm thinking aloud now. "Or maybe Duncan can buy him out, since he's already an investor. Though an arm's length trade right now would result in a rubbish price for Jem."

"Right," says Georgie after a beat or two. "I hadn't realized Duncan had invested in this place."

"Well, Lissa didn't have much to contribute."

"But Graeme's house must have been worth at least three million—"

I shake my head. "More like four, but mortgaged to the hilt, and I don't think his life insurance was up to much." I look at Georgie, her surprise laid bare on her features. "She didn't say anything to you?" How odd. I thought there was nothing Lissa wouldn't tell Georgie. On another day I might have felt a flash of something, some small triumph that would not have reflected well on me, to have been the recipient of a confidence that wasn't shared with Georgie, but today I'm beyond such pettiness. "Maybe she was embarrassed... Anyway, she felt bad that she couldn't match Jem in terms of equity investment in this place. Duncan stepped in and made up the difference, I think."

"Oh." The surprise is gone, replaced by a slight frown. I wonder if it upsets her that she didn't know.

We all fall silent for a moment, then Adam speaks up. "Are you going to be okay here on your own tonight? Wouldn't you rather sleep in the same villa as us?"

Us. They *are* a pair; he's not even trying to hide it. Can they really have leapt from a random hookup over a year ago at the end of a week's swimming holiday to this? What's been going on in the meantime, and why didn't Georgie tell me? "It's okay," I demur. "If I get freaked out, I'll go to Jem's; his villa has a couple of spare bedrooms."

Georgie's green gaze sits on me expressionlessly, and I wonder what I've said to warrant such deliberate nonresponse. But what she says is, "Ring if you change your mind." She stirs on the sofa, and Adam puts out a hand to help her lever herself upright. "You don't mind if I use your bathroom, do you?" she says.

"Of course not." I flap a hand toward the bedroom, with its en suite bathroom half visible through the open door.

"I'll tell Steve to make sure the security patrols pass by here, too," Adam offers, and I nod my thanks, but my attention is on Georgie, limping shoeless across the room. She's moving like every single step hurts. What on earth would be the point of all the effort to pretend if it weren't actually so? And then she closes the bedroom door behind her, and alarm bells ring for me once again. Closing the *bathroom* door makes sense, that would be natural—but the bedroom door? I gaze after her, my mind racing, only barely aware of Adam beside me on the phone again, instructing Steve to direct the patrols. What can she possibly be looking for? What can she think I have? Or am I now so steeped in paranoia that every single small action seems to me to be imbued with the deepest significance?

"Bron?" Adam says, and I realize it's the second time he's said it. I turn away from the closed bedroom door, arranging my face with a suitably inquiring expression. "That's sorted now." He looks around. "You're sure you want to be on your own?"

"Yes." I pause. "It was just an opportunist mugging, wasn't it?"

"Probably." But his unease belies him, and he seems to recognize that. "I don't know. Georgie didn't seem to think they were after her bag. It's a bit odd." Then Georgie is coming out of the bedroom. She's cleaned herself up a bit: the mascara smears are gone from her temple, and the sand has disappeared from her forehead, too, but she's moving just as awkwardly as before. I look at Adam, and for all he's ordinarily a closed book, it's as if I sense him wince with every step she takes, although I couldn't say that there's an expression at all on his face. If this is all a hoax, then he's the best actor I've ever come across.

Or Georgie is playing him, too.

After they've gone, I race to my room and survey the contents, trying to work out what Georgie was after. But nothing looks out of place, there or in the bathroom. I have the sense that my makeup bag has possibly been moved, but it was lying beside the sink, so it could easily have been knocked completely innocently when Georgie was cleaning herself up. Or maybe Georgie used some of the makeup. I could hardly begrudge her that, given the state she was in. I'm about to give up when I remember the slip of paper with the account numbers, and I quickly check the pocket of the dress I was wearing for it, but it's still safely tucked in there—and anyway, Georgie doesn't even know about that, so how could she be looking for it? Still, I can't shake the feeling that there was an *oddness* to her closing that door.

But standing in the doorway, gazing puzzled at the bedroom, isn't going to give me an answer. I shake myself into activity and lock the front door of the villa, which seems too scant a security measure, but it's all I have at my disposal. The aquamarine of the pool glows silently through the (locked) French doors. I sit down on the sofa with the branded hotel notepad and branded hotel pen to make my Venn diagram: two stark black overlapping ovals on the creamy paper. In the left oval: all those who had access to the kids' account numbers. In the right one: those who had access to Jem's business systems. I force myself to be blankly unemotional about it, to ignore the voice in my head that tells me I'm being paranoid, that there must be some reasonable explanation. Everyone who meets the standard makes the left oval. That's Rob, my parents, our twice-weekly cleaner, Georgie and everyone who has stayed the night in our house—I consider that a reasonable metric for the amount of time you'd need to go sneaking off upstairs to the study; it would be too noticeable from someone who'd just dropped by for coffee or even for a dinner party—which pulls in Lissa and Jem, too, but not Duncan or Adam.

The right oval is harder. Perhaps it should just be Jem and Cristina, but I'm not certain. I don't have enough familiarity with how Jem has been running the business to know who else might have had the necessary access. I put them both down and add a question mark below. Then after a moment's thought I add *Lissa,* too. I'll have to check if all the payments were made before she died, but even if some happened afterward, they could have been set up in advance.

I look at my ovals, assessing the matches. Then I take the pen and score a hard black line through the two names that appear on both sides, methodically scoring out each name twice, once left and once right, before rewriting them just the once in the space defined by the overlapping ovals. Two names. Jem and Lissa. It's patently ludicrous, to even be considering them, but the logic is inescapable. I look at the names again, as if they might miraculously morph into something— or someone—else, but they don't change. Jem and Lissa.

Then after a moment I add Georgie. Because if Lissa is there, Georgie must be, too. That's just the way it is.

Jem. Lissa. Georgie.

HOW TO KILL YOUR BEST FRIEND

Method 4: Electrocution

Hair dryer dropped in a bath tub? I suppose it's just about believable—and I could probably engineer such a situation. But I Googled it (not on my own device, of course), and it seems that it's actually very unlikely to be fatal. Electricity is lazy; it seeks the path of least resistance. The current will almost certainly run to ground through the bathwater and the bath plug, rather than through the cardiac tissue, meaning that the only thing that gets successfully fried is the bath salts.

How else can you engender a fatal electrocution? With difficulty, according to the Google search results. There are too many variables. AC or DC current. Wet or dry hands. The material of the shoes the person is wearing. Whether the current finds a way to breach the skin to reach the soft, vulnerable, unresistant tissues inside—and how much water and how much fat are in those tissues.

The more I look at this, the more I realize how exceedingly difficult it is to kill a person—without immediately getting caught, I mean. Which is, ordinarily, a good thing, one supposes. Though not much help to me now.

TEN

GEORGIE

The walk from Bron's villa back to mine feels like a hundred miles, though it can't be more than a couple of hundred meters; I'm soon regretting turning down Adam's suggestion of calling for one of the buggies. Beyond offering to carry me, which I refuse on the grounds that it would probably be more painful for my shoulder and neck, Adam doesn't try to talk. He just offers an arm to cling on to, and I do, transferring as much of my weight to him as possible, yet still gritting my teeth with every step. I won't cry. I didn't cry earlier, and I won't start now.

Finally we reach my villa. I head straight for the bedroom and flop down on the bed, lifting my bad leg up onto it with my hands. I'm so very, very tired, with the extreme and total exhaustion of a child. Even just getting ready for bed is an impossible effort. Adam surveys me from the bedroom door.

"You'll stay?" I ask, then wish I hadn't when I hear how pathetic it sounds.

"Damn right I will. On the sofa, if need be."

I waggle my head as if considering it. "I'm willing to share the bed, under the circumstances."

His lips twitch a little. "Stay there," he instructs, moving toward the en suite bathroom. "I'll bring you water and a toothbrush."

"And a facecloth," I call after him, trying to focus on the mundane, rather than on the flutter of panic at the edge of my mind, because he's going to stay the night, and he can't possibly be thinking that we'll have sex, not with the state that I'm in. Staying without any prospect of nookie seems even more intimate than daylight sex. I force down the panic by trying to think of something else, though the other topic that crowds my mind isn't any more reassuring. "There's something up with Bron," I say when Adam returns, sitting up to take the facecloth from him and wiping my face. There's still sand in my hair; it will get all through the bed, but I don't have the energy for a shower. "I've tried asking her, but there's only so many times you can say, *Are you okay?*"

"Yeah. She was really off at dinner; I asked, too, and got nothing much back." He passes me the toothpaste and toothbrush in return for the flannel. "I thought it was from that thing in the water." The serpent. The toothbrush momentarily halts in my mouth. The serpent: it feels like that was days—no, weeks—ago. Was it actually just today? And what had it been, really? It would be easy to dismiss it in comparison to the very recent horror of those skinny arms holding me like a vise, a hold that felt terrifyingly futile to try to break free from— but that long, dark, sinuous shape flowing beneath us in the blue waters was no invention. "Whatever it's from, she's definitely very rattled," he says thoughtfully. "Spit?" He holds out a cup, and I obligingly empty my mouthful into it.

"I saw her hide something at Jem's place." Jem's place, now, but with two bikes and photos as mementos of a time he can't remember, because he wasn't even there. Does it feel like his place to him? "She put a piece of paper in her pocket." He raises his eyebrows; he knows there's more. "It was still in the pocket of her dress when I went to the bathroom." I close my eyes for a moment, remembering those frantic few seconds, looking round the bathroom and the bedroom until I finally spotted the dress she'd been wearing, hung up in the closet. If it was me, it would have been on the floor somewhere, but Bron has always been tidy. The closet should have been the first place I looked.

"And?"

"I've got no idea what it means. It just had three numbers on it; I wrote them down." I pull up the hem of my dress, and he blinks in surprise to see digits scrawled in Bron's eyeliner pen across my upper thigh, like a crudely drawn tattoo. "It was the only thing I could find to write with, and the only thing I could think to write on."

"Impressively resourceful," he says appreciatively, humor lurking around the corners of his mouth. He takes out his phone. "I think we need a more permanent record, though. For personal use only, I promise."

"Careful how you angle that thing," I warn him with mock severity, and his mouth twitches again while he takes the photo, then checks the result.

"What do you think?" he says. "Phone numbers? The first two both start with seven; they could be London numbers without the 020 prefix."

"Could be, though the last one can't; it's only six digits. Dial one of them." So he does, twitching up my hemline to see the number he's copying, and prefixing with +44 20. He puts the mobile on speaker, and it starts to ring out, once, twice, three times . . . After seven or eight rings an answerphone kicks in: *Your call has been forwarded to an automatic voice message system. Extension 6622 is not available. Please leave a message after the tone.* He shrugs and tries the other eight-digit number. There's a single beep. "Call failed," he says. He tries again, with exactly the same result.

"Well, that wasn't exactly conclusive." I flop back on the bed again. "But perhaps they're invoice numbers?"

"Or payee references, or staff identification numbers. Can I borrow your toothbrush?"

I nod because I can't not, under the circumstances, though my stomach tightens: it's yet another step down a path I've never tread before, nor taken an active role in choosing now. I hear him begin to brush in the bathroom. My eyes are starting to close. A minute passes, or ten, or many more, before he spits, and says, "Or a supplier reference. Could be almost anything."

I open my eyes again. "They obviously meant enough to her to write them down. And to not tell us, which is weird. She's been acting weird this whole trip."

Adam snaps off the bathroom light. "It's not a normal trip, though, is it?" I can hear him moving around, presumably undressing, before I feel his weight settle onto the other side of the bed. I wonder if he's wearing underwear. I should take off my own clothes, or at least my dress—my ruined, misshapen dress. Even if I could get the blood out of it and mend the strap, I could never wear it again; the very thought makes me feel nauseous. That sudden disgust at the dress, at what it signifies now, gives me the strength to shimmy it up over my head and toss it onto the floor, then slide under the covers. No, this is not a normal trip. Not in any way, shape or form.

I lie on my back, somehow too exhausted to drift off. Adam is on his side in the dark, facing toward me, one arm extended to gently link his fingers through mine. His thumb rubs over my wrist, back and forth, then stills. He's breathing rhythmically, but I don't think he's asleep yet, either. Then he says, half muffled into the pillow: "There's one thing I've been wondering: why didn't you come?"

"Come where?"

He releases my hand and rolls over onto his back—mere inches away, but no longer touching. "The last swim trip. Why didn't you come?"

I gaze at the darkened ceiling. "I was going to. My flight was booked and everything." Not *everything*, in truth. I never actually requested the time off work. "But in the end I was just too busy. I was going to come out a month later instead." He makes a noise, some kind of strangled puff of air. "You don't believe me?"

"I'm sure you were very busy. I'm equally sure you could have made it work if you'd wanted to."

I could say, *You don't understand.* I could say, *You have no idea what my life is like.* I could say those, and other things, but I don't. Because, of course, he's right. "It wasn't because of you."

He laughs a little, a soft sound in the darkness, but he sounds weary rather than amused when he speaks. "Don't worry. I wasn't kidding myself that it was." I don't know what to say to that. I never know what to say to things like that; there's a language that everyone else is fluent in, but somehow I missed the lesson. Perhaps parents teach it; parents who aren't numbing their disappointment at life with alcohol and interminable, unwinnable fights, that is. But without any kind of Rosetta stone, all I can do is recognize there's a foreign tongue being spoken. Finally he speaks again. "It was about Lissa, then."

"Yes." I'm almost bewildered that he feels the need to ask that question. Of course it was about Lissa. It's always been about Lissa. But now there's no Lissa . . . My head aches and aches.

"What were you afraid of?"

"I wasn't—" But I can't finish the denial: I *was* afraid. "She'd been saying stuff for a while. On the phone and in emails. She was starting to sound . . . She was starting to worry that Jem . . ."

"That Jem was having an affair?"

"I—" I finally turn my head to look at him. His head is turned toward me; I can just make out the outline of it. There's a faint gleam where his eyes should be. I count two breaths, then two more. He's waiting patiently, but I can tell he won't let me off the hook. My throat is almost too tight for any words to escape. "Yes."

"And that scared you." Like mine, his words are a whisper.

I nod, turning back to look toward the ceiling once again. *Yes, it scared me. It scared me so much that I became an ostrich rather than risk seeing anything that might confirm my suspicions. I told myself I was doing the right thing in delaying, that it would be clearer if I visited by myself, but really, I was just scared. I thought I was better than that. I should have been better than that.*

"Because of what she might do?"

"No. Well, yes, but . . ." I can't say it, but I'm somehow helpless, unable to dissemble, either. I'm starting to feel mildly dizzy, as if the bed is spinning, but I can't see anything in the darkness.

"But what?"

"There are responsibilities. That we have." Every word speeds up the spin. It's beginning to feel like riding dodgems when drunk.

"Responsibilities?" I can tell he's frowning; he doesn't get it. I close my eyes briefly. I don't want to imagine the look on his face when he finally understands.

"If I saw, if I thought—if I *knew* she was going to . . ." I can't utter the words.

"If you knew she would . . . then what?" He's genuinely baffled. It's unlike Adam to be lagging behind. "You'd report her?" I can't help it; I laugh softly. It must be the tension, or the feeling that everything is careening out of control. But even though I'm ahead of him, he's catching up. "No, of course you wouldn't report her. No. You'd— you'd stop her." There's a sudden urgency in his voice, though he doesn't raise the volume. He sits up abruptly and reaches out a hand to snap on the bedside light beside him. I protest a little at the sudden brightness, but he ignores me. "How would you stop her, Georgie? What were you planning to do?" I finally glance at him, just as the penny drops and the dodgems crash. Hard. "Oh my God," he says slowly, visibly stunned. I look away quickly. "You were going to kill her. You were going to kill your best friend."

I open my mouth, but before I can say something—what? what can I say?—he jumps in. "Don't lie to me, Georgie," he says roughly. "Whatever you say now, don't lie to me."

"I wasn't going to lie." It's true. I am many things, and I have been many things, but a liar has never been among them.

"I'm right, then?" He's still stunned.

"Well." *You were going to kill your best friend.* It sounds so ridiculous, hearing him say it out loud, as if airing it exposes it for the nonsense it must be. Who, after all, thinks about killing their best friend? It must be a temporary piece of insanity, the sort of thing that hides in the dark corners of a mind; it surely can't withstand the open air. But this—well, this is more resilient than that. More real. I risk a glance at him. He's recovering his usual control. Only his eyebrows rise slightly to urge me on. "I'd been giving it some thought. In case it came to that. I was planning to come out a month later, just me. I thought maybe if it was just me visiting I'd get more time with her, and I might get a better sense . . ." I trail off. That's what I'd been telling myself. I'll never know now whether I would have choked on that visit, too, or whether fear for Jem's safety would have forced me onto the plane.

"Jesus fucking Christ." I can hear his breathing, short and fast, then he spits out, as if a challenge: "All right then, how were you going to do it?"

"That's the thing. It's remarkably difficult to come up with the perfect solution." I can't bring myself to say *murder. Kill,* maybe. Not *murder.*

"You don't say."

"You don't think I would have done it." I sound accusing. I could laugh at myself for that, except that we're talking about killing Lissa here. Specifically, me killing Lissa. Me feeling forced to kill Lissa. Only now she's already dead.

He waggles his head side to side as if weighing it. "No, I actually think you might have." Then he shakes himself suddenly, as if saying that aloud has delivered an impact that he's still reeling from. "Jesus Christ. You're like a child; you have no idea. You are literally the most fucked-up person I know—"

"Thanks," I say acidly, stung.

"—and even so, I didn't twig you were thinking *this*. So tell me, how were you going to do it? What were you considering? Poison? Assault and battery? Was drowning on the menu?"

"Yes," I fling back, grateful for the opportunity to be angry in return. "All of the above. And strangulation, electrocution, hit-and-run—"

"Is that part of why you wanted to come out alone? So you could quietly murder Lissa without your friends inconveniently getting in the way?" His delivery is rapid-fire, each word hitting the target unerringly.

"Yes, if I had to." I'm almost shouting.

"For fuck's sake, Georgie. Murder? Really? You don't even *like* Jem much."

"You think it would have stopped with Jem?" There are responsibilities that we have. Whether we'd choose them for ourselves or not.

He makes a sideways jerk with his chin—a grudging acknowledgment—before shaking his head, almost his entire body, like a dog might. "You couldn't just settle for warning him?"

The abject disgust in his tone is excruciating; the sear of it fans my anger. "You know he wouldn't have believed me. He'd have gone straight to Lissa—"

"So you'd rather *kill* her than tell on her?"

"I—" I stop. *Yes. Killing her would have been less of a betrayal.* He releases a sharp huff of frustration, and then we're both silent for a breath; for two, for three. My anger begins to slip away, mingled with the air of each exhalation. "That should have been why I didn't come with the rest of you," I admit at last. "Logistically, everything would have been easier on a solo trip—not least of all, finding out where her head was at." I think again of her email: *It's as if history is trying to repeat itself.* Which part of history? If only I had been here to ask her directly. "But really, I didn't come because I just wasn't ready to face it."

"And that extra month would have made all the difference?" I shrug; there's no way to counter his biting sarcasm. "You do know you would have destroyed yourself, too, right? Even if you'd managed to bring yourself to do it, and somehow get away with it? You'd have been writing your own death sentence, too. You don't carry that around inside you afterward and be just *fine.*"

Something cracks inside me, and things that I've been stamping down, keeping far from the light, push up against the sudden weakness, forcing their way through the sliver of a gap and spilling out of my mouth in a strangled gasp. *"Fine."* I lie utterly still on the bed. There are tears on my motionless face, running straight down from the corners of my closed eyes to the bedsheets as if a current running to earth, but I will win the battle. In a minute or two. In a minute or two, the crack will be patched. "I've never been *just fine.* I've never expected to be *just fine.* The only person that made me forget that was Lissa." *And Maddy.*

Adam is quiet beside me. I'm almost certain that he will reach out a hand to touch me, and if he does, I will shake him off angrily. I wait with my eyes closed, the tears already slowing, the crack repairs underway. But the touch never comes. Instead he says quietly, "If you thought Jem was in so much danger, you must think she killed Graeme."

His logic is impeccable. I try out possible answers in my head. But it's a black-and-white question, and all my answers sound like what they are: equivocations. Shades of gray. The moment stretches and stretches, and every second I don't reply is another answer in itself, that's neither one thing nor another. And now I can't speak, because I'm listening to Lissa sobbing down the phone line, four years ago:

He's dead, he's dead, he's dead. I can't say sorry, I can't fix things; he's dead. If I'd jacked in my job to give the IVF a better chance of working, we wouldn't have been fighting so much—

No, honey, no—

It's all my fault—

No, honey. It's not your fault. It was an accident, just an awful, tragic accident—

All my fault—

Lissa, it was an accident. A beat. *Wasn't it?*

But she didn't answer then, and she's not here to answer now. Beside me, Adam breathes out a long sigh. Of disappointment, presumably. This must be why I don't do the relationship thing: I can barely manage my own expectations; I can't possibly live up to someone else's. I should say something. I know I should say something; but I don't have the right words, and anything less than that would be meaningless. He sighs again, and moves as if to switch off the light, but stops suddenly. "Did Lissa suspect?" he asks. "Could she have known what you were thinking of doing?"

"I don't see how." But the idea settles uneasily around me, coating my skin and sinking slowly through; it won't be dislodged. A betrayal of that magnitude—would that have been enough to topple her fragile balance and send her into the waters at Kanu Cove?

He reaches out to the lamp switch again. "Get some sleep," he says evenly as the room goes black again, and I know from his tone that I've fallen badly short in his eyes, and it's not because I've been mulling over how to kill my best friend. And then I fall asleep, because I'm too physically exhausted not to, though at first my dreams are too panicked and frantic to allow me to sink into a proper oblivion. But then a dark creature arrives to flow like liquid through the fragments, winding in and out of the corners of my mind, cool and silent and *other.* It coils itself around me, it coils itself inside me, and drags me down implacably into the darkness that lies below. In the very last moments before unconsciousness claims me, I look out through eyes that I somehow know are both mine and the serpent's, and see Lissa's face looming out of the darkness, locked in a soundless, horrified scream.

ELEVEN

BRONWYN

I wake the next morning in a tangle of sheets wrapped round my whole body, even my head, and have to fight my way out, sleep befuddled, with the boat and the propeller and that sickly cold touch of the thing in the water in my mind . . . It's a shock to come out blinking into a quiet bedroom, sunlight streaming in through the open curtains. Deliberately left open, I remember, lurching upright to peer out at the pool area. But there's nobody there. And then I remember that there never was: that was my subterfuge.

I'm not good at this lying stuff.

A glance at the clock shows it's midmorning, already later than I would have expected. I take myself into the shower for a pep talk, the warm water streaming over my upturned face, washing away the last remnants of whatever murky dreams still hover. Right: no more defeatist attitude. Looking at things objectively, I must actually be very good at lying. After all, nobody suspected anything when Graeme and I were slipping in through doorways that each other's spouse had just walked out of. The benefit of being wysiwyg, presumably: nobody believed I was capable of anything more. Even Graeme was impressed by my attention to detail. Maybe if he'd had kids himself, he would have taken pains to be more careful. I had had to be careful enough for the both of us. Afterward, when there wasn't an *us*, I had to be careful enough for Rob; for Kitty and Jack.

And mothers are always careful. There's a plan A, B, C—and the rest of the alphabet, too, if need be. What mother ever says, *I don't know what to do*? It's not permitted; your children cannot be allowed to see such uncertainty in their bedrock. Their little worlds couldn't withstand such an earthquake.

I dry myself and find a dress to wear. It's tempting to dispense with hair and makeup, but that will be noticed. So I go through my normal routine: attempting to tame my frizz as much as I can before the humidity can have its way with it; attempting to lengthen my lashes and widen my eyes even though it will all end up wiped on a beach towel long before the day is out. But it's all armor now—the armor of normality. Someone has been planning an elaborate framing. I have a different plan.

And my plan starts with Duncan, who sits in neither oval, and who is too clearheaded and clear-eyed and, frankly, too rich to be part of whatever is going on here. Should I force myself to go to breakfast first, or would I be expected to check in on Jem at his villa first? Jem, I think, on balance. And Duncan might well still be there, too, anyway, given he apparently passed out on the sofa. Perhaps I can get on Jem's computer again. Kill two birds with one stone.

Well. Not kill.

There's music playing as I approach Jem's villa, something gritty and streetwise that I don't recognize; not my cup of tea, though it's exactly the sort of thing that Duncan professes to love—as if his deep knowledge of hard-core hip-hop and his black wife might suddenly make him look less like the kind of middle-aged white guy who would leap onto the dance floor for *Livin' On a Prayer*. Anyway, the door is ajar, which is how Jem habitually leaves it—he makes a point of telling all the staff that he literally has an open-door policy, and they can come to him on anything. If I was Lissa, that would have annoyed me; shouldn't your home be your private sanctuary?

"Knock knock," I call as I push open the door to be faced by Lissa: someone has rested the photo from the memorial on the table in the hallway, obscuring the photos that I know lie behind of both of Lissa's weddings (though none from Jem's first marriage, seeing as it ended in divorce). Up close there's both too little detail and too much: I can see separate strands of hair, yet there's no shape to the color variations. It's the sort of photo that needs a certain distance to resolve itself.

"In here," calls a voice over the music, which I now realize is in French. Jem's choice, then, presumably, though the voice is not Jem's. It's Duncan, sounding as if he smoked a thousand cigarettes last night. Which he may have done—well, not a thousand, but he's partial to a naughty cigarette or four when he's drinking. I follow his voice to the lounge. He's in last night's clothes, sitting hunched forward on the sofa, his elbows on his knees, cradling a cup of coffee, though there's a glass of water on the table in front of him, too. He looks up as I enter. "Morning, Bron," he says blearily.

"You look rough."

"I feel rough. I don't do this enough anymore; no tolerance." I stop myself from making the obvious point that increasing the frequency of his drinking is not the solution. He contemplates his coffee again. I look around. The curtains are open on the wide wall of glass, exposing the view over the entire resort. The computer in the corner sits quiet and dark.

"Where's Jem?"

"In the shower."

"Is he okay?"

"Surprisingly so. Unlike me." Duncan grimaces. "Though actually, maybe he's still drunk."

"Does he know about Georgie yet?"

Duncan looks up from his coffee, his thick, sandy brows aloft. He doesn't know yet, either, I realize. So I give my secondhand account, and Duncan, being Duncan—even hungover Duncan—asks forensic questions that I can't answer, which make me realize how little I asked last night. Jem comes to join us partway through my account, his hair still wet from the shower and unshaven, and I have to start again.

"Jesus," says Jem when I've finished. He's wearing his usual clothing, a white linen shirt and tailored shorts, but he's not his usual self. The jawline he's rubbing is unshaven; his eyes are bloodshot. And he seems smaller, somehow. "I'd better call Steve."

"Can you put me on the computer again first?" I ask quickly. "I'll do some more digging."

"Yeah. You know, I've been thinking," he says over his shoulder as we cross to the desk. "Since it wasn't me, it must have been Cristina. I guess she thought she was about to be found out when I asked Duncan to go through the budgets with her. That must be why she left." Ever the gentleman, he pulls out the chair for me, then shakes his head slightly. "Though I wouldn't have believed it of her."

I look up at him, at the hollows lying behind his eyes, and put my hand on his arm. "Jem, it's going to be okay."

He finds a smile, but it's his practiced manager smile. "I know. Thanks, Bron." He pats my hand. "Right, let's get you logged on."

He gestures to the chair, and I sit in it obediently. He *will* be okay, even if it doesn't feel like that to him right now. People like him always are. Women want to sleep with him, and men want to be him; it's a gift in life. Even now, I'm conscious of how close he is as he leans over to open up all the right applications. I'm conscious of the hint of alcohol still on his breath, of the smell of his lemon shower gel, and something else underneath, something that's just *him*. It's not that I want to sleep with him—I've learned my lesson on that score. It's just that in another lifetime, in another universe, some world in which Rob and Kitty and Jack never came to be—in *that* universe, I know that I would.

Jem leaves me to it, and I start my hunting: methodically, carefully scanning for any other payments that look awry while simultaneously waiting for an opportunity to speak to Duncan alone. But Jem switches off the music and makes his phone call to Steve in the living room, and a couple more calls after that, too. Duncan stretches out on the sofa with his eyes closed, his head on one of the arms and his bare feet extended out over the other. I check first of all whether there are any payments that have been instructed and not yet paid, in case there's more thievery waiting silently to be enacted, but nothing. There's nothing particular of note about the payments that have been made, either; certainly there's no way of telling who exactly instructed them. Then I concentrate on the numbers, flicking between the different systems to follow the flows and find the patterns. Once you have the measure of that, whatever doesn't fit sticks out, even if you don't know why. Just like how you can know a word is spelled wrong, even if you're not familiar with the word itself. The minutes stretch out with Jem murmuring quietly in the background.

"Have you eaten breakfast?" asks Jem, suddenly behind me. I hadn't heard him approach.

I shake my head, then look at my watch. "Haven't we missed it?"

"Yes. But I can do something here. Scrambled eggs on toast okay?"

"Great. Thanks."

He turns and shakes the prone Duncan by the toe, causing him to murmur sleepily in protest. "Duncan, eggs?"

"Mmmm."

"I'll take that as a yes."

"Yes. Please." He sits up and yawns widely, then glances over at me. "Have you found anything? It must have been Cristina, right?"

So he's the one who has been putting that thought in Jem's mind. Jem is in the kitchen now, safely out of range. "It's not Cristina."

"Well, you don't know—"

"Duncan, it's not Cristina." I spin on the chair and pull myself over by the heels toward where he sits on the sofa, the casters rolling easily across the smooth wooden floor. I'm careful how I pitch my voice. I don't want Jem to come in and think we're whispering about something, but equally I don't want him to hear me. "I've traced the money. I know where it was moved to."

"What? Where?" He's awake enough to be careful with his own volume.

"My children's Child Trust Fund accounts." He looks at me blankly for a moment. "You know, the government-backed tax-free scheme? The money is legally blocked in there until they're eighteen. And Cristina wouldn't have had a clue what those account numbers were. I doubt she even knew I have children."

His mouth falls agape, but his brain is working. "You're sure?" I nod. "I take it you didn't move the money yourself," he says, though it's barely a question. It sounds more as if he's talking to himself.

"Of course not! I'm being framed."

"Yes. Yes." He's nodding seriously; he'd already reached that conclusion. "Okay. Right." He looks round the room as if taking inventory of the contents. "I don't get the impression that anyone other than Jem and Cristina had access to the business systems."

"And Lissa. At least, I think she did."

His eyes meet mine sharply. "Lissa?" He glances around the room again, though this time I think he's checking whether anyone can see or hear us. "Yes, Lissa had access, too. Jem said she was much better on that side of things than he was." He taps his teeth thoughtfully with a thumbnail, before focusing on me again. "It wouldn't be Jem," he says positively. "And Cristina makes no sense, even if she somehow had those account numbers. But . . . Lissa makes no sense, either. I mean, why would she have wanted to frame you?" He looks at me, perplexed, and I put every ounce of my being into trying to look similarly bewildered, but he suddenly says, his mouth twisting, "Oh God, Bron. Tell me you didn't."

"Didn't what?"

"Tell me you didn't sleep with Jem."

"No!" I'm able to be suitably outraged only because of my surprise at the speed at which he reached that (erroneous) conclusion; my own hypocrisy hasn't escaped me. "Of course not, I—"

But I can't say anything else because someone is calling hello from the front door. I spin away from Duncan such that when Adam enters the living room, I'm back in front of the computer and Duncan is on the sofa, picking up his coffee mug from the table.

I twist in the chair. "Morning, Adam." I look behind him, but no Georgie.

"Morning," Duncan says, putting the mug down again. The coffee must be cold by now anyway. "I've just heard what happened. How's Georgie?" He's taking it for granted that Adam would know. I suppose they must have talked about his relationship with Georgie, insofar as men ever talk. "Freaked out?"

"Well. She's Georgie," says Adam wryly, with a small shrug. "I don't know that I'd go quite that far." Duncan chuckles a little, and I smile, too, but it's forced. Everything I do is forced, second-guessed before I do it. "She's certainly stiff and sore, though."

"What was she doing at Kanu Cove?"

"I don't know," he says uneasily. For once I can read his emotions clearly: anxiety. "She seems a little obsessed by it. Which is not exactly healthy for someone like Georgie . . ." *Someone like Georgie?* I don't understand. But he's already changing gears. "Steve has arranged for the chief of police to come over. There wasn't much point last night; the attacker had already scarpered."

"That won't look good for the guests," I comment.

Adam shrugs again. "We're the only guests left now." We look at one another in silence for a moment. It's inescapable. The hotel is done for. Nobody says it, but we all know it. Should I say it, though, given I'm supposed to be unflinchingly blunt? Is my silence uncharacteristic? But Adam is speaking again. "How is he?" he asks Duncan.

"Resigned, I think. He knows he needs to take some time to regroup." He runs both hands through his hair. "He's going to have to speak to the staff. He's arranged a meeting with them all later." Silence falls between us again.

"Where is Georgie anyway?" I ask Adam, after a respectful interval.

"Swimming," he says. My mouth opens in shock. "In the pool, not the sea," he says quickly, forestalling my alarm. "No kids to dodge and no head-up breaststrokers to annoy. She thought it might help her loosen off."

"The holy grail of a pool to yourself," Duncan says lightly. "See, there's always a silver lining."

Not just an empty pool. An empty resort, too. And no need for staff in an empty resort. I look out through the glass wall, at the tropical idyll it displays, so perfect that it almost seems fake. The cloudless blue of the sky, the vibrant greens of the sun-drenched leaves wafting in a gentle breeze. The short lawn in front drops steeply away, and the foliage that lies beyond is so dense that it obscures most of each of the villas, even though we're at the highest vantage point of the entire resort. I expect there's quite a program of maintenance to keep the vegetation from running rampant. I wonder how long it will be before it invades the paths and gardens and the villas themselves. I wonder how long it will be before there's barely a trace of the resort to be seen.

—

It's much, much later before I can find a moment alone with Duncan. We all hang out at Jem's villa until the middle of the afternoon, fortified by Jem's (surprisingly good) eggs on toast; I don't know why I had thought he wouldn't be able to cook. After all, Rob is a very good cook—though he does tend to use absolutely every pot, dish and utensil in the kitchen and is apparently physically incapable of cleaning up afterward. Georgie makes an entrance after a bit, moving stiffly, but certainly easier than last night, and with a much larger bandage over her knee. I work on the computer for a bit longer, but if there's something to find, I'm not up to the job—which, without blowing my own trumpet, means it's overwhelmingly likely there's actually nothing to find: this is what I do—what I did—and I am very, very good at it. But all the patterns I see make sense: a downward spiral of swirling clouds of figures circling a drain to be spat out into the waiting mouths of the suppliers, the staff, the insurance, the taxes, the booking system fees . . . the list is almost endless, but it's a completely normal list for a business like this. The only abnormalities are the payments I've already discovered. The payments that are sitting in my children's accounts.

The others have moved outside to the pool area, and there's nothing much more I can do on the computer, so I join them, feeling restless and uncomfortable, as if this indolence is *wrong,* as if there is something I ought to be doing, but what? Nothing springs to mind. I'm careful to stay in the shade—my skin won't thank me for any more sun—but even in the shade the heat is relentless today. I take regular dips in the water to cool off and pretend to read my book, a no-thought-required airport thriller, even though I can't concentrate for more than a line or two, and I keep a watchful eye on Duncan for any chance to continue our conversation. But the opportunity doesn't present itself: Duncan is largely comatose facedown on a sun lounger. Jem is not much different. Georgie applies sunscreen liberally and stretches herself out to soak up the sun, catlike and separate behind her enormous dark glasses. Adam watches Georgie's application of the sunscreen, his face inscrutably blank, then takes a book from Jem's shelves and settles down to read in the shade beside me. I'm conscious that he's making much better progress than I am with his reading.

Midafternoon, Adam suggests a late lunch, and Jem telephones ahead to warn the main restaurant, an unspoken admission that things aren't quite running as they should be.

"Are you okay?" I ask Georgie. She's shrugged herself into a complicated kaftan thing that seems to float as she walks, though the effect is marred by a purpling bruise on her shoulder roughly the same size and shape as the marks a bag strap would leave, and she's moving much more stiffly than when she arrived. "Did you do too much in the pool earlier?" She grimaces; as much of an acknowledgment as she's prepared to give. "Maybe swim with a pull buoy next time?" With a pull buoy between her legs, helping to keep them afloat, she could drag them and use her arms only.

"I didn't bring one."

"Jem," I call. "You must have a pull buoy Georgie can borrow?"

"For sure," he says disinterestedly. "Go raid the cupboard by the pool; that's where everything swimming-related is kept." He waves a vague hand toward a cupboard with a louvered door.

"You should grab it now," I suggest, simultaneously willing Jem to nip into his bedroom to pick up something, anything, so that I can have a few minutes with Duncan. But she shakes her head and says she'll pick it up later, and Jem appears in need of absolutely nothing, so I have no choice but to join the others in ambling en masse along the path, adjusting our pace for Georgie. As we reach the fork in the road that leads to my villa, inspiration strikes. "I'll catch up to you; I just need to pick up some sunscreen." I glance at Duncan, and he picks up the baton seamlessly. "I'll walk you," he says. "After the thing with Georgie, it will make me feel better."

"It's perfectly safe," insists Jem.

"Do you know how many security guards are working today?" This is Georgie. It's not said maliciously, but Jem's face darkens mutinously. I'm only seeing small flashes of it, but Adam is right: there's a very real enmity toward her brewing inside Jem.

"We'll see you at the restaurant," Duncan says, and we peel off, Duncan falling in step beside me. Neither of us says anything until we're out of earshot. Then Duncan starts, as if there hasn't been an hours-long gap in our conversation. "So. Transferring the money specifically to those accounts smacks of revenge. But it doesn't make sense; it doesn't seem like Lissa had a reason to want revenge."

"I know." I don't look at him, focusing on the path instead. If he had asked me directly about Graeme, what I would have done? Would I have owned up? I don't think so: I told myself long ago that I wouldn't fall foul of that. You shouldn't entrust your friends with that kind of toxic secret; it's like giving a child an ice cream and telling them not to lick it. It's just setting them up for failure.

Georgie knew, though. I never did work out how she knew, but she did. She promised never to tell anyone. I can't imagine her breaking that, not even to tell Lissa. I can't believe she would have done that.

Duncan is still thinking. "Unless she *thought* she had a reason," he ruminates. He glances at me. "Jem does flirt with you, you know."

"He flirts with everybody."

"Not with Georgie."

"But you say he doesn't *like* Georgie."

"True. He doesn't. Bad example." He thinks for a moment. "He does flirt with everyone. But he flirts with certain women more. You. Cristina." I almost cringe. Cristina was half in love with Jem; that was obvious to me. I'm sure Jem knew it, too, and I'm equally sure he took advantage of that. Was it just as obvious that I find him attractive? Has he been taking advantage of me, too, in ways I haven't even noticed? "It must have been Lissa," he says. "It can't have been anyone else. You're right; she must have thought she had a reason."

"And a pretty big one, to do something like that." Flirting wouldn't be enough. Duncan is right: she really must have thought Jem was sleeping with me. I'm not outraged; I'm not hypocritical enough for that. When did Lissa think Jem and I were having this affair? When would we have had an opportunity? I find myself replaying on fast-forward reels of memory of time spent with Lissa and Jem. There hadn't been many occasions, though they did both stay with me whenever they were in the UK. And there was that night when Lissa was off visiting a friend and Rob didn't get back till late, so it was just Jem and me together for the evening. I remember the awkwardness of it: almost like a date, in my own home, with my own kids asleep upstairs. Drinking red wine and talking, feeling too aware of him to properly relax. I suppose Lissa could have imagined something happened then. "I suppose that must have been it. A stupid misunderstanding. And she wasn't always reasonable— I mean, she always seemed a bit more, I don't know, *fragile* after Graeme died."

"Yeah." He's quiet for a moment, then he says, with an air of finality, "Yes, she could easily have gone down a rabbit hole in her head. And I do believe she was capable of something like this, if she was put under enough strain. I never did believe the acid, or the car rumor, even, but that thing with the knife . . ."

"Acid? Car? What are you talking about?"

He shakes his head quickly. "Later; we don't have much time." He hesitates awkwardly. "You know, you can tell me if there has been anything. Between you and Jem, I mean."

We're at my villa now. I turn to him and look him straight in the eye, one hand on his arm. "Duncan, believe me. There has never been anything between me and Jem. Truly."

He bobs his head awkwardly. "I believe you. I just—I just want you to know that you could tell me that kind of stuff."

"I know. I know I could." He's so uncomfortably earnest; it's rather sweet. I'm half smiling, even though it's not true: I can't tell him that kind of stuff. He has limits he doesn't even know he possesses. If I told him about Graeme he'd be horrified—and probably hurt that Graeme hadn't told him himself. All that time we've spent together, all of us, and particularly the way we've spent it—training and swimming together, where you really get the measure of a person, of the amount of fight that's within them and where their limits are, where you see them laid bare—gives us the impression we're transparent to one another, but it's a fallacy. We all have hidden spaces within us. Secrets have to be kept, for everyone's sake. "But there's nothing to tell."

"Okay." He ducks his head again awkwardly.

"Come on." I unlock the door, and we go in; I really do need sunscreen, as it happens. "And actually, there's more." I explain about the writing on the mirror; I even show him the photo on my mobile.

"Oh my God. That's awful." He takes the phone off me to peer at the screen, while pulling me against him for a quick, one-armed hug. There's a thickening in my throat at his physical demonstration of support, which is entirely uncharacteristic. Except when very drunk, he's really terribly British about public displays of affection. "Why didn't you tell us?"

I shrug. "I didn't know who left it. I didn't know who to trust. I still don't, except for you. Sunscreen, sunscreen . . ." Duncan stands just inside the door as I hunt for it. "I've been thinking I should make some excuse and get the first flight out of here," I call over my shoulder. "Isn't there another Lufthansa flight before ours?"

"It's been canceled."

"Canceled?" It's almost a wail. I hadn't exactly been pinning my hopes on getting a seat on it, but still . . . Then I wonder how he knows that. "You were looking at going back earlier yourself?" I finally spot the bottle of sunscreen lurking under a book; I grab it and shove it in my bag.

"No, it was Ruby. It's just that the twins are teething and she's having a rough time with them at night." He sounds slightly embarrassed; I remember that Duncan has always been sensitive to any suggestions that he might be "under the thumb." The male ego is such a fragile thing. "She always says you don't so much have twins as get ambushed by them. Look." He pulls out his phone and shows me a photo of the babies looking tearful and woebegone, their usually gorgeous milk chocolate skin sallow. "But as I said, that flight's no longer an option. So instead, she's getting the same night nanny we had for the first few months to come back for a bit, which at least means she'll get some respite. And to be honest, the nanny is a much better help than I could be." I grit my teeth a little at that. Kitty and Jack are well past teething issues, and both are generally very good sleepers, but it's hard not to feel a little affronted at the casual ease with which Duncan throws money at problems, and even more affronted that it actually works.

"Anyway," says Duncan, switching gears. "You're stuck here." He's tapping his teeth again with that same thumbnail. "You know, that message may not have been meant for you. Don't you remember, when we checked in? We all just grabbed keys. I'm not one hundred percent sure any of us are in the rooms allocated to our names." Tap. Tap, tap, tap. Not meant for me? I hadn't even considered that. I stare at him. That simple possibility takes pounds off the weight dragging at my internal organs. "Though surely it must have been meant for either you or Georgie, given the word *bitch*." True. Some of those pounds drop back in place. Though . . . I think of Jem's antipathy toward Georgie. I don't really think he has any reason to blame her for Lissa's death—at least, no reasonable reason—but still . . . Tap, tap, tap. "I think we need to speak to the chief of police. You're implicated in fraud: the best thing you can do is be open and honest. Probably best not to tell anyone else just yet; let's make sure we aren't muddying the waters accidentally for any police investigation. You've done nothing *wrong,* so you've nothing to fear." I stare at him. He said *wrong* in a way that had me expecting it to be followed by a *but* . . . "There will probably need to be a police report to get the money transferred back from the kids' accounts. And the police ought to know about that charming mirror message." He frowns. "I'm not too comfortable about you in this villa by yourself, you know."

"Well, let's figure that out later. Come on, we'd better get to lunch before we're missed." I almost say, *Before we start rumors;* it's something I might have jokingly said before. But the way he said *wrong* has put paid to that. He thinks of me differently now, even though nothing happened, even though he knows that it didn't, even though he would state categorically that he believes me. The thing is, he's considered that it *might* have happened—*Tell me you didn't sleep with Jem*—and he can't unthink that. It's there, in his mind, nudging his opinion of me askew and casting a shadow. I expect he thinks of himself differently, too, now: he's the generous, forgiving, understanding friend, willing to be supportive in the face of unforgivable behavior—even though the unforgivable behavior didn't happen. Or, in fact, did, but with a different husband, only he doesn't know anything about that. I'm being hung for a crime I didn't commit, but getting off scot-free with one I did. It's difficult to know how to react to that.

I usher him out the door and lock it, then we amble toward the restaurant. A welcome breeze has built up through the afternoon, taking the edge off a brutally hot day. I couldn't live here, for all it's supposed to be paradise; I would melt into a puddle of sunburn and headaches and lethargy. A bright spring day in Surrey is my kind of paradise.

"It's odd, though," Duncan says suddenly.

"What?"

"What was Lissa's plan? She must have meant for you to find the payments in the account at some point. And then what? If she hadn't had the accident, what was supposed to happen next?"

"I suppose…" I stop, trying to think it through slowly. "Yes, you're right, I would have found out, at some point. I'd have had to contact the bank to get the money returned. I suppose I would have found out where it came from, then, and Jem would have found out about it, too. He would have to have figured out that Lissa was to blame; it would make no sense for it to be Cristina. So…"

We've both stopped walking. Duncan is nodding. "So she was planning to leave Jem. She must have been planning that anyway. This was to be a fuck-you to the both of you. She must have been relying on him wanting to avoid any publicity that might come if he went after her for prosecution."

I want to say, *Poor Jem,* but I don't. Because then I'd have to suffer the sidelong glance that Duncan would give me, as he quietly added that comment to the ledgers in his mind, balancing the debits and credits of what there might or might not have been between Jem and me, based on absolutely no information whatsoever. Instead we walk on. I'm trying to find a way to venture the tiny tendril of suspicion that has occasionally inveigled its way into my thoughts when my defenses are low. "I suppose … I suppose she *is* dead, right?"

He glances at me sharply, assessingly, and this time I have no idea what that quick brain of his is thinking. "There was the fisherman who almost retrieved her body. The probability that there were two blond corpses"—I flinch at the word; how can he deliver it so calmly?—"in the sea wearing red TYR swimsuits has got to be vanishingly small."

"Yes." He's right, of course. And that's both a good thing and a bad thing; like most things in life, it has to be weighed and measured. Of course I want Lissa not to have died, but on the other hand, an *alive* Lissa hell-bent on vengeance doesn't bear thinking about … I think of the story of Lissa with a knife in hand, terrorizing Scott Mayhew. I'd heard other stories, of course, that I'd always taken with a pinch of salt—but nothing so extreme as *that,* and Georgie doesn't lie. If I'd known about that, would I have been more cautious with Graeme? Surely I would have been; though even acknowledging that feels like somehow legitimizing her behavior.

We're nearing the restaurant now. The others have picked a table at the center; Jem lifts a hand in a desultory acknowledgment. "Bron," Duncan says, putting a hand on my shoulder to halt me before we climb the two steps up to the raised restaurant floor. "It seems to me Georgie doesn't want to believe Lissa is dead; she would give anything for some kind of miraculous alternative universe in which Lissa is still alive. But you're smart enough to realize that her judgment is clouded right now." I look up at him. The sun is on his back, and his face is in the shade. He flips up his sunglasses to catch me in his earnest, naked gaze. Small beads of sweat are sitting proud on his sunburned nose. "Lissa *is* dead," he says gently. "And whatever she had planned has died with her. Don't let Georgie put you in a spin." I nod and manage an approximation of a smile, and he smiles back. "Come on, then, let's have some lunch."

The others are involved in a conversation that doesn't break for our arrival. "Nobody knows where she's gone, and the police will want to interview her, for sure," Jem is saying gloomily, nodding to us as we settle into chairs. "I asked all her closest friends, and either they're not telling or they really don't know." They're talking about Cristina, I realize. "I think most of my local staff are blaming that thing you saw in the water. The village elders have invited me to a ceremony this evening to appease Kanu."

"Appease? Appease how?" asks Georgie, visibly unsettled.

"No idea. I'll tell you after tonight. I'd be hugely fascinated if it weren't for the fact that right now I'm hugely fucked. Without Cristina . . ." Jem drains his glass of water and bangs it carelessly down on the table, his frustration evident.

"Well, if she is to blame, no doubt she's hightailed it off to somewhere like, I don't know, Switzerland or something," replies Adam.

"Switzerland," Jem snorts. "It's landlocked; there's literally no beach. Why would anyone want to go there?"

"Well," says Georgie seriously. "The flag's a big plus."

I'm looking at Adam as she says it. He turns to her with the most open and uncomplicated look of amusement that I've ever seen on his face, half a second before everyone else catches up. Her lips curve in a sly half smile as the laughter erupts around her. What she's said is funny enough that the tears in my eyes can be dismissed as tears of laughter, but really, they're from relief. It's finally sinking in that I don't have to doubt Georgie, my clever, loyal friend. I don't have to doubt Adam. I don't even have to doubt Jem, and I never did doubt Duncan—thank God I told him about all of this; thank God that I'm now armed with the benefit of his objectiveness. I don't have to doubt anyone. Lissa is to blame, and Lissa is dead and these people here are my friends. Steve was wrong when he said swimming was the connection between us all. It might have been the reason we met, but there were plenty more people on the swim team than Duncan, Lissa, Georgie and me, and I don't go on holidays and keep up with all of those. These people here are my friends.

And I won't think about that message on the mirror. It surely wasn't meant for me anyway.

TWELVE

GEORGIE

The chief of police arrives when we are finishing lunch—a pleasant lunch, or at least it would have been before . . . well, before. I've been trying to map the undercurrents since I got here. On the surface, all currents, deep and otherwise, appear to have stilled, but that's only on the surface. Jem is simply going through the motions; there's a mechanical feel about all that he says and does. Duncan is preoccupied, his eyes unintentionally roving over each member of the group as his mind ticks away. Adam seats himself beside me, briefly catching my hand in his to squeeze it, then letting go. He apologized this morning in such a general way— *I'm sorry about last night*—that I had wanted to ask: *What for*? For being angry at me for contemplating killing my best friend? For being angry at me for not answering his question about Graeme? But I was too stiff and sore and raw, so instead I said: *Me too*. Platitudes, both his words and mine, and we both know it—the reckoning is yet to come. But in the meantime we're operating on a surface level of civility that's nothing short of excruciating. Only Bron is a very good approximation of her usual self. Up until now she's been drawn so taut, like an overtightened string apt to snap at any little disturbance, but now her smile comes quick and easy and tension-free.

But the arrival of the chief of police puts an end to this short reprieve. He introduces himself in a long jumble of soft sibilants that I'm not quick enough to catch, but Jem calls him Jimi when he offers him a drink, and I'm positive that wasn't anywhere in the jumble. He's a small man of stocky build, with an open, friendly face. I wonder how much the chief of police, on a small island such as this, has to do. I should think the ability to charm and appease a major source of employment, such as a hotel owner, is high on the required skills list; he and Jem are joshing with each other like old fishing buddies. Are dogged investigative skills somewhere on that list? I can't tell. I watch them talk as a bead of water snakes down the outside of the chief's cold glass of Coca-Cola to catch on his thick fingers. There's an odd incongruity to his casual stance, drink in hand, with the gun sitting on his hip. Even after years of living in New York, I haven't got used to the sight of armed policemen. I wonder how it changes you, to have that kind of firepower at your disposal. Would I have been a different person last night if I'd had a firearm strapped to my body?

A second policeman, obviously of lower rank than the chief, joins them. Except for an additional six inches in height, he looks so similar that they could be father and son, but again, I don't catch the name. Jem doesn't appear to know him, though; that, or he's not worth joshing with. They stand together at the end of the table, too far for me to be able to catch what they're saying, but nevertheless I see the point at which Jimi switches into business mode. Then Duncan, who is closer than I, suddenly looks up and says, "What's that about Cristina?"

"Jimi thinks they're going to have to treat her as a missing person case," Jem tells him wearily. He has all of our attention now.

"What?" says Duncan. "Why? Surely she's just gotten on a plane?"

"One of her friends called it in," says Jimi. He's now projecting his voice for the whole table and has his face arranged into an expression of serious concern. Mini-Jimi's is an exact copy. "She hadn't packed anything, and her passport is still in her room."

"Maybe she's off on a bender," argues Bron. "Or she got lucky."

Jimi shrugs. "It's possible. But I understand that would be out of character. It's not been twenty-four hours yet"—he reflexively looks at his watch—"but it will be soon, and if she doesn't turn up before then, we'll have to start an official search." He sets his shoulders to signal a change of subject and looks at me. "Shall we move somewhere more private?"

"I don't mind," I say to him. "They can all hear it."

He nods a tad reluctantly, and I see that he had meant to interview just me, without an audience, but it's a nod nonetheless. He crosses to my end of the oval table and pulls out a chair at the head of it, a deliberate choice. His minion lounges against a pillar, arms crossed. Jem has put himself against a different pillar, just within Jimi's field of vision. It's a statement: he's claiming authority by not sitting at the table. Not as much as that of Jimi or Mini-Jimi, but certainly more than the rest of us.

Jimi looks round the group, then clears his throat and starts with the questions. Where was I, what happened, what did I see: exactly the questions you'd expect, in a calm, encouraging manner. Though one of his first questions is the hardest of all: what was I doing at Kanu Cove?

"Pardon?" I ask, playing for time. Why am I feeling put on the spot, when I've done nothing wrong?

"Kanu Cove. What were you doing there? You left the dinner to go there. Were you meeting someone?"

I shake my head. "No." It feels like every set of eyes is resting upon me. "I was just . . . getting some air."

He raises an eyebrow. "All the way over at Kanu Cove?"

I raise my chin. "It's a good place to go. To feel closer to Lissa." He blinks and moves on, like I knew he would; it's hard to challenge other people's grieving mechanisms. And besides, what I've said is true, even if I didn't want to say it. But I can feel Jem's gaze fixed on me, heavy and dark and *injured,* somehow—though how can I have injured him?—yet when I glance at him, his face is deliberately expressionless.

The questions move on. When I mention the lights going out, Jimi glances at Jem, who nods and immediately pulls out his mobile and murmurs orders to find the maintenance engineer. It's not my first recital of the incident, and by now I've got the hang of it: I don't try to describe in precise detail the panic I felt, which still seems only a short step away—far too easy to stumble into. There's no need to render in words the specific moments I can recall in vivid clarity, like stills from a film in ultra-saturated color: wrenching myself sideways to avoid the shadow bearing down on me; crying out as I dropped hard onto my knee; scrabbling desperately for my phone. Those are burned into my mind, yet I know I couldn't string together a coherent narrative of exactly *how* he grabbed me, or which direction I twisted in, or which hand was where; it all happened so fast. Instead, I stick to broad brushstrokes that seem wholly inadequate to me as a description of the event, but seem to satisfy Jimi.

"What happens now?" I ask.

Jimi spreads his hands, and it's clear he's going to do nothing. Perhaps there really is nothing he can do—to be fair, I can't think of anything myself—but nonetheless it rankles. "We are looking, of course, but with such a vague description . . ." He trails off as he sees my expression, then regroups. "But we will be sending regular patrols until the hotel is shut down. You will be safe."

Safe. I think of those viselike arms. I'm not sure I will ever be safe again. In truth, I never really was; I was just deluding myself.

Adam speaks up. "The hotel shutdown: when is that happening?"

"Right after you leave," Jem says expressionlessly, as if he has lost the energy to show emotion.

"Would you be able to show us where it all happened?" Jimi asks me.

I nod. "Now?"

"Yes please." His open, friendly demeanor, never far from a smile, has returned; I feel my fingers clench in irritation. No amount of pleasantries can wipe away what happened or the fact that he plans to do absolutely nothing about it.

"I'll come, too," says Adam. I extricate myself from the chair, a little awkwardly as my knee stiffens whenever I sit for long; Adam reaches out a hand to steady me. I take it, but I think: *I should never have started down this path. And, having started, I should never have come this far.*

"I wanted to ask: are you still looking for Lissa's body?" Duncan asks Jimi as the policeman passes behind him, in a casual aside that I only just catch.

Jimi's smile has dropped. "No." He shakes his head sadly. "There's no point. With the currents . . ." He spreads his hands wide. "The area to search is just too great. Like looking for a needle in a haystack."

"If the needle was wearing a bright red swimsuit and all the hay was blue, you mean," I say. Both Duncan's and Jimi's heads swing toward me; both, I think, were unaware they were being overheard.

"But bodies don't always float at the surface," Jimi says, his tone carefully regretful. "They actually sink to start, but the gases from decomposition make them go up and down." He waves a hand as if mimicking a plane moving up and down, but I think instead of the undulating serpent. "When the gases escape, they sink again, but the decomposition continues, so they sometimes resurface." Bron takes an audible breath in, one hand touching her lips. "Apologies," Jimi says quickly, turning to her. "I didn't mean to cause distress." *Except he did,* I think. He meant to distress me in particular, to shut me down. His eyes, flatly expressionless against the general goodwill of the rest of his visage, slide back over me again.

Jem levers himself off the pillar. "I've got a few things to do," he says to Jimi. "Come to my office afterward; the maintenance guy should be there by then."

Adam, myself and Jimi-Junior start along the sandy path by the restaurant, but Jimi-Junior calls to us to wait, and I realize that Jimi hasn't followed us. I look back to determine what the holdup is and see Duncan standing, talking urgently with his serious business face on. Bron, still seated, is looking upward at them both. I glance at Adam and see that he's clocked it, too. Then Jimi looks across at the three of us hovering on the path and calls out: "Go ahead, please. I'll catch you up."

Jimi-junior turns to me. "Can you take me to where you were when the first rocks started falling?" he asks, in almost unaccented perfect English.

"Um, sure." I look back at the restaurant tableau. The three of them are seated now, Duncan and Bron side by side, and Jimi in his head-of-the-table interviewer chair. "I—uh, I didn't properly catch your name," I say, stalling.

"The equivalent in the United Kingdom would be something like sergeant. Sergeant Lenny."

"Lenny?"

He half nods, half tips his head, in a way that tells me I haven't quite got it right, but it's close enough. I look back again. Bron is speaking now, and Chief Jimi is listening intently.

"Is it this way?" presses Lenny.

"Ah. Yes, that way." I reluctantly turn away.

"What's that all about?" asks Adam under his breath.

I shake my head: *No idea.* No idea at all, but a deep, cold unease is soaking through me, permeating every cell in my body and only adding to the icy lead in my belly. What can Bron and Duncan be saying to a policeman—the chief of police, no less—that they wouldn't say in front of the rest of us?

The walk is more than I would have chosen for my knee, given I've already swum with it today, but it doesn't complain too much. There's nobody at Kanu Cove when we get there, which shouldn't have surprised me but somehow does. I find myself looking around from the vantage point of the stone pier, as if scanning the area for someone; perhaps I subconsciously expected the old man to be there again? The water looks clean and clear and glassy in the middle: a perfect deception. Who could guess at the lethal undertows beneath such an idyllic scene? Or perhaps I'm focused on the wrong danger. Perhaps even now the serpent is there, stretched languorously in the depths, hidden by the light scattered off the deceptively innocent surface.

"You were standing here when the power cut happened?" Lenny asks.

I try to judge it, looking back at the inland curve of the cove, where the path lights must have been shining before they abruptly snuffed out. "Yes, around here." I look at the ground. There's plenty of loose gravel on the stones that could have been dislodged by the intruder, but there's no way to prove it; I don't see that it helps. Adam is looking up at the cliff face. "There's a path there, I think," he says, squinting even though he's wearing sunglasses.

I look at the water again. I wonder if whatever lies beneath can hear us talking. Can sea creatures hear the strange and alien—to them—beings that only ever briefly visit their world? "There was an old man here, once, when I came." Lenny looks across at me, surprised. "Oh no, not last night. It was when I came in daytime. He told me . . ." Lenny's eyes, so dark that they almost seem entirely black, are fixed on me, waiting. He isn't wearing sunglasses. "He told me Kanu takes who wants taken." I enunciate each word clearly. I want him to hear it as it was said. Adam looks across at me for a second, as if measuring me for something I don't understand, then back at the almost-path he's trying to trace.

"Ah." Lenny nods slowly, seriously. I was wrong to pigeonhole him as being just like his superior. This, now, is his natural demeanor, I think; the other was an act. Ordinarily, I would imagine his smiles are slow and hard-won. "It's a well-known local spot. You have, I think, Beachy Head?" I stare at him, flabbergasted. How does he know about a suicide spot on the south coast of England? "It's like that."

"Is that what you think Lissa did? Committed suicide?"

"It's recorded as an accidental death." His face is shuttered. That alone tells me what he thinks.

"Kanu takes who wants taken," I mutter again, but to myself. Then, to him, "Kanu takes: do they mean the cove, or the serpent?"

He shrugs. "Does it matter? They're the same thing, really."

Metaphorically, he's right, of course, but that shadow that slid through the water beneath us was not remotely metaphorical. "It matters," I say defiantly. "Accidental death and suicide are not the same thing."

"Of course," he agrees, and yet somehow, despite the shutters, I know he doesn't agree with me at all. If he spoke freely, he would say that anyone who climbed into these waters was committing suicide, one way or another. I want to shake him and shake him and shake him until he sees the truth, the self-evident truth, that Lissa did not commit suicide, could not have committed suicide, would not have committed suicide. I look to Adam for assistance, but he's some distance away, his eyes still tracing the almost-path; I have to turn away from Lenny before I erupt with the frustration and anger that's boiled up inside me with frightening speed. "Do you need to rest?" he asks politely, from behind me.

By the time I turn back, I have my face under control. "No, thank you, I'm fine," I say, and the words sound as they are meant to: polite, indifferent, calm. But he looks at me for a moment, and I see that neither of us is fooling the other, and we both know it.

"Presumably the attacker came from up here," Adam calls. I turn to see he's ascended a number of stone steps on a narrow staircase in the cliffside that I hadn't paid much attention to before. "There's a couple of paths leading from the top of this staircase."

Lenny starts toward the stairs. "I'll stay here," I say, gesturing with a grimace toward my knee.

"Perhaps stand on the pier," Lenny suggests. "Then we can check if you could have been spotted from above."

I nod and move myself back to where I must have been standing, looking out over the water, and wondering yet again about the serpent. Does it sleep at night, or during the day? Does it sleep at all, in fact? Perhaps it's watching me, even now, from its watery kingdom. I take a step toward the edge of the jetty to peer into the depths. The heat is rolling up off the baking-hot stone of the pier; ordinarily I would sit on the edge and dangle my feet in the cool of the ocean. Would the serpent see those feet; would it uncoil from its resting place beneath the waves as it sensed the intrusion into its underwater world? I have an urge, reckless and nihilistic, to try it—like the urge to step out into the void when at the top of a very tall building. My feet take me a step closer to the edge, I even start to slip off my sandals—and then I hear Adam's voice, calling indistinctly to Lenny, and it's like a shock of cold water: *What am I doing?* I step back hurriedly, shocked at myself. I should be afraid, like Bron—wild horses couldn't drag her into the sea right now—and I *am* afraid, but I'm other things, too: terrifying things. Curious. Defiant. Still a loose cannon, however much I might have thought I'd grown past that.

I have an urgent desire to escape from here, before any more ridiculous notions take hold of my mind, but Adam and Lenny are engaged in conversation high on the cliff, almost at the top; it looks like they will be a while yet. I could leave them both to it—but perhaps that would be interpreted badly; perhaps better to stick it out on the pier, though staying well away from the edge . . . There's a tiny piece of shade at the farthest end, the end that's closest to the open ocean, where a fold in the cliff face casts a shadow: it's not much but surely better than nothing. I move that way, and a small breath of wind dances around me; I stand still for a moment and close my eyes, savoring the brief sense of cool as the breeze licks at my damp skin. All too soon the breeze dies, and I reluctantly open my eyes again and turn for the small patch of shade—but something snags at my gaze, something on the rocks at the base of the cliff. I shade my eyes with one hand and look again. An indistinct bundle, too distant to make out, though I can see that it's moving—wait, no, it's not moving independently, it's merely rising and falling with the movement of the sea. It's so far away I might never have seen it except for the movement and the color: red. My stomach lurches. I blink, then rip off my sunglasses to see the color unadulterated by any filter, but it's not the red of the TYR swimsuit; it's a different red, only I know this red, too. It's the red of the reception staff uniforms.

"Adam," I yell. I'm turning to look for him. "Adam, there's something there; come quickly. Adam, Lenny." I hobble back along the pier to find them both clattering down the stone steps at pace, Adam ahead of Lenny. "There's something at the base of the cliffs; something red. I can't quite see what it is, but I think . . . I think . . ." I stop. Adam has reached me now.

"Where?" he asks, shielding his eyes to look in the direction of my pointing finger. "I can't—"

"Farther left. There."

"I can't—wait, yes." I hear his sharp intake of breath, then he turns to Lenny. "We'd probably get a better view from the path."

"I'm coming, too," I say quickly. I can't countenance being left alone on this pier again. Adam looks down at my knee and opens his mouth as if to say something, but whatever my face holds stops him, and instead he offers an arm to lean on.

The climb is grim. Every step results in stabbing pain. The treads are uneven heights and roughly hewn; even without a bad knee it would be an awkward climb. In places there's a rope balustrade to hold on to, but more often than not there's nothing but loose rock or bushes on either side. One could slip and land tens of meters below on the jetty, with only the hope of a bounce or two on the rocky staircase to break the fall. Lenny is climbing quickly and is far ahead of me in seconds. Behind, Adam takes to unceremoniously shoving me upward with a strong hand under my backside, and I'm horribly, humiliatingly, grateful. Still, the top is miles away and not getting any closer.

But Lenny doesn't go to the top; he takes a path that looks like nothing more than a rabbit trail, which, whilst uncomfortably narrow, is at least more or less flat. I adopt a sort of uneven shuffle which covers the ground at a reasonable pace and try not to think of where I'll end up if I slip. Ahead of me Lenny has stopped and is peering down the cliffside to the sparkling blue waters below. As we approach, he takes his phone out of his pocket and starts to dial. He turns as he hears us and starts to shake his head, one hand outstretched, but at the same time his call connects and he has to speak—and then it's too late for him to stop us; we are peering over the cliffside, too. From this vantage point some thirty meters above, we can see the red bundle clearly, and it's not a bundle. It's a person, except that it can't be a person any longer; no person would lie like that, awkwardly rising and falling with the water, half on and half off the tumbled heap of rocks at the base of the cliff, occasionally partly submerged by the brilliant white foam of the waves that intermittently break and froth over the red skirt fanning out in the water, tugging insistently at the scarlet material, and at the long, dark hair that clouds around an indistinct face; tugging her out to sea. *The waves will win in the end,* I think. *The rocks cannot keep her. She isn't theirs.*

Adam is gripping my arm. I'm not sure when he took hold of it. "Cristina?" I ask, and the word sounds absurdly clumsy and loud.

"I can't be sure at this distance but—probably." I look at his face, at the grim white line of his tightly pressed lips, then back at the dazzling riot of color at the base of the cliff: the turquoise blue of the sea, the scarlet red of the skirt and the snow white of the foam. It's hypnotically striking. "Georgie. Georgie, come on," Adam is saying, though it sounds as if he's far away. In another land, perhaps. "We should get you down from here; get that knee some ice and some rest."

I'm still looking over the cliffside, my eyes narrowed against the sunbeams that lance off the waves. "I suppose there's no chance that she's still—"

He's shaking his head. "I doubt it, but the boat will be here as quick as possible."

"Boat?" *Boat. They will drag her out of the water, flopping her over the side like a dead fish, but she isn't theirs. She should be left for the sea. Or for Kanu, or maybe that's the same thing . . .*

"Yes. Steve is on the way; didn't you hear Lenny say?" Suddenly reality floods back in, breaking whatever awful trance I've been in: *Poor Steve.* She's a person, or she was; not an offering, or a sacrifice. She was a colleague here at the hotel; a friend to many, presumably. How utterly awful for Steve to have to help recover her body. And then other questions rush in: *What happened to her? Surely she didn't trip and fall?* I look up the cliffside, to peer at the path leading from the top of the staircase, which is much wider and more established than the trail we're on, and then down again, calculating the likelihood that a fall from there would result in landing where she currently lies. Not likely, as I judge it. That path sits back from the edge of the cliffside, and in any case the initial slope is gradual. You'd have to be several meters off the path before you'd be in danger of sliding so quickly that you couldn't stop. From where we are standing, though . . . I kick at a stone and watch it bounce—once, twice—then fly through the air until it splashes into the water below with minimal fuss, some five meters to the right of the body. Yes, from here it's perfectly possible. Only this path doesn't lead anywhere: one couldn't even get to the main reception on it; it just peters out. She wouldn't have been walking on this tiny trail as a route to her staff quarters. Perhaps she was taken here by force? And then I finally make the connection that I should have made immediately, and a shudder runs through me. *Those arms, banded like steel around me . . . Would he have dragged me up here just so he could watch me tumble and fall?*

Adam is looking at me, his head cocked. He takes my hand, his mouth still in that tight, grim line. "Are you okay?"

"Yes." I pause. "I don't know." I start to move back along the path. "Do you think it was an accident?"

"No. And nor do I think it was suicide."

"Oh." I hadn't even contemplated that. "Me neither." I'm watching my footing carefully; I can feel Adam watching me, too, hovering, ready to grab me if I make one false move. "It could have been me. It must have happened last night; it could have been me."

He doesn't deny it, and I feel my stomach clench. I had been wishing he would protest, that he would find some fault with my logic. "The police will have to take the attack on you rather more seriously now."

"You'd think so." I need to get off this damn cliffside. I need a cool drink in a locked room: somewhere safe to stop, to calm down and think. Only—is anywhere safe? Without knowing what's going on, how can I tell?

"Georgie," Adam says, catching at my hand to make me halt reluctantly. "I don't know what's going on, but this is serious." I can't see his eyes through the dark lenses of his sunglasses, but I don't need to;

the tension around his mouth is unmistakable. "Promise me you'll be careful. No more running off alone to Kanu or anything stupid like that. Promise me."

"I—" I stop: there's the faint buzz of an engine. We both turn to see the familiar shape of the resort speedboat making its way through the mouth of the cove, buffeted by the ocean waves before it reaches the relative calm afforded by the shelter of the inlet and makes for the cliff wall. Steve is at the helm, with two other members of the water sports team in the boat, and the distinctive stocky, uniformed figure of the chief of police, too. Steve pulls back on the throttle and spins the wheel to turn the pristine white craft broadside. I look away; I don't want to see them manhandling her into the boat. She would have been more peaceful out at sea. For a moment I picture her, drifting slowly with the relentless current under the water, silent and calm in the embrace of Kanu's kingdom. But her long, dark hair won't stay dark; it turns to blond as I watch, and as she turns in a lazy spin under the water, I see that she's actually Lissa.

"Georgie," says Adam insistently. "Promise me. Nothing stupid."

"Oh." It takes me a moment to follow what he means; I'd lost track of that conversation. "Yes, I promise." Of course I promise; who wouldn't? Though I doubt it will make much difference. If you don't know what's going on, how can you tell what's stupid?

HOW TO KILL YOUR BEST FRIEND
Method 5: Shooting

Shooting. As in, with a gun. An actual gun. I mean, I can see that it scores pretty highly on effectiveness, but . . . Well, I suppose you could make it look like a robbery gone wrong, so it's got believability going for it, too. The problem is execution: could I get hold of one? I have to think that it's actually possible: there's a couple of people I know who might know someone . . . And right there is the problem: it's far too traceable. I'd cause too much of a stir just sourcing the weapon.

Could I steal one? I suppose that's possible, too. There's one or two idiots I know of whose gun cabinet is not as secure as it should be. I couldn't travel with it, though. She'd have to come to me. Which would happen at some point, but when?

A gun. It bears thinking about, actually. A gun.

THIRTEEN

BRONWYN

A body. On the rocks. At Kanu Cove, no less—Kanu again. It was Kanu where Lissa went missing, and Kanu where Georgie was attacked, and now Kanu where a body has been found. If I was at all superstitious, I might be inclined to give some weight to all the local legends about the cove. I'm not, of course, but even so, nothing on earth would get me to take a stroll to Kanu Cove right now.

For probably the fifth or sixth time, Duncan has got up from the table and is peering over the edge of the terrace balustrade, as if he might magically see round the headland. His left leg is visibly jiggling as he stares out, watching for the return of the boat that took the chief of police out to see what his colleague found; but for that twitching leg, he could be an advert for the resort, leaning thoughtfully against the stone barrier, with his white shirt in sharp contrast to the backdrop of the sea, so brilliantly blue that it hurts the eyes. That is the holiday I want to be on, the one promised by an ad just like that, where my most pressing mental calculation each day is whether to apply factor 30 or factor 50. Instead, I'm sitting here at the table worrying about a body, for God's sake: an actual dead body. Presumably

Cristina. Who else could it be, after all? And if it is Cristina, what does that *mean*? Is it a tragic accident, or foul play? Is it related to everything else, or is this just a horrific confluence of events? I'm trying to think it all through, but my mind won't settle; it skips around, as jittery as Duncan's left leg.

Perhaps there's no point in trying to analyze until we have more facts. I press the heels of my hands to my temples, conscious that this oppressive windless, airless heat is bringing on a headache, though it seems inappropriate to complain of that when Cristina may be dead. *Dead.* Her face swims into my mind: somewhat pretty in a very high-maintenance kind of way; I don't imagine anyone ever saw her without lashings of heavy mascara, perfectly coiffed hair and bright red lipstick over those startling white teeth. I close my eyes briefly and refuse to think about what the seawater will have done to all that mascara.

Dead. It's scarcely credible, and yet, here we are, awaiting the return of the chief of police. I should have known that our pleasant lunch was too good to be true; if I'd closed my eyes, it could almost have been any one of the meals we've had on so many previous swimming holidays. But only if I closed my eyes, and I couldn't do that, even metaphorically. With them open, it was impossible to miss the gaping hole where Lissa should have been. But if Lissa had been here, then what? The lunch would have been more raucous, I suppose; Georgie would surely have been drinking, too, as would I. Or perhaps she would have been in one of her nervier states, and then we'd all have been drinking even harder, for a nervy Lissa is like having a constant background noise of nails dragged down a blackboard: it puts everyone on edge. But either way, it wouldn't have been better if Lissa was still with us, because what she was doing, doing to *me,* would still have been bubbling away under her carefree facade. I would have been like those animals in the nature programs—antelopes or some other kind of horribly vulnerable grazing beast—

calmly milling around in the sunshine, blithely unaware of the predator only meters away. Which, in fact, is exactly how I feel right now; except I'm not blithely unaware. I know there's a danger, a terrible, implacable danger; only I don't know where it's coming from.

A familiar whine from one of the electrical engines turns my head; Adam and Georgie are arriving on the back of one of the laundry carts. Georgie looks positively exhausted; Adam physically lifts her down.

"Duncan," I call, and he turns, then leaves the balustrade at once.

"Is it her?" he asks Adam urgently, as soon as the pair reach the table. "Is it Cristina?"

"Most likely," Adam says with a grimace. Duncan drops into a chair with an indistinct exclamation; his leg is finally still. "I was too far away to see her face clearly, but everything fits: hair color, build, uniform. Have you got any water?"

"Here." I pass across a bottle, only a third full, and he pours a full glass for Georgie then takes the remaining mouthful or two straight from the glass bottle before looking round to order some more, but there are no waiting staff to be seen. "Could it have been an accident?"

"Highly unlikely," says Georgie, between glugs of the water. She has tiny beads of perspiration on her upper lip and tracing a line down the center of her sternum.

"Wait," says Duncan, leaping up again. "That sounds like the boat. Should we go down to Horseshoe Cove?"

"It's not a spectator sport." The acid in Georgie's tone is unmistakable; Duncan colors at her words, and for a moment I think he just might try to mount a challenge, but after a second he subsides in his chair. Then he pointedly asks Adam, rather than Georgie, what they saw, but the snub is rather lost on her, as she's busy arranging two chairs so that the seats face each other in a makeshift bed. Before long she's slumped down, legs outstretched and eyes closed, though I'm absolutely positive she's not sleeping. Duncan runs out of questions rather quickly. Even with Adam and Georgie here, too, the known facts are limited, and nobody seems keen to indulge in speculation.

"So, what, we just wait here?" I ask.

"Jimi and Lenny are coming here when they've finished with the body," says Adam. Out of everyone, he has remained the most like himself on this trip except, if anything, even more watchful, as if permanently half turned to check on Georgie. I wonder if Georgie quite knows what she's got herself into; Adam is not the sort of man that can be picked up and put down at whim. "We might as well wait."

I lean back in my chair and wonder what the police will do with the body when they've "finished" with it. Will they take it away with them or will a coroner's van need to be arranged? If the latter, where will they put it until the vehicle arrives? Will it need to be somewhere cold, like the walk-in fridges that I assume all hotels have, or will they lay her out on one of the pristine white beds in an empty villa, like a guest who has just forgotten to leave? Will she stain those pristine sheets, with all the salt water and the smudged mascara and the smeared lipstick . . . I shake my head to dislodge the train of thought, but that only serves to remind me that my headache is getting fiercer. I'm not sure I can take any more of this hideous inaction. "I'm going to find some water," I say, pushing my chair back decisively.

That gets attention from both men. "I'm not sure—" begins Duncan, but then he stops. He's looking over my shoulder; I twist to see the junior policeman—Lenny?—approaching, and sink back into my chair.

"Georgie," says Adam quietly, and she sits up immediately.

"Is it Cristina?" asks Duncan, when Lenny is still meters away.

Lenny waits until he has reached the table before answering. His face is grave. "Yes. Steve was able to confirm for us."

"What happened? An accident, surely?" The words tumble out of me. Georgie glances at me briefly, and her expression—something akin to pity—causes color to rush into my cheeks, as if I'm being embarrassingly gauche and naive.

Lenny is shaking his head. "Not an accident." He catches sight of something and turns slightly. "Ah, it's the chief." He clasps his hands behind his back as if waiting respectfully for the senior officer before continuing, but Duncan dives in anyway, voicing exactly my own thought: "Surely you can't tell that without an autopsy?"

"Au-autopsy?" Lenny stumbles slightly on the unfamiliar word, frowning slightly, by which point Chief Jimi has reached the table, too. He rattles off a phrase in the local language, and Lenny's face clears in understanding. Then the chief turns to the rest of us. "Normally, yes, you are right, there would have to be an autopsy, as you say. But in this case, it's clear that we must proceed with a murder investigation. Because she was shot."

FOURTEEN

GEORGIE

Shot. The stark finality of that is the most shocking thing to me. Lissa's death is like a picture with no hard edges: each possible scenario blurs into the next, and you can't interpret it without bringing something of yourself to it. By contrast, Cristina's death is a pin-sharp photograph, with everything clearly defined. She is dead because a bullet tore through her—through her stomach, actually; when I hear that, I find that I'm pressing one hand to my own vulnerable belly and the other to my mouth. She probably wasn't dead when she went over the cliffside, but she would have bled out very quickly in the water; or so Chief Jimi said. A forensic team is combing the cliffside right now, looking for any blood that might show her path down, whilst we continue to sit in the restaurant, with the others attempting to answer questions that I can't, seeing as I never met her in life. Questions like: *When did we last see her? How did she seem? Can you think of anyone who would want to harm her?* And all the while, I see the riot of color at the base of the cliff, only this time the skirt is not the only red in the image. A ribbon of deep scarlet streams endlessly from her abdomen, even as the featureless face grows paler and paler until it matches the white froth of the breaking waves.

Only, perhaps I don't need to have actually met Cristina to answer that last one: *Can I think of anyone who would want to hurt her?* Well, no, except . . . *Jem.* There's a pregnant pause after Jimi voices that question. I look around the table. It makes no sense not to say it, even if it's ridiculous to think of Jem actually shooting anyone; a fight, a push, a tragic accident—that I could believe, but not a gun. Duncan is studiously looking at his glass, and Bron is methodically shredding a napkin; I can't help thinking that both of them are deliberately avoiding my eyes. Adam meets my gaze, though, and I can see that he's thinking exactly the same thing. He shrugs minutely, and I take it as a cue to speak up. "Well, there seems to be some money missing from the company," I say awkwardly. "Jem's company, I mean; has he told you?"

Jimi inclines his head. "I'm aware of it."

"Well, I'm not suggesting he killed her, but I suppose if Jem thought Cristina was behind the missing money, he wouldn't exactly be thrilled with her—"

"There's a big difference between being pissed off and actually shooting someone," Duncan objects.

"I know, I know. I'm just trying to be—"

Duncan talks over me. "Jem would never have hurt Cristina; he adored Cristina—though not in a romantic sense," he adds hurriedly to Jimi, color flaring quickly in his cheeks as he realizes how his words could be misinterpreted. "Purely professional. Surely this was some kind of madman, and Cristina was just in the wrong place at the wrong time."

"Perhaps," says Jimi. He has nothing in his hands; no notebook or pen. It irritates me that he's not even taking notes. Lenny is, though. "The company; that is the company owned by Jem, Lissa and yourself, Duncan?" Duncan nods. "If I remember rightly, Lissa's shares went to Jem, is that correct?" Duncan nods again. "And she owned a sixth?"

I look sharply at Duncan. Only a sixth? Surely Lissa had owned much more than that? "That's right," Duncan says, somewhat reluctantly. "Together Jem and Lissa owned fifty-one percent." Bron looks up from the napkin, her hands momentarily stilled by that. Fifty-one percent. Which means that Duncan holds forty-nine percent: a much bigger investment than I had imagined. I'm surprised Lissa never told me that. I'm surprised Duncan didn't, either. I look across at Adam and find that he's studying Duncan thoughtfully.

"Miss Ayers," says Lenny suddenly, as if he's just remembered something. "I may have something for you." He reaches into a pocket and pulls out what looks like a paper bag—

"My phone!" The screen is miraculously uncracked, despite having been hurled with force into the undergrowth. Lenny explains that he found it, and several other items—a hair clip, a hairbrush, a lens cloth so sandy that its lens-cleaning days are over—that must have fallen out of the ripped bag to lie strewn along the path from Kanu Cove.

"Will all of this stop us getting on the plane tomorrow?" asks Bron suddenly. It might be the first thing she's said since we heard Cristina had been shot, and even for her, it's a remarkably tone-deaf question. Duncan glances across at her, mild surprise registering on his face.

Jimi takes a second or two before he answers. "I don't think so," he says carefully. "If we have more questions, we can contact you by phone." He pushes back his chair to rise. "Well, thank you for your insight," he says, despite the fact that I can't think of a single thing any of us have said which was particularly insightful.

"Presumably you'll be looking at whether this is linked to the attack on Georgie," Adam says, rising himself. A complicated dance of handshakes begins.

"We'll be pursing all avenues," Jimi says blandly, and my fingers curl into my palms at the anodyne response.

Lenny proffers his hand to me, and I take it distractedly. "And Lissa," I say loudly, to break through this absurd charade of politeness. Lenny glances at me, his dark eyes quiet and wary, my hand held for a beat too long in his firm, dry handshake before he thinks to release it. Everyone else is looking at me, too. "Surely you'll be reopening the case now."

Jimi shakes his head. "There's no reason to do that."

"No reason?" I'm genuinely incredulous. "Two deaths and one attack in one small remote resort, and you're not even going to look at whether there's a connection?"

"Miss Ayers," he says, in words so deliberately patient that the condescension is unmistakable, "do you have any evidence to suggest a connection between this crime and the unfortunate accident that befell Mrs. Kateb?"

"I—no evidence, no, but surely—"

"No evidence," he repeats, nodding. "Exactly. You must understand, Miss Ayers, that we are policemen. We cannot just reopen a case without any new evidence."

I turn away, struggling to collect myself, to prevent my anger from spilling out in wordless vitriol, or worse, in furious hot tears. By the time I turn back, they've taken their leave, both of them, Lenny awkwardly matching his longer stride to his superior's.

"You okay?" Adam murmurs.

"Yes." Except of course I'm not. How could anyone be okay? "I'm not wrong," I mutter defiantly.

"Come and sit down."

I look at the table, which is big enough for six, and yet we are only four. We should have been six; if Lissa was still alive we would be six. We haven't just lost Lissa; we've lost Jem, too, I think—if he was ever truly a part of the group. *Lost.* What a stupid expression. As if the person has been misplaced; as if you might walk into a room and find them after all. Maybe Jem feels like that; maybe he expects to see Lissa in every room he enters in that villa; maybe *lost* feels like the right expression to him. But I didn't *lose* Lissa. She was taken. Cristina, too. It beggars belief that there wouldn't be a connection.

"Your knee needs a break. Sit down," urges Adam again, and I allow myself to sink into a chair. He's right; my knee is aching. All that hiking up and down the cliff certainly hasn't done it any favors.

Duncan clears his throat. He's about to take charge, as if that's his birthright as a male. In a deliberate show of disinterest, I pick up my phone and start to scroll through all the messages that came in through the night—junk mail, mostly; with all the vociferous complaints about the aggressive firewall, the IT department seems to have dialed back its efficiency to essentially nil—whilst lending half an ear to Duncan's bid for authority. "What with all of this—Cristina, the attack on Georgie—I don't much like the idea of Bron or Georgie sleeping in villas on their own." I look up at my name and find Bron looking at me, her mouth parting as if she's about to say something, but then she closes it again. I return to my phone. "I was thinking we should all move into one villa," Duncan continues. "That would surely be easier for Jem, too; he can get started on closing up our villas. The presidential villa has enough bedrooms for us all, right? What is it; four, five bedrooms?"

"Four, I think," offers Adam.

Sender: georgieayers698@gmail.com. It's another email released from quarantine—I've been getting them in dribs and drabs; last night's batch included the email with the white dress code for the memorial—but it's weird; that's my exact name, with the right spelling, but that's not an email address that I own. And why would I be sending myself an email? The title is: *Wish you were here.* I can feel myself freeze. My pulse is beating so loudly in my ears that surely the others must hear it. I'm only dimly aware that Duncan is still speaking. "Georgie," he says testily. "Right, Georgie?"

I look up. "Sorry—what?"

"The presidential villa, Georgie. Four bedrooms, perfect for the four of us. Right?"

I look at Bron, who nods quickly in agreement. "Uh, sure."

"Makes perfect sense," I hear Adam say easily, but I'm already looking back at the email, hunting through the quarantine information at the top to find the date it was actually sent. The night before she died. Actually, very late that night, probably only a few hours before she disappeared. It's possible it was the last thing she ever typed. The world has narrowed to the small screen of my mobile phone. I start to read: *Seriously, honey, you should be here. You were meant to be here.*

"Okay then," Duncan is saying, starting to push his chair back. *I need you to keep me in check.* "I'll go and speak to Jem about it. I'm sure it'll be fine; it's just one more night." *Actually, I needed you a while ago. I've not been entirely honest in my emails; I thought I could guilt you into coming out here. Alas, no. But this one is the unadulterated truth. I've done a bad thing and I'm not sorry.*

"Wait," I hear Adam say, and his tone is sharp enough to yank me away from the email. "What were you and Bron discussing earlier with the chief of police?"

It should have been my first question after the police left the four of us alone, but Cristina's death derailed us all. Duncan pauses awkwardly, halfway between sitting and standing, and I see him glance involuntarily at Bron, and I see that he was the first person she looked to, also—and I know we aren't four. We are two twos, except who am I kidding? I glance back at the email. The only two I've ever been part of was Lissa and me. We are two, and one, and one, and the math of that is very, very different.

FIFTEEN

BRONWYN

"What were you and Bron discussing with the chief of police?"

Of course Adam and Georgie were bound to wonder. Of course they were going to ask that very question. Duncan drops back into his seat and starts to explain. Ordinarily I would be irritated beyond measure by someone else taking charge of a narrative that relates to me, but on this occasion I'm perfectly happy to let Duncan do the talking. In fact, I'm curious to see how he'll edit the message. He took charge with the local police, too, and was very insistent that the fraud be kept a secret—*no need to publicly air the laundry of the dead, and it certainly wouldn't help the hotel's reputation*—though perhaps Cristina's death has put paid to that.

Death. Murder, actually. Horrific and awful, of course, but surely completely unconnected to the fraud, or that vile message on the mirror? Now that the shock has had a chance to subside, it strikes me that this tragedy has actually lessened the threat level, as it relates to me. I expect Georgie is right in her assumption that the same man who attacked her must have killed Cristina. Perhaps she's even right that the same person killed Lissa, but clearly we will never know.

Either way, the safest thing we can do is leave; and we're doing that tomorrow. Even the chief of police has approved our departure. I think again of Jimi's reaction to Duncan's precise, undramatic description of the fraud. I could swear he looked at me more carefully, when he understood what Duncan was saying about Lissa's motivation, as if he might discern something he'd previously missed, as if he might suddenly spot the reason why Lissa—svelte, gorgeous, glamorous—would have become jealous of me. Me, the boring housewife.

But I *want* to be the boring housewife; I want to be *happy* being the boring housewife. If all of this can be resolved without Rob needing to know anything, I'll go home and be the perfect wife, mother, daughter-in-law, friend. I'll put my hand up for every parent rep post, and I'll make fairy cakes and cookies for every bake sale; I'll have coffees and arrange kiddie playdates, and I'll make sure I never again wish I hadn't thrown in my job. Rob's mother never worked, which can go either way for influencing a son's expectations, but in Rob's case, the outcome is clear. He never pressured me to give up, but he comments at least once a week on how much easier it is for him to just concentrate on his career instead of worrying about whether he's supposed to be doing a nursery drop-off or preschool pickup.

When Duncan drops the bombshell of where the money has been funneled to, for once Georgie's eyes stop flitting down to her phone and grow comically round, and when I turn to look at Adam, sitting right beside me, I see that his jaw has literally dropped open. They didn't know; I'm certain of it.

"But—why? Who?" asks Adam, bewildered.

"Not Cristina, then," Georgie says definitively. Her mouth is a tight straight line, and each word is a sharp bite. "Lissa, I presume. *Fuck.*" She's cross, I realize. Furious, in fact; it seems like it's all she can do to stop herself from exploding in anger.

"Lissa? But why? Why Bron? She's . . ." Even as he's saying it, I see

Adam's eyes swing round to me, and my cheeks redden in some kind of Pavlovian response. He's doing the same kind of math as Duncan. "You and *Jem*?"

"No, of course not! Why would you even think that?"

"Lissa thought it," says Georgie, with, if anything, more anger. She looks down at the phone in her hand. "She said she did a bad thing—*fuck*."

"What?" I stare at Georgie. "Lissa said what? When?"

Georgie glances at her phone again, then sighs. The fight goes out of her slowly; it's like watching a balloon deflate in slow motion. "I got two emails from her, sent in the days before she—she died. I only just got them; they were caught in my work's ridiculous firewall. She was totally fed up with Jem flirting with all the female guests. And with you, Bron. Sorry."

"He didn't," I protest. My cheeks are reddening again. Duncan didn't even take a breath before assuming I was having an affair with Jem, and Adam was only a beat or two behind. "He doesn't."

"He did and he does," says Adam unequivocally. "It's like breathing to him."

"I . . ." I swallow. I can't immediately think of a comeback; I change tack. "But there's never been anything between us!" I rally hotly. "Ask Jem. We've never been even close to doing anything!"

I look at Duncan. His face is contemplative, but when he sees me looking, he holds up his hands. "I know," he says. "We all know that."

Georgie shrugs. "Sure, but it doesn't matter." Does Georgie believe me? I suppose she of all people has the most cause to doubt. "In her last email, Lissa said—well, she strongly suggested you and Jem were fucking. She was pretty upset about it."

I can't help it; I flinch. It's the word choice as much as anything. All week I've noticed how much unnecessary swearing everybody else indulges in. Maybe the change is in me, not them; maybe I used to be equally potty-mouthed. Probably it jars with me now because

I've got young kids and I hang around with other parents and nobody—nobody decent anyway—swears around young kids. But even so, I don't think I would ever have used the verb *to fuck* to describe whatever sexual relations I might have been having. I wouldn't even use it to describe what Graeme and I were doing. *To fuck* is . . . clinical. More than that: repercussion-free. No, we were absolutely not *fucking*. "When is this torrid little affair supposed to have started?"

"I don't know. Maybe when they stayed with you in Surrey? I'm not sure. She didn't sound . . ." She falters. "She sounded not herself."

"What do you mean?" asks Adam.

Georgie looks down at her phone. "Well, here's an extract." She starts to read, deliberately putting no emphasis into the words, which somehow makes them land with all the more weight. *"I swear he's needling me on purpose now. He's all: Bronwyn, your kids are so gorgeous! You seem like such a great mother! I really . . ."* She stumbles. "Sorry, her spelling has always been atrocious, it's throwing me off . . . *I really want to cum on your enormous freckled lactating tits! Okay, he didn't say that last one, but I know he's thinking it."* Georgie looks across at me. I must be scarlet from head to toe, and I'm fighting the urge to cross my arms across my chest. *Enormous freckled lactating tits.* It's about the only body part I possess that I've been consistently happy with, and in one fell swoop Lissa has made me feel like a cow with gigantic udders—an impressive feat from beyond the grave—despite the fact that I haven't been *lactating* for almost two years. "Um, sorry, Bron," Georgie says again, after a pause. "It says far more about her state of mind than it does about you. Or, um, your tits." I nod without speaking. I'm not sure I can speak. So Lissa was horribly jealous over the wrong husband. I feel simultaneously both utterly guilty and also one hundred percent unfairly persecuted. And also just plain hurt: to write that in an email—it's so *mean*. "No wonder it got caught in the firewall with that kind of language," she mutters. I put the heels of my hands up to my eye sockets.

"I personally have never considered ejaculating on your tits," I hear Duncan say, mock seriously. "I mean, your stomach, maybe; but not your tits." A short laugh escapes me, though my eyes are perilously damp behind my hands.

"I'm an ankle man, myself," Adam says. "Though I confess I do like a freckle or two. Are you freckled *all* over, Bron?" We're all laughing now; it's like a warm bath around me, easing the sting. I put a napkin up to my eyes and bend over, and Georgie slides over to put an arm round me, squeezing me around the waist. She doesn't let go until I have dried my eyes and sat upright again.

"So it was a *fuck-you* to both of you then, I guess," says Duncan, businesslike once again. "That at least makes some sense; two birds with one stone, et cetera." He looks across at me. "To be honest, if Lissa thought you were screwing Jem, I think you got off lightly, all things considered. And—not to speak ill of the dead or anything—she doesn't sound like she was at her most balanced when she wrote that."

"In retrospect, I'm not sure she's been balanced since Graeme died," Georgie says, in a thoughtful tone.

"Poor Jem," says Adam, with a grimace. "He'll put two and two together and realize that she could hardly have been expecting a happily-ever-after with him after stealing from the business."

Stealing. The word jars almost as much as *fucking* did. It *is* stealing, for all that the malicious intent makes it seem . . . other. Like a deadly sin—wrath, perhaps—something undesirable as a character trait, but not necessarily illegal. Duncan nods. "Yeah, I thought that, too. The money will get returned, though it might take a few weeks. Jimi said there's a financial crime team that will handle it."

"Oh, one more thing." I get out my phone. "This was written on my bathroom mirror. I found it the morning after the memorial." Adam peers over my shoulder, then takes a sharp breath in. He takes the phone off me and hands it to Georgie, whose puzzled expression turns to shock.

"Oh, Bron," she breathes, looking again at the screen. Then her eyes find mine. "But why didn't you say anything?"

I feel like I'm squirming. "I don't know, I—"

"I'm not certain that it was meant for Bron," interjects Duncan, thankfully moving the conversation off me as he explains his theory of the room keys. Georgie's laser gaze doesn't budge from me, though she doesn't say anything. Her eyes are very green against her newly tanned face.

"If not Bron, then Georgie, surely?" says Adam, his brow furrowed.

"I can't imagine who's behind it, if it really was meant for me." Georgie looks at the screen again, squinting as if she's trying to perceive a three-dimensional image within the stark two-dimensional words on the screen. They weren't two-dimensional on the mirror; the browny-pink lipstick jutted out in thick lumps and proud streaks.

"But wait, does that really make sense?" Adam asks, his brow furrowed. "We did just grab keys, but Georgie wasn't even here yet when the rest of us checked in; her room shouldn't have been among them." He's right. I feel my stomach drop as if I'm on a roller coaster. I hadn't thought it through; I was too busy clinging to the hope that that awful, brutal message was nothing to do with me. "Though I suppose the graffiti artist could just have made an honest mistake on the room number." He moves a hand, recognizing the incongruity of his language—*honest mistake*—but nobody bothers to respond. "If it was meant for Georgie, was it somehow connected to the attack on her?"

"When we spoke to Jimi, he thought that was just an opportunistic mugging. The people who come to this kind of place are often decked out in expensive jewelry, watches, et cetera," Duncan replies. "But that was before Cristina . . . I'm sure he's keeping an open mind."

"That'll be a first," mutters Georgie. Duncan glances at her but chooses not to engage.

"*It's your fault*. What do you suppose is the *it*?" says Adam, as if musing idly on the meaning of song lyrics.

"Lissa's death, surely," Georgie says. "What else could it be?"

"But how is that anyone's fault? You heard the chief; all the evidence suggests that was an accident," I protest. Or suicide. For the first time I truly consider that. Was Lissa so distressed by Jem's shenanigans, by him pushing her buttons, that she actually decided to end it all? She was always complicated: her highs were very high—usually fueled by alcohol or drugs—and her lows were crashingly low, but still . . .

"An accident," repeats Georgie. "So I keep hearing." She's silent for a minute or two. We all are, sitting slumped in our chairs like bored teenagers, completely sapped of all energy. "It doesn't make sense. None of this makes any sense," she mutters. Then she shakes her head and looks at me. "So that's everything? Nothing else to share?"

I nod. "That's everything. You?"

Her eyes shift to Adam, who is right beside me so I can't see his face, but whatever is on it causes her to falter. "Nope," Adam says for her. "That's everything,"

"Okay, then," says Duncan, pulling himself to his feet like it's an enormous effort. "I'll go and speak to Jem about the presidential villa."

So now we are four in a villa with exactly that number of bedrooms, although I suppose that's one too many under the circumstances. Or perhaps not—I can't quite tell: Adam and Georgie are certainly taking a very low-key approach. Maybe there's trouble in paradise, or maybe that's just how they are. Georgie was never really *with* anyone at university, so I can't exactly rely on past performance. Georgie fucked, though. Georgie certainly fucked.

The villa itself is extraordinarily impressive. Having lived in London, anything with space seems remarkably decadent, and this place is enormous. The open-plan living space has three huge sofas and a dining table comprised of a slab of repurposed driftwood that could seat twenty, and there's still enough space between the furniture for a game of indoor cricket. I take a quick glance at the kitchen, which Duncan told me knowledgeably is kitted out to professional chef standard (how can one tell?), and spot every appliance I can think of and a few more that baffle me as to their purpose. It should be fun, all being together: like a grown-up dormitory, except with separate bedrooms for each of us and luxury private bathrooms stocked with expensive toiletries. I would have loved it at university: zero chance of missing out if you're all under the same roof. But if there was ever any fun to be had on what was always a funeral trip, Cristina's death has ruled it out. Beautiful weather, perfect beaches and empty swimming pools be damned; we're all just counting the minutes until we can get on the plane home. Except Jem, I suppose. I can't think that there's any light at the end of the tunnel for him, not for a long, long time. Though I feel myself redden even thinking about him: how *embarrassing* that anyone would think I would be naive enough to be seduced by Jem. Though in truth, if I hadn't been hauled back to my senses through the interlude with Graeme, would I have been vulnerable to exactly that? Not that Jem would have tried anything. Or would he—was Lissa right? Did he have a soft spot for me?

Oh God. It's going to be impossible to speak to him without excruciating awkwardness from now on. On the bright side, though, there's just one more night to get through, and then tomorrow, we fly away and leave all of this behind us. I hope. Please let that be how this works out.

Nobody much feels like dinner after the dreadful events of today, so we go for a drink at the small bar right on the beach. I'm tired of the same company, the same faces; I'm missing Rob and the kids and *home,* but there's safety in numbers. There was no way I was going to decline and remain in the enormous villa all by myself; for all that we seem to have an answer on the money stuff, the message on the mirror still nags at me, and the idea that there might be a crazed psychotic gunman on the loose doesn't much help, either. We all shower and change as we would for any dinner on any of our holidays together, but it feels like going through the motions. I can't bring myself to care that my hair is frizzy; I don't even contemplate trying to style it. I reach for any old dress, then realize that all of mine emphasize my cleavage, and then spend five minutes dithering about that before I tell myself to stop being an idiot and put on a damn dress. When I finally emerge, I see that Georgie looks like she's suffering from a similar level of malaise: she has scraped her shower-wet hair back into a messy bun and applied the barest minimum of makeup, though on her the effect reads like an off-duty ballerina. She seems uncharacteristically absentminded, too: she has a pull buoy in her hand, presumably borrowed from Jem, and I swear she'd have brought it to the bar if I hadn't pointed it out.

There isn't a bartender when we get there; Adam hops nimbly over the counter and bows to the rest of us, perched on the barstools. "Good evening, ladies, sir; I hope you're enjoying your stay at our fine resort," he says drolly. "What can I get you?" Georgie only wants sparkling water, and I'm after a simple white wine, but Duncan throws out the challenge of a dirty martini, which Adam sets about providing with a look of relish.

"You know, Dunc, I had no idea you owned forty-nine percent of this place," Adam comments, as he amasses the right glasses.

Duncan ducks his head, mildly embarrassed. "Don't shout about it," he says awkwardly. "Not even to Steve; I'd rather the staff just thought I was a bog-standard guest. I wouldn't want to muddy Jem's authority."

"I guess you really believed in the business model," Georgie says, half teasing and half thoughtful.

"Actually, I really did. And I still do; this is just a temporary setback. Luxury eco is the future for the hotel business, in my opinion, and Jem really knows what he's doing. He's the majority shareholder, I might as well be a silent partner. Although . . ." He stops, as if struck by something.

"What?" I ask. "Oh, thanks, Adam." I take the white wine he's holding out.

"Well, I was just thinking. There's a clause in the shareholders' agreement . . ." His mind is still ticking over; he's muttering as if speaking just to himself. "Technically it won't apply if nobody formally charges Lissa over the fraud, which I suppose they won't given the circumstances . . ."

"What?" I repeat.

He glances across at me. "Oh. It's something I insisted on." He sounds almost shamefaced. "It's just—well, I insist on it in all our private equity deals. If any partner commits fraud, then their shares are automatically offered to the other partners on a pro rata basis, for a dollar each."

I do the math. "So technically you ought to own roughly seven twelfths now. *You* ought to be the majority shareholder." I see Adam and Georgie exchange another of those glances.

Duncan looks uncomfortable. "Yes, but I'd never enforce it." He shrugs. "I can't anyway. They won't charge Lissa." But I can still see him thinking. "They won't charge Lissa," he mutters again.

"Evening, folks," calls a voice. I look up to see Steve ambling toward us. "Oh dear, we can't have the guests serving themselves. Let me take over," he says.

"Don't you dare; I'm having far too much fun," says Adam. It's true: he's almost smiling.

"Are you okay?" Georgie asks Steve gently.

He runs a hand over his face. "No," he admits. "It's a shock. When we got her in the boat . . ." He stops, his mouth working soundlessly for a second. Georgie is closest to him; she places a hand on his arm, and he goes on. "I couldn't—I couldn't bear to be on my own, to be honest. I'm not intruding, am I?"

"Not in the least," she assures him, to murmured assent.

"Lager?" Adam suggests.

"Thanks. No need for a glass."

Adam pops the cap on a bottle and passes it across the counter to Steve, then turns to Duncan. "Your drink, sir," he says, proffering the glass, complete with olive on a toothpick, with a bow. He's even laid out a coaster for it. "Are you planning to leave soon?" he says to Steve.

Steve takes a swallow of his beer and shakes his head. "I'll stay and help Jem shut up shop." How does one shut down a hotel? Presumably all the linens and movable equipment will have to go into storage; it must be a massive job. "Nothing better to do anyway."

"You're a good man," says Duncan earnestly.

"Well, I don't know about that." Steve reddens and drops his head as if physically shouldering away the compliment. "It's not entirely altruistic. Jem will reopen; I'm sure of it. And I like it here, today notwithstanding." He grimaces sharply. "I'll want my job back when he docs."

"I'll drink to that," says Duncan. He takes a suspicious sip and then raises the glass appreciatively to Adam. "Good martini. If the bike shop business doesn't work out, I think you've got an alternative career in tending bar."

"How did Jem's staff pep talk go?" Adam asks Steve. "That was before everyone heard about Cristina, right?"

"He gave it a good crack, but . . ." He shrugs. "People are scared;

they have families to feed. There's a hotel on the other side of the is-land that's hiring, and I heard the fish factory has jobs going, so—"

"There's a boat coming in," Georgie says suddenly. She's swiveled on her barstool so that her back is to the counter, one elbow behind her resting on its surface. "Look." She's pointing with her other arm toward the closest of the two wooden jetties that jut out into Horse-shoe Bay. Her eyesight must be excellent; I can't see anything myself, though I can just make out the faint strokes of an engine.

"There shouldn't be anything coming in without permission." Steve is frowning as he stands up to get a better look. Georgie has already scrambled down from her seat and is walking toward the wa-ter's edge. "Where's her bloody lights? It's ridiculous coming in dark like that." He turns and places his beer on the bar. "I'd better go see what's going on." He leaves, but he doesn't follow Georgie; instead he jogs off down the path, surprisingly light on his toes for such a big man. It's a longer route, but paved—he'll beat Georgie there; she's tracking along the shoreline through the sand, but at a walking pace. I slide off my barstool, too, and hurry to catch up. I can see glints of reflected light off the boat—which is now perhaps only sixty meters away from Georgie and me, and much closer than that to the jetty—enough to make out its shape: the familiar long-nosed shape of all the local boats, but even so, something about it nags at me. It's headed directly for the jetty at a low speed, with minimum noise and wake, but suddenly, as Steve reaches the pool of light from the jetty lamps, there's an indistinct shout. The engine revs up, and the boat wheels round in a flurry of spray and white water and noise, just dipping into the arc of the jetty light as it turns. I see that its hull is dirty blue.

I clutch Georgie's arm. "It's the same one."

"What?" She glances at me, then back at the receding boat, which has already put tens of meters of distance between us, and then back to me again. "Same what?"

"That's the boat that almost ran me over."

"No, it can't be," she murmurs, almost desperately. Then, louder more urgently: "You're sure? It's pretty dark. You couldn't have got more than a glimpse of it."

I feel my teeth catching my lip. "I know." I try to analyze, to weigh and measure. There must be hundreds of boats of that particular style and shape just in the local area. Presumably blue is a fairly common hull color. But still, that particular blue, with exactly that level of shabbiness to the boat . . . "I *feel* sure, but you're right, there's no way I ought to be." But I am sure.

"It was going to dock until the driver saw Steve," she says. I'm not sure if she's talking to me or herself. Steve is coming over to us. "Did you recognize the driver?" she calls to him. "Or the other person?"

"Were there two on it?" he asks. "I just saw the driver."

"I think there were two," she says.

I shrug. "I didn't see."

"Anyway, did you recognize the driver, Steve?" she presses.

"Sort of. I could swear I've seen him before somewhere." He's silent for a moment, then shakes his head in frustration. "Nope. It'll come to me. I'm sure I know him from somewhere."

"He certainly knew you, or at least knew he shouldn't have been there," I say.

"Yeah. I'd better call Jem and have him find some extra security. Until this place is properly closed down, it's going to be a looter's paradise." He turns for the bar, but Georgie doesn't follow. There isn't enough light for me to see her face properly, but I can see that her eyes are still searching out to sea, as if she's tracing the wake of the speeding boat, though there's nothing to see out there now except blackness. Then suddenly she turns her head to me. "I'm sorry, Bron," she says urgently. I can feel her hand gripping my forearm. "If I'd been around more, if I'd been there for her, I could have—I could have . . ." She trails off. Her eyes are gleaming in the dark. Are they full of tears?

What is she talking about? "Don't be silly. None of this is your fault." I twist my forearm, palm upward, and grip her back. She shakes her head, not speaking. "Georgie. Do you mean Lissa? Really. It's not your fault. If anything, it's Jem's—I mean, what was he doing antagonizing her like that?"

"I know, but I should have been there for her. I had a responsibility," she says, half wildly. This isn't like Georgie. She's starting to scare me.

"Rubbish. Lissa was a grown-up. She made her own choices." I try to inject some humor. "If anything, blame the parents."

"Oh, believe me, I blame them, too."

She hasn't laughed, like I thought she would; instead the bitterness in her voice could sear through steel. I try again, but I can't think of different words to say. "Georgie, really, none of this is your fault. She was a grown-up. She made her own choices."

"Yes. I suppose." She takes a deep breath. "It doesn't feel that way, but yes. Of course you're right." I can feel her trying to quell her agitation. I don't quite understand why it's erupted now. "Except for the grown-up part," she adds wryly, sounding far more like herself. "She wasn't ever that."

I huff out a small laugh, though I know it's too soon for both of us: every memory has a sting. "Yeah, except for that part."

HOW TO KILL YOUR BEST FRIEND

Method 6: Hit-and-run

It has some merit, I suppose. One could rent a car—something ten a penny, your average small, ubiquitous car, the sort of thing that umpteen rental companies rent out by the dozen—and obscure the number plates, and wear a disguise. You'd have to know where she'd be, though. You'd have to know you wouldn't cause any hurt or injury to anyone else. It's really just as bad as the cliff thing: what are the chances that she'll be walking alone down a quiet road, at precisely the time that I need her to be? It's too vanishingly slim. And even if, by some remarkable coincidence, there was indeed an opportunity, you couldn't be sure it would be one hundred percent effective. What if she simply ended up paralyzed? Or merely scratched? It's all or nothing. It's always been all or nothing.

SIXTEEN

GEORGIE

Fuck. Fuck fuck fuckity fuck.

I got this wrong. I got this so very wrong—how could I have been so stupid? I was too fixed on what I thought I knew; I was too wedded to the things that I believed to be true. I look at my watch. Less than twenty hours until we all get on a plane. Less than sixteen before we leave the resort.

Strategy. Is there an immediate danger? I can't tell. It doesn't quite all hang together yet. It's like watching an artist in the moments before the crucial brushstroke is applied, the one that makes sense of all that came before, the one that causes your brain to say, *Aha, I know what it is now.* I can't see what's to come, only what has been. The boat is the problem. Without having seen it, I could believe it was all over. That we could get on a plane and all would be fine. But I have seen it, and it means something, only I can't quite make it fit.

But is there an immediate danger? Probably, if I make it clear what I know. Is that what happened to Cristina? Did she suspect something? Did she let that slip to the wrong person?

Strategy, though. I need strategy. Safety in numbers? It's what

Duncan has suggested after all. Does he know more than I think? Or am I second-guessing everyone now? Duncan, Bron, Adam, Jem, even Steve. I should tell someone, surely. But who?

Sixteen hours. Fuck.

"We should talk," Adam says mildly. Duncan, Steve and Bron are playing cards at one of the tables that should be filled with suntanned hotel guests but isn't. I declined the invitation to play; I wouldn't be able to concentrate, and it would be noticed, since I'm the acknowledged card sharp of the group. So instead Adam and I are both still at the bar, sitting side by side, our legs almost but not quite touching, while Jack Johnson croons melodiously in the background (Adam found the sound system). His body language is loose and careless— he has his elbows on the counter, and he's holding a bottle of beer lightly between finger and thumb, as if it's neither here nor there to him as to whether he drinks it or not—but there's a thrum of tension in the gaze that rests on me.

I want to say: *Really? Now? Aren't there more important things to worry about?* But, of course, he doesn't know that; he doesn't know that I'm counting off every second, every minute until we get away from here safely. So instead I say, "What do you want to talk about?" It's a genuine question; I'm not being difficult. Or at least, I'm not trying to be difficult, despite the instinct to buck and kick— not only against the timing but also against the statement: nothing good in the world ever started with the words *We should talk.* But this is Adam: in the interest of future friendship, or at the very least, future civilized conversation, I should honor whatever pathway he's alighted on to put distance between us.

"A few things. But first, I wanted to say sorry."

I look at him, but I can't hold his gaze. Instead I swivel on my seat to look out to the ocean that I can't see. There can't be much moonlight, or my night vision has been destroyed by the lights of the bar: I can't even pick out where the waves are breaking, or any difference between sky and ocean. I wonder if the boat is still out there: circling, waiting. "What for?"

"How about you tell me what you want me to be sorry for, and we'll start from there?" he says gravely, but somehow I know he's both teasing me and mocking himself. I wasn't expecting that. Unexpectedly, I feel the corners of my mouth twitching upward.

"Starter for ten, then." I keep the tone light, mild; I keep my eyes on the invisible ocean with the possibly invisible boat. "You said I'm the most fucked-up person you know."

"Yeah. Um. Sorry. Though in my defense, I didn't say it was a *bad* thing."

My gaze jumps to his face, and then just as quickly away again. "How could it be a *good* thing?"

"Because . . . because it's just a thing. Like green eyes. Or blond hair. It's just one of many things about you."

"That I'm fucked-up?" I want to be cross, I want to work up a good head of steam, but it's hard in the face of this, this—whatever this is. I don't have the words to describe it. Nothing about this conversation is going the way I expected from *We should talk.*

"Totally fucked-up. Also smart and funny and sexy as hell, but yeah, totally fucked-up. And I was in active combat in the army; I know a lot of screwed-up people. Believe me, I know how to recognize it. I had counseling. I mean, I'm practically an expert."

I'm laughing out loud now, and when I turn to look at him, I see tiny crow's-feet are crinkling at the corners of his eyes and his lips are curling up. "Would you recommend it?" I ask, when I've stopped laughing.

"What?"

"Counseling. Lissa was very dismissive of it. Though to be fair, that may have been because she hadn't found the right therapist. It's not like there's an enormous pool of them here." I try not to look at my watch, I try not to count the minutes that are passing, but I can't help looking out toward the sea again, still wondering about the boat. It was coming in to meet someone, surely. Or to drop someone off.

"You've never tried it?" I shake my head. "I suppose it depends on who you see, but I've had a good experience with it." He pauses and takes a swig of the beer. "The way I think about it, it's a method of getting an objective look at what pushes your buttons. It's up to you what you do with that information afterward." He moves as if to take another swallow of beer but pauses with the bottle near his lips. "You really stopped drinking without counseling?" I nod. "How?"

"I moved to the States."

He makes the connection frighteningly fast. "Because it took you away from the people you drank with. It took you away from Lissa."

I don't even need to nod, because he knows it's true. It was a good career move for me—it would probably have taken me a couple more years to make partner without it—but that wasn't why I leaped at the opportunity. "Everyone drank at uni; everyone drank to excess. We weren't so different to everyone else—except I always knew we were, really. I could never see the point of just one glass of wine; I still can't. For me, the goal was always complete annihilation; Lissa was like that, too—you know that." I take a sip of my sparkling water. "I was in a pretty crappy headspace when I got to uni. Lissa and me—it was like we saved each other; I can't explain it any other way." *Complete unconditional love.* "Only, everyone else calmed down after they left uni, and we didn't. I started to feel like . . ."

"Like the cure was going to kill you."

"Something like that." *And that unconditional love is dangerous. There should be limits and boundaries. I did betray her, but not how she thinks. I betrayed her twice: first, by not being strong enough to stop her in her mad schemes; she relied on me for that, and I couldn't always deliver. And second, by leaving her.* I yield: I look at my watch. Almost fifteen hours now. Surely if I can share all of this with Adam, I can share my suspicions? I take a deep breath, but suddenly he says: "If you thought that Lissa killed Graeme, why didn't you go to the police?"

"I couldn't do that. Not without being sure." *If I had been sure, what would I have done then?* I look across: he's taking a swallow of beer. There's that vulnerable triangle on show at the base of his throat again. "You could have gone to the police yourself."

"I know." He stops, beer midway to his mouth, thinking. "That's fair. But I couldn't put a motive to it, not one that would stack up for the police. They were fighting a lot, I know, but that's not exactly con- clusive." The bottle of beer travels down rather than up, unsipped. He looks at me. "Did you have something more?" I shake my head. It's true: I didn't. I'm certain Lissa didn't know about Bron. And it's clear Adam doesn't know, either. He goes on: "I mean, if Graeme was hav- ing an affair or something, I would have had something to hang it on, but . . ." *I can't spill Bron's secrets. I made a promise.* I look away, and then I wonder if that's too telling, and make myself look across at him. He lifts the beer to his mouth and actually swallows this time, his eyes looking into the past and taking absolutely no notice of me.

I rest my eyes on him, once again weighing whether I should tell him what I know. I'm so *exhausted* by the secrets. But there's still that odd thrum of tension that makes my stomach tighten in dread; a dif- ferent kind of dread to that which is already there. "There's some- thing else you wanted to talk about," I say.

"Yes."

I look across to the left, to the pool of light from the lamps on the jetty on that side of the bay. "Out with it, then."

I hear him sigh; I hear the clunk of the bottle as he places it on the bar. "Her email," he says quietly. I glance across, taken by surprise. "You lied about what was in it. I've been trying to work out why." I freeze. Every single muscle in my body has instantly clenched tight.

"You made out like it was all about her suspicions of Bron and Jem, but it really wasn't. It was about something else entirely."

Slowly my muscles are unclenching. "How exactly do you know what was in her email?"

"I read it on your phone when you went to the loo," he says bluntly. I stare at him blankly. "Which is an unforgivable invasion of privacy, I know." There's a burst of laughter from the table; I glance across to see Steve tossing his cards down in mock disgust.

"You read . . . But—my phone locks automatically. It has facial recognition."

"Yeah, but your PIN code for when that doesn't work is really obvious. Two, five, eight, zero: straight down the middle, all the digits. I've seen you do it a hundred times."

"That is . . ." I really can't find the words. I'm also trying to work it through. If he's read the email, what does he really know? What was implied and what was actually in black and white?

"Unacceptable. Unforgivable. I know." I risk a glance at his face. He's utterly impassive.

"You don't sound sorry for *that*," I say tartly.

"I'm not, really. I thought you weren't being entirely truthful. I needed to know. I'm not proud of it, but I'm not sorry. Now I want to know why you were lying."

It's such a straightforward delivery: no-nonsense, direct, unapologetic. I'm more confused than upset. "How on earth do you think I can ever trust you?"

"Come on, Georgie." He sounds weary. "You already don't trust me. Or anyone else. Otherwise you wouldn't have lied."

"Well, with that kind of circular logic you can really justify anything." My fingers are kneading my temples, my eyes now on my knees as I perch on this ridiculously uncomfortable barstool.

"And what's your logic? You don't trust anyone so you can lie to everyone?"

"Actually, no." I keep staring at my knees, my fingers working furiously at my temples. "I wasn't lying." Not exactly. "I was just trying to keep a promise."

This, at least, startles him. "A promise? To who? To Lissa?"

"No. To Bron."

"Bron? But that makes no sense."

I shake my head. "Just—okay, stop. It doesn't matter. That's not what's important right now." I glance at the card players again.

Adam follows my gaze. "We can go for a walk," he suggests.

I shake my head minutely. "We shouldn't be apart from the others. It isn't safe."

"Isn't safe? Because of what happened to you and Cristina?" He looks at me for a beat. "No, that's not it. What's going on here, Georgie? What do you know?"

I should think this through, I should strategize, I should play every scenario through in my head before I say a single thing . . . but I'm just too *tired*. Bron would be able to do it—more than that, Bron would be incapable of *not* doing it—but I'm not Bron. I start speaking almost without deciding to. "I don't know what I know. I went back to Jem's, after I picked up my stuff to move into the presidential villa. I wanted to get the pull buoy, so I wouldn't have to disturb him by picking it up if I decide to swim early tomorrow." I glance at the card players. Duncan is smirking about something, and Bron is half groaning, half laughing. The table is now littered with empty beer bottles. I wonder where Jem is. Was the boat meant to meet Jem? Does it mean anything that Jem is so tight with Jimi? Adam waits for me to continue, his face watchful, but one leg, hitched up on the bar of the stool, is jiggling to a frenzied beat. "I saw . . ." I take a deep breath. I see it again: my hand opening the louvered door. The cupboard has one large space up to around waist height, in which boogie boards are stacked, then several shelves above which apparently have no order to them. I see my hand ferreting through the jumble of snorkeling masks and flippers and swim floats and swim paddles and swimsuits and goggles and caps and trunks; through all the detritus of water-related paraphernalia, looking for the distinctive blue-and-white or yellow-and-black stripes of a pull buoy. "I saw her red TYR swimsuit." I almost miss it: it's slipped down the back of the lowest shelf, and is obscured by the boogie boards below, but the fire-engine red catches my eye. "It's in Jem's pool cupboard. Right at the back, behind a load of other stuff." I glance at him, trying to keep my own agitation under wraps. It's hard not to whisper; it's hard to trust that the music will cover my words if spoken at a normal volume. "Don't you see? She couldn't have been pulled from the ocean wearing it. I doubt she was in the ocean at all. He must have paid the fisherman to say that. He—"

"He. Jem?"

I nod jerkily.

"Jem." He looks at me seriously. "She could have had more than one *Baywatch*-red TYR swimsuit."

I shake my head definitively. "No. She only had one, and she couldn't have got a second. Bron and I really liked it; we looked to see if we could get one ourselves, but they'd discontinued that style. And there hasn't been anything similar available since from TYR. All three of us have been on the lookout; we've literally had WhatsApp chats on it."

"Not entirely conclusive, but okay, I'll buy it." He's scanning the area whilst endeavoring to look calm. "So, what do you think happened?"

I shake my head. "I can't quite string it together." *If only I'd made her confide in me; I could have talked her out of whatever madness pushed Jem along this path. If only I'd been there for her.* "Maybe he figured out she was planning to leave him."

"And what? Killed her? That's an extreme reaction to the threat of divorce."

"Or maybe he thought she was going to kill him."

"If she'd been going to kill him, he'd be dead." He delivers this in such a matter-of-fact manner that I choke back a half-hysterical laugh. "Anyway, why would he think she was going to kill him?"

"Because . . ." I stop. Why would he?

Adam is nodding. "Exactly. How would he know about her past vendettas?" I remember what Adam said the other day about Graeme: *He wasn't under any illusions about her. He just loved her anyway. Like you did.* My throat is hot and closed tight. I look out into the darkness and tell myself I'm tracing the horizon line, even though I can't see it. *I should have been here. If I'd just been here . . .* "I'm sure Jem knew nothing. Just look at his reaction to that story with the knife. He was drunkenly mouthing off about it the other day; he thinks you made it up."

"No, he doesn't." I hear the caustic note in my voice. "He's trying to convince himself I made it up, but deep down he doesn't believe that." Adam tips his head briefly in silent agreement. "But you're right, he had no reason to feel in danger. An argument, then? A fight with a tragic accident?"

"Maybe. And then what? How would he dispose of the body?" He thinks for a minute and then answers his own question. "Off the side of a boat in deep water, with weights attached. That's what anybody round here would do."

"So she'd have ended up in the water anyway, but probably nowhere near where the search had been taking place." And not wearing a red swimsuit. She's spinning gently underwater again, her hair swirling around her, obscuring her face. But this time she's naked and vertical, held in place by a rope bound around her ankles that snakes down to a rock on the seabed, with her arms half raised, as if she's about to start conducting an orchestra.

"But, remember: someone saw her swimming," Adam says. "Though I suppose she could have, and then she returned. Or maybe he was paid to say that, too . . . We'd have to question him, and the fisherman. And there's no way that I can think of to do that without going through Jimi."

"I know. And Jimi is so close to Jem, I can't imagine that he'd listen to us."

"Steve?" Adam suggests.

I shake my head. "He's loyal to Jem. And he wants his job back. He won't go out on a limb."

"The blue boat from this evening. You think it was coming to meet Jem?"

"Maybe that's the fisherman's boat. Or maybe it has absolutely nothing to do with anything." Only I don't believe that; not with how the driver spun away from Steve. It fits in somehow; I just don't understand how yet. I glance at the ocean. If the boat is out there, circling, I wouldn't hear it above the music.

We sit quietly for a moment. "Follow the money," I murmur. Adam looks at me. "You know, it's so weird what Bron said about Graeme's house. I distinctly remember him saying that the mortgage on it was next to nothing."

"Yes, that's right: he inherited some money when his great-aunt died, and paid almost all of it down."

"So it doesn't seem to make sense that Lissa didn't have enough of her own money to invest fifty-fifty with Jem. Unless she didn't want to—maybe she was more cautious on the business plan than I thought."

Adam shakes his head. "No, I spoke to Duncan about that. He was absolutely sure she couldn't afford it, and Jem thinks the only thing in Lissa's estate is her share of the hotel."

"That can't be true." Could she have spent it? Thousands, certainly; maybe even hundreds of thousands—but not millions, surely? Not without people noticing. "But regardless, the only thing Jem really wants is control of his own hotel. Which he had either way, whether she was alive or dead."

"Probably not if they divorced," Adam reasons. "Duncan and Lissa could have ganged up against him."

"Yes, I suppose. If he thought she was going to divorce him, killing her would have guaranteed himself control." Killing her. We're talking about this as one might discuss whether to get take-out for dinner. I glance at the ocean again. Perhaps the boat is out there, idling above the waves, whilst beneath it the long, dark shape of the serpent ripples silently through the depths. "Assuming he didn't get caught."

"True, but if he did, what would happen?" His brow furrows. "I'm sure the law says you can't profit from your own crime. Would her share go to her parents instead, then?"

"I suppose. But I expect Duncan would buy them out. I can't imagine that they would want anything to do with this place."

"So Duncan would benefit more than Jem in that scenario."

"Yes. But not intentionally, right?"

Adam shrugs. "Once you suspect one of us, you have to suspect all of us," he says mildly.

I close my eyes briefly. He's right. It's like a poison—no, a virus with no cure, spreading and infecting all it touches. *We can't go on together with suspicious minds* . . . Some more noise erupts from the card table. Bron's smile is wide and loose; she's several glasses of wine down and it shows. Steve is getting up from the table and heading our way. "Another beer?" asks Adam, climbing down from his stool and moving behind the bar.

"Please. And one for Duncan. Excellent service here," he says jocularly.

"What are you playing?" I ask, though I have absolutely no interest.

"Shithead. Though I always knew it by the much less offensive name of Threes. Duncan is cleaning up."

"Only because Georgie isn't playing," Adam says, passing across two beers.

Steve takes a drink from one of the bottles. "Is your flight tomorrow morning?"

"No, midafternoon," I say.

"You'll want to keep an eye on the weather. There's a cyclone that might or might not head this way. Even if we just get the tail, those things can really do some damage. It might be worth heading to the airport pretty early; the last ten kilometers of the road down to this place can suffer landslides if the rain is really heavy."

"Good advice; we'll keep an eye on it." Adam immediately starts tapping on his phone, searching for a weather website. I watch Steve make his way back to Bron and Duncan. They have their heads close together, but as Steve approaches, they break apart in what looks like a transparent change of subject.

"Shall I try and figure out the coffee maker?" Adam suggests eventually.

"Please." I turn to face him as he studies the complicated silver machine, but I have to adjust to be side-on; I can't turn my back on the sea, on the double threat it represents. So I sit awkwardly, half looking out and half studying Adam. It's interesting to watch him ponder a problem. He's like Bron in a way: fiercely analytical. He likes to gather the facts; I'd bet he had the most detailed business plan ever seen before he embarked on his bike shop business. He starts to amass what he has deduced he needs, and I glance idly at my phone, wondering if I ought to change the PIN code now. I'll only forget the new one, but I probably should on principle . . .

Adam is flattening off the coffee grounds in the portafilter. "You know, the emails." I look at him inquiringly. "How can we be sure they were from Lissa? You said yourself that she sounded . . . off. Not

her normal self. And, not to throw myself straight back in the dog-
house or anything, but it was a cinch for me to break into *your* email
account, and we're not even married . . ."

"Yes." I don't even bother trying to pretend I'm still cross at his fla-
grant breach of privacy. I stare at him, thinking. Then I grab my phone
and unlock it, scrolling quickly to the email from georgieayers698@
gmail.com. He twists the portafilter into the machine as if he's been
a barista all his life, sets it running, then comes to look over my shoulder. I turn my head to look at him archly.

"Oh, come on," he says, off my look. "It's not like I haven't seen it
already."

I shake my head disapprovingly, but I don't hide my screen from
him. We both start to read.

Subject: Wish you were here

Seriously, honey, you should be here. You were meant to be
here. I need you to keep me in check. Actually, I needed you
a while ago. I've not been entirely honest in my emails; I
thought I could guilt you into coming out here. Alas, no. But
this one is the unadulterated truth. I've done a bad thing and
I'm not sorry. I can't tell you what it is right now, but you'll
find out anyway.

The therapist I was seeing, the one I told you about with the
ridiculous skirt suits that are too small for her and shoes that
are too big for her (like I've said before, you can't be choosy
about your therapists on an island in the middle of nowhere)
thinks I should seek forgiveness for past transgressions. (I've
been amusing myself by recounting some of my exploits.
She pretends not to be horrified, but she is.) Apparently,
seeking forgiveness is an important step in moving forward,

in starting anew. A clean slate and all that. I think of it more like a level playing field. Mine's not level, but we differ substantially, her and I, in our opinion on the direction of the slant. I'm owed, and I've never been one for forgiveness.

I miss you. I know I shut you out after Graeme died, so you could say it's my own fault, but I miss you. Graeme died. It's still hard to write that, to think that, to live with that. And you think I killed him—I know you do, no matter what you say or have said. I was never upset that you thought that. I could have, under certain circumstances. We both know that. I'm upset because of why you thought that. You took a side, and it wasn't mine. That's betrayal. I've tried so hard to cast it in another light, but I can't. I lost you at the same time as I lost Graeme. I just didn't realize it. It's ironic actually; it was the fact that you questioned me, that you thought I might have done it, that led me to hunt for clues. I'm not sure I would ever have found out if not for that. Would I have been happier not knowing? Maybe. But maybe not. I'd have been blaming myself, and now I know who I should be blaming.

There are countless versions of this email that I've drafted and deleted, most of them full of tirades of vitriol against Bron and Jem. (I swear he's needling me on purpose now. He's all: Bronwyn, your kids are so gorgeous! You seem like such a great mother! I really want to cum on your enormous freckled lactating tits! Okay, he didn't say that last one, but I know he's thinking it. To hear him tell it, she's a "voluptuous Titian painting" rather than a fucking Picasso.) But all of that is just background noise for the purpose of this particular email. This is about your betrayal.

So. I've done something. It's taken a long time to put it all in place. You'll find out soon enough what it is. I really wish you had been here to stop me, but also, I really don't. It's probably better this way. My jellyfish therapist (no brains, no spine) thinks I need to move on, which is the one point we actually agree on, but I can't do that until everything has been leveled off. When the dust has settled I can start again. You won't be part of my new life. I love you, you know I love you, but I can't forgive.

I expect you'll call as soon as you get this. Don't bother. I won't answer.

The impact is no less significant for this being a second read. If anything, it's greater; the blows have the time to properly land. I finish a few seconds ahead of Adam. I can feel him looking at me when he's done. "Are you okay?"

"No."

He absorbs that. "What do you think?"

"It's definitely her. And she doesn't sound in the slightest like someone who's planning to either kill herself or go out swimming somewhere known to be highly dangerous in the dead of night."

"Yeah." A beat passes. "Would you have called her if you'd got it when she sent it?"

"Yes." I look at the ocean again. It makes no sense to rage at an overenthusiastic email firewall, but nonetheless I'm filled with it. If only. If only the email had got to me. If only I'd been able to call her. "She'd have picked up. I think. I think she'd have picked up."

I can feel him nodding. "Yes. She says otherwise, but I'm sure deep down she wanted you to stop her, whatever it was she had planned." He pauses. "I guess Jem stopped her instead. Maybe Cristina figured it out. Maybe he . . ." *Shot her.* He doesn't say the words. He doesn't have to.

"What do we do now?" I thought I would feel better, sharing this with someone—with Adam—but I don't. I can no longer kid myself that I've simply got myself worked up inside my own head, that's there's a reasonable explanation just waiting to be heard. The reasonable explanation is that my best friend's husband is a killer.

He sighs. "I don't know. I suppose we ought to get proof on the swimsuit."

"I should have taken a photo. I can't think why I didn't." *Because it was such a shock. Because the instant I saw it I wanted to run and not ever stop running, bad knee be damned.* "I can do that when I return the pull buoy."

"The safest thing would be to send the photo to Jimi when we're at the airport."

"Yes." I look at my watch. Less than fifteen hours.

I can feel him looking at me again. "Why did she think you betrayed her?" he asks diffidently.

I want to tell him, I really do. Wouldn't it be so much simpler to open myself up and let everything blow out of me, like dust in the wind? *But I promised.* I shake my head. "Not my secret to tell."

SEVENTEEN

BRONWYN

My wineglass is empty. It's possible I've drunk too much again—probable, even—but I'm actually *having fun,* for what feels like the first time since I got here. Steve is making a valiant effort to drink away the truly awful day he's had, and Jem hasn't joined us, for which I'm eternally grateful—that would have been a buzzkill, if ever there was one. Quite apart from the fact that he would have been—understandably—reeling from the shock of Cristina's death, I'd have been supremely self-conscious and awkward around him, wondering if the others were analyzing my every word and gesture. And they would have been; at least, Adam and Georgie would have been, for sure. They're up at the bar now, their heads together in that way they have that seems to shout that the rest of the world isn't welcome. Georgie and Lissa had that, too. When they were together, you knew that everyone else was just the sideshow, in their opinion. In everybody's opinion, actually. You never quite knew what might happen when you were around them; it felt wild and reckless to even be along for the ride.

Ooh, I'm about to win. "And I'm out," I say, dramatically laying down my ace to groans from Steve and Duncan. "I'm going to get another glass whilst you two battle it out for second place." I put my right hand up to my forehead in the shape of an L. "Losers," I sing-song. "How many have you actually won, Steve?"

Steve shakes his head at me, smiling ruefully. "It's rude to mock the afflicted. But can you grab us two more beers whilst you're there, please?"

"Sure." I'm a little unsteady on my feet as I head toward Adam and Georgie at the bar, but I'm not sure anyone would notice. Georgie smiles at me as I approach. I slip my arm round her waist. She's so slim, Georgie, but there's nothing insubstantial about her. She's like rope.

"Come and play, Georgie Porgie," I wheedle, whilst nodding to Adam, who has already retrieved the wine from the fridge to fill up my glass. I tug at her gently, but she resists, holding on to both the barstool and the counter, and shaking her head.

"Sorry. I can't quite get into the frame of mind today."

"Beers for the boys, too?" Adam interjects.

"Yes, please." I take Georgie's hand off the counter and use it to try to pull her off the barstool. "Please come. You'll get into the frame of mind; you just need more to drink. What are you having?"

"Sparkling water."

"That's your problem. Come on, have a glass of wine. You used to be *fun*, you know, before you gave up drinking." Her eyes leap to my face, shocked; shocked, and something else: hurt. Adam is suddenly still, on the other side of the bar, in a way that seems almost menac-ing. I'm acutely aware that I've crossed a line. "I—I'm sorry, I—"

"Here are the beers," says Adam evenly. His face is implacable, as it always is, but his eyes are flint. He's holding the bottles out to me. I want to keep apologizing, but it's clear he won't brook it. After a second I take the bottles, awkwardly in one hand, so that my other can scoop up the glass of wine. I turn and head back to the card table, feeling their eyes upon me, and their silence, too: they won't speak whilst I'm in earshot.

"Thanks," says Duncan, reaching out to take the two beers off me. Then he glances at me again. "You okay?"

"Yes," I say brightly, settling back down at the table. Duncan starts to deal, and I take a sip of my wine, glancing sideways toward the bar. Their heads are together again, and Adam's forearm is stretched across the bar, the back of one finger gently stroking down her arm. *He's timed it to perfection,* I think. There wouldn't have been space for him if Lissa was still alive.

"Up we go," says Duncan. We're back at *the ranch,* as Duncan has taken to calling the presidential villa, in a nasal imitation of an American accent. He has an arm around me, and I am dependent on it to an embarrassing degree as we navigate the steps to the front door. It's a big door; heavy, wooden and almost twice the width of a normal front door in the UK. I like it.

"You should live here, you know," I tell Duncan. "You'd have no trouble getting the double buggy through this door."

"One day. Right now the commute would be a killer."

"You practically run the company. You can work from anywhere." I slither from his support onto the white sofa and fight not to close my eyes. I can't imagine ever having a white sofa. The impracticality of it is jaw-dropping.

"I actually do run the company." Did I know that already, or did he get promoted recently? "And to run it, you need to be on the ground. Water?" He doesn't wait for me to reply; he starts pouring from one of the courtesy bottles that have been left out.

Georgie and Adam are just behind us. "The weather report is looking worse," says Adam to nobody in particular. "I checked the British Airways' site, and they haven't put up any kind of notice about it, though." *Of course you did*, I think. *Be prepared: isn't that what they teach you in the army?*

The sofa, for all that it's white, is very comfortable. I've slid down on it, and my eyes are starting to close. Suddenly I feel a gentle tapping on my head. "You'll feel much better if you sleep in your own bed," Duncan is saying.

For a moment I consider staying where I am, but I know he's right. I groan and lever myself upright. "Here," he says, offering a glass. "Best get some water down you." I drink it all obediently, and then he takes it off me and refills it whilst I struggle to my feet.

"Thanks, Dunc," I say, taking the glass back and weaving wearily toward my room. "Night, all."

"Night, Bron," says Georgie. There's nothing in her tone to suggest she hasn't forgiven me, but nonetheless, what I said sits between us. I hadn't even imagined that the words that came out of my mouth— *you gave up drinking*—were true until I saw her reaction, because surely I've seen her drinking plenty of times lately? Well, every swimming holiday, at least; I wouldn't know what she does in Manhattan. Regardless, I hadn't meant to hurt her; I don't think I knew that I could. It throws everything I've ever thought about Georgie off-kilter; all those wild, reckless times at uni when she seemed invulnerable, having the time of her life. I have the sense that everything is shifting and sliding in my mind, but I don't quite understand it yet. I'll speak to her in the morning. Things are always better in the morning.

At the door of my bedroom, I fumble for the light switch with one hand, half facing the wall. I find it, and the dim hotel lighting gently switches on: mood lighting, completely useless for real life. I turn toward the main body of the room, and—I drop my glass. Even as it's smashing on the hard tiled floor, into one large piece and a myriad of small shards among a puddle of water, I recognize the cliché from a thousand movies. What has caused me to drop the glass is a cliché, too, but no less effective for all of that: sprawled across the wall of my room, in a line of foot-high black spray-painted letters that cross both the painted wall behind the bed and the ceiling-high cupboard doors on either side of the bed, is:

HAVE YOU TOLD THEM WHAT YOU DID, BITCH?

Underneath the letters, there's a large knife stuck in the wall, pinning something to the plaster, some sort of scrap of material, in a pattern of blue and purple diamonds that faintly tugs at recognition in my brain, but it's so incongruous that I can't place it—and then all of a sudden I realize what it is. It's one of my swimsuits. The knife is a cleaver, almost a machete; a rectangular blade attached to a sleek black handle with a pleasing aesthetic curve to it. It's the type of knife one might use to chop meat; I expect my swimsuit offered little resistance, but only the top corner of the knife is buried. The wall must be quite unexpectedly hard, I find myself thinking.

Duncan gets to me first. "Are you al—" He breaks off. "What the—" I grab his arm as he starts to step inside, intending to explain that I smashed a glass, but the words don't come. Instead I gesture at the floor. He looks down wordlessly, then back at the wall. Georgie and Adam have joined us in the doorway by now, their own questions dying in their throat. The size of the letters, the sheer abandon of spraying paint with no care or regard to the decor, somehow demands silent homage. I stare at it. There can't be much doubt that the message is meant for me. Once could be a mistake, but twice is beyond coincidence.

I realize I'm being gently shaken. "Bron, come away," Georgie is saying. She might have been saying it for a while; it's as if I've gradually become aware of a radio in the background, and also simultaneously aware that it's been on for some time. "Bron, come now; come away, honey. Come now." She shepherds me gently to the pristine white of the living room, with its snowy sofa and unblemished walls. For a moment I consider refusing to sit down—surely I will besmirch the sofa?—until a small iota of sense prevails: the writing is on the wall, not on me. Adam hands me a can of Coca-Cola, one of the small ones from the minibar. Rob would never let us take drinks from there: *Daylight robbery,* he would say. But Rob isn't here, so I take the drink mechanically and sip it, and the sugar which rushes through my system is like a light bulb turning on, or a muffler being removed: suddenly sound and light flood back in.

Georgie sits beside me on the sofa, her worried eyes focused on my face. Duncan and Adam are hovering anxiously in front of us. "I'm all right," I say, because that's what one says, no matter whether it's true or not at the time. Just saying it is a talisman: it will become true at some point.

"We should call the police," Duncan says. "I'll call Jem. He can sort it out." He takes a few steps away and starts to talk into his phone in a low voice, pacing around the room as he speaks.

"You can sleep in my room," Georgie says to me. "We ought to leave yours untouched for the police."

"Thanks." I wonder if she intends to be in the room, too, or if she'll be with Adam. Then I realize it doesn't matter: I won't be able to sleep anyway. Not when someone has buried a knife through my swimsuit into the wall; not when someone is out there who surely wants to put that blade through me, with or without the swimsuit.

Adam has gone to the kitchen; in a few seconds he reappears. "That knife is from the kitchen here. There's one missing from the knife block. I take it that's your swimsuit?" I nod. "Then at least we know who the messages are meant for," he says grimly.

Duncan rejoins us. "Jem is calling the police. But he's not sure they'll be able to come out anytime soon; the other end of the island is getting battered pretty hard." As if on cue, there's a sudden flash from outside. All four of us turn toward the long wall of glass that separates the indoor living space from the outdoor space, which is beautifully lit and equally well provided with sofas and tables and the like in the open area between the villa and the pool. From nowhere, rain starts to hammer down, hitting the ground improbably hard, as if it has been flung there with force and malice. The noise is extraordinary, a constant tattoo of a million drumbeats. It takes another flash, and the crash of thunder several seconds later, for me to realize that the flashes are lightning. I should have twigged to that before now; I must be still drunk, for all that I thought the shock of the bedroom scene had tipped me into full sobriety.

"Wow," says Georgie, wide-eyed. "If this is just the tail, I'd hate to be close to the center of the storm."

"Did anybody leave anything outside?" Duncan asks, in a remarkable moment of practicality. "The wind is picking up; you might lose it if you did." Nobody moves. The rain is mesmerizing. We watch it for what might be seconds or minutes or hours. I have an urge to go outside and stand in it, face upturned; to feel it hammering on my skin, washing me clean. Another movie cliché.

"I wonder if the road will be passable with all of this," Adam says. "Steve said it's prone to landslips." I'm watching the drops bounce back up from the ground. There's so much water in the air that there's a haze around all of the outdoor lights.

"I, for one, am absolutely in favor of leaving early for the airport," I say. I want to leave and never ever come back. I want to leave and have it all be no more than a memory, not much different to a bad dream.

"Bron," Duncan says gently. "Have you any idea what that message is about?" It's difficult to wrench my eyes away from the rain to look at him. "It's just, you know, it's just—it seems very personal. Surely you must have an idea."

I can feel Georgie's eyes upon me. It occurs to me that she's waiting for me to tell it; and that she won't say if I don't. And if she won't say now, then she never did; not to anyone. And that, suddenly, is the scariest thing of all: Georgie didn't tell. And then I finally see it, the bigger picture, and I almost say, *Aha!* For the briefest of moments I have the same elation I would have at work when I finally found the error in a spreadsheet, the mistake I'd missed that was throwing all the calculations off, but that elation is immediately swept away by the subsequent wave of fear that engulfs me. I have the bigger picture now, but not the detail, and the devil is always in the detail. I look at Duncan, his earnest eyes fixed on me. *You could tell me that kind of stuff,* he said. But I knew I couldn't, and I still can't, not while I haven't quite pinned it all down. I've got to move carefully, right now. Maintain a balance. I scrub a hand over my face, deliberately obscuring my expression. "I've no idea. It doesn't make any sense." I try for a weak joke. "You'd think that if I'd done something deserving of that kind of vitriol, I'd at least remember it." Georgie is still watching me, her face very still, though I either see, or imagine that I can see, disappointment in her eyes. That's another of Georgie's contradictions: she's disturbingly secretive but also inordinately honest.

"A madman, then?" Duncan sounds dissatisfied with that.

"Or woman," says Georgie, rather tartly.

Duncan sighs. "Mad person, then. Believe me, I wasn't meaning to suggest that males have the monopoly on madness."

I rush in. "Georgie, can I borrow your charger? My phone is almost dead, and I want to speak to Rob."

"Of course," she says, getting up. I follow her into her bedroom. The ferocity of the rain hasn't lessened in the slightest. If anything, it's even wilder and more blustery out there. Periodic gusts drive the rain almost horizontal; it's like seeing the wind drawn in contour lines. "Are you going to tell him what's happened?" she asks over her shoulder, as we enter her room. "Won't he worry?"

She's leaning over the bedside table to unplug the charger. I take the opportunity to nudge the door until it's just a few inches ajar. Closed would be too obvious. Then I cross the room and grab her wrist when she straightens to pull her into the en suite bathroom. "What—" she starts, but then falls silent as I shake my head. I close the bathroom door behind us.

"We're in danger. Or at least I am; I can't quite figure it out." I'm whispering, which is stupid in this enclosed bathroom, but nonetheless I am. Georgie's eyes are huge in her face, her brows drawn close over them. "I think . . . I don't know how to say this. I think Lissa is still alive. I think she planned all of this; I think it's retribution for sleeping with Graeme, though I don't know how she found out. I know I sound crazy, but actually it's the only thing that makes sense, I—"

"Yes."

"I—what?" That's the last thing I expected her to say.

"Yes. I think so, too." She closes her eyes briefly and sighs, expelling what must surely be all the air in her lungs. "I found her red TYR suit in the pool cupboard. I have to go back and photograph it; it was stupid of me not to. I must have been in shock."

"You found . . ." I stop, thinking that through. The mirror is slightly tinted. An unnaturally brown version of me scratches at my hairline. "But the fisherman—"

"Yes, I know. He must have been lying, which means someone must have paid him to." I had always thought it odd that the fisherman particularly noted the brand of swimsuit, not just the color; there's only one small logo on that suit, on the upper left breast. I'd wondered if it was a reaction to the shock: had the image been seared in his mind? But no, he remembered the brand because he was parroting what he'd been told to say. Georgie is still speaking. "Lissa, I suppose. I thought it was Jem; I thought maybe he killed her. But nobody but Lissa would do *that.*" She gestures toward where my bedroom lies, the bedroom with the foot-high letters and the knife in the wall, which I'll never sleep in.

"Yes." It's worse than I thought, having her agree with me. It means that all of this is *real.* It means that I'm not being stupid, or paranoid, or hysterical; not that those are things that I usually am, but today I'd take any one of them over being right.

"I thought I would be so happy if Lissa was alive," she mutters.

"We could be wrong," I say, which sounds like a backward sort of comfort. "But surely it's safer to act as if we're not."

She nods silently then shakes herself before I can say anything further, and she looks at me gravely. "Whatever she's up to, she's not doing it alone. She couldn't move around the hotel; she'd risk being recognized. She must have an accomplice."

"I know. We can't trust anyone." But then, I never thought I could. Not even Georgie, as it happens. I feel a flash of absolute gratitude toward her now, and then a terrible, awful pang for having ever allowed myself to doubt her, but neither lasts. The fear is too great; it doesn't allow room for anything else. "Not Jem. Not even Adam or Duncan."

"Wait—I meant that she must have had local help. You can't truly suspect Adam or Duncan are helping her?"

"No, but . . ." I hesitate, rubbing my hairline again. "I just don't know. You heard Duncan; he gets ownership of this place if Jem is convicted of anything. Maybe he made a deal with Lissa." I don't really believe that, but I just can't bear to tell Duncan what is behind Lissa's enmity. He would be so disappointed with me on both counts: for doing it, and for not telling him.

"That's ridiculous." But she is less vehement about it than she might have been. "And what can Adam possibly have to gain?"

"Adam? He'd be more than happy to have Lissa disappear. Then he gets a clean crack at you." She opens her mouth and then shuts it silently. "Then there's Jem. I mean, he was willing to obstruct justice with the swimsuit. What if he's actually on Lissa's side? Helping her disappear in exchange for her shares in the hotel?" Her eyes widen. She hadn't thought of that angle. "And I bet there's life insurance he can collect on her, too. So. I don't really suspect Adam or Duncan, not truly, but if we tell them, there's always the chance they'll say something to the wrong person, and who knows what danger that would put us in. Until we know more, we don't share anything with anyone. Deal?"

"I . . . All right, deal." She looks as if she wants to swallow the words back as soon as they come out of her mouth, but it's too late. And Georgie keeps her promises; I know that beyond doubt now.

A thought suddenly occurs to me. "Wait: do you think she shot Cristina?"

She doesn't flinch; she must have already wondered that. "I don't know. Maybe the guy who attacked me is working with her; it could have been him who shot her. We have to be really careful. Nobody should ever be alone."

"And we have to get away from the resort as soon as possible. Now, if we can."

"Yes. If we can convince the others, somehow." She sounds doubtful, though. "I don't know how we do that without telling them—"

"No. We're not risking it." She doesn't nod, but she doesn't try to press her point again. "What do you think Lissa's plan is?" I ask hesitantly. "What does she want?"

"What she always wants." She grimaces. "Justice, as she sees it."

"What does that mean?"

"I don't know. But it can't be good for either of us."

I'm frowning. "Either of us? Why, what did *you* ever do?"

"I didn't tell her. About you and Graeme. Which in her eyes means I chose you." She closes her eyes briefly. "I was trying to choose both of you."

"She wouldn't . . ." I try again. "She wouldn't really hurt me, would she? I mean, it's just not *reasonable*." Even as I say it, I can hear the flaw in my logic, that assumption that Rob always cautions me against: that everyone will behave *reasonably*. Cristina is dead; shot. That's not *reasonable*.

Georgie is looking at me with an expression that suggests she can't quite believe I said that. "Bron," she says patiently, as if speaking to a child. "She has engineered a situation where she's technically dead. She's thrown off all connection with any of us that might curb her; there is literally nothing to limit her. She has probably already killed, or at least ordered a killing. At this point I really don't think she'll give a solitary fuck about what you or I or anybody else might consider reasonable."

"Yes." There's something wet on my hand. I look down absent-mindedly to see blood running from the cuticle of my thumb. I don't remember picking at it, but there's blood under the fingernail of my first finger, too, so I must have. "Fuck."

HOW TO KILL YOUR BEST FRIEND
Method 7: Strangulation. Assault. Battery.

A blow to the head, or suffocation—or both. The problem is that it's so very personal. Direct. Which I suppose it should be; if you're going to kill someone, you shouldn't be insulating yourself from the process. That was always my objection to the use of drones: warfare ought to be immediate; it ought to be bloody, to be close combat. You should be forced to witness, to feel, each and every impact. You shouldn't be allowed to put it at arm's length.

But I digress. Again. I keep doing that. Because it's so awful to contemplate, I suppose: her eyes looking into mine, with full knowledge and horror at what I'm doing. She would see it as a betrayal—except, would she? Some part of her has always relied upon me to reel her in. That's the contract: I have to love her absolutely and save her from her worse instincts. And in return I get—what? Redemption, I suppose. So perhaps she would understand what I was doing.

EIGHTEEN

GEORGIE

We exit the bedroom to find Adam and Duncan on the sofa, in close conversation. Duncan looks up. "I just heard from Steve," he says. "He thinks we should head to the airport ASAP, in case the road gets blocked." The weather is playing into our hands. I manage not to exchange relieved glances with Bron. Our plan is a simple one—keep quiet, never be alone, and leave as soon as possible—but it was the last step that I'd been most concerned about. We could be wrong, of course: perhaps I'm just seeing what I want to see. Bias confirmation, they call it at work: that tendency to only take notice of evidence that supports your preferred thesis. Do I want Lissa to be alive so much that I've lost all objectivity? And then another thought comes: *Do I want Lissa to be alive at all?*

"Is there anyone who can drive us?" Bron asks Duncan. Some of the tension has leached out of her since our tête-à-tête in the bathroom. I suppose she feels that every passing minute takes us closer and closer to leaving for good, but that isn't having the same effect on my own stress levels. If anything I feel stretched tighter. Every minute that nothing happens takes us closer to the point when something will. Lissa hasn't set this all up for nothing.

"He's found someone who can do it. He said he would have driven us himself, but he's had way too many beers. Can you be ready in forty-five minutes?"

"I can be ready in about three minutes," I say. "I've not unpacked after the move here." For once there's a benefit to my lack of industriousness where my wardrobe is concerned. I pause, glancing at Bron. "Bron would have to go into her room, though. Which kind of messes up the, um, crime scene." *Crime scene.* We are in a villa with a crime scene, with a bedroom that holds a scrap of chlorine-resistant nylon dangling from a butcher's cleaver. *But we have a plan.* I keep telling myself that I feel better with a plan. You would think that knowing Lissa so well would mean that I would be in the best possible situation to figure out what she might do, but I can't fathom it. She isn't reasonable, but that doesn't mean she lacks reason: there is a point to all of this, but we just don't know what it is yet.

Duncan shrugs. "If we stay and get stuck, the police won't get to us for a while anyway, and you'd surely have to go in to get some clothing."

"We could photograph it first," Adam suggests. "I know it's not ideal, but it's better than nothing. Did you unpack much?" he asks Bron.

"Everything," she says, as I knew she would. "I always do." It wouldn't have crossed her mind not to unpack, even for just one night.

"I'll confirm forty-five minutes from now, then; at the reception," Duncan says. He looks at his watch. "That would make it twelve thirty a.m."

"Better make it twelve forty-five," Adam replies. "We ought to go by Jem's place first and explain to him that we're leaving."

"No, stick to twelve thirty," I say quickly. "Adam and I can get our stuff sorted and then go and explain to Jem—I have to return some-thing anyway—and Duncan can stay here with Bron while she packs. I'm sure he'll come to the reception with us to see us all off; you can say your goodbyes then."

"Makes sense," says Adam, quickly backing me up; he knows I need to photograph the TYR swimsuit. I look at Bron with a question in my eyes—*Okay?*—and she nods back in a short jerk. I had won-dered if she would demur, if she would find some reason for a private goodbye with Jem; even as the thought crossed my mind, I knew it was unfair, but I couldn't unthink it. For a moment, when Duncan asked outright about the message, I thought she would spill all, but no. Perhaps I'm being selfish in wanting it to be out in the open; per-haps Bron is right, and it benefits no one. But if I had kept fewer se-crets, would we have got to where we are now? I keep thinking of Diane, right back on that first evening, and the words that she spoke so bitterly: *Was it something I did? Or didn't do? Or Philip? Or you?* She had the right of it: I am me because Lissa is she; she has made me who I am, and she must bear some responsibility for that, although it's the corollary that's really biting here: I have made her who she is. That responsibility lies with me, with every action I did or didn't take, with every blind eye I turned. The blame sits with me.

But right now, I have to focus on the present: Jem. Jem, who I thought killed his wife, but didn't. Probably. Perhaps this will be the last time I ever see him. I expect Duncan will keep in touch, given the business connection, but I don't see why I should or would. Nothing on earth could persuade me to come back here again, and certainly there's no reason for him to reach out, to suggest grabbing a drink if he happened to be in New York. He doesn't like me, and there's no social pressure to spend time with your dead wife's friends that you've never liked.

Except that the wife isn't dead after all. And he might even already know that.

There's still enough staff on hand that Adam manages to rustle up a porter to take us to Jem's villa in one of the electric buggies. The storm's onslaught continues unceasingly, and the buggy's rain protection is not much better than that of a child's pram, consisting of clear plastic sides rolled down to fasten with Velcro against one another and the frame of the buggy, but the wind is so fierce that the Velcro is no match and they keep snapping apart; we will be soaked long before we get to Jem's place. I climb in to sit side by side with Adam, conscious of his watchful eyes upon me, directly behind the driver, who is a young man that I remember working as a waiter at breakfast. And then we're off, Adam and I trying to hold the plastic sides down as we go. The puny headlights of the buggy illuminate the rain such that it seems to become as solid as glow sticks, blurring and smearing when viewed through the flimsy plastic windscreen. There's standing water almost the entire way, and at times I'm not quite sure where the path is, but the driver takes it all at a speed that suggests he has no such doubts. It is not a comfortable journey.

I hear a crackle of the driver's handheld radio as we pull up at Jem's villa. "One moment, please," he says. He lifts the radio from his belt to his ear and holds a rapid conversation, then turns to face us all. "I wait for you?" he asks hesitantly, looking expectantly from Adam to myself and back again. "Or can I go and . . . ?" He gestures with the radio, and I deduce that he is needed elsewhere.

"No, that's fine; you crack on, mate. We'll call again when we're done here," says Adam.

"Okay. Thank you." He smiles genially in a remarkable display of Colgate-white teeth.

The short dash of ten meters or so from the buggy to the shelter of Jem's porch is long enough that my shoulders and hair are soaked, and the two enormous puddles that I have to run straight through make my sandals treacherously slippery underfoot. Adam gets there ahead of me and holds the door open, simultaneously swiping at the rain on his hair; drops fly from his flicking hand in a way that's somehow reminiscent of a dog shaking itself after a bath.

"Hello? Je-em," he calls loudly once I'm inside, making the name into two syllables. There's no response. The portrait of Lissa is still propped on the table in the hallway, her pale, featureless visage almost luminous in the dim lighting. There's something odd about it that's nagging at me. Adam calls Jem's name again, but my attention is still on the portrait. "Wait here a moment," Adam says. "I'll just check in case he's asleep or not decent or something."

Not decent. I almost laugh. We both know he's not a decent man. The fire-engine red swimsuit in his pool cupboard is proof of that. But I suppose he might be in bed; after all, didn't Lissa complain he wasn't as much of a night owl as she was? Is. But I should say was. *Oh dear God,* I caution myself, *I'm going to trip myself up here if I'm not careful.* Even the use of tenses is fraught with danger.

The portrait is still insistently claiming my gaze, and as I stare at it, suddenly something moves inside me, like a tumbler dropping into place inside a lock, and I see what it's been trying to tell me. *It could be Maddy.* The same delicate china features; the same coloring. It could be a grown-up Maddy. Did I truly never see the resemblance before? Surely at some level it must have registered with me. I hear Adam's voice from the lounge, and seconds later, a deep murmur that must be Jem, and their voices drag me away from the bewildering revelation; there will be time to process that later, I tell myself. "Come on through, Georgie," Adam calls to me.

"Hey," I say to Jem, as I enter the lounge. He's wearing his usual uniform—tailored shorts, white linen shirt—but the sleeves are carelessly rolled up, his feet are bare, and he has what looks like tortoiseshell reading glasses tipped up on his head. There are no guests left for him to be on point for, I suppose. I half expect to see a glass of something on the coffee table, or a bottle, but there's nothing in plain view. The curtains are drawn, but I can still hear the rhythmic pounding of the rain outside, with occasional cascades of stronger beats when the wind throws the drops at the long glass wall hidden behind the drapes. Adam is putting his phone is his pocket; I realize he must have been showing Jem the photos of the vandalized room. "Sorry, I think we're dripping all over your floor. It really is quite a storm." *What utter banality.* But really, what else do I have to say to him? He doesn't like me, and now I don't trust him. Before, I wouldn't have said I disliked him, but I also wouldn't have said I had a great deal of time for him, either. When we first met, when he and Lissa were only newly coupled up, I thought, *Well, that won't last. Rebound relationship.* Their engagement was a shock.

"Is Bron okay? That message—" He's shaking his head.

"She's okay," I say. I see it again, in my mind's eye. The lettering, bold and large. The swimsuit, the knife. "Shaken, obviously."

"It's so . . . *weird.* Cristina, and now this . . . We've never seen anything like that before; I can't imagine what's going on. I'm so sorry that this has sullied your experience of this place." He appears genuinely troubled, but for some reason I think of him at the memorial service, barely inhabiting his own skin; the very embodiment of a man grieving. Surely that wasn't an act? Bron has me doubting everyone and everything. "Though I can't help thinking that the storm is a blessing in disguise; much better for you guys to get away from whatever that is all about as soon as possible. And, of course, silly for you to get stranded here if the road becomes impassable." He turns back to Adam. "Can you send me those photos? I'll need to pass them on to Jimi."

I sidle toward the kitchen, where there's a door that leads out to the pool area. "I'll pop the pull buoy back in the cupboard while you're doing that."

Jem looks up from his phone. "You can just leave it here."

"It's no trouble," I say, quickly dashing out through the kitchen before I can hear him reply. The lock on the kitchen door that leads outside is a simple turn-and-release mechanism; I'm outside in a flash. Like the presidential villa, the first floor of Jem's villa partially protrudes over the pool terrace, providing protection from the unending rain, which cascades in a steady curtain from the overhang, colored yellow-gold in patches from the outdoor lighting. The cupboard is in the dry area, thankfully. I pop the pull buoy back on the same shelf I originally found it. Then I turn to my real motivation: taking a photograph of the red TYR swimsuit. I pull the boogie boards forward so I can get a better look, but the cupboard is too dark. I fish in my pocket for my mobile and activate the torch function, then sweep the beam over the back of the cupboard, but I can't see any telltale flash of fire-engine red. I bend to take a closer look.

"Now what exactly would you be looking for?"

I whirl round. Jem is standing a few feet away from me, his hands in his pockets and his expression unreadable. The pool lights paint one side of his face golden.

"Jem," I gasp. "I didn't hear you."

"I know you didn't. What were you looking for?"

"Nothing, I was putting the pull buoy back, like I said." I can feel myself flushing. I wave an arm at the cupboard and try for joviality. "And, you know, trying to be a good citizen by leaving this shocking mess in some kind of order."

"Bullshit." He's no longer unreadable; there's an ugliness to his expression now. He's trying to intimidate me.

"Jem, I—" *Where is Adam?*

"You were looking for this." He draws his right hand out of his pocket, and with it comes the red swimsuit, bunched in his fist. "You found it earlier, didn't you? You found it before I did. You think I killed her."

"No, I really don't—"

"Bullshit!" he roars. I almost flinch at the violence of his delivery.

"Don't lie to me! Ever since you got here, you've been needling away, picking at every little thread. You'd love to show that I killed her, wouldn't you? You could have just asked, you could have just approached me, but no. Not you. You're looking for any chance to cut me down." Surely Adam must hear him—except no, he won't hear a thing above the noise of the storm, I realize; the pounding of the rain is cocooning us. And with the curtains closed, he can't see us from the living room, either. Jem takes a step toward me, and I find myself backing up a step, like a dance—but I don't want to dance. Not with him, and not like this. He's a strong man, Jem: barrel-chested and gorilla-armed, and he likes his gym sessions. The strength in the skinny arms of the man who attacked me would be nothing compared to that of Jem. "You'd love to see me behind bars, stripped of my hotel, my livelihood. You couldn't bear it that she chose to marry me—me!" He thumps his chest and moves one more step forward. I take another step back and feel a cupboard shelf butting into my rear. He has hemmed me in. Panic is rising: I can't breathe, I can't concentrate on what he's saying, I just need to get away from here. Can I rush him? But he's so much bigger than me. And decently agile, whereas I have a damaged knee and, in any case, I lean more toward endurance than sprint. "She chose me. I don't know what the two of you did to each other before, and I don't care, but she chose me. Me. And—"

"Don't you come a step closer," I explode, borderline hysterical. "Don't you dare touch me."

"Touch you? I'm not going to fucking touch you." But he takes a step back, as if shocked into suddenly realizing how much he's advanced. There are tears streaming down my face. I don't remember starting to cry. "I'm not going to hurt you." He looks at me properly, and something in his face changes. His ugly righteous anger falters. "Shit. Georgie. It's okay. I'm sorry. Really, I'm not going to hurt you." He takes another step back and extends a hand, palm down, as if soothing a cornered animal. *I could run now,* I think, except that I'm not sure if I can. My head is curiously light. It's almost floating, yet my heart is pounding, my breath is coming in rasps and my feet feel rooted to the spot. "And for the record I didn't kill Lissa, either."

I take a deep breath, then another. Then another. "Then," I say, with difficulty. Each breath is an effort, let alone forming speech. It must be a form of panic attack, a logical part of my brain recognizes. It doesn't particularly help to know that. There's a tingling in my fingers, as if I've gone to sleep on them. "Then how . . . come . . . a fisherman . . ."

He nods. "I know. It was wrong, I know." He clenches his jaw as if temporarily grinding his teeth. "I just—I just needed it to be over. She obviously went swimming and got swept out, but without a body . . ." He shrugs. "Well, without a body the whole thing was— God, it was awful. It wouldn't end, it was just *lingering*. No closure. And business was suffering. I thought that—well, I thought that maybe if there was a sighting of a body, that would draw a line under it. So I found a guy and paid him a few hundred dollars." He shrugs and his mouth twists. "Though it didn't make any difference in the end. I'm still having to close the hotel."

"Did . . . Jimi . . ."

He cottons on instantly, shaking his head. "No. No, he thought it was all legit." He looks down at the red swimsuit in his hand, almost bemused. "I really did think she must have been wearing this. The police asked, and it was the only suit I could think of that I couldn't find. I only spotted it today." He shoves it back in his pocket, but a stray strap hangs down in a loop. His brow furrows. "I really don't know which swimsuit she could have been wearing instead." He's silent for several seconds, as if hunting in his head for the answer. As if knowing what swimsuit she died in would make all the difference. I breathe and breathe. It's getting easier. And reason is returning. He paid the fisherman. Did he also pay the worker who said he saw her swimming?

"The worker. The one who . . . saw her . . . in the . . ."

He shakes his head quickly. "No, I had nothing to do with that. He really did see her. She really must have been swimming in Kanu Cove." He looks at me. "She really did drown, Georgie," he says gently.

Kanu takes. Kanu takes who wants taken. But no, Lissa had too many scores to settle. She wouldn't let herself be taken. Lissa didn't drown. I shake my head, but he doesn't react. He watches me sadly. "Are you okay?" he asks awkwardly, after a moment.

"I think so." My breathing is almost normal. Speech is becoming easier now, too.

"I'm sorry," he says. He truly seems it. "But I hate that you were closer to my wife than I was. I can't look at you without thinking that, and it makes me so . . ." He twists his head away, his jaw clenched tight. I think he's waiting for me to protest, to say *No, no, you're wrong; you and she were soulmates,* but I neither believe it nor have the stomach for the lie. The unfilled silence settles between us. "Anyway." He directs those remarkable sea glass eyes back at me. "Do you believe me? That I didn't kill her?" I nod. "Are you going to tell the police about the swimsuit?"

I consider it. "I doubt there's any point." *And in any case, your wife is most likely still alive, and bent on a vengeance that never had anything to do with you.* "I expect you're about to burn it."

He nods shamelessly. "Yes. At the earliest opportunity."

Suddenly Adam's voice calls out, "Georgie? Georgie, are you all right?" He's clattering out of the kitchen door at pace, but he stops abruptly when he sees Jem and me standing together. "Georgie," he says warily. "Is everything okay?" Then he spots the strap hanging down from Jem's pocket. Jem follows Adam's gaze and sees it himself.

"I suppose she told you," he says fatalistically.

"Yes."

"I didn't kill her. She really did go swimming and drown. It's just, without a body . . . I just—I just needed it to be over."

"Yes." But Adam's eyes are on me, checking me over. "I'm sorry, Georgie. He told me he was going to the bathroom—"

"It's okay. I'm okay," I say quietly.

"Jesus, Adam, I would never hurt her. I just wanted to talk to her." But Adam doesn't respond. Jem looks at him for a moment and then turns away, his face hollow. "Come on, guys, let's go back in."

Something occurs to me. It's been bothering me, in the scenario in which Lissa is still alive: Lissa's cavalier treatment of Jem. What has he really done to be so thoroughly screwed over by his wife? Lied to and stolen from, and his livelihood reduced to rubble. "One question first." Jem looks at me warily. "Did you ever cheat on Lissa?"

"What? Why?"

I shake my head. "It doesn't matter why. Just answer me." He looks like he's about to refuse. "You owe me for that little display before." Adam looks as if he's about ask what I mean by that, but I shake my head minutely at him.

"I—oh, okay. Whatever," Jem yields. "Then: No. Never." Those sea glass eyes meet mine without any hesitation. I believe him—and then suddenly he checks himself. "I mean, when we met I was still with my ex-wife; I don't know if that counts. But ever since we decided to be together, it's just been Lissa. One hundred percent Lissa." I exhale sadly. There it is. He cheated to be with her. Their marriage never stood a chance. He looks away again, and suddenly he seems much smaller. "I really loved her, you know. I know we fought sometimes, but I even loved that about her, that she would never back down. She was . . . God, she was extraordinary." He looks around again, as if his vision extends through the golden rain curtain, as if he can see throughout the entire resort. "This was our dream. We were going to grow old together here, you know?"

"I'm sorry," I say, and I actually mean it, in a way that aches at my very bones. I'm sorry for things he can't possibly know that I'm sorry for. He nods absentmindedly, still looking out through the rain. "Come on. Let's go back in."

NINETEEN

BRONWYN

Packing. That's what I need to focus on. Packing up all my things in a bedroom I didn't even get to sleep in. After faltering in the doorway, I take a deep breath and force myself inside, though with the door left wide open; I can hear reassuring thumps and bangs as Duncan opens and closes drawers and wardrobes in his own room. I take another deep breath, then pull out my suitcase from where I'd pushed it under the bed. There's no reason to look at the wall, at the tessellated blue-and-purple-diamond-patterned swimsuit still pinioned by that weighty blade, drooping down sadly like a lifeless flag; there's no reason to allow my eyes to take in the black spray-painted letters as I open the wardrobe doors. Instead I glance at my watch. In twenty-five minutes we'll be gone. Just twenty-five more minutes, and all of this will be nothing more than a bad memory, and I know how to lock those down. I've had practice.

Clothes from hanging rail, shoes from the bottom of the wardrobe, and jewelry and passport from the little safe inside. Underwear from the drawers. Chargers, for my phone and laptop; mustn't forget those. Toiletries: I head into the (unsullied) bathroom to collect them, mildly regretful that I didn't get a chance to enjoy the enormous tub that sits by the sliding glass doors that lead to a private outdoor space with a second shower.

The sliding doors are open. I stare at them for a second, trying to make sense of that, and then I realize, with dawning horror: *I've miscalculated.* I whirl round, meaning to scream, meaning to head straight for Duncan's room, but it's too late.

She's here.

TWENTY

GEORGIE

"I'm so sorry; he must have snuck round to you through the bedroom French doors. I should have realized sooner . . . What did he say?" asks Adam quietly, turning himself so that he partially shields me from Jem. We're back in the living room of Jem's villa. Jem is on the phone, presumably ordering a buggy to take us to the reception, but I'm not really listening closely enough to follow his conversation. I'm too aware of time passing by, second by ticking second. Another and another and another. Each one brings us closer to . . . something. A reckoning. An awful, fateful reckoning.

And I'm aware, too, of how fragile I'm feeling. Before the attack, I would never have thought I would have crumbled in the face of a threat. But, even now, I can still feel an echo of the intense rising panic that struck me when Jem hemmed me in. If a reckoning is coming, I have no confidence I can withstand it.

"Georgie?" prompts Adam, barely above a whisper.

I shake my head. "I'll tell you later." My voice is equally low.

Jem is coming off the phone. "Sorry, we only have one driver at the moment. He's at the presidential villa, presumably picking up Bron-wyn and Duncan and your bags, but he'll come here afterward."

"I'll ring Duncan's mobile and find out if they're nearly ready," says Adam, pulling out his phone. I lower myself carefully onto the sofa, wincing a little as my knee is forced to bend. Jem watches me, then turns away, shoving his hands deep in his pockets, but that brings them into contact with the swimsuit; with a muffled exclama-tion, he yanks them back out as if burned. "He's not picking up," Adam says. "I'll try Bron." I twist my head to look up at him, seeing the unease growing in his face with every unanswered ring.

"Jem, you need to ring," I say.

"Ring where?"

"The presidential villa. Now." The urgency in my voice spurs Jem into action. He moves swiftly and wordlessly for the conference-style phone that sits on the desk next to his computer. It's on speaker: we hear every electronic digit as he punches in a number and then the loud *brrring* of each peal of the call. My heart leaps as someone picks up—*She's there! She's answering the phone!*—but then I realize from the words that emanate from the phone that he's simply called the reception. "It's Jem. Put me through to the presidential villa," he barks. Seconds later, the conference phone is making the same abra-sive peals. One, two, three. No answer. *Pick up, pick up, pick up.* Seven, eight, nine.

"They're probably on the buggy on their way here," Adam says, but his eyes are tight with tension.

"Radio the driver, then," I say impatiently. "Can you do that, Jem?"

"I don't have a radio here." He cuts off the call and dials again, speaking over the polite rote script that the receptionist answers with. "It's Jem again. Can you radio to check where the buggy is?"

"Just a moment," replies the disembodied receptionist. There's a clunk that sounds like a receiver being set on the desk.

Jem looks across the room. "What's going on?" he asks, his eyes unerringly fixed on me.

"I don't know. But Bron and Duncan are missing, and someone put a knife through Bron's swimsuit into a wall, so I'm thinking that's not good."

"Someone," says Adam. It's a statement, not a question, but I can see in his eyes what he's really asking. I close mine. I can't bear to say it.

"I don't understand," Jem says testily. "What am I missing?"

I open my eyes to find Adam still looking at me. He rubs his hair with both hands, short and sharp, an uncharacteristic display of consternation, and then he nods briefly as if we've had a full conversation. Perhaps we have. "Lissa," he says baldly to Jem, though his eyes are still on me. "It must be Lissa. She can't have drowned after all."

"What?" says Jem uncertainly, and I turn to see a myriad of emotions crossing his face—bewilderment, anger, despair—but not a one of them is hope. Perhaps he daren't let himself hope. "But that's . . ." And then he starts to put it together in earnest. "Is that who you think did that sick nonsense in Bron's room? That's completely ridiculous. Come on, you both knew her. Lissa would never be capable of something like that." He looks around at each of us in turn. The dead silence that meets his words drenches him like a wave of ice-cold water: he takes in a sharp, ragged breath and shakes his head. "I . . . You . . . Look, even if she wasn't actually dead, why the hell would she have it in for Bronwyn?"

The phone crackles into life. "Mr. Jem, sir?"

"Yes?"

"Rafi says Mrs. Miller is gone." I hear rather than feel my sharp intake of breath. "He's been looking for her with the other sir—"

"Duncan?"

"Yes, sir, with Mr. Duncan, sir. They have both been looking for her. They have checked through every bedroom and bathroom and outside. He doesn't know where she's gone." Jem looks across at Adam and me. "Mr. Jem, sir?"

"Yes. I'm here."

"What should Rafi do?"

"Tell him to come here," suggests Adam. "Tell him to come and pick us up. We can go there on the buggy and search."

Jem nods quickly and relays that message. "And radio all staff to be on the lookout for Mrs. Miller," he orders. Then he stabs a button to disconnect the phone and turns savagely to us, his face dark. "You're fucking nuts about this Lissa rubbish, but I'll deal with that later. Right now we need to find Bronwyn. I'll go to reception; I can better manage things from there. I've got my mobile." He doesn't wait for an answer; he simply heads out of the door of the lounge. Seconds later we hear the front door bang.

Suddenly Adam's phone chirps into life. "Duncan," he says, stabbing at the phone to put it on speaker. Duncan is already in full flow: "—don't know what's going on. We were both packing, I could hear her, and then when I went to see if she was finished, she was just *gone*. We've looked everywhere." Despite the tinny sound of the mobile, I can hear frustration and concern warring in his voice. "It makes no sense."

"Duncan, listen, the driver—Rafi—is coming to collect us, and we'll help look for her," Adam says.

"Dunc, be careful," I add. "We think—we think Lissa is still alive."

There's silence. Then a puzzled, "What?"

"We think it's Lissa behind all of this."

"You can't really think—"

"Yes," I say, simultaneously bending over to unfasten my sandals. "But her body—"

"Red herring." Truly red, in this case. Fire-engine red.

"What are you doing?" Adam asks me, directing his voice away from the phone.

Duncan's voice crackles out of the phone again. "That can't . . . But why would Lissa even want to target Bron? Because of Jem? Bron told me there was nothing between them."

"There was nothing between them. She never slept with Jem." I don't have time for the explanations. One of the buckles is fiddly, and I can't quite get it to release; my fingers are too jittery and unsteady. *More haste, less speed.*

"*Graeme?*" asks Duncan. It's impressive how quickly he has revised his calculations. There's silence from our end. "Oh," says Duncan faintly. "But he never said anything. Did—did *you* know, Adam?"

"No," Adam says briefly. His eyes are on me. "What are you doing?" he asks me again.

"I'm going to take the bike. I can't move fast enough right now with my knee." I straighten up, my feet finally liberated. Those sandals are so lethal in the rain, I'm better off without them. I take the phone off Adam and put it close to my mouth. "Duncan, change of plan; we're not coming to you. You need to check every inch of the villa again, and then go check Horseshoe Cove. I think Lissa is moving by boat; the same boat we saw at Horseshoe Cove this evening. Adam, when Rafi gets here, get him to take you to Steve's place. Drag him out of bed and sober him up any way you can; the pair of you have to get his boat and bring it round to catch up to me."

"Catch up to you where? Where are you going?"

There's a grim inevitability about my answer. "Kanu Cove," I say.

Please don't be there. Please be there. I don't know what I'm hoping for more.

I haven't been on a bike for years—I wouldn't dare in the Manhattan traffic—but here I am riding along in the dark, hunched against the rain that's plastering my hair against my head, with the skirt of my sundress tucked up in my knickers so as not to get entangled in the chain, and my bare feet pressed uncomfortably against the ridged pedals and a nagging pain flaring in my knee with every rotation. I don't know the pathways nearly as well as Rafi, the breakneck buggy driver from earlier, and even being the unseasoned cyclist that I am, I can tell that the tires are too soft and presumably the brakes won't work well in this weather, which makes me cautious. Plus it's difficult riding through wet sand, even when the sand is covering a harder surface beneath; I'm puffing from the exertion, though it feels like my open mouth drags in as much rainwater as air. Am I really moving so much faster than I would on foot? I can't tell.

Please don't be there. Please be there.

But in truth I have made progress. I've already passed the reception, catching a glimpse, through the curtain of rain, of Jem in his white shirt behind the counter, barking orders into a phone. He must have run there to have arrived so quickly. I wonder if he's thought to close the entry gates, but I don't stop to tell him. If I'm right, she's not traveling by road. I hope I'm not right; intellectually there's no reason to think that I would be—but I *feel* that I am. I feel it in the cold dread that fills my stomach, sending ice through my veins. Even the panic that infuses me has no heat in it. And the cycling, unfamiliar though it is, works the same way all exercise does for me: it wipes away the noise and focuses the mind. I am full of dread for a reason. I am doing the only thing I can do about it, and as quickly as I can. Nothing else is material right now.

There's a fork in the pathway that causes me to screech to a halt, the rusty bike protesting loudly. Everything looks different in the dark and the wild weather. I can only really see ten to fifteen meters ahead; I've been relying on the lamplights ahead springing into view as I approach them. But now I'm unsure as to exactly where I am. There are two paths that one can take to the cove. One circles round to finish on the beach area of Kanu Cove, descending in a fairly steep slope, but something that I can probably manage on the bike. The other heads toward the top of the headland and finishes at those steep steps cut into the cliff, that Lenny, Adam and I climbed only hours ago. But have I really reached that point already? I don't remember passing the junction where a fork leads off to the staff quarters; is that where I am now? I peer through the deluge and the darkness, searching around for any kind of clue, while simultaneously flexing my fingers; I've been gripping the rubber handlebars so tightly, so as not to be jettisoned from the bike by any unexpected potholes or tree branches, that my hands are starting to cramp. When I glance at them I can see in the dim light of a nearby path lamp that my fingers are a bloodless white and puckered from the water. I'm cold now. The air temperature must still be tropical, but the wind chill on wet skin is substantial.

Pick the path that's on the coastal side, I decide. I can't risk being diverted to the staff quarters. I settle back onto the saddle, hopping on my left foot as I struggle to get the bike moving on the wet sand, and feeling a different kind of lancing pain through my knee as I do so. And then I'm off again. Either the wind has picked up again or the foliage here is less effective at protecting me; a couple of gusts of wind almost knock me off.

Please don't be there. Please be there. And then: *What am I going to do if she's there?*

I ride on, the rain streaming continuously down my face. My dress is so wet that I don't have to worry about the skirt of it tangling in the chain any longer; it's plastered to my upper thighs. The path has switched from groomed sand to tarmac and is climbing instead of descending, and after a couple hundred meters of climb, I can't deny it: I'm on the path that goes over the headland. I'm going to have to ditch the bike at some point. And then the decision is taken out of my hands when a particularly strong gust of wind veers me sideways, causing the front wheel to jackknife on some kind of obstruction—a rock, presumably—and I'm tipped off, landing in an unceremonious sprawl half on, half off the tarmac path. I struggle back to my feet, ignoring the tears in my eyes, barely even checking myself over, because what is the point? It's not as if I can stop. I don't bother to pick up the bike again, and instead I start to run, trying to place my bare feet lightly on the hard path, though I soon have to drop back to a walk, pushing down on my thighs with my hands as I stride forward, as the path kicks up much more steeply. I will be on the top of the headland soon, but I'll be able to see only the far side; not the side I want. Not the nearside, which has the jetty where a boat with a dirty blue hull might pull up.

And then I've reached the top and the onslaught I've been under from the storm is nothing compared to the ferocity that greets me now. I'm buffeted so hard that it's a genuine battle to move forward, and the drops of rain that continually strike my skin actually sting. I dip my head and push on, ignoring the pain and trying to break into a run now that path has flattened out, though it's really not much better than a fast walk; I'll be faster when I get onto the stone steps, I tell myself. The lighting here is much more infrequent, but the tarmac gleams wetly in whatever light there is, so it's not hard to follow, even with my eyes half shut against the violent gusts. After a hundred meters or so, I realize that I'm moving downhill a little. And then the path veers sharply left, and I see the start of the wet stone steps. If anything, they seem more daunting here at the top: rough slabs of stone, narrow but deep, and desperately uneven, of such ridiculous proportions that I can't help wondering what kind of being they were designed for—a giant perhaps, but one that's ludicrously narrow in beam? A rivulet, born of the storm, is coursing down one side of them. I take a deep breath and start to descend. Each step is a leap of faith. There's no handrail that I can see, and scant few lamps, either; and each step is deep enough that weight has to be transferred before the new tread is found, so that each stride involves an odd sort of hop down, praying for rock to meet my bare foot, praying that it will be

flat and smooth, not pitted or scattered with the gravel that occasionally bruises my soles, my breath humphing out of me at each landing
and my knee screaming. More than once I stumble; once I have to
catch myself on a low bush growing at the side, or I would have fallen
who knows how far down. After twenty or so steps, I notice that the
wind has eased off a touch, and the rain is lashing less ferociously.
Then I see the pathway we took earlier, the one that's no wider than
a rabbit trail. If the man who attacked me took it in the dark, he's
much braver than I. I wonder how long he had been watching me
from above, biding his time. I wonder, too, how he fits in at all—but
I can't spare the energy for speculation. I have to keep climbing
down, one giant step after another.

Please don't be there. Please be there.

I'm so focused on my footing that it dawns on me well after it
should that I'm now able to see the lights of the stone jetty; that I have
only ten meters left to descend. And therefore I'm not focused on being quiet, though it's not as if my strategy relies on that, because I
have no strategy. The last steps are over in seconds, and then I'm
stumbling over the rough gravel path onto the blessedly smooth surface of the jetty, looking back and forth, my attention initially caught
by the boat that's tied up only a few meters from me, rising and falling
jerkily with the wild waves, but I can't see anybody on board—and
then I see a figure. A misshapen figure, about to clamber on board—
but no, it's two figures, clamped oddly together, their faces turned
toward me, the jetty lamplight fighting through the rain to extend
just enough illumination for me to be certain: It's Lissa. It's unmis-
takably Lissa. Now it's no longer a thought experiment, or intellec-
tual conjecture; now it's solid fact. Lissa is alive. And she's jamming
something metallic into the side of a very wet, bedraggled and scared-
looking Bron. It can only be a gun.

HOW TO KILL YOUR BEST FRIEND

Method 8: Drowning

Drowning. It's quite an arresting thought. I suppose it's the poetic tragedy of the idea that a champion swimmer's heart might beat its last in her own arena.

But . . . drowning. Difficult to do—and yet, not. Executable and believable, it ticks those boxes; of course I could engineer an opportunity for just the two of us to swim together. That's not the difficult bit. The difficult bit is the actual doing of it. I suppose I would have to hit her on the head with something to disorient her—a rock, maybe; I could claim a freak wave bashed her against some rocks—and then hold her underwater. Except she's strong; she would fight; she would judder and jackknife and kick. And even if she didn't, even if the rock knocked the senses clean from her head and the seawater swept them still farther away . . . even then, I don't know that I could do that. Not in the water. Water, swimming, the clarity of it, the cleanness of it: that's what's been saving me. It's sacred, in a way. I don't feel I can sully it.

So, no. Not in the water. Not there.

TWENTY-ONE

BRONWYN

This can't be happening. This can't be happening.

That's all I've been able to think from the moment she appeared in the villa —Lissa! Lissa, alive! But this can't be happening. She *is* Lissa, but also she isn't: there's something *wrong* about her. The gun, to be sure, but that's not all of it. She isn't listening or engaging or reacting to any of my questions, a stream of *whats* that become *whys* that become *wheres:*

What are you doing?

What do you want?

Why are you doing this?

Where did you get that?

Where are you taking me?

There's something robotic about her. It's more terrifying than any display of fury ever could be. More terrifying even than the gun, because a gun is only ever as dangerous as the hand that holds it.

It was the gun that stopped me from crying out to Duncan, that allowed her to slip me out the French windows of the bathroom, then through a gap in the wall of the outdoor bathroom area, out to the back of the villa, and then on through a gap in the hedge to the next property where a small buggy was waiting. *Don't ever get in the vehicle,* I remembered from some old safety briefing about kidnappings (Why on earth was I receiving such a safety briefing? I don't remember). *Once you do, you're done for.* But I got in. There really wasn't anything else to be done. I drove, as she directed, half considering crashing into a tree, but the cold, hard barrel jammed against my side made me think twice; it would probably go off as we crashed. In fact, any pothole might jolt her finger . . . I drove very carefully after that particular thought. I followed her instructions. She knew which paths to take to avoid any staff, which also served to confuse me as to where we were going. Though I really should have guessed. Kanu Cove. Of course.

And here we are, and there's the same boat with the shabby blue hull, pitching horribly against the jetty in the swell. Could I throw myself in the water? But no, getting enough distance to be safe from bullet fire would put me into the path of the rip; I'd surely be swept away.

"You tried to run me over with the boat," I call over my shoulder, as she directs me along the path toward the boat. She's only a foot or so behind me. I'm trying to look around for any kind of way out, but to my left is a sheer cliff face, to my right is the water, and behind me is a woman with a gun. And the heavens continue to assault us with the lashing rain.

"Not really," she calls back. "We weren't trying that hard; we were just having some fun." She sounds as if she's starting to have fun herself, now. The robotic tone is melting away.

"We? Who's we? The man who attacked Georgie?" I risk a glance behind, but she simply gestures with the gun. It would take out my liver right now.

"Keep walking."

"Are we going on the boat?"

But she doesn't reply. We're nearly on the pier. The steep escarpment to our left seems to be warding off the worst of the wind and rain: I can hear Lissa's footsteps behind me. She's wearing some kind of hiking boots—much more sensible than my sandals, but then, I didn't know what I was dressing for—and dark-colored shorts with an army green tank top, and a baseball cap that's presumably keeping the rain off her face. She looks like she's channeling G.I. Jane. All those advantages, and a gun, too.

How can I get myself out of this? I keep scanning around, looking for options—and then I see a flash of something high on the cliff face, perhaps thirty meters above us. A slender bare calf stepping down in a pool of lamplight. I struggle to see more without making it obvious that I'm looking, but the pale blue dress that follows the calf gives me an answer. Georgie. A flood of hope springs up like a fountain inside me. Georgie is on her way, and if Georgie is on her way, then surely there is hope yet. Surely she'll be followed by the cavalry.

I try one of my previous questions again, hoping to distract her, to keep her from noticing Georgie's progress. "Lissa, why are you doing this? I thought we were friends."

"So did I. But that friendship ended when you started fucking my husband, so no, I don't think we're friends anymore. You deserve this."

"Nobody deserves this."

"An eye for an eye."

She can't mean . . . "An eye for an eye? Georgie, it was just a brief affair."

"A brief affair? You destroyed everything. Every good memory I've ever had with him. If I'd found out when he was alive, maybe I could have at least salvaged something. Maybe he could have made me believe that it didn't mean anything. But he's dead, and I have nothing, and you have everything. Does that seem fair to you?"

"For God's sake, Lissa, I have children!" My voice is rising.

"I wanted children," Lissa says. She sounds almost thoughtful. "I wanted children with Graeme. I don't think you deserve to enjoy your children."

Her last sentence robs me of breath and sends icy dread coursing through my spine. I can't pretend it was uttered in anger. She's horribly, terrifyingly dispassionate. I can't pretend she's not being herself, either. Lissa has never struggled for courage in her convictions; she's always been binary. True or false. Right or wrong. Life or death. We're by the boat now. I feel her clamp my right arm with her left one. I could pull away; she wouldn't be able to maintain her grip given how slick and wet my skin is, but the gun is ever present, both in my mind and, at this very moment, jammed against my side. She turns us so that we are looking toward the cliff face. "Let's wait for Georgie, shall we?" she says, as if suggesting a stop for coffee.

"How did you find out?" We both have our eyes on Georgie. The lamps along the steps are quite widely spaced, but now that we've spotted her, it's easy to follow the pale shape. She's dropping heavily onto each step, but always on the same leg; presumably she's trying to protect her bad knee.

"Georgie, actually." I turn to her, horrified—*What?* But she shakes her head. "No, no, she didn't tell me anything. But I realized she was wondering if I'd killed him. Which made me wonder if I had had a reason to, that I didn't know about. So I checked his phone *very* carefully. You know he was always useless with technology. He'd accidentally taken a photo of one of your Snapchat messages." She shrugs. "At least, I presume it was accidental; he regularly took photos of his own ear when he was on the phone. It wasn't even that incriminating a message, it was just—strange. Then I started looking back at all the odd little things and it started to fit."

"It didn't mean anyth—"

"Rubbish. It meant everything, to me."

Her words are a sledgehammer. There is nothing I can say, but I try it anyway. "I'm sorry. I'm so very sorry."

She laughs. It sounds like she's genuinely amused. "We're well beyond sorry. We're a *really* long way past that. My husband died, and I thought I couldn't go on living. And then I found out that even before that, you'd stolen him from me. There's not enough sorrow in the world to atone for that."

I need to keep her talking. I'll think of something if I can just keep her talking. "I don't understand what your plan was."

"It hasn't quite gone as intended," she admits. "I've been improvising pretty well, though. Nobody was supposed to see me swimming, and there certainly wasn't supposed to be a body spotted. Ideally I would have just disappeared. The police would have suspected Jem; they always look to the husband first. They'd have found my emails and concluded that you two were having an affair—and that you were stealing from the company. Rob would have had to hear about it; you couldn't have kept it under wraps. Then when you threw yourself into Kanu Cove after my memorial it would obviously have been suicide, out of guilt at your terrible behavior." I draw in a sharp, ragged breath. So that is the plan: I'm to drown in Kanu Cove. I look at the water. If she tosses me in here, I can probably get to the side; the most dangerous water is in the center of the narrow inlet. But if she tosses me in from the boat . . .

"But they wouldn't find any evidence we were having an affair, because we *weren't,*" I argue.

"Weren't you? I was never quite sure. But anyway, they'd have found evidence, if they'd looked. It's pretty easy to plant evidence." She turns her head from the cliff face to look at me. "And you'd be gone and no one would miss you because everybody would know what a little snake you are, though with the wrong husband. But I'd get what I wanted—I'll still get that. An eye for an eye." In the darkness, her own eyes might as well be made of obsidian. "It's not hard to commit murder, is it? It's the getting away with it that's difficult. Much easier to do that if you're technically already dead."

"Lissa," I manage. "Lissa, please listen—" But Lissa isn't listening; she's watching Georgie on her last couple of steps. We watch her reach the flat ground, stumbling a little then straightening, looking round—and then she sees us. "Lissa," she says. Her voice is cracking. Her face is cracking, too. "Lissa."

"Hey, Georgie. You look like shit," Lissa says matter-of-factly.

It's true. Her dress is soaked through, streaked in places with dirt, and hitched up strangely as if she's caught it into her knickers in the bathroom; almost the entire length of one of her lean legs is on display. There's blood mixed with the rain streaming off one forearm. Georgie glances down at herself, but she doesn't seem to see; she just looks back at Lissa. "How could you? How could you let me believe you were dead?"

"It was the only way," she says dispassionately.

"Bullshit."

Lissa doesn't say anything.

Georgie tries again. "I didn't betray you. I didn't. It was an impossible situation. I didn't want to put you in the position of hating Bron." *Thank you, Georgie. Thank you, thank you.* "And their fling was over so quickly, and I was scared of what you might do to Bron—"

"You chose Bron." I wonder if I could pull away now. I wonder if Lissa is involved enough in this exchange that I could take her off guard. But she's still gripping my arm, and the gun is still nudging my side.

"I didn't—"

"You betrayed me. You did." Lissa is yelling now.

Georgie stops, all the fight dropping out of her. "All right," she says in a tired voice. "Maybe I did. But I don't know what else I could have done."

"You could have told me. And then maybe he'd still be alive."

"That makes no sense." Lissa doesn't reply. Georgie tries again. She's trying to run out the clock, I realize. She's trying to give the others a chance to get here. "How long have you been planning this thing anyway?"

"Since I found out about Bron. Though it took meeting Jem, and hearing about this place, to figure out exactly how to do it."

"But . . . Jem loved you," Georgie says, almost bewildered.

I risk a glance at Lissa, feeling the butt of the gun scrape across my ribs as I turn to her. Her mouth is tensed in a straight line. "Jem does whatever is best for Jem. Jem might *think* he loved me, but it was convenient to him to love me. I daresay he would have kept thinking he loved me right up until the moment it became more useful to him to screw someone else."

"You're wrong about him," I say quietly.

Lissa shrugs, and I tense as I feel the movement through the metal of the gun. "Maybe. But I doubt it."

Georgie changes tack. "You know, I didn't get your emails until much later. They got stuck in my work firewall."

Lissa ignores her. "Come on, Bron, time to climb aboard." She lets go of my arm but moves behind me, pushing me toward the boat.

"Is that why you had your guy attack me? To punish me?" Georgie asks.

"Actually, no. Sorry about that. He thought you were Bron. He was taking advantage of the power cut; to be honest, he's none too bright. He used to work here, but he got let go for suspected theft; that's how he knew how to move through the villas, where all the keys were kept and everything. He thinks we're going to live together in the lap of luxury in Thailand now. By the time he figures out that isn't happening, I'll be long gone." I feel a shove at my back. "Come on, Bron, don't dawdle," she says impatiently.

"And what about Cristina?" I ask, looking to stall.

"That was unfortunate. I do regret that somewhat. She saw me, on the clifftop; she realized it was me. I didn't have a choice." She shrugs, which once again makes my insides ice-cold as I worry about what that movement might do for her pressure on the trigger. "She had always been dying to get into Jem's pants, though, so maybe I'll just mark it down as a preemptive strike."

"She'd already quit," I say. "She wasn't going to be going anywhere near Jem in the future."

"Really? I didn't know that." But she's not at all interested; I can feel her focus slide across to Georgie. "You were supposed to come on the trip, you know."

"To stop you?" Georgie asks.

Lissa laughs again. "No, there was no stopping me. You were supposed to make sure they investigated. But by the time you came out it was too late, and anyway, you were too busy fucking Adam. I had to kick you to get you even slightly suspicious of Jem. Get on, Bron." She's pushing me; I have no choice but to step from the jetty onto the pitching and yawing speedboat that's slick with rain and sea spray. I'm planning to go straight over the other side, into the water, but she yanks on my dress, hauling me back, and the moment has passed. "You're going to drive, Bron. Go grab the wheel." I stumble along the boat, one hand bracing me against the gunwale.

"Adam is on his way here. And Steve is bringing the boat," calls Georgie from the jetty. I look desperately across at her, through the side of the windscreen, our panicked eyes meeting. She's only a few meters away from me, but it's a yawning gap. She might as well be miles away.

"Then we ought not to delay. You can cast us off, Georgie." She jabs me. She's standing right behind me. Presumably the gun is now in her left hand, because her right is hanging on to the handle in the side, but she's so close that even a wild shot would hit me. "Do you remember how to drive? Switch on the engine."

"You don't need Bron," calls Georgie desperately. "It's all over now. Leave her and go. Live on the money I presume you've squirreled away from Graeme's house. You've scared us all, you've won, you've had your justice—you can just go."

"Justice? Graeme is dead. And now I know what was ruining our relationship. Bron has to pay." I hear a warning note creep into her voice. "Cast us off now, Georgie. Do it, or I'll shoot her. She's going to die either way."

I look at Georgie desperately. She looks down at the bowline, nearest to her feet, then bends to start untying it. She throws it messily onto the bow of the boat. I realize I'm shivering, even though the rain seems to be abating. And possibly the wind, too.

"Now the other one. Bron, get ready to pull us away."

The engine is idling in neutral. I have a hand on the throttle and twist to watch Georgie. Is there a way I can gun the engine and cause Lissa to fall? Or will she just end up firing the gun anyway? Georgie is unwinding the rope, then coiling it in her hand, ready to toss it onto the craft. She starts her throw, but at the very last minute she leaps across, too, landing heavily on one side of the boat just as I engage the engine and we lurch away from the pier.

"Georgie, you weren't invited." Lissa is not pleased.

"I'm gate-crashing."

"Your funeral." I glance back in shock. Lissa laughs as she sees the look on Georgie's face. "Not literally. At least, not for you. That wouldn't be fair. I'll drop you somewhere."

"Where am I supposed to be heading?" I ask. Right now I'm headed for the beach. Could I run us straight onto dry land?

"Out to sea." Reluctantly I turn the wheel. I've barely put the engine above idle; we're being tossed around like flotsam. I haven't driven a speedboat for years; I'd be nervous even without a storm and a gun pressed into my back. "Come on, give it a bit more welly. You know there's supposed to be a serpent that lives here?" yells Lissa above the engine noise, for all the world as if we're on a day trip.

"We saw it," Georgie yells back.

"Did you really?" Lissa is genuinely energized. "I thought I did, too, once, but Jem didn't believe me. What was it like?"

"Really long. Dark. Really fast."

"That's what I saw, too!" It's the oddest thing to hear them talk. It's as if nothing has happened, as if they're exactly how they've always been. "The locals think it ate me."

"The locals think you wanted it to."

"Not really my style."

"How did you survive?"

"I had fins and a boat waiting just behind that headland." Fins. No wonder Arif thought she looked like she was kicking hard and swimming fast. She gestures to the opposite side from the cliff that Georgie descended from. "Put it in neutral now, Bron. And it was a slack tide, too. Even so, it was a scary swim; I bloody hate night swims, as you know. All right, Bron, this is where you get off."

I turn. "You're joking," I say desperately, even though it's perfectly clear that she isn't.

"Nope. Over the side with you."

"I'll—I'll drown." *Or the sea creature will get me.*

"Yes. That's the point." I don't move. She sighs. "Well, okay, I can shoot you instead. Though frankly I'd take the water, if it were me; at least there's *some* chance."

"Lissa, stop. This is crazy." Georgie sounds crazy herself. "Everything can be okay if you just *stop.*"

"No. It can't. It's too late for that." She's circling round, one hand on a windscreen strut, and the other holding the gun, her arm extended, reaching out until the barrel is on my belly. She looks at my face. "Do you want me to pull the trigger?"

"No!" *This can't be happening. Rob, I'm sorry. Kitty, Jack: I'm sorry. I'm so sorry.*

"Back away then." I take a step back, twisting to slip past the driver's seat, one hand steadying myself on the side. "Now jump in."

"No." I put all the authority in my voice, all that I can muster from my years of being a mother. Because, after all, Lissa is just a child. A child who needs to know where the boundaries are. "I won't. I won't do it."

"Okay," she sighs, and in horror I realize that she's closing an eye to aim, and I throw myself sideways just as there's an earsplitting crack from the gun. The boat is so very slippery from the rain and the sea spray that I find I'm hanging half over the side, the gunwale pressed into my hip bones and one hand on a fender cleat, with just enough purchase to stay on. But then I realize that I'm being lifted up and over, and then my wrist is twisting awkwardly and I have to let go—I'm falling into the ocean. There's no shock on entry; the water barely feels any colder than the air temperature, but the strength of the waves is utterly terrifying. I'm lifted up and down, and pulled left and right, in what seems like a random fashion, except that I can already see I'm being swept away from the boat. I kick my shoes off and start to swim front crawl desperately toward the boat, my eyes stinging and blurry without goggles, but when I stick my head up to check my progress I can see that I'm losing the battle. It's like swimming in a washing machine. Turning my head to breathe is a lottery: I might equally find a face full of water rather than clear air. The current is already tugging me away frighteningly quickly; I can feel how it wants to sweep the skirt of my dress away. I should take it off, but I don't want to lose ground in the seconds it would cost me to do that; if I can't get to the boat in the next minute or two, I never will. I'm sprinting as hard as I ever have, but it's a crazy sort of swimming: sometimes I can't get an arm out the water because of waves crashing over me, and sometimes my arms are pulling through open air when the sea drops away beneath me, and all the while I'm trying to keep myself as high on the surface as possible, as if that might protect me from the sea creature. Three strokes, breathe and look. Three strokes, breathe and look. But I'm losing ground quicker than ever, or the boat is deliberately moving away; I can't tell. And then I realize that I'm going to exhaust myself doing this and I still won't get back to the boat, but I keep going and going because I can't think of what else to do; I'm terrified to stop. When I next stick my head up to sight, Georgie is leaning over the back of the boat, shouting something. She's so far away now that I can barely make out her features. I tread water for a moment, rising and falling with the waves that sometimes obscure the boat, gasping for breath, straining to hear, but I've no chance with the water in my ears and the wind whipping away her words—though I think it's the same word, over and over again. The same word, though I can no longer see her making it.

And then, from nowhere, my brain makes sense of the movement of her mouth, and I turn away from the boat, lifting myself high in the water with eggbeater kicks right at the point when a wave lifts me up, to have the best chance to get my bearings. I'm scanning the water for the one thing that might save my life, the thing that Georgie was trying to tell me: the buoy. The buoy in the middle of the cove. If I can see the buoy, if I can grab hold of the buoy, then I have a chance. Unless I've already been swept past it . . . It has a light on it at night; I remember that. Is that—yes, it's there! It's farther out toward the cove mouth than I am; I shall have to aim inland of it to take account of the current. I start to swim, and as I do, I realize that the boat has switched course: it's fore of me, rather than aft. Hope throws a shaft of light through me: has Lissa come to her senses? Are they circling round to pick me up? I stick my head up again, using the eggbeater to lift myself. But no, that light is just as quickly snuffed out: they're not looking in my direction, not even Georgie. I can see Lissa at the wheel, and as I watch, Georgie suddenly flings herself at her, both arms wrapping round Lissa. For a moment they hover improbably, somehow balanced together on the top of the gunwale, and I strain to watch over the waves as they continue to teeter there—but I know that their small moment of equilibrium cannot last; they have to fall one side or the other. And then they topple together over the side of the gunwale into the sea.

And I think: *Well, we're all in the same boat now.*

TWENTY-TWO

GEORGIE

I know now. I know how you kill your best friend. You have to go down with her; there isn't any other way.

We hit the water together, one of my arms wrapped tight around her from the side, her frantic breaststroke kick tangling in my own legs as we sink beneath the surface. Then I have the presence of mind to release her, and I pull down and kick hard for the surface, emerging to find that the rain hitting my face is colder than the sea that envelops me. I scan around quickly, trying to get my bearings: we're already meters away from the boat, which, absent a driver, is pitching crazily in the storm-whipped waves. Then I spot her, only meters away, at a forty-five-degree angle on her back with her feet drawn up and her hands busy: she's trying to take off her boots. Smart. It prompts me to duck under the water to pull my dress over my head and discard it, and my bra, too, as the padding in it allows it to fill and flap, though I know none of it will help; not me, not Lissa. Neither of us is strong enough to withstand this. When I come up again, I can't immediately see her, but then a wave lifts me high and I spot her again, farther away from me this time; simply a featureless, pale face-

shape against the dark ocean. For a second I think she might be trying to shout something to me. But it's too late. We're too far apart. I
can't hear.

I tread water, keeping only the minimum of my head above water,
obeying the number one rule—don't fight a rip—whilst I consider
my options. I know I won't survive this, but I have to at least try. I owe
it to—well, to whom? Really, to whom do I owe anything in life, in a
world where Lissa doesn't exist? But still. I have to try. The problem
isn't being in water, or the storm, or even the cold—even at this sea
temperature, hypothermia will set in eventually—but getting onto
dry land. I know I can float or tread water a lot longer than the average person, but I can't do it indefinitely. What we thought had happened to Lissa, when she was the Lissa in the red swimsuit, caught in
the riptide, swept into that vast expanse of ocean with no land for
hundreds of miles, thousands even; what we thought had happened
to her is about to actually happen to me. All those years of open water
swimming experience, and look where it has got me.

Adam might find me. It's a small chance, but it's possible. He and
Steve might bring the boat round and somehow spot me. But it's
more likely that they'll be able to help Bron, if she's managed to grab
the buoy—I use urgent eggbeater kicks to raise myself up and look
for it, but I'm sure I've already been swept past it—though I don't
think she heard me, so there's only the very slimmest of chances.
Sod's Law suggests the only person they will rescue is Lissa. In my
experience, the universe has exactly that kind of sense of humor.

Where is Lissa? She will fight; I know it. Perhaps she will fight
more than me. Which of us, really, is the stronger? I'm not sure I've
ever known the answer to that. I have a better swimming pedigree,
but survival here is not going to hinge purely on that. Lissa will fight
tooth and nail, to the bitter end. I'd better start figuring out how to
do that myself.

I lift myself up with eggbeater for a count of five, ignoring the odd grinding in my bad knee as I do so, trying to assess my surroundings. I don't really know where I am, given how dark and wild it is—and then suddenly I realize that I can make out certain outlines, changes in darkness. Is that the cliff face? It could be. And the water hitting my face might actually be sea spray rather than rain now. One shouldn't fight a rip, but one can swim sideways within it, and try to break out of it that way. So I have perhaps two opportunities. One is to move sideways out of the rip and reach land before I'm swept out of the mouth of the cove into the open sea. The other is to reach the shore of the nature reserve before I'm swept past the tip of it. How far is it? Four miles? Five? I've swum farther, no question. Though not in storm conditions in the dark, with a wicked current, no goggles, and no support boat . . . I'd need to manage my energy for a sustained hard effort. I try to make sense of which way I'm moving, but the tumbling and churning of the waves isn't helping much, so I turn to face what I'm guessing is the mouth of the cove, where I can possibly detect a certain dark grayness rather than the pitch black of the cliffs. I'm closer to land on my left, I think. I'm not sure of it, but I think so. I start to move that way. I will do one hundred strokes, I decide. One hundred strokes in that direction. Surely the rip can't be wider than one hundred strokes. One hundred strokes, and then we'll see.

I start to swim and count. *One, two, three, four, five, six . . .* I quickly realize I can't breathe to my left—the waves hit me in the face every time, choking off the chance to drag in air, whereas perhaps one in three breaths to the right results in the same. So I breathe on every second stroke, to the right, and I decide that I will sight every ten strokes, to make sure I'm still heading for the cliffs, roughly perpendicular to the flow of the rip. But it's so very hard to sight; I can't see well enough with my salty, bleary eyes, through the sea spray and the darkness. I renege on my own deal after sixty strokes, switching to eggbeater to lift myself up on the surge of a wave to try and get a better idea of where I might be.

It's already too late. The storm must be abating; there's intermittent moonlight now, enough for me to see, during a fortuitous cloud-break, that I'm almost at the mouth of the cove, and there's no way I can reach the cliffs in time. There's no point in even trying; I need to preserve my energy now. I'm going to be in the water for a long, long time. Maybe forever.

So, plan B. Except really, it's plan C, since plan A was to topple Lissa overboard and take control of the boat, then pick up Bron and, hopefully, a far less murderous Lissa, too; a long shot, for sure, but what else was I supposed to do? Sit meekly in the boat and let Lissa drop me off somewhere nice and safe, whilst Bron thrashed and flailed in the water until exhaustion overtook her and she slipped silently beneath the waves forever? *Yes. That's surely what anybody else would have done.* And then, with an odd pang: *That's what Adam would have wanted me to do. Too late now.*

Plan C, then. I briefly consider whether I can fight my way out of the current eastward to get back to the resort, or at least the same island as the resort, but then I remember the shape of the coastline on the map. Horseshoe Bay, then a headland, then the narrow tongue that is Kanu Cove, then another headland, and then a bay with a small town, where many of the staff come from; and then after that, the land starts to fall sharply away, curving round because that's the northern end of the island. The current between here and the nature reserve flows west-northwest; I could use up all my energy fighting to get back east and simply find myself too far north with the land receding away from me. Better to go mainly with the flow but try to direct myself farther westward, to hit the nature reserve before I run out of island to land on. Which is all well and good, but how the hell am I supposed to navigate? Bron would be all over the velocity vectors; she'd have the math done in a trice—*If the current is moving four miles an hour west-northwest, and Georgie is moving two miles an hour westward, exactly how fucked is Georgie? Give your answer to two deci-*

mal places—but even she would struggle without a fixed point to orient herself.

Bron. God, I hope she found that buoy. That's her only hope now. I don't want to think of Kitty's little face, pinched with misery; I don't want to think of Rob, broken. And all of it my fault. If I had realized what was happening to Lissa, if I had found a way to stop her mad descent . . .

I need to move. Every moment that I'm not traveling west increases the likelihood that I'll overshoot the island. I need to move, but I need to get it right; the combination is paralyzing. *I can't do this.* Even were it daylight, this is too much to attempt. The waves are too massive, now that I'm out of any protection of the cove; I've never swum in conditions as wild as this. The waves have a strength that simply can't be fought, or tricked, or reasoned with; they're inexorably bearing down on me, again and again and again. Panic is building up inside me, threatening to steal my breath, threatening to flood through all my systems, to put me back on the sandy ground, my arms bound tight by my attacker; threatening to put me back in Jem's villa, hemmed in against the cupboard. Only if I let it take me this time, I will die.

I will not die without a fight. Lissa will be fighting. I am going to fight.

I flip onto my back and breathe. Three long breaths, in and out; as a calming exercise, it's hampered by a particularly ferocious wave smacking against my face, but I try three more, looking up at the sky. And suddenly I realize I can see stars—not just one or two, but lots. Not the whole sky, to be sure, but still . . . The visibility must be markedly improved. And if the visibility is improved, I ought to be able to see the lights of the hotel. Or if not, perhaps of the small town. If those are behind me, if they're visible on my left side when I breathe, then I must be cutting hard enough left. I'm lifting up to look now, and immediately I spot the town. It's terrifying how far north I've drifted already. I need to start swimming.

So I do. Stroke after stroke after stroke. I'm not in the least bit sure I'm making any progress at all, but I keep the town's lights behind me, on my left side. They don't seem to get any farther away. I keep the tempo as high as I think I can manage for, say, a two-hour swim, though this will likely end up a lot longer than that; I'm not wearing a watch, so I have absolutely no way of judging the time. My arms pull through the darkness beneath me, my hands disappearing in the gloom to reappear again at the start of their next stroke. Stroke after stroke after stroke. Check for the lights under my left arm: still there. Stroke after stroke after stroke. I resist the urge to look ahead. There's a long way to go before there will be any point in doing that.

Time passes, punctuated only by strokes and breaths and glimpses of lights. Sometimes I think I'm simply swimming on the spot, being washed back by the waves. At other times it feels like I'm swimming up a wave only to crash into open air from its crest. My arms already ache, but there is nothing to be done but to keep on turning them over. The irregularity of the waves makes it hard to get into a rhythm, but eventually it comes. My brain, though, won't allow itself to be scrubbed clean. The abject panic, hovering just in the periphery, prevents it. I wonder how Lissa is doing. I wonder if she's made the same calculations that I have. She hates night swimming; is she panicked? Of course she's panicked. But, more than that, I bet she's furious with me, for what I've done to her. What I've done to us both. This isn't how this was supposed to play out. She was supposed to have her level playing field now, all proportionate vengeance neatly ticked off.

Proportionate vengeance. It sits in my mind for stroke after stroke after stroke. I don't know what counts as proportionate vengeance. I wonder if she even knows, or if she's still too blinded by the horror of losing Graeme. I thought she was pulling herself out of it—marrying Jem, making a life out here—but instead she was burrowing into it. How could I have missed the fact that she was planning this all along?

The lights, when I look under my left arm on a breath, are farther away; I'm sure of it. I finally allow myself to lift my head and look forward on a stroke. All I can see are waves. I break my stroke and tread water instead, my legs moving into eggbeater automatically, though my bad knee isn't really taking its fair share of the load. There is a long, low, dark shape on the horizon. It's very, very far away. I twist my head to look back at the lights. They seem closer. I'm not even halfway. Probably not even a third. I am never, ever going make it. The despair isn't particularly devastating. I always knew I wasn't going to make it.

I hope Lissa isn't panicking.

I stick my head down and start swimming again.

I hope Bron found the buoy.

I keep swimming. My eyes aren't open, except when I breathe on the left side, to check for the lights. I think the waves may be subsiding. Perhaps they died down a while ago. Time is as liquid as the ocean; it seems to both ebb and flow. Am I swimming forward, cutting through the water, or is the water rushing backward around me? Which way am I moving through time? I see people and events from the past—or is it the future? I see Lissa and me, in a bar, in a café, in a pool, waking up together in a bed somewhere. I see Maddy, as a toddler, holding out her arms to be picked up, her face ecstatic with joy at seeing me. I see Bron, holding a tiny newborn Kitty, her face somehow immeasurably changed, though I couldn't say how. Sometimes I see a dark shape slipping sinuously through the depths beneath me, and I keep seeing Maddy floating some meters below, only occasionally I can't tell if she's Lissa. There's the same slightness of build, the same blond hair floating and billowing around a face with features that aren't filled in enough for a definitive identification, exactly like the portrait. Whoever it is, they don't speak to me—but why would they? There's no point.

I keep swimming.

At some point it occurs to me I ought to check my bearings again.

I can see the outline of the nature reserve far ahead of me, just a low humped shape that's darker than the sky. It drops away into the ocean on my right; I'm going to overshoot. Nothing but a monumental, impossible effort can get me there, and I don't have a monumental effort left in me.

I keep swimming.

I see the dark, sinuous shape again, so alien in its effortless movements, undulating through the water as if merely air. It's the serpent, the Kanu serpent; I see that now, but it doesn't scare me. It edges left in my field of underwater vision, and I follow it, entranced. It comes closer to me now: I can see overlapping scales on its skin, like a snake. It's not black, exactly, or if it is, it's a kind of black with patterns within it, some kind of elegant mottling that I could never describe, that seems to change from moment to moment. It's so long that I can't see its head or its tail. It's always moving to my left, sometimes coiling itself right round to return when I am very slow, but even then I can't see the head or tail. It's endless, I think. Endless and timeless, and extraordinarily alien in its beauty. Gradually it dawns on me that it means for me to follow it, that there's an urgency to the way in which it repeatedly moves ahead and returns. It wants me to speed up, too, I think. It seems like I ought to obey. I don't have any energy in my arms—my right one is barely clearing the water on its recovery—but I start to at least kick harder, which in turn increases the cadence of my strokes. There's no Maddy or Lissa now: I've left them behind, or ahead; anyway, I've left them. Or they've left me.

I keep swimming, harder, with all that I have left, because Kanu wants me to and that seems to make sense.

I keep swimming.

TWENTY-THREE

BRONWYN

The buoy is not just a buoy; it's so much more than that. It's a goal, something to focus on; it allows for planning and strategy; it wards off the panic. Not completely; nothing could do that, as the situation is too manifestly dire for there to be no panic. But with the buoy to focus on, I can squash that panic down so that it doesn't erupt into the gut-wrenching sobs and gasps that linger, dangerously close to breaking through.

The serpent. No, I won't think about that.

But seeing the buoy and reaching it are two very different things. For one thing, the buoy is dwarfed by the waves, and I can only see it when the relative positions of it and myself—both being constantly either raised up or abruptly dropped down by the swell of the ocean—are exactly right. For another, I know that the current here is fast, so fast that I must aim significantly closer inland than its actual position to have a chance of reaching the buoy, but I can't tell where I am in relation to it. And the third, completely unexpected hazard, is the boat. I can see it, in the intermittent moonlight, and occasionally hear it, too. Lissa couldn't have been wearing the kill cord: the engine is still running, but without anyone to control it, it's entirely at the mercy of the waves, jerking and twitching randomly with no sense to its course. If I stick my head down and swim, I'm liable to be run over. I'll have to swim water polo–style—head-up front crawl—which is more tiring, but much better for visibility. But which direction?

I'm about to pull off my dress, when I realize that it can be a help rather a hindrance. I sink a couple of meters below the surface, to get out of the surface effects of the wind, and try to use it like a wind sock by judging which way the skirt is being dragged. It's very clear. Now I have the equivalent of a compass: I know the direction of the rip, and from that I can work out the entire topography of the problem.

I can do this. This kind of challenge suits me. I don't have Georgie's stamina: she comes into her own after a couple of kilometers, and I couldn't match her then even at my fittest, but I've always been able to smash out shorter efforts. I look for the boat, which is jinking around some four or five hundred meters from me, then scan for the buoy again, catching a quick wink of the light perhaps three hundred meters from me. I run a calculation in my head, trying to work out where I should aim given the relative angle of my trajectory to the current, and my speed, and the current speed, but I don't have all the information. All I can do is a best guess and then adjust as I go on. I start, turning my arms over hard and fast, kicking strongly, my head held high. My dress is a hindrance, but I daren't take it off in case I need it for a compass again. The kids and Rob try to nudge into my mind, but I can't allow for that. I can't focus on anything but the task at hand. And I'm gaining on the buoy; I can see that. Hope flares inside me, and I redouble my efforts just as I catch a glimpse of the speedboat out the corner of one eye. It's heading straight toward me. For a moment I wonder if I can grab on to it, but sense prevails: I'll probably end up cut to shreds by the propeller. I don't break stroke; I swim on, hoping that it will be jerked off its current path by a large wave. If not, I can sink beneath it—though, will I be able to see well enough in the dark waters to come up in a safe area? It's closer now, only twenty meters or so away. I stop swimming and tread water. It's growing larger, taller, more menacing; on the crest of a wave it seems enormous, like facing off against a cruise liner. Part of me registers that the fact I can see it so clearly means that the cloud cover must be receding. Ten meters, and still coming. Oh Jesus. I'm going to have to duck.

I take a deep breath and duck-dive as fast as I can, pulling down strongly with my arms, farther and farther into the depths, until my ears are sore with the pressure—surely that's deep enough? I scull to maintain my position, and I look up, starting to count. *One, two, three* . . . There's nothing but blackness above me, though I can hear the metallic rhythm of the engine, distressingly loud for something I can't see; surely it must be right above me? Though it would be loud even if it weren't, sound travels so well through the water. *Six, seven* . . . I can already feel my lungs starting to buck at the lack of oxygen. How long can I stay here? *Nine, ten, eleven* . . . I start to rise, slowly, carefully. Then out of the corner of my eye, I see a faint sparkle of silver that when I turn my head to look resolves into a rush of moonlit bubbles that can only be caused by the propeller; I twist and dive down again, my lungs bursting, twisting onto my back after two strokes to look up. The bubbles are still there, but I desperately need to breathe. I start to swim laterally under the water, away from the bubbles: using three, four, five big breaststroke pulls, fighting the spasms in my chest. I'll have to aim upward soon. I have no choice, propeller or no propeller. I have to breathe or I'll pass out. And then something cold—*what?*—slithers against me, and conscious decision is slain: I shoot like an arrow for the surface, my arms above my head for protection.

I surface intact—*yes!*—with a huge gasping intake, looking frantically all around me for the boat and also frantically under me for any kind of creature, not sure if I should be readying myself to dive again or to swim. I see the boat immediately, only ten meters from me, but heading away from my position. I'm whimpering—I can hear it; it breaks through my panic somehow, and I force myself to lie back and breathe, filling my lungs again and again while the pulse hammering in my ears begins to slow, sense gradually catching up with me. It could have been anything that touched me. Seaweed, a plastic bag; anything. There's no reason to assume it was the creature. Then the real danger strikes me again, and I come upright: the buoy. Where is the buoy? I can't see it, I can't see it anymore—and then I spot a flash of light. I've definitely lost ground on it. I quickly duck under, to test the current direction, and then start my head-up front crawl again, faster than ever—well, probably not, given how tired I am now, but at least with even more effort than ever before. At first I think I'm simply keeping myself stationary, as the buoy doesn't seem to get any closer. And then a fortuitous wave picks me up, and I find I'm surging on it, clearly getting closer, and it gives me just that glimmer of hope that I need. I can do this. It's getting closer. Perhaps thirty more strokes. I can do this. I can do this—and then suddenly I'm upon it, reaching out with grasping arms toward my floating savior, relief flooding through me.

But the buoy itself is clearly not designed for a swimmer to hang on to it. I try to wrap my arms around it, but it's too large a sphere for them to reach easily around it—certainly I can't link my hands—and it's also covered in a sort of slimy algae that makes it extraordinarily slippery. I try to hold on, but lose my grip in the swash of a large wave; I have to fight hard to get back to it. Even the light on top has a smooth casing which offers no fingerholds. I feel down underneath it for its tether, hoping for a rope rather than a chain. I'm in luck: it *is* a rope. It has the circumference of one of my wrists, and it's thick with slime, but I can get my hands around it easily. I wrap my legs around it, too, crossing them at the ankles, and I hold with arms outstretched, so that I can partially lie back and float. The strongest waves tug hard at me, and I get submerged from time to time, but I can hold on. For a very long time, I should think. Not forever, but for a very long time. Absent other factors, that is.

Other factors. I try to list them. The boat remains a risk; I should keep checking around for it. I suppose I could fall asleep and unconsciously let go, if I allow myself to close my eyes: no eye-closing allowed, then. There's the cold, too: now that I'm stationary, I'm not keeping myself warm through moving, so hypothermia could set in, but in these sea temperatures that will take a long time. It will probably be daylight before that happens, and surely I'll be spotted by then? Georgie said Adam and Steve would be bringing the boat. Surely they'll find me long before morning?

The sea creature. Now that I'm not focused on a task, it's nudging at my mind. The fear isn't rational—I know that—but that doesn't make it any less potent. Every single reasonable argument I can construct simply fails when faced with the pitch-black, bottomless depths below me and all the nameless terrors that are concealed within.

Think of something else. Rob, Kitty, Jack: but no, I can't think of them, either. Not now. It's too unforgivable: I've jeopardized my life with them, I've jeopardized their well-being—but no, I can't think of that now. Not until I'm safe.

The sea creature—

Stop it. Keep your eyes open, look around and keep holding on. Just keep holding on.

Keep holding on.

TWENTY-FOUR

GEORGIE

Somebody is shaking me. I really wish they would stop. I'm far too tired; I want to sleep some more. But something very uncomfortable is being jammed into my side with every push. Come to that, everything I'm lying on is uncomfortable, and gritty, and . . . sand. I must be lying on sand. I'm lying on my back, though not on a flat surface. I'm sloping awkwardly to one side.

"Georgie. Georgie," a voice keeps saying, along with the shoves, and I realize that it's Adam. Why is Adam here? I start to open my eyes, but pain stabs through my left eye. I clap a hand up to it. For some reason that seems to elicit a cheer, though from whom I can't tell. My tongue seems to be about the size of a whale, and desiccated, furry and cracked. I cautiously try to open my eyes again; the pain is still there, but less severe. It's very bright, and Adam is grinning at me. I've never seen him with a smile so wide.

"Water," I try to say, but it comes out as a grunt. He seems to understand anyway and brings a bottle to my lips; one of the glass reusable ones from the hotel. I move my head as he brings it to me, and it chinks against my teeth.

"Sorry," he says. He's hunkered down beside me. I'm still lying down, so half of the water splashes out of my mouth, running in rivulets down my cheeks. "Sorry," he says again. Now he snakes an arm under my shoulders and brings me up to sitting. I see that I'm just under the shade of some foliage, not far from the waterline. Judging from the light, it must be almost midday. I realize that the cheers came from Steve and three of the hotel staff in the hotel speedboat that's hovering nearby, as close as its draft will allow. I also realize that I'm only wearing teeny tiny knickers.

"Shirt," I say, and this actually comes out sounding like I mean it to. Adam grins again and pulls his own shirt, a gray T-shirt advertising his bike shop, over his head, then sets about pulling it over mine and moving my arms around to get it on me, like one would with an infant. His nose is sunburned, I notice. It wasn't yesterday. I take the water from him and drink again. I can almost feel it moving through my body, seeping into every space, invigorating the cells. My eyes are instantly less sore.

"Can you move?" asks Adam. "Are you hurt?"

"Don't know." I think about it. Then I give up for more pressing questions. "Lissa? Bron?"

"Bron's fine." *Oh, thank God.* "We found her last night, clinging on to the buoy." I hadn't thought she'd heard me. "She wasn't actually in the water very long; maybe only three-quarters of an hour, tops. She said you saved her life, telling her to do that."

"Lissa?"

He shakes his head grimly. "Not so far. Though if anyone finds her, I'll kill her myself."

Steve is coming across to us. I wonder if he was waiting until I was decently covered. "Can't tell you how pleased I am to see you," he says to me, pleasure beaming across his broad face. I try a smile back, but there's a danger it might crack my lips. "Should have known that if anyone could survive that swim, it would be you."

I didn't expect to. And I almost didn't. The horror of it is too near. I can't smile back at that. "It was . . ." I don't know how to describe it.

"Tell us later," suggests Adam gently. "For now, let's get you back to the hotel."

"The flight?"

"We'll miss it. It takes off in an hour. You couldn't get on it anyway; the police need to speak to you. And Bron. She told us what happened."

"Are you okay to walk, or shall we carry you?" asks Steve.

"I think I'm fine." My body's response to the water is nothing short of remarkable, like a desert responding to rain. I am blooming, I am an oasis, I have become verdant. I will never take fresh water for granted again. Together they help to lever me to my feet, and I find that I can indeed stand. I'm sore and I'm stiff, but not much more so than after any really long, hard swim. Adam runs his eyes over me as if he's doing an inventory. "I'm fine, really. Ten fingers and ten toes." I start to walk and have to put a hand out to grab him for support as my knee buckles. I look down at it; it's definitely badly swollen. "And one dodgy knee." I look at the boat, and beyond it, expecting to see a suggestion of land on the horizon behind, the island where the hotel is nestled, but there's nothing but ocean. "Where are we, by the way?"

"The farthest tip of the nature reserve," says Steve. He's hovering on my other side, ready to lend support if I buckle again. He shakes his head. "If you hadn't landed here—"

"Well, she did," says Adam quickly. "She's here."

I'm here. How extraordinary. *I'm here.* I look out at the ocean, as if I might see the serpent there, but the water is clear and calm and blue. I have Kanu to thank for being here; I'm sure of it. There's a haze around my memories, but I do remember that, at least. I would have never veered left enough; I would never have picked up the pace when I needed to—not without Kanu.

We're sloshing into the water now. The waves are so meek and mild that I fancy they're sheepish after their tantrum of last night. The salt stings on grazes I hadn't realized I had. Some are in odd places, like my hips: that must be from dragging myself across the sand to get clear of the waterline. The speedboat looks impossibly high to get into, but the lads on board take an arm each and haul me straight up as if I'm a feather. Once we're all on board, Adam tucks a towel around me and hands me a fresh bottle of water. "Do you have anything to eat?" I ask nobody in particular.

"Now that's a good sign," says Steve with a smile as he powers up the engine. Everyone and everything is smiling as we set off, moving slowly as we are technically in the area where speedboats aren't permitted, though I suppose they would make an exception under these circumstances. The sun glints off the waves. The sky is scrubbed clean blue. One of the staff members hunts in a bag and hands me a packet of biscuits. They are manna from heaven; there is no better nutrition to be found in all the world.

One of the staff in the boat says something to Steve in the local language, grinning. "Really?" says Steve, and he looks across at me.

"What?" I manage.

"Joyo says his grandfather told him that we would find you."

"His grandfather?"

The lad, who can't be more than eighteen, says something more. Steve translates. "You met him, once, apparently? At Kanu."

"Yes! I did. I remember." He must mean the wizened old man with the rotten front teeth. *Kanu takes who wants taken.*

"He saw his grandfather when we refueled the boat. He says his grandfather said you are . . ." He turns back to Joyo, as if checking something. "Sorry, my translation skills aren't brilliant, but the best I can do is: daughter of Kanu. Or maybe, daughter of serpent. Yes, that's better."

"Daughter of serpent." I lean back against Adam. He loops an arm over my shoulder, across my torso. My shoulder groans at the weight, but I don't complain. Everything hurts anyway. "I saw it, you know," I say quietly to him, in between mouthfuls of biscuit.

"The serpent?"

"Yes." How to explain what I saw, what I felt? I start another biscuit. I can feel Adam's chin on my hair, and the press of his expectation, as he patiently waits for me to say more. But I can't think of how to start. "I saw Maddy and Lissa, too, though, so . . ." I shrug.

"Maddy? Your sister?"

"Yes." I wonder how he knows that. Perhaps my secrets haven't been so perfectly cached after all.

"She—um, she died, right?" He's feeling his way through this. It almost makes me want to hug him, the care he's taking.

"Yes."

"I'm sorry." I nod, knowing he will feel the movement. "Quite a night, then," he says dryly, but there's a smile in his words, too.

"Quite a night." I start on another biscuit. I might finish the packet, all by myself.

"Bron said something odd," he says after a pause. There's something in his tone that I can't identify. "She said it looked like you went into the water on purpose. To take Lissa with you." That press again, that weight. He wants something from me. "But she was in the water, herself; maybe she couldn't see clearly," he adds hopefully.

He wants me to say no, it wasn't like that. But I'm done with that. No secrets. Not for anyone. "I knew it could have gone either way."

He sighs, a long controlled sigh. He's trying to tone it down, under the circumstances, to come across as exasperated rather than angry, but I know him now. He's furious with me. "What the hell were you thinking?"

"I was thinking that if I could get control of the boat, I could pick up Bron. I tried to keep a hand on the windscreen strut, but I couldn't hold on. So I ended up going over with her." It was always a Hail Mary play. I know he knows that. And I know he knows what I was prepared to do.

He sighs again. "For fuck's sake, Georgie. You always find a way to make things *impossible*."

"I know." I eat another biscuit. I'm not entirely sure what he's saying, but it doesn't sound good. I don't want to face that now. Right now, the world is smiling. "Maybe it's because I'm the daughter of a serpent."

He laughs, unwillingly, but he laughs. "You really are the most fucked-up person I know."

"I know."

TWENTY-FIVE

BRONWYN

I move to the front door with a smile when I hear the bell ring, but Kitty streaks past me, elbows out in her determination to be the first to greet our visitor. "Georgie! Georgie!" she clamors as she drags the heavy wooden door open. Georgie doesn't disappoint: she opens her arms out wide and scoops up her little goddaughter, swinging her round and round while somehow managing to exclaim how she's grown and tickle her all at the same time, and the little girl positively fizzes with the attention. Then there are new bedrooms to inspect, seeing as Georgie hasn't seen the house before (Kitty is inordinately proud of her bunk beds, even if I won't let her sleep on the top bunk yet), and Jack, solemn faced and suspicious with a thumb in his mouth, to be won over, and presents from Georgie to be opened; all in all, it's a good twenty minutes before the two of us even manage to say a proper adult hello.

"This is a lovely space," she says appreciatively, looking around as I lead her into the kitchen. "You suit it." A typically Georgie backward way of putting it, as if I'm bending to the house rather than vice versa. Though maybe I am: to the house, and to this suburban life. I made it home from the trip in once piece, after all, so I'm doing what I promised: I am being the perfect boring housewife. I'm even on the parish council. Treasurer.

"Thanks. Coffee?" Kitty and Jack are on the living room floor, engrossed in the toys Georgie brought. One of them makes an extremely loud chirruping every twenty seconds or so. I silently hope it has an off switch; otherwise the batteries might mysteriously go missing very soon.

"Please. I haven't really adjusted to the time zone; I need all the caffeine I can get. You look really well," she says, leaning on the kitchen counter as I run the new all-singing, all-dancing coffee machine. Rob likes his coffee. He didn't quibble about the expense for that, at least.

"Thanks." She means I look thinner. Which I am. "I've been keeping up the swimming. You never know when it might come in handy," I joke. She winces theatrically. "Too soon?"

"Just a little."

I take the cups across to the table, and we settle opposite each other. The French doors are open onto the garden. I can hear a bee moving lazily around the lavender near the doorway. "You look well, too," I say. She does. She's got a nice hint of tan, and she looks relaxed, as if she's on holiday, though apparently this is a work trip. She's come straight from the office; she's wearing a superchic short-sleeved shirt-dress that's the perfect office-to-social-occasion choice.

"Well, it would be hard to look worse than when we last saw each other, I suppose." Eight weeks ago. We all said goodbye at Heathrow Airport, dead eyed with exhaustion from the flight, and from everything else, too. Poor Georgie had a connecting flight to catch and not much time to do it in, particularly with a bad knee. A memory pops into my mind of her walking away from Adam, Duncan and myself down a long airport corridor, her back ramrod straight even while she limped off, completely alone; we watched her together, all three of us, but she didn't so much as glance backward. I'm not sure it had struck me before what a big step she took in moving to the US on her own, leaving all friends and family. Well, friends, at least. She left family a long time ago.

"Is your knee okay now?"

"Mostly. It still twinges on a breaststroke kick, but then I've never been much of a breaststroker." Neither of us says what we're both thinking: Lissa was the breaststroker.

"Where are you staying? Has your firm put you up in a nice hotel?"

She blushes a little. "They would have, but actually I'm staying with Adam."

Interesting. And the blush makes it even more interesting. "So are you two doing the long-distance thing?"

"We haven't really talked about it." She stirs her coffee for absolutely no reason, seeing as she hasn't put any milk or sugar in it. Then she surprises me with candor: "I think he wants *me* to say something."

That's smart of Adam, forcing her to make active choices. "Well, what do you want?"

She covers her face with both her hands. "Oh God, I don't know," she moans. "I'm basically a novice at this." I can't help laughing, and she removes her hands. "Don't mock, you annoying, smug married person."

"Married, but not smug." I can't joke about that. "Never smug, now."

Her face sobers instantly, and she nods. "How much did you have to explain to Rob?" she asks delicately. We haven't really had a chance to catch up on this. We've spoken a few times, but I've always had either the kids or Rob within earshot. I did manage to find some privacy when I called her to let her know that Lissa's body had been found in the water—for real, this time—some five hundred miles away from the hotel, but that was a short conversation. You can't really segue from something like that to anything at all.

I shrug. "Nothing. Lissa was unstable. For some reason, she got the wrong end of the stick about Jem. There's nothing else for him to know." He hadn't really questioned much anyway. He'd always thought Lissa was a bit loony tunes—and Georgie, too, back in the day—so it fit perfectly into his worldview.

"Did Jem do anything? When they got the body back?"

"No. There wasn't any point; there'd already been a memorial. And with the circumstances being so murky . . ."

We watch an unusually large bee fly through the open doors. It moves left, then right, then figures out its mistake and flies straight back out again.

"Have you spoken to him much?" she asks.

"Jem?" She nods. "A few times. I think it's fair to say you're not on his Christmas list." She nods again and sips her coffee, not in the least surprised. Jem's complicated view of Georgie certainly hadn't been improved by her tipping his not-dead wife into the water: Jem thought she should be standing trial for murder, or at least manslaughter. Given he should have been in the dock for obstruction of justice, I couldn't find a lot of sympathy for him on that score. "He should be opening up the hotel next season, though. Duncan is helping him rebrand. Oh—and Kanu Cove is becoming a nature reserve; some marine biologist found evidence of—"

"The serpent?" Her eyes are wide, expectant. Almost hopeful, which is odd.

"No, not that." She visibly deflates. "Some rare type of mollusk. It means the government will purchase the land from the hotel estate, and Jem won't have to worry about it in terms of guest security anymore."

"That's great for Jem." She really sounds like she means it; the antipathy doesn't seem to travel both ways.

"Would you ever go back there?" I find myself asking. It's a question I've been asking myself.

She doesn't immediately answer. "I don't . . . I don't know," she says at last. "Maybe one day. But I don't know."

"Mummy, can I have a drink of milk?" It's Kitty, at the kitchen door.

"Magic word," I say repressively.

"Pleeeeease can I have a drink of milk?"

"Of course you can, sweetie." I get up from the kitchen table and cross to the cupboard where the kiddie beakers are kept. I threw out all of our mismatched crappy plastic ones when we moved and got ten of the Emma Bridgewater polka-dot melamine ones; it's a small thing, but they make me smile every time. "More coffee, Georgie?"

"Please." Kitty is scrambling onto Georgie's lap, without any care for where her sharp elbows or knees might make contact. Georgie doesn't seem to mind at all. It crosses my mind that if she does become a mother, she may well be incapable of discipline. And then it crosses my mind that I've never thought of Georgie becoming a mother before. That hadn't even seemed in the realm of possibility.

When I turn back to the table to deposit the tumbler of milk, Kitty isn't on Georgie's lap anymore. She's scrambled onto the counter to reach the naughty cupboard. "Kitty!"

"Georgie wanted a cookie," she says irrepressibly.

"She told you that telepathically, did she?"

Georgie laughs. "I would like a cookie, Kitty," she says.

I roll my eyes. "All right." I collect Georgie's coffee from the machine. "Don't forget plates," I call to Kitty.

"I've got the bags instead." I turn to her in alarm, my breath catching in my throat. Kitty, oblivious, places the cookies on the table on the brown paper bags and scrambles back into Georgie's lap. "You can't have them if you're allergic to nuts," she says seriously to Georgie. "Mummy always puts hazelnuts in them."

I watch Georgie register the two cookies, each on their own brown paper bag as a substitute for a plate. I watch her lift her head wordlessly, her shocked eyes meeting mine across the unkempt blond head of my daughter. It's too late. The connection has been made. I could lie, but she wouldn't believe me; whatever she's already seen on my face won't allow that. I see the horror dawning on her as she works it through, making link after link. Her eyes haven't left mine; I feel my cheeks burning. She makes a reflexive movement, as if to push away from the table, but then stops helplessly, pinned by the presence of my daughter on her lap.

"Kitty, maybe you could take Georgie's cookie to Jack," I say quickly. "I think Georgie is feeling a little sick after all."

Kitty nods and scrambles down. Georgie breaks eye contact to watch her tiny figure disappear through the doorway. *That's why I did it*, I want to scream. *For her, for Jack, for Rob.* For the life that was about to be destroyed through absolutely no fault of theirs.

Georgie turns back to me slowly. She no longer looks so tanned; in fact, she looks ill. But she's Georgie: she won't pull any punches. She's a rip-the-"Band-Aid-off-in-one-go kind of girl. "But you knew he was allergic," she says shakily, almost bewildered. Those green eyes, warm and filled with laughter only moments ago, are looking at me as if she can't comprehend what's in front of her.

"Yes. We all did."

"And yet . . ." She stops, as if it's too appalling to even vocalize, and then steels herself to try again. "And yet you gave him the cookie." I look at the table. I won't cry. I won't cry.

"Bronwyn." *Bronwyn.* Not Bron. Her shock is receding; there's a whipcrack in her tone, and yet she hasn't raised her voice at all. I take it back: she'll be perfectly capable of disciplining her children. But I am not her child; she cannot discipline me—she hasn't the right. I did what I had to do under the circumstances. I lift my chin.

"Yes."

"Wait: his EpiPen." She looks at me with fresh horror, and other things, too. Disbelief, disappointment. I could drown on the wave of hot shame that floods through me. "You—you removed it?"

I can't help it; I look down at the table again. That's the crux of it, really. The rest could just about be accidental: one could feasibly have forgotten about the allergy, or have forgotten there were hazelnuts in the recipe. And it *was* accidental—sort of; I didn't go there intending to give him it. He had a sweet tooth; he spotted the cookie bag and tweaked it out of my handbag and I just . . . didn't stop him. I see him taking the first bite, my mouth opening to say words that could have sent my life one way—but I didn't say them. I closed my mouth, I was silent, and my life took a different turn. But the EpiPen: that was deliberate. Excusing myself to use the bathroom and instead searching quickly for his jacket to find and remove his EpiPen: one couldn't call that an accident. I lift my head and square my shoulders. "He was going to tell Lissa. He wasn't leaving her or anything; just the opposite. He wanted to start over with her, with a clean slate. We weren't meeting for, for—well, you know." I can't say *sex* with my kids in the next room. "All of that was over. I was trying to talk him out of it."

"Because you knew what she would do."

"And I wasn't wrong! Look what she *did* do. I was just—"

"I know," she interrupts. "You were just cleaning up the mess. It's what mothers do. Isn't that what you always say?" Her head is cocked, and now she's looking at me like one might consider a piece of art that you haven't quite decided where you stand on. Shock was preferable to this detachment. Suddenly I'm scared.

"You can't tell anybody. Please. You can't—"

She shakes her head. "No. I don't keep secrets anymore." She's pushing back her chair. "I kept yours, and look what it did to Lissa and me. I thought maybe Lissa killed Graeme—did you know that? I wasn't there for her, and it was you all along. So, no, I don't keep secrets anymore."

"I—" She can't mean that. She can't. "Nobody will believe you. There's no evidence." The bags aren't even from the same shop; we've moved since Graeme died, and I get them from a different place now.

She looks at the brown bags as she leaves the table and shrugs. "I expect not."

"Georgie—"

"I'll say goodbye to the kids now."

"If you say anything, Georgie—if you say anything, just think what it could do to the kids. To Kitty. Your goddaughter—just think—"

"Goodbye, Bronwyn." She's turning for the door.

I fall silent, tears running down my cheeks though I'm not sobbing. I stand in the kitchen, watching her leave. Her back is ramrod straight once again, and she doesn't look back. She never looks back.

TWENTY-SIX

GEORGIE

I walk down the street toward the lido. It's been the kind of summer's day that showcases England at its best: a warmth without any fierceness that extends into the long, still-light evening. Even though it's gone 8 p.m., the people on the streets are in short sleeves, and I've no need of the cardigan that's in my bag.

I call Adam. "Hey, you," he says. I can hear his almost-smile. "I'm still at the shop. Are you still at Bron's?"

"No, I left ages ago."

He pauses, intuition flickering. "Is everything okay?"

"Actually, no. Not really. I've just come from the police station."

"What?"

"I figured it out. She killed Graeme. The paper bag, the cookie with the nuts. It was Bron."

"On—on purpose?"

"Yes. He was going to tell Lissa."

"Wait—Bron admitted this to you?" He sounds incredulous. I explain. It takes far less time than it should. Surely the reason for a man's death—a good man, a man we all loved—should consume more than fifteen seconds of phone time. "Oh my God," he breathes. There's silence down the phone line. I pause by a park and loll against the fence. I feel very tired, yet my head feels oddly light. Another effect of jet lag, I expect. Or perhaps of having reported my remaining best female friend to the police for murder.

"And, what, you went straight to the police?"

"Yes. I told you, I'm done with secrets." There are still kids playing in the park, shouting as they whiz down the slide, though it seems late to me for that. Surely they should be in bed by now? An old poem floats into my head: *In summer, quite the other way, I have to go to bed by day.*

"I . . . Jesus."

"I don't expect they'll convict her; they probably won't even charge her." I think again of the face of the doubtful desk sergeant that I spoke with. He seemed very young for the job. Though that probably says more about me than him.

"You know it means that Rob will find out." There's no accusation in his voice.

"Yes." Of course that has occurred to me. And it has occurred to me that I may not have many friends left after this. Certainly not Bronwyn. I don't know which way Duncan will tip, either. Will he think she did a terrible thing and should be punished? Or will he think that punishing her won't bring Graeme back, and would hurt Rob and the kids? I can't pick it. Adam is the only one I can count on. At least, I'm presuming I can count on him. "Not just Rob, I expect. Everyone will find out."

"You didn't ring me before you went to the police," he says mildly. "Did you think I might talk you out of it?"

Did I? "I don't know. I just knew I had to do it, so I went and did it." *Like pulling off a plaster.* "Would you have tried?"

He's quiet. I imagine him in the shop, with some kind of strange bike-specific spanner in his hand; he'll be spinning it unconsciously as he thinks it all through with the same kind of deep, careful con-centration that he applies to his work on the bikes. "I don't know. I might have suggested you sleep on it. But I think we'd still have ended up at the same place." *We.* Something loosens within me. I was right: I can count on Adam.

"It's not vindictiveness, you know."

"God, I know that; you've never been vindictive. You're done with secrets."

"Yes—and more than that. It's not for me to decide if she should be tried or punished or any of it. It can't be my responsibility; I'm too close." *I've learned my lesson on that score.* Diane was right: there were things she didn't do, and Philip didn't do, and I didn't do. And maybe if we had done those things, Lissa wouldn't have gone as far as she did, and she'd still be alive, but I can't really tell. I'm too close for any perspective. I've always been too close for that. "It's like—it's like why doctors should never treat family members."

"A new Georgie."

"Yes." I pause. "You'd better like this version."

"Does this version still live in Manhattan?"

"Yes." A small boy trips; a fraction of a heartbeat later comes a mournful wail. I watch as a young woman rushes over to scoop him up. I take the plunge. "Though I'm thinking that my neighborhood could use a good bike shop." There's absolute silence down the phone. I am literally holding my breath. The sunshine isn't reaching my skin anymore. I watch as the woman soothes the boy; in seconds he is off, running full pelt toward the sandpit. Adam is still silent. I can't take it; I have to say something. "You could—you could come for a recce."

Still nothing. *I've got this wrong; how can I have misread this so com-pletely?* Then: "I could," he says cautiously. "But it would depend. Are you going to throw yourself into certain death again? Because there's fucked-up, and then there's suicidal. It's just . . . I'm just not up for the latter. You have to want to be here."

"I know. Things are different now." Lissa is dead; really, really dead this time. Everything is different now. "I'm different now. And anyway, I'll have you know that I had to fight really hard to live. Even with being the daughter of a serpent and all that." I'm trying for humor, but we both know that it wasn't funny at the time. That it's never going to be funny.

"Yeah, I'll give you that." There's a lightness in his voice now. "I could come check out the bike scene in Manhattan, I suppose. Maybe I could even fly back with you, if Mick can look after the shop."

"That would be perfect." It's an extraordinarily beautiful day. I start to walk again. "I'm going for a swim at the lido; it's open till ten tonight. Want to join me?"

"Sure. I'll get there as soon as I can. See you in the water."

The woman at the lido kiosk looks flushed and entirely lethargic; she takes my money without bothering to say a word. Behind her, I can only see a small section of the pool, but it sounds fairly empty, and when I get to the changing room I find it busy, but everyone is dressing to leave rather than to swim. I change quickly and emerge to find the late-evening sunlight still warm on my skin and only three other people in the lido. I dive into the cool, clear, sterile water, so different from the water at Kanu Cove, or even at Horseshoe Bay, and break into a relaxed front crawl, and below me, a long, sinuous shadow uncoils itself to slide effortlessly through the water, always just out of the reach of vision.

ACKNOWLEDGMENTS

So, this is book number three. An interesting number, that: big enough that I ought to have known what I was embarking on but not so large as to suggest that I might be an old hand at it. It's true that *How to Kill Your Best Friend* was, in certain practical ways, an easier writing experience than book two—not least because I'd already had the experience of writing to a deadline with *The Missing Years*—but I'm beginning to suspect that, on an emotional level, it will never get any easier. My inherent levels of neurosis simply won't allow that; I don't think I will ever feel like an old hand. Therefore, to my family, who have the dubious pleasure of living with this anxious, insecure author, I can only say—with apologies—that this is probably as good as it gets! And, thank you: your love and support is a gift beyond all measure. I must also say an extra-special thank-you to my gorgeous boys, Cameron and Zachary, for the gusto and relish with which they offered up (highly inventive) suggestions of how one might kill a person for the "Method" sections; not the most conventional after-school conversation topic, it's true, but so far they don't show any sign of being scarred for life . . .

To my wondrous agent, Marcy Posner at Folio Lit, a galaxy of thanks. I've said it before and I'm sure I'll say it many, many times again, but I genuinely couldn't have managed it without your steadying hand, keen eye for detail and thoughtful advice. How lucky I was to be on the same train as you all those years ago! Thank you also to Anna Shapiro for her thorough reading and intelligent comments, and to Maggie Auffarth for her continued, and much appreciated, help with all areas of the social media universe.

For me, *How to Kill Your Best Friend* will not sit in my memory as a Covid-19 novel, as the main bulk of it was written before the pandemic became apparent. However, a certain amount of editing, and the vast majority of the work on the publishing side, has taken place under the shadow of the disease. So, to Kerry Donovan and the excellent team at Berkley and Penguin Random House, my sincere thanks. In these most trying of circumstances, and in the face of a seemingly endless stream of obstacles, I've been so impressed to see everyone working tirelessly with the same commitment, dedication and professionalism as ever, and (even more impressively) with no loss of enthusiasm. Thank you so much for your support of this book and of my writing career. Thank you also to Sarah Hodgson for her very helpful comments on the manuscript, and also to the rest of the team, too, at Atlantic Books, who, besides being wonderfully professional, are also extremely good company over a glass or two of wine!

To all my friends: I have not seen enough of any of you, and it's not even my fault. I'm so looking forward to a time when we can plan coffees, lunches and dinners with abandon; I think it will be all the more special when that time comes. To the swimtrek gang: we really have to start planning another trip soon; it's been far too long . . .

Lastly, I want to thank my readers. Covid-19 has, for many of us, highlighted the importance of the basics. Health, shelter, security, family and relationships—the pandemic has constantly reminded us not to take these for granted. For many of us who have faced, and may still be facing, restrictions that prevent us from seeing friends and family or traveling, books have been a welcome refuge: another way of meeting people, of stepping out into different worlds; another way of feeling connected in a time of isolation. I always enjoy hearing from my readers, but the messages I've received during this period have been especially welcome and particularly poignant: a shining strand of connection in these difficult times, and a reminder of the power and reach of the written word. So, to all of you, dear readers: thank you so much for choosing to take my books into your lives. It's an honor and a privilege that I will never take for granted.